I took my eyes away from that shiny blade with a conscious effort of will. What I saw next wasn't any better. The black man, Clement, was holding my beautiful little Beretta automatic pistol. Not pointing it at anyone. It was just dangling casually, his forefinger through the trigger guard.

But what was worse was what I saw on the floor, stacked neatly at Donahue's feet. Project X. My secret manuscript. The complete record of my Big Caper.

"What do you want?" I asked hoarsely.

"That's obvious isn't it? We want you . . . but before we get into the whys and wherefores, let's get some ground rules straight. Either of you get any ideas of suddenly shouting, screaming, making a fuss—don't. You saw how fast Angela is with her sticker. Clement can be even faster with that nice piece of yours, Jannie. Make a peep, you're dead; it's that simple. No joke. No threat. Just the truth. You try to fuck us up, you're dead and gone."

CAPER

LESLEY ANDRESS

PUBLISHED BY POCKET BOOKS NEW YORK

POCKET BOOKS, a Simon & Schuster division of
GULF & WESTERN CORPORATION
1230 Avenue of the Americas, New York, N.Y. 10020

Published by arrangement with G.P. Putnam's Sons
Library of Congress Catalog Card Number: 79-17559

ISBN: 0-671-83385-5

First Pocket Books printing January, 1981

10 9 8 7 6 5 4 3 2 1

POCKET and colophon are trademarks of Simon & Schuster.

Printed in the U.S.A.

CAPER

How It All Began

I was in bed with J. Mark Hamilton, my brother-in-law. We had spent the night together because my sister, Laura, was in Park Central, recovering from plastic surgery. She'd had her tits elevated.

So there we were in the morning, J. Mark and me, his unshaved jowls scraping at me. *"Bon appetit,"* I murmured, and then the phone rang.

It was Sol Faber, my literary agent.

"Morning, doll," he said brightly. "We got a meet with the man at tennish. Remember?"

That's the way Sol talks.

"I remember," I said. As a matter of fact, I had forgotten. I have that frailty: I lose the remembrance of unpleasant coming events.

Sol told me to meet him in the lobby of Binder Publications a few minutes before ten. Then we hung up. My brother-in-law raised his bald head to stare at me.

"Who was that?" he demanded.

"Your wife," I said. "She asked me to remind you to pick up the drycleaning."

1

His face went white before he realized I was ribbing him. J. Mark is not the fastest wit in the world. He does, though, possess certain skills, even if I don't allow him between my sheets solely because of them. It's a form of hostility directed against my sister. Laura is the pretty blond, petite one. I am constructed more along the lines of a Marine drill instructor, and I have a profile that belongs on postage stamps.

In all modesty, I am not a gorgon, but I am large. Five-ten, to be exact. J. Mark Hamilton was my sister's height: five-four. Like most tall women I inspire dreams of conquest in short males. Simply, I suppose, because we're *there*.

I am extraordinarily slender, but hardly fragile. My breasts are not as large as Laura's, lifted or descended, but I have strength in my shoulders, arms, back, and legs. I work at it: jogging, yoga, swimming, sex. My health is indecently good.

I wear my hair quite short. It is a rather indeterminate shade of dark brown. My eyes are brown too.

I am twenty-eight years old, and was born in Lima, Peru, where my father was serving as consul. Laura, who is three years younger, was born in Paris. Of course. She would be.

My father died when I was twenty-two, in a manner so ridiculous that I blush to mention it. A golf cart he was riding tipped over and fell on him, breaking his back. Near the sixth green. My mother waited a decent interval (five weeks) before remarrying. Juan, my stepfather, is two years older than I, very Spanish, and can't decide whether to be Picasso, Manolete, or Cervantes. He and my mother live on the Costa del Sol in a seafront condominium. My mother's name is Matilda. She is called Matty, and we exchange Christmas cards.

I visited them only once, and fled after Juan made his interest clear. He is quite short.

I have never been married. I don't live a celibate life, but neither do I sleep around. I like men better than women.

I think that concludes the vital statistics. Oh, one more thing: I have very long feet. I offer this only as proof of my intention of making this narrative as honest as possible.

I still feel I did nothing wrong. The New York Police Department and the Manhattan District Attorney's office, of course, feel differently.

Who Am I?

~~~~~~

My name is Chuck Thorndike. My name is Mike Cantrell. My name is Buck Williams. My name is Pat Slaughter. And, God help us, my name is Brick Wall.

All pseudonyms, of course. My real name is Jannie Shean. But I am the author of hard-boiled mystery-suspense thrillers, and Aldo Binder, "the man" at Binder Publications, is convinced that since men are the big puyers of this genre, the author's name should also be male. And not only male, but ruggedly, toughly, two-fistedly masculine.

"Like Mickey Spillane," he told me.

"Like Raymond Chandler?" I said. "Like Dashiell Hammett?"

But I was so anxious to sell my first novel that I agreed to be Chuck Thorndike. Then, when I got in the swing of things and began turning out four pot-boilers a year, along came Mike, Buck, Pat, and Brick.

I make no claim to creating literature, but I do strive for intelligent entertainment. My books are tightly plotted, with the required dollops of sex and

4

violence, and they have found a faithful readership. I have had two movie sales, and last year I grossed almost a hundred thousand dollars. As Brick Wall might say, "That ain't potato pancakes, sweetheart."

I'm lucky and I know it. For every novelist able to support himself on his earnings, there are a hundred who must earn bread teaching Creative Writing in New Hampshire girls' schools, writing ad copy on Madison Avenue, or slicing pastrami in an Orchard Street deli. Probably I made it because I found a formula I enjoyed writing and a lot of people enjoyed reading. Not that it's a formula original with me. It's called the Big Caper, and involves looting a bank vault, a kidnapping, hijacking an airliner, a raid on an armored truck—something large enough to require a gang of four to a dozen bad guys.

The first third of a Big Caper thriller is spent gathering the personnel: delineating their strengths, weaknesses, and their relationships to each other; and planning the caper. The second third of the novel describes the actual commission of the crime. In the final third, the whole thing falls apart through bad luck, clever police work, or from the personality defects, failure of brain or nerve, and antagonisms of the gang members. They are not the master criminals they fancied themselves. Justice triumphs.

How many Big Caper novels have you read? A dozen? A hundred? I hope some of them were mine. Or, rather, Chuck's, Mike's, Buck's, Pat's, or Brick's.

Together, we turned out books like link sausage, until, about six months ago, it all began to come apart like . . . well, like a Big Caper. The final sales on Mike Cantrell's latest, *Mayhem on Mother's Day,* were down, way down. And the bookstores were returning unsold stacks of Pat Slaughter's *Massacre on Division Street.*

Worse, I had recently turned in Chuck Thorndike's new opus, *Murder for Breakfast,* and after three weeks of chilling silence from my publishers, Aldo Binder's secretary called Sol Faber to set up an appointment with the great man himself. I fancied I heard, faintly, the sounds of a guillotine. Creak of pulley. Rasp of rope. Whistle of blade's descent. *Chonk!*

Editorial Bullshit

The offices of Binder Publications were in a seedy
building overlooking Times Square. On a clear day
you could see the massage parlors on Eighth Avenue.
Our meeting was held in the Editorial Conference
Room, which had all the ambience of a Central Park
Comfort Station.

Besides me, the cast of characters included:

Sol Faber, my agent. Sol tried *so* hard with his California leisure suits and blow-dried hair. He was thin,
jerky, with horn-rimmed glasses, a pinkie ring, and a
habit of snapping his fingers to call a waiter.

Aldo Binder, my publisher. Aldo was the only man
I knew who wore double-breasted vests. He was a big,
lumpy man with gloomy eyes, much given to brooding
silences. He smoked black cigars. It was said he got his
start publishing porno. He was shrewd and knowledge-
able. Had the same secretary for thirty-three years.
There were stories about *that* too, with references to
the spavined leather couch in his office.

Simon Lefferts, my editor. Lefferts was a shithead
and a snotnose. He was supposed to have a PhD in
American Literature, and he treated every manu-

script that came across his desk like the first draft of
Farewell to Arms.

So there we were, four nutcakes, sitting around an
old oak table that must have been bought from a de-
funct fraternity house. The top was carved with
names, class numerals, Greek letters, and one "Fuck
you." Simon Lefferts had the manuscript of Chuck
Thorndike's *Murder for Breakfast* in front of him,
along with three pages of single-spaced notes. I figured I was in for a two-hour personal pogrom.

Lefferts took charge immediately.

"This," he said, pointing at the manuscript but for-
bearing to touch it, "is totally unacceptable."

"Now wait a minute," my agent said. "We're con-
vened here for a nice family get-together to consider
ways and means—am I right? I mean, a little cutting
here and there, a little rewriting here and there, a
little—"

"Totally unacceptable," Lefferts repeated. "Totally
incompetent."

"Aldo!" Sol said in anguished tones. "You read the
book?"

My publisher's round head nodded. I was afraid it
might roll off that fat neck.

"And . . . ?"

"Stinks," Binder said.

Then the editor got down to nuts-and-bolts. The
plotting was juvenile, the dialogue jejune, the characterization banal, the motivation hackneyed, the
description puerile, the exposition illogical, the tran-
sitions erratic, and so on, and so on. . . .

I came close to stalking out. I can't take criticism—
who can?—and I couldn't believe the novel could be
that bad.

"Let's not talk generalities," I told Lefferts. "Give
me specific examples, page and paragraph."

"Delighted to," he said maliciously. "Juvenile plotting: On page 54, you say the girl took a cab because it was raining heavily. Two pages earlier you describe the night as crisp and clear with a full moon shining. Jejune dialogue: On page 134, the muscle, the dumbest one of the gang, a real moron, says, 'I have a feeling of *déjà vu.*' How would he know what that means? Banal characterization: The cop is fat, Irish, and drinks. The bank president wears a pince-nez and is fussy. The gang leader is lean, dark, and cold-eyed. Stock characters all. Hackneyed motivation: On page 98, the gang moll doesn't show up for a rehearsal of the caper because her daughter is having a Sweet Sixteen party. Oh my God. Puerile description: On page 52, quote, 'The moon hung in the sky like a ripe melon.' How original! Illogical exposition: On page 162, you say—"

"All right," I interrupted him, "you've made your point."

"Points," he said cruelly.

"Roscoe," Aldo Binder said.

"What was that, Aldo?" Sol asked.

"Roscoe," Binder repeated.

"On page 211," Lefferts explained, "the safe-cracker fires his gun at the bank guard. You write, '*Ka-chow* went his roscoe.' Handguns haven't been called roscoes since Black Mask Magazine. And *Ka-chow?* Since when does a gun go *Ka-chow?* Bang, maybe. Or blam. A gun snaps, or pops, or roars, or thunders. But *Ka-chow?* Sounds like a sneeze."

I try not to take myself seriously, but despite what I may have told you about running a sausage factory, I take my work very seriously indeed. So it was hard to sit there and hear my novel being put through the shredder. I was close to tears, and only the fact that I knew Lefferts wanted to see me blub kept me outwardly unshaken. Inwardly, I was figuring how I could nail his balls to a stump and push him over backward.

We all sat in silence after his lecture on the sounds of gunfire. Then Aldo Binder took a deep breath, so deep the buttons on his waistcoat seemed threatened. Then he exhaled. He took one of his black cigars from his breast pocket and began peeling it.

"You and you leave," he said, jabbing the cigar in turn at Sol Faber and Simon Lefferts. "I'll talk to Jannie in private."

God had decreed: They filed from the room. I fumbled for a cigarette. Binder held a match for me before lighting his cigar.

"I knew Lefferts hated me," I said, trying to laugh, "but I didn't know how much."

During his frequent silences, Binder had the habit of tipping back his fleshy head and opening his mouth wide. The entrance of the Lincoln Tunnel, with teeth. Not the most appetizing sight in the world.

Finally he snapped his mouth shut with a *click* that startled me. Then he regarded me gravely.

"Simon doesn't hate you," he said. "Simon resents you."

"*Resents* me?"

"You're a successful author."

"Oh," I said faintly, beginning to feel a little better, "I didn't know he wanted to write. It's a bad sign in an editor, no?"

"*All* editors want to write," Binder said. "They see trash make a fortune, and it looks so easy. However, his personal pique doesn't make his criticism wrong." He waved toward the Thorndike manuscript. "It's a lousy novel, Jannie. I won't publish it."

"A complete rewrite?" I said, gritting my teeth.

"No, I don't think so. The plot's preposterous."

"Well . . ." I sighed, "then I guess this is the parting of the ways."

He shifted his bulk round on his uncushioned chair, then settled down with fingers laced across his corporation. Corporation? That mound was a conglomerate!

"Jannie," he said, "you've made a lot of money from Binder Publications."

"Oh sure," I said hotly, "and Binder Publications has made a lot of money from me."

"True," he said, nodding his head. "And that's why I'd hate to see our relationship come to an end. Of course, under the terms of your contract, after our rejection you're free to try the book elsewhere. Do you want to?"

The sudden question took me by surprise. I stalled by stubbing out my cigarette and lighting another.

"You smoke too much," he said.

"You eat too much," I said. "I don't know what I'll do with this thing, Aldo. I'll have to think about it."

"Before you make up your mind," Binder said, "will you resent it if I tell you what's wrong with the novel? And with your two previous books?"

"No, I won't resent it," I said, lying stoutly.

"Jannie, novels in the detective-mystery-suspense field are essentially fantasies."

"All right," I said, "I'll go along with that. But—"

"Wait," he said, holding up a pudgy hand. "Let me finish. They're fantasies. But when a man picks up a paperback by Brick Wall, he isn't looking for *Little Red Riding Hood*. He wants a hard, tough, realistic, *believable* story. Oh, it's all imagination. You know it, and I know it. It's all a creation of the author's mind. But the reader must believe the author is doing nothing but detailing actual events in familiar language.

Reporting. One misstep, one flight of fancy too many, and the writer betrays the reader's trust."

"And I've been betraying my reader's trust?"

Binder tapped the ash from his cigar, blew gently on the glowing tip. "You've lost all contact with reality," he said. That '*Ka-chow* went his roscoe' may sound funny now, something easily eliminated in editing, but it's symptomatic of what's happened to your writing. You don't seem anchored to the real world anymore. Your readers have sensed this. That's it in a nutshell, Jannie: You've lost contact."

We sat in silence again. I looked down, tracing with a fingertip that "Fuck you" carved into the oak tabletop. I wasn't ready to accept what Binder had said. Lost contact with the real world?

"Well," I said finally, "what do you suggest?"

"There are things you could do. Interview cops. Take a night tour in a patrol car. Such things can be arranged. Try to meet some criminals, active or behind bars. Read the reports of sociologists and penal officials. Read the tabloids. You're a clever lady; you'll find ways. All I'm suggesting is that you get your head out of the clouds and your feet back on the ground."

"If I wrote a sentence like that," I said, "Lefferts would blue-pencil it with a notation: 'Unacceptable cliche.' "

"Think about what I've said. I see no reason why, with a little effort, you can't get back to the kind of novels your readers have enjoyed in the past."

"And bought," I reminded him.

"And bought," he agreed. "Jannie, Binder Publications is *not* a nonprofit organization. Not deliberately, it isn't."

First Stirrings

~~~~~~~~~~~~~~~~~~~~~~~~~~~~~~~~~~~~~~

Sol Faber ushered me from the offices of Binder Publications holding my elbow as if he expected me to collapse with the vapors. He snapped his fingers at an empty cab and, remarkably, it stopped. He told the driver to take us to the Four Seasons.

"My treat, doll," he told me grandly. "We'll have a few drinks to repair our egos and then we'll have some of those little sausages and shrimps on darning needles."

"Thanks, Sol," I said gratefully, "but I'll split the check with you."

"Okay," he agreed immediately. "Listen, don't let what El Jerko said about the manuscript put you in the pits. He was just running off at the mouth. What did you and Aldo talk about?"

"More of the same," I said. "He just doesn't want to publish the book. Says we're free to try it elsewhere."

"Uh-huh," he said, looking out the cab window. "Well, we'll talk about that while we eat."

Sol wangled a table in the Grill Room, a section

that's almost wholly occupied during lunch by the book publishing crowd. He snapped his fingers for the waiter.

I usually drink white wine, but at the moment I needed a martini. Sol had something pink with tequila and shaved ice.

We weren't exactly in a festive mood, and exchanged only a few words while gulping down the first round. Sol knew some of the people at nearby tables. He smiled, waved, told me who they were.

"You know a lot of people in the business, Sol."

"The name of the game, doll; that's how an agent operates. Personal contacts."

"So you have contacts at other houses where we could send this Thorndike book?"

"Well, uh, sure. Lots of places."

We ordered another round.

"Sol," I said, "I seem to detect a lack of enthusiasm for sending the novel somewhere else."

"No, no," he protested. "No, no, no. Where'd you get that idea?"

"Because you just used five no's. Sol, did you *read* the book?"

"Read it? Of course I read it."

"All of it?"

"Well, listen, doll, maybe not *all*. I mean, I know your work; I know how professional you are."

"How much of it did you read, Sol?"

"Oh . . . I don't remember, exactly. Maybe the first fifty and the last fifty pages."

"And what did you think of it? Tell me the truth now."

"Jannie," he said, turning sideways to look sincerely into my eyes, "I've got to level with you. I didn't think it was up to your usual high standard."

I laughed.

"Sol," I said, "you've got more crap than a Christmas goose."

"Yes," he said happily, "that's true."

We ordered. I had the chef's salad, and Sol got his shrimp and sausages broiled on skewers. While we were at it, we asked for another round. I was beginning to relax. The world wasn't really coming to an end. Not that morning.

"All right, *doll*," I said, "let's have it—what's wrong with the book?"

The poor dear really looked perplexed, blinking frantically behind his horn-rims as he tried to estimate how truthful he could be without losing a client.

"Look," he said, "I read enough of the beginning to know what the caper was and who the main characters were. Then I read the last part to find out how it all came out."

"And . . . ?"

"Well, listen, Jannie, you know why people read books like this? Crime stuff, spy stuff? Because it's *neat*."

"*Neat?*"

"I mean, it's like a package. Say you got this bunch of guys involved in a big crime. They plan it, then they pull it. And then there's the end."

"They get caught or killed, and justice triumphs."

"Not necessarily. I read a novel last year where the bad guys got away with it, grew mustaches, and took the loot down to Rio to live happily ever after. It was a good read. A very satisfying book. You know why?"

"No. Why?"

"Because it has a *neat* ending. No loose ends. When it's all over, readers want it finished, resolved. Because everyone is looking for something that just doesn't exist in real life."

"Form?" I said. "Everyone wants form and order?"

"My very words," he said gratefully. "Everyone wants form and order. Either the law catches up with the crooks or they escape. Who cares? But what's important is that the whole thing is resolved. That's very fulfilling. Now I read the last fifty pages of your Thorndike thing and, Jannie, it just left me with my thumb up my ass. Two guys get killed, one guy gets caught, one guy commits suicide, and one guy—you never do say what happened to him. The ending is such a mishmash, the reader doesn't know what the hell happened. Doll, this book doesn't end; it just stops."

I didn't say anything. I forked away at my salad, thinking about what Sol had said.

Binder had said the modern fairy tale had to be built on realism. But how could you be "true to life" with Sol's neat, tidy ending?

A puzzlement.

"I'll think about it," I told him.

We finished lunch with a vodka stinger. We left, feeling no pain, and Sol put me in a cab. I went back to my apartment, sharing the seat with Chuck Thorndike's *Murder for Breakfast*. When I got out of the taxi I had a sudden desire to leave the manuscript behind. Maybe the next passenger would get a few laughs. But no, I lugged it upstairs.

The phone was ringing when I came in; I dashed to grab it. I had the wild hope that Aldo Binder had changed his mind. But it was only my brother-in-law, J. Mark Hamilton, burbling with happiness. It seemed that Laura was being kept in the hospital another twenty-four hours, and how about a replay of last night?

"Oh, fuck off," I snarled. And slammed down the phone.

My apartment wasn't palatial, but I thought it was

great, with a lot of polished wood and green plants. It was a two-bedroom layout, but the smaller bedroom had been converted into an office den. I did my writing in there. It was much more cluttered than the rest of the apartment and maybe more comfortable.

I kicked off my loafers and settled back in a distressed oak swivel chair I had bought in a junk-antique shop for $29.50. It was comfortable enough and squeaked musically every time I turned.

Then I began to read *Murder for Breakfast* by Chuck Thorndike.

I rarely used to read or reread my stuff. I typed "The End," then sent it off to Sol Faber and after a while the checks began coming in. I really didn't care if Binder Publications changed the titles and I wasn't much interested in the covers they slapped on my books. I had done my job: the writing. The production, promotion, and selling were up to others. That may be a short-sighted attitude for a writer, but it was the way I felt. I had never been on a TV talk show and had never been interviewed by a newspaper or magazine. I couldn't care less.

So reading Chuck Thorndike's Big Caper was like reading something written by a stranger. I hadn't looked at it for almost two months, and meanwhile I had been working on Buck Williams' newest.

I didn't have to read more than ten pages. I've never been so ashamed in my life.

It was a piece of cheese.

I mean it was *bad*. I started out squirming, and ended up laughing. It read like S. J. Perelman and Woody Allen collaborating on a classic put-on. I had everything in there, from the shifty-eyed villain to the whore with a heart of gold, from the Irish cop with his "Begora" and "B'Jasus" to a private eye with snap-brimmed fedora and soiled trenchcoat.

I started reading about 2:00 P.M., determined to finish the damned thing. The outside light grew dim. I switched on the desk lamp and read on; I can endure pain. I finished at about 7:00 in the evening. Then I straightened the manuscript pages, tapped them neatly into a smooth bundle, and dumped the whole thing into the wastebasket. Then I felt my cheeks. I was blushing.

I went into the kitchen for a chilled, half-bottle of Gallo chablis and brought that and a glass back to my office. I peeled off my pantyhose and settled in the swivel chair again. I poured a glass of wine, and sipped.

My Writing Career

During my relatively brief and successful writing career, I had been like someone who builds houses without knowing anything about engineering or architecture. He builds simply by observing how other houses are constructed—beams here, rafters there, shingles on the outside.

I had written my novels the same way, by reading and observing how other people wrote similar books. Never once had I considered the theory or *philosophy* of the detective-mystery-suspense genre. I wasn't even aware they were important enough to warrant a theory or philosophy.

The comments of Aldo Binder and Sol Faber that morning were a revelation to me. I had been a lucky blunderer, grinding out imitative books people wanted to read. Now, because I really didn't know what the hell I was doing, my luck was running out.

Aldo Binder had been right: I had lost contact with

the real world. Sol Faber had been right: I had for-gotten, if I ever knew, what my readers wanted.

Still, I wasn't about to toss my hands in the air and seek employment as a domestic. It never occurred to me to stop. Obsession? Possibly.

I Was Hungry

These deep, deep thoughts were interrupted by a very human need: hunger. I'm a big woman, and a chef's salad at noon really isn't enough to see me through the day. I went into the kitchen to inspect the larder. Dismal. The best possibilities seemed a half-dozen eggs and a small, canned ham. Not the Four Seasons, but it would do.

The kitchen clock showed a few minutes to 8:00 so I called Dick Fleming.

"Richard," I said, "am I interrupting?"

"Nope. How are you, Jannie?"

"Miserable. Eat yet?"

"I was just looking in the fridge. How does a hunk of greenish cheddar and a few slices of gray baloney grab you?"

"I can do a little better than that—ham and eggs. Want to share?"

"Be right over," he said.

I met Richard J. Fleming at Sol Faber's New Year's Eve party, two years ago. . . .

"Listen, doll," Sol said excitedly, holding on to him,

"you've got to meet this gorgeous guy, Dick Flemmer his name is, and he's the new—"

"Dick Fleming," the man said, smiling.

Sol snapped his fingers. "Right! Dick Fleming. He handles children's books for Mayer, Markham. Dick, this beautiful lady is my favorite client, Jannie Shean."

"Jannie Shanahan," I said soberly.

"What?" Sol said, worried. "Oh, I get it! You're putting me on. Right, doll? You're putting me on?"

Dick was a few inches taller than I, and almost as skinny. That helped. Also, it turned out, he was a quiet, sweet, amusing, un-pushy man, and he became my closest and dearest friend.

He was not gay, exactly, and he was not straight, exactly. He edited children's books, and there was something childlike about him: sudden and brief enthusiams, fits of stubbornness, an occasional tantrum. But generally he was smiling and serene, as if he had come to terms with himself and could live with what he was.

He spoke little of his background, but I gathered he'd been raised by a widowed mother and an unmarried aunt. He came from someplace in Ohio, and in the two years I had known him, had never returned for a visit.

He was lanky and loose-limbed, fair-headed, with pale, freckled skin. He moved gracefully and had a pleasing singing voice. He played a passable piano and guitar, and spoke three foreign languages. He was also an excellent cook and a marvelous host. He doted on parties.

Dick's apartment was three blocks from mine, on East 74th Street, and we frequently dropped in on each other, but never without calling first. During the previous summer we had rented a place together in Easthampton, and it worked out very well. He was easy to live with: quiet, neat, self-effacing. He was there when you wanted him, and gone when you wanted to be alone.

When Dick came over, he volunteered to fix dinner. He scrambled the eggs with chives and found a can of pineapple slices in my cupboard to add to the baked ham. So that, plus an endive salad with a vinaigrette sauce, made a feast that we both tucked into with fervor.

While we ate, I told him what had happened to me during the day. He listened closely, asked very perceptive questions and, as usual, seemed genuinely interested in my problems.

We took our coffee and brandy into the living room and sprawled side by side on my chesterfield.

"Well," Dick said when I'd finished my tale of woe, "sounds like you've had a full day."

"Yeah," I said sourly, "full of bullshit." I sometimes used words like that. Dick didn't.

"What are you going to do, Jannie?"

"I don't know. I'm about a hundred pages into a new book. I read those over, too. Just as bad. I'll have to junk them, I guess. What did you think about what Binder and Faber said? About mystery-suspense novels?"

"I don't read that kind of thing," he said. "You know that. But I'm always suspicious about profound pronouncements. Maybe they're right; I'm not saying they're not. They could just as easily be wrong. But what disturbs me most is that you yourself think the book is bad."

"It's bad, Dick. I read it over. I trashed it."

"All right. You're entitled to a flop now and then. No one hits it all the time. But don't let one turkey make you feel you're a failure as a writer. Get started on something new, right away."

"That's what Sol told me. But Binder told me I've lost contact. He was talking about reality. So how do I make contact with reality? I don't know what to do. Spend the night?"

"Sure," he said. "You haven't been shaving your legs with my razor, have you?"

"I bought new blades."

"Good. Jannie, I shouldn't even venture an opinion on your books. You know I don't read anything written for anyone over fifteen years old. But I've found a factor in children's books that may be applicable in the detective-mystery-suspense field. Kids are hooked by adventure. Risk and adventure. Unknown lands. Unexplored continents. Seas no one has sailed, uncharted galaxies. I think the same holds true for adults. Men and women read crime fiction for the adventure, the risk.

"Did you see the results of that poll where they asked people what they thought of their jobs? The huge majority said their jobs were dull, boring, and offered no satisfaction, no fulfillment. They didn't ask me, but I'd have said exactly the same thing: dull, boring, unsatisfying."

"I didn't know you felt that way."

"Well . . . sure. But what else can I do? The salary isn't great, but it's okay. I suppose someday I might get a similar job in some other house at more money. Or even become an editor-in-chief. So what? It's all such a drag. I try not to look ahead because it depresses me so much. But that's my point: If you can get a feeling of risk and adventure in your books, I think you're home free. Readers have a longing to experience what life denies them."

"Bed?" I asked.

"Okay," he said. "Let's take the brandy."

That suited me fine.

Dick feel asleep first, head on my shoulder, his fine hair tickling my nose. But I couldn't sleep. My brain was churning. I went over again and again what Aldo Binder had said, what Sol Faber had said, what Dick Fleming had said. What I should do and not do, write or not write. A woman's curse: worrying unnecessarily about what men think.

Dick was sleeping soundly. I kissed the tip of his nose. I moved his head off my shoulder as gently as I could. I disentangled arms and legs, pulled away and slipped out of bed. I pulled sheet and blanket up and tucked him in. Then I went padding naked into my office, snapped on the goose-neck desk lamp, closed the door.

It was warm in there, toasty enough so that I didn't need a robe. I sat down in the swivel chair, trying to keep it from creaking. I wondered if the seat cushion would leave button marks on my bare ass. I got out a long, yellow legal pad and a ballpoint pen. But I didn't write down a word.

It started out as something wild, ridiculous, nonsensical. Then harebrained. Then merely insane.

How long I sat there, brain-storming, I don't know. At some point the door opened. Dick stood there, naked as a pin, rubbing his eyes and yawning.

"Dick," I said excitedly, "sit down and listen."

"What time is it?"

"How the hell should I know? Two, three in the morning. Sit down and listen to my great idea."

Grumbling, he folded himself into the armchair on the other side of the desk. He shook his head from side to side, trying to clear the sleep away.

"Okay," he sighed patiently, "I'm awake. Go ahead; what's your sensational idea?"

I told it to him.

"How's *that* for making contact with reality?" I said, laughing excitedly when I was done. "How's that for getting back to 'true-to-life' details? I can't make my next book any more realistic than that, can I?"

He looked at me queerly.

"And get caught and do twenty years?"

"I'm not going to *commit* the crime," I said, "I'm just going to find out how to *plan* it. At the final step, just before the breaking-and-entering, I'll bring the whole thing to a screeching halt. I can imagine the rest of it; the *actual* crime will write itself. Don't you see what I'm doing? I'm going to put myself in place of my chief villain. I'm personally going to go through everything he'd have to go through: all the problems, difficulties, fears, delays. I'm going to experience everything I've been writing about and didn't *know* about. My God, Dick, I'm going to become a Master Criminal!"

He took a deep breath and blew it out, staring at me with that same look I couldn't fathom, as though he thought I had flipped.

"You're going to recruit an actual gang?"

"Right," I said, nodding. "Bad guys. Bent noses with a lot of experience. Felons."

"And how are you going to find them—put a want ad in *The Christian Science Monitor?*"

"Dick, that's just the *point*—don't you see? I've got to find out how you'd go about recruiting a gang. Who you'd have to contact. How you'd find him. For instance—a gun. If I'm going to be a modern Ma Barker, I'll need a gun. How do I go about getting a gun in New York City? I'm sure it can be done, but *how?* That's the kind of problem I'll have to solve. But look at what I'll be learning!"

"Jannie, are you serious about this?"

"Of course I'm serious!"

"Do you know what you're getting into, getting a gun and hiring a gang of crooks? What happens when you hire your thugs and rehearse them for your Big Caper, and then call it off at the last minute? What do you think their reaction will be?"

"Oh hell, Dick—I can handle that. They're all morons. I'll just tell them it's off and disappear. If I pay them for a week or two of rehearsals, I'm not hurting them, am I? But that's just a minor detail. I haven't yet figured it all out. I'm just drafting the grand concept. What do you think?"

"Jannie, there may be danger. Real-life danger, not pretend."

"Of course there will be danger! There *has* to be danger. How else can my Big Caper be realistic? How can it ring true? I want to learn about the danger. I *want* to be afraid. That's what the whole idea is about. Where are you going? Back to bed?"

He had uncoiled his naked length from the armchair and was starting for the door.

"Be right back," he said.

He returned in a moment with the brandy bottle and our two glasses. He set the snifters on my desk blotter and poured us hefty shots.

"Jannie," he said, "I want in."

"What?"

"I want in. I want to be the first member of Jannie's gang."

"You're crazy."

"No crazier than you. How about it?"

I stared at him, trying to understand.

"Dick, this has nothing to do with misguided chivalry, does it? The macho male joining up to protect the weak, defenseless woman from the big, bad men?"

"Do I look like a macho male?" he asked reasonably. "Use your brain, Jannie; what do I know about guns, knives, or physical combat?"

"Then *why?*"

"The adventure," he said. "The risk."

"I'll drink to that."

Hot Ice

~~~~~~

The following evening, Dick came over after dinner. I had dined with Laura and my brother-in-law, and had to endure a two-hour replay of the great tit-raising. It was recited in excruciating detail while their live-in housekeeper served us quivering hemispheres of salmon in aspic.

I got home before Dick arrived and prepared for our conference by setting out scratchpads and ballpoints, glasses, a bucket of ice, and a chilled bottle of vodka.

Despite what Aldo Binder thought, I *did* read the tabloids, and like most writers in my field, I clipped everything relating to crime—specific cases, statistics, new developments in police procedures, etc. I kept all these snippets in a series of bulging file folders, and the one I pulled out that evening was labeled Current Crimes.

What I was after was the type of crime that offered maximum gain and minimum risk. After Dick was ensconced in the armchair in my office, we divided Current Crimes into two roughly equal stacks of clip-

pings and began breaking them down into classifica-
tions: homicides, robberies, burglaries, kidnappings,
extortions, blackmail, hijacking, etc. Then we combined similar piles and started eliminating. Homicides
went first, of course. Small potatoes. We also discarded
blackmail and extortion. Both required a special
knowledge, or leverage, we simply didn't possess. We
eliminated kidnapping because it was distasteful and
hijacking because we wouldn't know what to do with a
747 or a trailer-load of cigarettes if we stole one.

That left burglaries and armed robberies. We mixed
another drink and divided the two stacks of newspaper stories by target: individuals, offices, stores,
banks, armored trucks, hotels, etc. Some of these,
such as banks and armored trucks, were thrown out
because of the expertise involved.

Individuals, offices, stores, or hotels seemed to both
of us to offer the best opportunities. But robbing an
individual or burglarizing an individual apartment or
house scarcely qualified as a Big Caper. It would require one criminal, two at most. We were looking for
a crime demanding a gang.

We considered a luxury hotel as a possible target.

"The trouble with looting a hotel," Dick said,
skimming the clippings, "is that that too requires inside information. The crooks obviously know when the
safe deposit boxes are loaded. That hints of some hotel
employee being in cahoots, doesn't it?"

"Also," I said, "there have been at least five big
hotel heists in Manhattan in the past few years. Security has been beefed up. I think there's a special
squad in the NYPD just to keep an eye on hotels, and
for all we know there may be permanent stakeouts of
hotel desks at night."

"Then let's put hotels aside for the time being. Ditto
offices. Offices sound small time, especially since most

payrolls are paid by check. That leaves stores. Jannie, you take half these store robberies and I'll take half. See if we can come up with something."

We divided the clippings and began flipping through them.

After a while Dick said:

"Jannie, how far back do these stories go?"

"About three years. Why?"

"Just wondering."

We read along in silence for a few more minutes. Then Dick said:

"That's interesting."

"What is?"

"Do me a favor: Put aside any clippings you find about jewel robberies. Just stores. Not couriers, cutters, messengers, and so forth; just stores. Anything to do with jewels. Mostly diamonds."

He poured us each more vodka and we went on with our task. A half-hour later, we had a fat little stack of reports on jewelry store robberies all over the country. Dick started going through this specialized pile.

"What are you doing now?" I asked him.

"Eliminating all those where the reported loss was less than a hundred thousand dollars."

It didn't take him long. When he finished, he had a fistful of newspaper stories, some consisting of several clippings on the same case stapled together. Dick counted the individual cases.

"Fourteen," he announced. "Fourteen jewelry store thefts in the past three years in which the take was more than a hundred thousand."

"That's wild," I said. "And there may have been more; I can't guarantee that my newspaper clipping is one-hundred percent efficient."

"But the number of robberies isn't the most unusual

factor," he went on. "You'd think most of those four-teen thefts would be in New York, in the diamond district on West 47th Street. That's diamond head-quarters for the whole country. But only two of the robberies took place there. The other twelve were all over: Chicago, Beverly Hills, Dallas, Atlanta, Miami, Denver, and so forth. And here's something just as odd: most of the fourteen took place in the past year, and only one bundle of clippings shows the crooks were caught."

"I may have missed the solution of the crime," I confessed. "The original theft usually gets a big play in the papers, with a headline and long story on page one. If the case is broken a year later, it usually rates a few inches of type on page fifty. I could have missed it."

"Maybe," he said doubtfully, "but according to your file, *most* of these recent jewelry store capers are still unsolved."

"Let me see," I said, and he handed over the clip-pings.

I went through them swiftly. Then I reported to Dick:

"Practically all were armed robberies during the daylight hours when the stores were open for business. Only three of them were breaking-and-entering at night. That makes sense; jewelry stores have good nighttime security, with electronic alarms to the local precinct house or to a private security agency. But the daylight robberies seem to have been practically all successful."

We looked at each other. Dick Fleming has a short upper lip. Now it lifted in a half-smile.

"They wore masks, of course?" he asked me.

"Usually," I said. "Ski masks or stockings pulled over their heads. Or maybe just disguises, like fake beards and mustaches. Wigs and crazy clothes. Things like that to confuse the witnesses."

Again we looked at each other. I added ice to our glasses and poured in more vodka.

"How does it sound to you?" Dick asked.

"Sounds good. Sounds like our best bet. You?"

"Sounds good to me, too. Jannie, if we did rip off a jewelry store, how would we cash in?"

"Two ways," I said. "One, we can sell the jewelry to a fence. Making sure he's not an undercover cop. If a fence gives you twenty to thirty percent of the retail value of the stuff you steal, you're lucky. The other way of cashing in is to sell the stuff back to the insurance company that carries the policy on the store. You understand? They'd rather pay thirty thousand to recover the jewels than shell out a hundred thousand if they were never found. In effect, in cases like that, the crooks are holding the jewels for ransom. The cops hate those deals between crooks and insurance companies, but there's not much they can do about them. But we don't have to worry about that. After all, we're not actually going to pull the job."

"That's right," Dick Fleming said, his pale eyes staring somewhere over my head. "We're not, are we?"

Having decided on the robbery of a jewelry store, we went on to a discussion of the type of store that would best fit the Big Caper concept. Not something as large as Tiffany or Cartier. It would take an army to pull off a successful daylight heist of those emporiums. But not a little mom-and-pop shop either; the take wouldn't pay for the expense of planning and the splitting of the profits among several gang members.

"A medium-sized store," I said.

"About four or five employees," Dick said. "Certainly not more than ten."

"A store on one level. With a single entrance."

"But an expensive place, specializing in high-quality gems. Diamonds, emeralds, rubies, sapphires."

"A place with an alarm system that can be cut or put out of order."

"With no more than one armed guard on the premises."

"Right," I nodded, making fast notes on my scratch pad. "A place like that. How many do you think we'll need?"

"Maybe three men," Dick said. "In addition to you and me. More than that begins to get unwieldy. We'd be running up each other's heels."

"We'll need someone outside in the car," I reminded him. "A driver for a quick getaway and to serve as a lookout."

"A fourth, then. Or perhaps one of the three I mentioned. It depends on the size of the store. Jannie, that'll have to be your job—locating a suitable target. I can help out on weekends, and maybe during lunch hours, but you'll have to do most of the scouting."

"Where should I start?" I asked.

"Try Fifth Avenue first," he said. "The crowds could be a help during the getaway."

"Or a hindrance," I said. "If we get hung up in traffic. Some nice shops on Madison, too. And 57th Street. I'll just have to cover the whole midtown section."

"A lot of walking."

"A lot of fun. Besides, I need the exercise."

After he left, I cleaned up the office, carried glasses, ice bucket, vodka to the kitchen, restored clippings to the folder, tucked folders back into the file cabinet. Then I sat down in the swivel chair again, read over the brief notes I had jotted down.

It occurred to me that I would be foolish not to keep a complete record of everything Dick Fleming and I did, said, thought. Such a journal would be an invaluable reference when it came time to start a new book.

"Here's looking at you, Aldo Binder," I said out loud. Then I threaded a yellow second sheet into my IBM electric, typed in yesterday's date at the top, gave it a working title: "Project X." I started writing. I subtitled the first section: "How It All Began."

I decided not to tell Dick Fleming that I was keeping a precise record of our activities. It would only make the poor dear nervous.

Learning the Trade

~~~~~~

I wish I had been wearing a pedometer during the following two weeks; I would have loved to know how many miles I covered. Back and forth on the cross streets from 34th to 59th. Up and down on the avenues from First to Sixth.

The weather was sharp enough to justify wearing my mink, for which I was truly thankful. What cop or jewelry store owner would suspect a tall, elegant lady in a full-length mink coat and a wide-brimmed black fedora with a band of pheasant feathers? With an alligator shoulder bag? I was a walking illustration of why the Endangered Species Act was passed. For instance, I began to look upon policemen, guards, and even the public as my natural enemies. Jewelry stores and their contents became challenges. Traffic flow was noted only as it might impede or assist my plans. Even the weather took on a new dimension; a bright, sunny sky might not be desirable, while a dark, rain-soaked day might prove advantageous.

It was a totally upside-down way of looking at the world and society, a little scary, constantly stressful,

but there was exhilaration in it, too. The senses were
constantly alert, the mind sharpened and restless. The
ordinary concerns of life were of no import. Food lost
its flavor, and even sex seemed a second-rate pleasure. Nothing was as important, as meaningful, as the
business at hand: the planning of a successful illegal
enterprise.

And what freedom! I glimpsed the anarchic world
of the criminal, and it shocked me with its excitement
and almost sensual delight. I began to understand why
people might deliberately turn to crime without the
spur of poverty.

I started out each morning at about 10:00 A.M.,
taking a cab to the corner I had left the day before.
Once afoot, I walked at a steady, purposeful pace: a
shopper out for early-morning bargains or an East
Side lady on her way to dentist or gynecologist.

I soon developed the ability to judge a jewelry
store's possibilities in seconds, merely by walking past
across the street. The hole-in-the-wall shops were out.
So were those featuring cheap costume jewelry and
watch repairs. So were stores located on upper floors,
or ground-floor shops with two interior levels, or those
with more than one entrance.

After the first week I realized how difficult a getaway by car would be in the traffic-clogged cross streets.
I decided to concentrate on avenues where traffic
moved faster and blocks were shorter.

I actually entered several shops. I asked to look at a
watch, a ring, necklace, whatever I spotted in the nearest showcase. I never bought anything, but the few
minutes I was in the store enabled me to make a quick
estimate of the size, merchandise, prices, number of
employees, presence of guards, and to discover if
the safe or vault was in the selling area or in a separate locked room.

I also tried to form a general impression: prosperity or seediness, a clean, glittering shop with modern fixtures and Muzak, or a grimy, threadbare store with worn carpet, dusty display cases, and the odor of disinfectant. The smartness of the employees' dress was another tipoff. So was the presence of a doorman. Some expensive shops, which I automatically rejected, kept their front doors locked and apparently admitted only familiar customers or those of prepossessing appearance. I couldn't see them buzzing the door open for a gang of hoodlums in ski masks.

I also inspected outside window displays in order to get a rough idea of the price range within. In the better shops, the jewelry on display carried no price tags or the tags were turned facedown. This was a clue to quality merchandise, and I had no hesitation in stalking in and asking the price of the most impressive item in the window.

I learned things about jewelry stores I hadn't known. Size was not necessarily an indication of wealth. Some of the most elegant and apparently most prosperous shops were simply one long, well-appointed room with armchairs for customers and no jewelry on display. The customer made known his desires, and the clerk went into an interior locked room to bring forth a velvet tray of rings, bracelets, earrings, or whatever was requested. If nothing on the tray satisfied, it was returned to the vault, and another tray brought out. At no time was the customer left alone with jewelry. Under that system, boosting would have been practically impossible.

Something else I learned: In several shops in the Forties, the armed guard or one of the clerks was equipped with a miniature radio transmitter, carried on belt or in pocket. I could only assume he had direct

contact with the local police precinct or a private security agency.

And in many stores, the silent alarm buttons were
in plain view. In fact, they were so obvious I figured
their public placement was deliberate. Would-be
thieves would concentrate their attention on the buttons in view, to make certain they weren't pressed,
giving employees the opportunity to use silent alarms
more cleverly concealed.

I already knew that the narrow strip of aluminum
foil you see around some street windows is wired to a
burglar alarm. But I also learned that in expensive
jewelry stores, individual show-cases are frequently
equipped with pressure alarms on the lid or door.
These must be deactivated before the case is opened.

As for the main vault or safe in the rear of the store
where valuable items were placed at night, the few I
glimpsed appeared to be left open during the day. A
comforting fact.

During the second week, Sol Faber called me in the
evening.

"Where have you been, doll?" he inquired anxiously. "I've been calling you for the last three days."

"I've been out, Sol."

"Doing what?"

"Research."

"You mean you're working on something new?
That's my doll! How's it coming?"

"Fine. Very realistic."

"Music to my ears!" he bubbled. "And remember,
neat and tidy. The ending should be neat and tidy."

I told him I'd try, and after he hung up, I brought
my account of the fake Big Caper up to date.

A Problem of Violence

Across the street from my apartment house, and down the block a few doors, was a French restaurant called Chez Morris.

Morris was a rough, tubby guy from Brooklyn who looked like a longshoreman, which he once was. There are about 100 authentic French restaurants in Manhattan, and I'd guess the Chez Morris ranked about 101st. You entered through a long, narrow bar where patrons without reservations waited until a table was available. But after 10:00 the bar became the gathering place of regulars from the neighborhood.

Morris, the owner, knew everything: old baseball scores, sports records, gambling odds, lyrics to ancient songs, casts of forgotten musicals, the vice-president under Coolidge. Morris could settle any argument, and his word was law. He also took bets now and then and handled a few cartons of bootleg cigarettes.

I timed my arrival for a few minutes after 10:00 in the evening. I figured the regulars wouldn't yet be clogging the bar, and I'd have a chance for a private conversation with Morris.

"Hey, Jannie," he said in his raspy, waterfront voice. "Long time no see. How you been?"

"I'm not going to tell you," I said. "Why should we both be miserable? A double brandy, Morris."

"What's with the brandy?" he said. "I never known you to dip your nose in anything but white wine. Something wrong, Jannie?"

"Ah, hell," I said. "I got mugged last night, and I still got the shakes."

I held out a hand and trembled the fingers convincingly.

"Son of a bitch," he said bitterly. "You're the third in the neighborhood this month. You get hurt, God fabbid?"

"No," I said. "Just the shit scared out of me."

"I can imagine," he said. "But you weren't hurt?"

"No, nothing like that. Just took my wallet. A little over a hundred. Didn't touch my credit cards. I guess I was lucky."

"You get a good look at him?"

"What can I tell you? A kid with a knife."

"The lousy creep," he growled and moved away to wait on a new customer.

"What did the cops say?" he asked when he came back.

"The cops," I said scornfully. "They took my statement and promised nothing. What can they do? A hundred muggings a night. The animals are taking over. Morrie, I just felt so helpless. He had a knife, and I had nothing. He made me reach into my shoulder bag for my wallet. I swear if I had a gun in there, I would have shot him in the balls."

"Just what he deserved," Morris said virtuously. "Your honest citizen, he can't carry a gun. The assholes can carry an arsenal."

"Morrie," I said, staring into his eyes, "I'm not going to get mugged again. Not without putting up a fight, I'm not. Do you know how I can get a gun?"

He froze. "Aw, babe," he said, "you don't want to do that. So what if you plug a guy trying to rob you? Then you're in trouble with the law."

"I don't care!" I told him furiously. "I want to be able to fight back. Listen, maybe the next guy will rob me *and* try rape as a little bonus. Morrie, can you help me? Help me get a gun?"

Again he moved away to wait on another customer. When he came back, he leaned across the bar. I leaned toward him.

"Well, listen," he said in a growly whisper, "I think you're doing the wrong thing. I mean, maybe you miss, and the bentnose decides to shoot you or cut you up, God fabbid. Who's to say?"

"I'm willing to take my chances."

"You know how to handle a piece?"

"I can learn. Point it and pull the trigger—right?"

"Well, yeah. Something like that. If your mind is made up, Jannie, maybe I can do something for you."

"How much?"

"Fifty, a hundred, more," he said judiciously. "It depends on the iron. Let me get in touch with this guy I know."

"When can I meet him?"

"Drop by tomorrow night," Morris said. "Or give me a call. I'll try to have some word for you. You're absolutely positive you want to do this, Jannie?"

"Absolutely," I said firmly.

"Okay." He nodded. "I'll see what I can do."

On Target

I now had three possible targets I wanted Dick to inspect. We started with a store on the east side of Fifth Avenue, between 54th and 55th streets. A relatively small shop, one entrance, three clerks, plus a manager and armed guard. Two display windows, with only a few items tastefully exhibited. The vault was in a back room, protected with a steel gate and solid door, both open during selling hours.

We took a look from across the street, then walked by once, then returned to look in the windows, then went in to stroll about. All the employees were busy with customers, so we had an opportunity to wander around and inspect the merchandise in showcases. We chatted, laughed, pointed out items to each other.

After we exited, I took Dick's arm and led him downtown.

"Well?" I asked him. "What do you think?"

"I don't know," he said doubtfully. "An awful lot of gold-plated costume jewelry and cultured pearls. I don't think it would be a big take. Maybe they keep the best stuff in the vault, but that four-thousand-dollar necklace of small diamonds was the most expensive thing I saw. I just don't think the place is worth the effort."

"All right," I said. "The second one's over on Park, just one more block south."

This was a larger, more elegant shop with a uniformed doorman, apparently no armed guard, and six clerks on duty, plus a cashier, floor manager, and an aged lady who apparently did nothing but gift-wrap. There were two small television cameras high up in opposite corners, so perhaps that missing armed guard was in a bulletproof cubbyhole, watching TV monitors.

This time we asked to see a diamond solitaire—"something in the moderate range"—and were shown a gorgeous rock like a miniature ice cube held in platinum claws. Only $18,000. We asked if something better was available. Indeed it was, we were assured, but the manager would prefer to take care of us personally. Unfortunately, he was busy. If we could wait a few minutes . . . ?

We told the clerk that we had another appointment.

Outside, to prove our innocence, we paused casually on the sidewalk to light cigarettes before sauntering away.

"What about that one?" I asked Dick Fleming.

"The money is there," he acknowledged. "Did you see what the manager was showing the woman in the white mink? The emerald bracelet?"

"Fifty-thousand minimum, I'd guess," I said. "Wonder where the vault is? In the back?"

"Or on another floor," Dick said. "Up one level or down one. But that's not what's bothering me. It's those TV cameras."

"Take a look at the last place," I said. "Then we'll discuss it."

My final possible was on East 55th Street, just west of Madison. But I was so impressed by it that I disregarded the business about traffic jams on crosstown streets. The outside was not prepossessing. There were small signs in the windows: "Watch and Jewelry Repair. We Buy and Sell Antique Jewelry. Silver, Gold, Precious Gems. Diamonds for Investment."

Dick turned to me. "What's this—a supermarket?"

"Take a look," I urged.

The place was called Brandenberg & Sons. It wasn't the newest or the most elegant of the shops I had cased, but it was furnished in a kind of quiet, subdued opulence: deep Oriental rugs, upholstered Louis XIV armchairs for customers, small polished walnut showcases with brass corners and hardware. There were three clerks, all handsome young men, wearing navy blazers and gray flannel slacks.

An opened door at the rear afforded a glimpse of an old-fashioned safe. No television cameras here, but there were several silent alarm buttons in plain view. No armed guard to be seen. Steel shutters that could be drawn down at night to protect the outside window displays. The whole place had a genteel, hushed, cathedral atmosphere.

The three clerks were busy. The manager himself approached us. "Good afternoon," he said, bowing deeply. "May I be of service?"

"I noticed your sign," I said. "I have a gold pocket watch—"

He spread his hands and raised one shoulder. "But of course," he said. "How old is it?"

"I have no idea," I confessed.

"Bring it in," he told me.

"Thank you," I said.

"Could we look around a moment?" Dick asked.

"Please do," the manager said, beaming.

We didn't stay long, just long enough to take a quick look at a dazzling display of gold, diamonds, rubies, sapphires, emeralds. Incredible Victorian jewelry in worked gold, and avant-garde designs in crystal, silver, platinum. We heard one of the clerks say to a sable-clad dowager, "With the matching bracelet and earrings, madam, the necklace would be two hundred and eighty thousand."

When we got outside, I took Dick Fleming's arm and walked him across the street to a luncheonette.

"That's it," Dick said. "The place is loaded."

I reached across the table to squeeze his hand.

"I'm glad to hear you say it, Dick. It's my first choice, too. It's not as flashy as some of the places I saw, but I think the loot is there."

"No doubt. And it has only one entrance. A total of six employees, counting the two repairmen in the back. Of course there may be messengers or others."

"Plus customers," I reminded him.

We were silent while our tea was served.

He shook his head.

"It just seems too good to be true," he said. "No TV cameras. No armed guard. The door of the safe open."

"Alarm buttons," I reminded him.

"I know, but still—in a place handling two-hundred-thousand dollar necklaces, the security seems awfully casual to me."

"Not to worry. All we've done is tentatively decided on a target. I'll check out the place completely before we go ahead. I like this luncheonette. I can sit here and see when it opens, when it closes, how many employees report for work, when it's crowded with customers, when it's empty, and so forth. Also, I'm going to pay them at least one more visit. I really do own that old pocket watch I told the manager about."

"And you're willing to sell it to them?"

"Why not? Help finance our campaign."

We both laughed. We were so light-hearted, so happy. All I can say in our defense is that we honestly had no intention of going through with it.

Jannie Gets Her Gun

Morris said his gun dealer promised to be at Chez Morris at 10:00 P.M. on Sunday night.

"If you wanna seriously negotiate, babe," he advised me, "you be here at 10:00 on Sunday. Don't be late; this guy is very punctilious."

"Punctual," I said.

"Whatever," Morris said.

When I entered Chez Morris at 10:00 on Sunday evening I went directly to the far end to talk to Morris. He leaned across the bar toward me, speaking in a conspiratorial rasp.

"He's at the little table near the kitchen door," he said. I turned slowly, took a quick look. I couldn't believe my eyes.

"The plump little guy?" I asked Morrie incredulously. "The middle-aged cherub? He looks like everyone's favorite uncle."

Morrie showed me a mouthful of teeth as big and yellow as salted almonds.

"That's what he's called," he told me. "Uncle Sam."

"What's his last name?"

"Just call him Uncle Sam."

"What do I do—just walk over and say, 'Hello, Uncle Sam'?"

"That's right."

So I walked to the small table near the swinging kitchen door, stood there nervously, and said, "Good evening, Uncle Sam. My name is Jannie Shean."

He leaped spryly to his feet with a beneficent smile, shook my hand firmly, pulled out a chair and held it for me.

"No last names, dear lady," he said in a light, chirpy voice. "No need for that at all. Would you care for anything?"

"A coffee?" I asked. "Black."

He held up a finger, and when a waiter appeared, asked for a pot of coffee for two.

"Well, well," he said brightly. "Here we are."

He was a twinkling little man, no taller than five-five, and rotund. He positively radiated health: sparkling blue eyes, a clear complexion, and alert, energetic movements.

He was wearing a handsome jacket of go-for-broke plaid, open-necked tattersall shirt with a paisley ascot, a suede waistcoat with silver coin buttons, beige slacks. He had a horseshoe of perfectly white hair about a bald pate that was lightly freckled.

"Dear lady," he said, pouring our coffee, "I can't tell you how devastated I was to learn of your recent misfortune."

I looked at him, puzzled, then recalled my fictitious mugging.

"I don't suppose it was all that unusual," I mumbled.

"Unfortunately not." He sighed. "These are perilous times in which we live. To what sad state has our civilization arrived when such wolves may prey upon an innocent public without fear of apprehension and punishment?"

I can recognize a rhetorical question when I hear one, and made no effort to reply.

"It is," he went on, "only natural to wish to protect one's person against these depredations."

"I want to defend myself!" I said, with all the anger I could muster.

"Of course you do, dear lady," Uncle Sam said. "What type of weapon were you interested in?"

This last was spoken in a perfectly ordinary tone. I would have supposed he'd prefer a place more private. However, I assumed he knew his business.

"Uncle Sam," I said, "to tell you the truth, I know very little about guns. I was hoping you might advise me."

"Of course, dear lady!" he cried, eyes sparkling. "How wise of you to put yourself in the hands of an expert. I shall be delighted to give you the benefit of my years of experience in this specialty. Now, may I make a few suggestions?"

"Please do."

"I find, in dealing with ladies, that many are interested in the decorative aspects of the firearm. Nickel-plated. Pearl grips. Things of that sort. But I counsel against letting the mere outward appearance to be the convincing factor in the purchase. I believe sturdiness of construction and reliability of function to be much more important."

"I couldn't agree with you more," I said, fascinated by his spiel. "What do you recommend?"

"Since you are, dear lady, a fine figure of a woman and, as I determined from the firmness of your handshake, you are the fortunate possessor of no little physical strength, I would like to suggest to you a

handgun perhaps a mite heavier and of more rugged
construction than I might advise for a frailer lady.
Added weight usually means greater reliability and
accuracy. In addition, I would urge the purchase of
an automatic pistol rather than a revolver, since the
technique of loading a well-designed pistol is easily
mastered, more shots are available when needed, and
the flat, streamlined shape makes it an excellent
weapon to be carried in a purse without snagging on
the lining in case a quick withdrawal is demanded."

"You seem to have thought of everything," I said
admiringly.

"I do believe," he said, lowering his eyes modestly,
"that I am by training, temperament, and experience,
well qualified to promise complete satisfaction to my
patrons. But I must tell you, dear lady, in all honesty,
that in most cases, a well-balanced revolver offers
more accuracy than a pistol of approximately the
same caliber. However, I do not believe long-range
accuracy is a necessity in your case since, if you
should ever make use of the weapon against an at-
tacker, the range would probably be quite short."

"Yes," I said. "Point-blank."

"Precisely," he said with some enthusiasm. "So I
have no trepidation in recommending an automatic
pistol to you. Now I will show you a small, private catalogue of various weapons of this type that are available . . ."

The spiral notebook he put before me had an illustration Scotch-taped to each page. The pictures
appeared to have been clipped from manufacturers'
catalogues. In addition to a photograph or line drawing of the weapon, there was a paragraph of descriptive material that included weight, barrel length,
number of rounds capacity, muzzle velocity, range,

etc. In all cases, a price had been inked on the border in an elegant, Spencerian hand.

I folded the catalogue open at a particular page and handed the notebook across the table to him.

"This one?" I suggested.

"Ah . . . no," he said regretfully. "I would not recommend that particular model to a lady of your sensibility, reasonable though the price may seem to you. A German design originally, it was a splendid, combat-proved officers' pistol. Unfortunately, it has been copied in several countries with inferior technology. My last shipment was not up to par. Definitely not up to par. No, dear lady, I cannot honestly recommend that weapon."

I retrieved the notebook and scanned the remaining pages. Then I turned back to an illustration that had caught my eye. Again, I folded the notebook open and returned it to him.

"It's a little more than I wanted to spend," I said, "but it seems to be a well-designed, compact weapon. In fact, it's rather sweet."

'Ah-ha!" he said delightedly, slapping the tabletop with his palm. "It is sweet indeed! The Pistola Automatica Beretta Modello 1951 nine-millimeter Parabellum. Magazine of eight. Weighing one pound, fifteen ounces. Muzzle velocity: more than thirteen hundred feet per second. Dear lady, an excellent choice. Excellent! In addition, I am happy to tell you that I can supply this particular model in a factory-sealed carton, complete with extra magazine, cleaning tools, instruction booklet, and so forth. A pirated model, I must admit, but of excellent quality and workmanship. I have test-fired this particular shipment personally, and I do assure you the firearm is equal to the original design and well worth the stated price."

"I'll need some, uh, bullets," I said faintly.

"But of course. Understood. At a very small additional cost. I suggest a box of fifty."

"Whatever you say."

"Then you are quite satisfied with this particular gun, dear lady?"

"Oh yes. As long as you recommend it."

"I do indeed. But you will be happy to know that should it prove unsatisfactory, for whatever reason, I stand ready to buy it back within a year of purchase at a mere twenty-five percent reduction of your cost. That is my personal guarantee to you. Now just let me do a little quick arithmetic here to arrive at the total cost of weapon and ammunition."

"Plus tax?" I said lightly.

"Pardon?" he said absently. "Oh no, dear lady, no tax."

He tucked the catalogue back into his attaché case and removed a small scratchpad. He figured rapidly with a gold ballpoint pen.

"One nine-millimeter Parabellum automatic pistol in factory-sealed carton, plus fifty rounds of standard ammunition for same . . . one hundred and . . . carry the six . . . and we arrive at one fifty-three, seventy-two. Oh, let's round it out to an even one hundred and fifty dollars. How does that strike you, dear lady? Is it within your budget?"

"I—I think so," I said hesitantly. "I'm afraid I don't have the cash with me," I said. "I don't suppose that you would take a check?"

"Well, ah, no, dear lady, I do not think that would be wise. Over the years I have evolved a system of payment and delivery that I think you'll find satisfactory. However, it usually involves a third person—in this case, Mr. Morris Lapidus, our estimable host. You trust Mr. Lapidus?"

"Morrie?" I said. "Of course. All the way."

"Excellent." He nodded, beaming. "My sentiments exactly. When can you deliver the total cash payment to Mr. Lapidus?"

I thought a moment. Then I said:

"The restaurant opens at noon tomorrow. I can have it here by then."

"Most satisfactory," Uncle Sam purred.

"And I'll pick up my gun from Morrie?"

"Oh no!" he said, shocked. "No, no, no, dear lady. I wouldn't think of involving Mr. Lapidus to *that* extent. You leave the purchase price with Mr. Lapidus at 12:00 noon. Return at approximately 2:00 P.M., and Mr. Lapidus will deliver to you an envelope. Within the envelope you will find a key to a parcel locker in Grand Central Station, along with a brief note giving you the number and precise location of the locker. Only one warning: Your purchase must be taken from the locker within twenty-four hours. Lockers closed longer than that may be opened by the authorities and their contents removed."

"I'll go as soon as I get the key," I said. I paused, looking at him thoughtfully.

"Ah, yes, dear lady," he said with a particularly gentle smile. "You are wondering if, after you have paid the sum required, I will actually leave a locker key with Mr. Lapidus. Or if it will be the right key for the locker designated. Or if the weapon will, indeed, be in the locker. Or if the cupboard will be bare."

"Well . . . yes, Uncle Sam," I confessed. "I was thinking along those lines."

"Trust," he said solemnly. "I can urge you to nothing but trust. One of the noblest emotions of which human beings are capable. You must trust in my honor and in my honesty."

I stared at the clear, guileless eyes and lips curved in a perpetual smile.

"I trust you, Uncle Sam," I said.

"God bless you, dear lady!" he cried joyfully. He caught up my hand and pressed the knuckles to his lips.

That next night, Dick Fleming and I sat at the desk in my office and tried to follow the instructions in the leaflet: "To load the 9-mm. Parabellum, it is necessary to depress the magazine release button (marked 3 in Diagram A), allowing the magazine to eject freely." And so on.

The gun, magazine, and bullets gleamed dully in the light of the desk lamp. They seemed very heavy, very solid. We were both surprised by their physical presence. They were—well, they were very *real*.

I picked up the empty pistol, gripped it in the approved manner, pointed it at the far wall.

"Not *ka-chow*," I said. "*Pow!*"

"*Pow!*" Dick Fleming said. "Now where's part 6 in Diagram C?"

Crime as Theatre

"Assuming we go ahead and recruit a gang," I said to Dick, "I'm not about to bring them up here for strategy meetings and arguments on how to divide the loot. I don't want them to know who I am, either. I don't want them to come looking for me after we desert them."

"Understood," Dick said. "But even if we set up another place to meet, and you operate under a phony name, what if you meet one of them accidently on the street after this is all over?"

"That means not only a change of name," I said, "but a complete change of identity, of appearance. So complete that even if they met me accidently later, when I've become Jannie Shean again, they won't recognize me."

"Can't be done," Dick said firmly.

"Sure it can. Change of hair color with a wig. A new makeup job. A different wardrobe. Even a different way of walking and talking."

"Playing a role?" he said dubiously. "You're not an actress, Jannie."

"The hell I'm not!" I said. "All women are actresses. How else do you think we've been able to survive in a man's world? Tell you what—I'll go ahead and create the new woman. You take a look, and if you say it won't work, I'll forget it and we'll try something else."

"Fair enough," he said. "Now what about this business of another apartment, a new home for the new woman?"

"Let's take it step by step. First the new appearance, then the new name, identity, background, apartment, and so forth."

"Jannie," he groaned, "it's going to cost a lot of money."

"Not so much," I said. "Besides, it's all deductible as a business expense: research for my new novel."

"I'd love to be there," he said, "when you try to convince the IRS."

I found a lingerie shop on Sixth Avenue that apparently catered to the wives and girlfriends of underwear fetishists and sex maniacs. In the window I saw brassieres with holes cut out around the nipples, panties with open crotches, and negligees embroidered with obscene suggestions.

"Good morning," I mumbled to a saleslady. "Do you have anything that will make me, uh, look bigger —up here?"

"Sure, dearie," she said promptly. "Single, double, or triple pads?"

"Uh, single, I guess."

"What size are you now?"

"About 34-B."

"Take the double," she said firmly. She craned around to inspect my derriere. "You could use some fanny pads, too. Come back to the dressing room; I'll make a new woman out of you."

She did too. A triumph of engineering.

I bought a lot of freaky stuff in that place. Including red babydoll pajamas that had, embroidered on the crotch, the legend "All hope abandon ye who enter here."

Elsewhere, I purchased two pairs of sexy sandals with three-inch heels. I could hardly stand in them, but the clerk assured me I'd soon learn to walk gracefully.

"They make you look like a queen," he gushed.

I was about to tell him that he was way ahead of me, but thought better of it.

I bought sweaters too tight, blouses too small, skirts too short.

In the Times Square Wig-o-Rama I bought a metallic-blond wig, shoulder-length, and one so black it was almost purple, came halfway down my back. Both wigs had the texture of steel wool and smelled faintly of Clorox. I figured a perfumed hair spray would remedy that.

Finally I bought two berets and a lined trenchcoat in red poplin. The salesgirl said the "in" way to wear it was with the belt casually knotted and the collar up in back. When I came out of the store, I passed a hooker wearing a T-shirt that said: "The customer always comes first."

I gave her a friendly nod. Sisters.

The only things left to buy were makeup and perfumes, and for these I went to Woolworth's, where the prices were reasonable, the selections enormous, and where I let an enthusiastic salesman show me how to apply false eyelashes that looked like a picket fence, paint on green shadow, and apply a small black beauty mark. You just licked it and stuck it on your chin.

"Makes me look like a skinny Madame Du Barry," I told the clerk.

"Precisely," he beamed.

This shopping spree lasted a week. At home, at night, with the door locked and chained, and the shades drawn, I practiced walking my three-inch heels, stuffing the cotton pancakes in my bra, and applying just enough eyeshadow so I wouldn't look like a victim of malnutrition. I started out giggling, but after a while I really worked at it, and rehearsed a voice change, too, striving for a husky, sex-inflected Marilyn Monroe whisper.

I was fascinated by what I saw in my cheval glass. Not only was my appearance utterly different, but I *felt* different. I looked like a floozy. I *was* a floozy. The falsies gave me a pair of knockers that came into the room three seconds before I did. My padded behind bulged provocatively. The ersatz eyelashes batted, the carmined lips moued, the long, long legs wobbled suggestively on the spike heels. When I added a cocked beret and tightly cinched trenchcoat, I could have seduced the United Nations. More than that, I felt seductive. Also, cheap, hard, available, and willing, willing, willing.

After a week of practice that included going out at night to learn how to negotiate steps and curbs in those hookers' heels (I received four propositions during those trial runs), I decided it was time for the final test.

I called Dick and asked him to come right over to discuss something important. I then went downstairs and sailed by the doorman, who knew me but didn't give me a second glance, being too busy with the first. I figured he didn't recognize me.

I took up station in the dim doorway of a Third Avenue store I knew Dick would pass. I lighted a cigarette, let it dangle from my lips. I stuck my hands deep in the trenchcoat pockets. I tried to jut my fake chest.

Along came Dick, walking fast. I blew out a plume of smoke from the corner of my mouth just before he came abreast of me. I stepped out into the illumination of a street lamp.

"Wanna have a little fun?"

He looked at me. I mean, he didn't just glance, he *looked*.

"Not tonight, thank you," he said primly and continued walking.

He took about three more steps, then stopped so suddenly he almost fell on his face. A classic double-take. He turned and came back. He stood in front of me, staring.

"Change your mind, buster?" I murmured.

He shook his head in disbelief.

"All right, Jannie," he said. "You win."

Casing

There were so many things I had written in those Chuck-Mike-Buck-Pat-Brick books of mine that I really knew nothing about. Like casing. I'd have my villains walk around the target twice, time the night-watchman's schedule, and maybe discover when the payroll was to be delivered.

But now, trying seriously to determine how Brandenberg & Sons might be robbed with profit and minimal risk required a laborious, minute-by-minute study, conducted with a stopwatch, that was gradually extended for almost a month. I filled two notebooks of observations, and from my jottings. Dick Fleming designed beautifully neat time charts of personnel flow, using a variety of colored inks.

By consulting these records, we could pinpoint the location of any one of the employees at any moment during the working day. Since we didn't know their names, they were designated Manager, Salesmen 1, 2, and 3, and Repairmen 1 and 2. Each was described physically so we could tell them apart. In addition I discovered the presence of a seventh employee: an aged black man who apparently doubled as porter and messenger.

Most of my casing was done from the window of the luncheonette across the street. I varied the tables at which I sat and the times I was present. Fortunately, the place was usually crowded and seemed to have a heavy personnel turnover.

I changed the luncheonette routine occasionally by driving from my apartment to East 55th Street and double-parking my XKE as long as I could, using it as an observation post. But the car was too noticeable to use frequently, so I borrowed Dick Fleming's black VW several times.

I noted several things of interest:

The store did not open for business until 10:00 A.M., but all employees arrived between 8:45 and 9:00. In the hour before the public was admitted, the store was dusted and vacuumed by commercial cleaners who arrived at 9:00 each morning. Also, during this preparatory hour, the interior steel shutters protecting the window displays were raised. I was bemused to note that despite this protection most of the valuable items were removed from the street windows at night and presumably placed in the vault, to be returned to the window displays in the morning.

The two commercial cleaning men were admitted by the manager, who unlocked the front door to let them in and locked it again after their entrance. They rarely spent more than forty-five minutes giving Brandenberg & Sons its spic-and-span appearance. When they departed with their vacuum cleaner, mops, brooms, etc., the manager unlocked the door, let them out, then locked the door after them. At precisely 10:00 the door was unlocked once again to signal the start of the business day. This routine never varied.

The employees were apparently on a rigid lunch hour schedule: never were more than two absent at the same time. I think the repairmen brought sandwiches. At least, both carried small black cases, like doctor's bags, when they arrived in the morning, and I never saw either of them go out to lunch.

Brandenberg & Sons closed promptly at 5:00 P.M. A few minutes later, the interior steel shutters were lowered, and I was unable to observe the routine of closing. I presumed the valuable items were put in the vault, and interior burglar alarms set. Whatever was done didn't take long, because all the employees had exited by 5:30. The manager was always the last to leave, and he not only turned a key in a conventional lock, but reached high to turn a key in another lock which, I assumed, activated another burglar alarm attached to the door. When he opened up in the morning, he reversed this process, first turning off the alarm, then opening the door.

When the manager locked up and departed at 5:30, he was always accompanied by clerk Number 3, who kept his hands in his topcoat pockets and was, I suspected, armed. They always followed the same procedure. They walked over to Park Avenue, then one block south. There at a corner bank, the manager took out a manila envelope from his inside jacket pocket and dropped it into the bank's night deposit vault. I supposed the envelope contained the day's receipts, cash and checks. The two men then went their separate ways.

During the weeks I was observing Brandenberg & Sons as closely as possible, I also tried to form a clearer idea of their clientele. For the most part they seemed middle-aged or older, and very few were window-shoppers. That is, they were not interested in the outside display windows, but came down the street and turned purposefully into the store. They knew exactly where they were going. Many of them arrived by taxi or private car, and not a few by chauffeured limousine.

I also became aware of a special type of visitor to Brandenberg & Sons. These were invariably youngish men, most of them well built, conservatively dressed, and all carrying black attaché cases handcuffed to their left wrist. There were three or four such men entering Brandenberg & Sons every week. I couldn't figure it out. Finally Dick decided they were jewelry salesmen or couriers from wholesale jewelry merchants delivering purchases made by Brandenberg & Sons.

Dick and I had several discussions about who actually owned our target store. Neither of us believed it was that rubicund manager. Dick said we could probably find out, if we wanted to go to the trouble, by looking up city records, leases, reports of property sales, bank references, membership lists of jewelers' associations, etc. But did we really want to attract attention to ourselves by such inquiries? Besides, what difference did it make to professional thieves whom they were robbing? Inevitably, it would be the insurance company, wouldn't it? So we made no effort to identify the actual owner of Brandenberg & Sons.

A bad mistake.

During my second week of casing, I dug out my grandfather's pocket watch from a bottom bureau drawer, slipped it into my purse, and made my second actual visit to the store.

I was approached by the salesman we had labeled Number 1, but I told him I wanted to speak to the manager.

"Mr. Jarvis?" he said. "He's busy at the moment. Would you mind waiting?"

He brought up one of the brocaded armchairs and seated me with all the deference of a headwaiter giving a duchess the best table in the house. Then, another customer entering, I was left alone: a marvelous opportunity to look around.

The door to the back room, where the vault was located and where the repairmen worked, was closed. I presumed the manager was in there. I estimated the interior of the store as approximately 60 feet long and 30 feet wide. The three clerks were all occupied with customers. Once again I was conscious of the hushed opulence of the place. No one, it seemed, spoke over a murmur. You couldn't hear footfalls on the thick carpeting. Showcase doors slid noiselessly, and merchandise was always exhibited to customers on squares of padded velvet.

I watched the three clerks at work. Although they had dissimilar features, they were all of the same physical type: tall, slender, with a whippy grace. Curiously, I fancied there was something almost sinister in their appearance: they had expressionless features but very sharp, alert eyes, with a kind of brooding intensity. I suspected I was looking for novelistic characters in quite ordinary salesmen.

The manager finally entered from the back room, leaving the door open. He was accompanying one of the conservatively clad, attaché-case-bearing visitors. The manager escorted him to the front door, they shook hands, the salesman departed, the manager came back into the shop. Some signal I missed must have been passed, because he came directly to me. He bowed and said, "I am sorry to have kept you waiting. You've brought the watch and chain you mentioned on your last visit?"

That last visit had been almost a month earlier. I was surprised he remembered me, and I told him so.

"I never forget a face," he said, with what seemed to me a cold smile. Then he added, with more warmth. "Especially such a charming face!"

I handed him the watch, and he asked if he might take it into the back room for a few moments to have one of his technicians examine it.

And off he went with Grandfather's watch and chain, closing the door of the vault room behind him. I spent the four or five minutes he was gone making a surreptitious examination of the ceiling and walls. Brandenberg & Sons was located on the ground floor of what had once been a five-story town house, and I suspected the store occupied the original drawing room. The ceiling and walls were wonderfully rococo, but unfortunately all that fanciful carving and ornamentation could easily conceal a small peephole or even the lens of a TV camera. In addition, there was a full-length pier glass set into one wall. If that was a one-way window, there could easily be an armed guard concealed behind it, keeping an eye on the shop.

Mr. Jarvis returned, thrusting his paunch confidently ahead of him. He told me he was happy to be able to offer me two hundred dollars for watch and chain. If that was not acceptable, Brandenberg & Sons would be willing to take the item on consignment, in which case I would receive 65 percent of whatever they were able to obtain for it.

"No," I said. "Thank you, but the two hundred is satisfactory."

"Excellent," he said. "If you'll just step this way, I'll get your money and prepare a receipt for you to sign."

I accompanied him to a discreet cashier's desk where the money was kept in a small drawer. Nothing so vulgar as a cash register. Mr. Jarvis paid me in crisp fifties, and I signed a receipt he prepared describing the watch and chain in some detail. I had intended to use a phony name and address, but at the last minute I feared he might ask for identification. So I signed Jannie Shean and scrawled my real address. He didn't ask for identification.

Mr. Jarvis then escorted me to the front door. He seemed a genial, voluble type. I was conscious of his fruity cologne. We shook hands when we parted. I thought he held my hand a little longer than necessary.

When I described this visit to Dick Fleming that night, he looked at me queerly.

"What's wrong?" I asked him.

"Two things," he said. "One: He didn't ask for identification. How did he know you didn't steal the watch?"

"Oh, come on, Dick! I was wearing my mink."

"You could have stolen that, too. But what bothers me most is why a place like Brandenberg's is fooling around with secondhand watches. It just doesn't make sense."

"Maybe it's a valuable antique."

"Do you really believe that?"

"No," I admitted. "Matty had it appraised when Father died. It's worth about what Jarvis paid me."

"All right, then, we're back to my question: Why is Brandenberg and Sons interested in stuff like that?"

"I don't know."

He looked at me thoughtfully.

The New Woman

~~~~~~

I was relaxing in Dick Fleming's apartment, wearing my tart's duds, hooker's heels parked up on his cobbler's bench.

For some reason I really didn't understand, Dick was turned on by my floozy costume. He liked the spiked heels, the net stockings, the padded bra. I wondered if I had suggested fun-and-games while wearing that getup, if he would, finally, be able to cut the mustard. I decided I didn't want to find out.

"Problem," I said, my nose in my glass of white wine.

"What's that?"

"When I come out at night in this Sadie Thompson disguise, I try to sail past the doorman as fast as I can. No problem there—so far. I think he thinks I'm a call girl balling one of those rich bachelors on the sixth floor. But tonight, as I was coming out of my apartment, my next-door neighbor was leaving at the same moment. I ducked back inside just in time. But if I keep coming out dressed like this, someone on my floor is going to see me sooner or later, and I'll have a lot of questions to answer."

"But after you get your new place, won't you be living there?"

"Sure, but not *all* the time. I'll want to come back occasionally to pick up my mail, write some checks, maybe change to have dinner with my sister. But I can't keep popping in and out in this clown's suit, particularly during the day."

We were silent a few moments, pondering. Dick topped off our glasses.

"I don't really think it's a problem," he said finally. "You'll drive back to your permanent apartment, and in the car, you take off the wig and false eyelashes and wipe off some of the guck. Then you button the trenchcoat up to your chin. You could even keep a pair of loafers in the car so you don't have to parade through the lobby on your stilts."

"Sounds good," I said, nodding. "You're so smart. And when I go from my apartment to the new place, I'll just reverse the process, park somewhere and put on my wig and makeup in the car. That solves one problem and brings up another. My car. That XKE is just too conspicuous. Also, the license number could be traced. Also, a crook hoping to pull off a successful heist wouldn't be driving a car like that."

"Borrow my VW," Dick suggested.

I shook my head. "Same objections. License could be traced, and a VW is just out of character. I think I better rent a car. Something that isn't worth a second look. A nondescript Ford or Chevy or Plymouth. Something ordinary."

That same night, we decided on a name—Bea—to go with my new appearance, then on an identity for her. We agreed I'd try to avoid volunteering any in-

formation about Bea's background, but if pressed I
would grudgingly reveal the following:

Beatrice Flanders was born in a small farming com-
munity near Terre Haute, Indiana. Both her parents
were dead, but she had an older, married sister in
Indianapolis, and a brother in the Navy. She was a
high school graduate who had also attended business
college for six months before she decided there was
more money to be made as a cocktail waitress. She
had been married to a nogoodnick who had intro-
duced her to the shoddier, least profitable forms of
larceny, including gas station holdups and the badger
game. Hubby had deserted for parts unknown, never
to reappear, and Beatrice had returned to hustling
drinks in bars, taverns, roadhouses. She had also, for
a few years, followed the convention circuit as a party
girl. At various times she had teamed up with strong-
arm thugs, safe-crackers, cat burglars, hotel thieves,
etc., learning as she went along. Finally, for the last
two years, she had been associated with Danny
"Woppo" Epstein, who specialized in jewelry store
holdups, working alone or recruiting local talent as
needed. Danny had taught Beatrice all the tricks of
his trade, although he never allowed her to go along
on his jobs. Bea and Woppo had cut a wide and successful swath through the Midwest until a gutsy
Chicago jeweler, reaching into an open safe at Danny's command, came out with a Smith & Wesson .38
and blew Woppo away. Now Beatrice Flanders was
in Manhattan alone, her funds running low, looking
around.

Bea's Place

~~~~~~

We parked the rented Fairlane on West 87th Street, making certain the suitcases were in the locked trunk, out of sight. Then we began tramping up one cross street and down the next, from Riverside Drive to Columbus Avenue. In that area, Beatrice Flanders looked like one of the World's Ten Best Dressed Women, but no one gave us a second glance. There were harlequins on the streets you wouldn't believe, drunks in the gutters, spaced-out addicts nodding in doorways.

We wandered from fleabag to fleabag, and after a while stopped asking each other how people could live like that. The answer was obvious: They had no choice. We saw crumbling walls, decayed ceilings, cracked plumbing fixtures, exposed electrical wiring. We saw one room that appeared to have decorative wallpaper until we realized it was an enormous roach colony. We saw a once-elegant hotel that had become a whores' dormitory. And always the diseased dogs, scabrous cats, cripples on crutches, wounded drunks with filthy bandages, and what seemed to be hundreds of mental cases talking to themselves, urinating on the sidewalk, howling at the sky, or sitting catatonically on the curb, fingering gutter filth.

Finally, late in the afternoon, we found what we were looking for on West 94th Street between Broadway and West End. The Hotel Harding. Someone had defaced the outside sign to make it read "Hotel Hard-On." It had once been a structure of some dignity, with a façade of gray stone and pillars of reddish marble framing the entrance. The lobby smelled of urine, vomit, old cigar smoke, hashish, and a disinfectant so acrid it made my eyes water. There were no chairs in the lobby—to discourage loiterers off the street, I guessed. In fact, there was nothing in the lobby but the scarred desk and the birdcage of an ancient elevator shaft. The elevator itself, however, was a self-service and relatively new, but already layered with the ubiquitous graffiti. The brass indicator showed twelve floors.

The man behind the desk, reading a tout sheet through a hand-held magnifying glass, must have weighed at least 300 pounds of not-so-pure blubber. He was wearing a blue, sweated undershirt. His transistor radio was roaring racing results, and he was annoyed at being interrupted.

"Five a day, thirty a week, a hundred a month," the fat man said, singsong, in a surprisingly high-pitched voice. The thirty came out "thoity," hundred was "undert," and month was "munt."

"With private bathroom?" I said in my husky whisper.

He looked at me disgustedly.

"Ja say so?" he demanded. "Seven a day, forty a week, one-thirty a month. You want it?"

"We'd like to take a look at the room," Dick said firmly.

The clerk took a key attached to a brass tab from a board of hooks and tossed it contemptuously onto the counter. It would have skittered to the floor if Dick hadn't caught it.

"Room 703," the man-mountain snarled. "Cross ventilation. Sheets and towels every week."

We waited for the elevator to descend, then took a leisurely ride to the seventh floor. As we inched past the third floor we heard loud screams of extreme anguish: either a murder in progress or a woman in labor. On the fifth floor, someone was playing acid rock on a radio or hi-fi, loud enough to make the elevator vibrate in its shaft.

Room 703 was on the east side of the hotel. I don't know how the desk clerk figured it provided cross ventilation, unless you left the corridor door open and there was a breeze coming down the air shaft on the other side. The room was about fifteen feet square, with one window (on the shaft) and a small, open closet. The walls were cracked, the paint rippled with age and peeling in patches. The floor was covered with slimed linoleum, so worn that in several places the brown backing showed through.

There was a single bed, a dresser, a tarnished mirror, an upholstered armchair, a small, rickety desk with a chair to match. Everything in that cheesy orangewood. There were no linens on the bed, and the mattress was stained in ways I didn't care to imagine.

The bathroom door had been painted so many times it couldn't be closed. There was a sink, a toilet, an open shower stall. The fixtures were yellowed and crackled, the sink rusted, the toilet seat cracked and peeling. Dick flushed the toilet. It sounded like the Charge of the Light Brigade.

We went back into the living room-bedroom-study-dining room-parlor, etc.

"Let's forget it," Dick said.

"Look for another place?"

"No," he said, "let's forget the whole thing. You can't live here or anywhere like it. Give it up, Jannie."

"Bea," I said. "Watch yourself. And I'm not giving it up. This is great local color. I can get a page or two of description out of this place. Very realistic. I'm taking it."

"Maybe you should go to a doctor first and get some shots."

We went back down to the lobby, and I told the fat man I'd take it. By the week.

"Week in advance," he said. "No cooking. No boyfriends sleeping over. No loud music. No wild parties. No pot-smoking. No hard drugs. No customers."

I was delighted. My disguise was a success.

I handed over forty dollars and got a furious stare when I asked for a receipt. But I stared back just as furiously, and finally got what I wanted. It was barely legible, but I figured it was something to show the IRS when they questioned whether a week at the Hotel Hard-On was a legitimate business expense. Then I signed a registration card with the name Beatrice Flanders.

On the way back to the car, we stopped at a Broadway supermarket. I bought roach spray, rat repellent, soap, soap powder, washcloths, Brillo pads, etc. Then Dick insisted we stop at a liquor store where he bought me a fifth each of vodka, scotch, and brandy.

"In case of snakebite," he said.

We drove back to the hotel, and Dick helped me upstairs with the suitcases and new purchases. It was then getting on to 6:00 P.M., and we decided to get something to eat in the neighborhood before Dick took a cab back to the East Side and I prepared for my first night alone in Room 703.

We went out into the narrow corridor and almost collided with a man coming from the elevator. He drew back politely to let us pass. He looked about thirty-five, but had one of those hard, young-old faces that made it difficult to estimate age. He was tall, at least six feet, slender as a whip, and very, very dark. Jet hair, strong, black eyebrows, a complexion so brown it was almost russet. When he smiled at us, he displayed a gleaming array of shiny white teeth, dazzling against his tanned face and beard-shadowed jaw.

"Just move in?" he inquired pleasantly.

I nodded.

"Welcome to Waldorf West," he said wryly. "My name's Jack Donohue. I'm in 705. If there's anything I can help you with, bang on my door."

"Thanks," Dick Fleming said gratefully. "Appreciate that. We're going out for dinner. Can you recommend any place in the neighborhood?"

"Most of them are ptomaine places," Donohue said. He certainly did a lot of smiling. Mostly at me. "Your best bet is to eat Chink at Tommy Yu's on Broadway."

"Thank you," I said in my boudoir murmur. "We'll give it a try."

He nodded and went down the hall to his room.

In the elevator, Dick said, "Good-looking guy. And he seems pleasant enough. Won't do any harm to have a helpful neighbor."

I didn't say anything. In many ways Dick Fleming is not with it.

After dinner we walked back to the hotel in silence. There were three men and a woman loitering on the steps of the Hotel Harding. They gave us a cold and silent appraisal as we walked by. We halted a few doors down. When we glanced back, they were still staring at us.

"You're sure you want to go back in there?" Dick asked nervously.

"I'm sure," I said, which was a damned lie.

"Good luck then." He kissed my cheek. "If you decide to run, then run. You don't have to prove anything, to me or to yourself."

He touched my arm, then turned and walked away, back toward Broadway, a cab, escape. It took a conscious effort to keep from running after him. But I returned to the entrance of the hotel and started up the steps.

"What's the matter, honey?" the woman said in a whiskey rasp. "Y'strike out?"

I shrugged. "You lose one, you win one."

They laughed, and suddenly they didn't seem so sinister; the Harding was just another dirty hotel, and I would survive.

When I got off the elevator and walked down the corridor (which, in honor of the graffiti, I had nicknamed the Tunnel of Love), I saw the door of Room 703, which I had locked, was now wide open. I peeped cautiously around the jamb. A wizened harridan was making up my bed with sheets that looked like the shrouds of a poverty-stricken ghost.

She looked up as I came into the room.

"Listen here, dearie," she whined, "I take care of this whole rotten place. Twelve floors, and I got no help. I ask for help, but that owner, he don't give me no help. I gotta do everything around here, people screaming for this and that, new sheets, fresh towels, and the mess some of these animals make you wouldn't believe—"

Her litany of woe went on and on as she spread

the tissue-thin sheets, a threadbare cotton blanket, and hung two towels in the bathroom. They looked like used flour sacks.

Finally, just to stop that whiny voice, I gave her two dollars.

"God bless, dearie," she said in a voice suddenly strong and vigorous. She folded the bills and stuffed them in her bra. "I'm Blanche. You need anything, you just ask for me. I'll take nice care of you."

She gave me a horrendous wink. Then she was gone. I closed and locked the door behind her. There was a chain on the doorjamb, but the slot in which it should have fitted was missing. There were four splintered holes showing where it had been. So I got the straight-back chair and jammed it under the knob.

I struggled with the air-shaft window for almost five minutes and finally raised it a few inches. A cool breeze came in. A breeze redolent of ripe garbage and burning rubber—but cool.

I flopped down in the sprung armchair, kicked off the spike-heeled sandals, flexed my feet and surveyed my kingdom. I knew I should unpack, try to scrub the worst of the scum from the bathroom sink, spray against roaches, and generally try to settle in. But I was too weary to do anything but lean back and wonder just what the hell I thought I was doing.

I wondered myself to the edge of depression. It was too late to back out, too soon to quit. I got up again and uncapped the bottle of vodka Dick Fleming had bought me. Then I looked around. No glasses.

I took the chair from under the knob, unlocked and opened the door and struck my head out. The hallway was empty. In stockinged feet I padded down the corridor to Room 705 and knocked on the door.

"Who is it?" A forceful voice, almost angry.

"Your new neighbor," I said to the closed door. "Room 703."

Sound of chain being slipped. Not one, but two locks opened. Then the door swung wide. He smiled at me.

"Hel-lo!" he said. "This is wild; I was just thinking of you."

"Listen," I told him, "I'd like a drink. I've got what goes in, but I don't have a glass. I was hoping you might have an extra you can spare until tomorrow when I can buy my own."

All this in my breathless floozy's voice.

He stared at me, the smile still there.

"I can't find Blanche," I explained lamely.

"Sure, sure," he said. "Your husband doesn't want to go out?"

"He's not my husband."

"Boyfriend?"

"Just a friend. And he's not here. Have you got that glass?"

The tension went out of his stretched grin.

"Then you took the place alone," he said. "Sorry, I didn't understand. Sure, I've got a glass you can borrow. Come on in; I'll wash it out for you."

"Oh, don't bother," I said hurriedly. "I'll rinse it."

"No bother," he said, the white teeth flashing again like a neon sign. "Come on in. Just take a minute."

I entered hesitantly, leaving the door half-open behind me. If he noticed, he gave no sign. He went into the bathroom and in a few seconds I heard water running in the sink.

His room was larger than mine and looked more lived in. He had *two* armchairs, *two* pillows, *two* blankets, a small TV set and smaller radio. Best of all, he had a refrigerator: one of those waist-high jobs that holds a six-pack, a pint of milk, a deck of sliced salami.

He came out of the bathroom, polishing a glass with a towel that was, I noted enviously, larger and thicker than the ones Blanche had given me.

"How about ice?" he asked casually.

"Oh, I couldn't—" I started.

"I don't even know your name," he said suddenly. "You know mine."

He said this in an odd, challenging way, as if we were making a bet.

"Beatrice Flanders," I told him. "Bea for short."

"But not for long, eh?" I didn't know what that meant, but it seemed to amuse him.

He went over to the refrigerator and busied himself prying the trays loose. I had a chance to inspect him.

It wasn't accurate to call him handsome. There was an inhuman regularity in his features. Each side of his face was an exact mirror image of the other, a rare thing in human physiognomy. The result was cold perfection. Only that frequent smile gave warmth and humanity to what otherwise would have been a chilling and disturbing mask.

He moved well, lithely and with grace. I imagined his body would be dark, smooth, all long muscles covered with soft, almost hairless skin. All his actions —bending, turning, lifting—seemed fluid and effortless; his gestures were just as light and flowing.

His voice was musical, with a remarkable range. He knew how to use it for effect.

He wore his slacks and knitted sports shirt well; he had the kind of relaxed body that makes clothes look good. His hands and feet were surprisingly small for such a tall man, tapered in a pleasing fashion; they completed him, as if he were enclosed in one artful, continuous line.

He emptied the ice cubes into a plastic bowl, then went into the bathroom to refill the trays.

"Where you from, Bea?" he called.

"Here, there, everywhere," I said casually after he came back into the main room.

"Yeah," he said. "Me too."

"What kind of work do you do?"

"This and that. Well, I've got the glass and the ice ready for you."

He looked at me.

The ball was in my court.

"Care for a drink?" I asked. "I have vodka, scotch, brandy."

"Thought you'd never ask." He grinned. "What are you having?"

"Vodka."

"That'll do fine."

"I'll bring it in here. Your place is more comfortable than mine."

"Sure," he said.

We drank the vodka on ice, with a splash of water. My first of the day. We sat sprawled in the armchairs. He had kicked off his loafers, and we wiggled our stockinged toes at each other.

"Just arrived?" he asked idly. "I mean in New York?"

"A few days ago."

"Who's the Tooth Fairy?"

"Who?"

"The guy I saw you with."

I tried not to smile, but it was a descriptive name for Dick.

"Friend of a friend. He helped me move in."

"He's a flit, isn't he?"

"I don't know. I don't think so. He's an okay guy."

"Uh-huh. Well, it's no business of mine. Live and let live. Where were you? Before New York?"

"Chicago. You?"

"Miami. I like the tracks down there."

"Now I know where you got the tan. You follow the horses?"

"My secret vice," he said, his smile a little tighter.

"You do all right?"

He flipped a palm back and forth. "I get by. The luck runs in streaks."

"How's it running now?"

"Out," he said ruefully. "But the only thing you can say about luck is that it'll change, sooner or later. Maybe meeting you will change my luck."

"I'll drink to that if you'll fill my glass."

We sipped in silence a few moments. He stared at me over the rim of his glass. His eyes were narrowed. He seemed a little puzzled, a little uncertain.

"Cocktail waitress?" he asked finally. "I don't mean to pry; I'd just like to know if I've got you pegged. Tell me to go to hell if you like."

"That's all right," I told him. "Yeah, I've been a cocktail waitress. But not recently. Not for the past two years."

"Boyfriend?" he guessed shrewdly.

"That's right."

"You split up?"

"Permanently. He croaked."

"Sorry to hear it."

I shrugged. "Those are the breaks."

"You come to New York to go back to cocktail waitressing?"

"No," I said. "Never again. Not for me. I'm going to take it easy for a few weeks. Look around. See what I can line up."

"Mmm," he said. He looked up in the air. "Maybe we can do each other some good."

"How's that?"

"Well . . . you know," he said cautiously, "sometimes there are more chances around for a couple than for a single."

"Yeah," I said, just as cautiously, "that's true. Got anything particular in mind?"

"Nooo," he said slowly, "not at the moment. Maybe we could line up something."

"Maybe," I said thoughtfully, staring at him. "How heavy will you go?"

If he was surprised, he didn't show it.

"Depends," he said. "On what's in it for me."

I never doubted for a moment that he was speaking about an illegal hustle.

"Fair enough," I said. "I've got one thing going. It's just an idea right now, but it may work out. If it does, I'll need help."

He was silent a long time, apparently trying to make up his mind. Then he decided . . .

"Help? You'll need help? You're talking about muscle?"

I nodded.

"I'd like to hear more about it. When you're ready."

"All right," I said. Then I took a chance. "You're not hurting, are you, Jack? If a few bucks will help . . . ?"

He shook his head, grinning.

"Not that bad. Not yet. But thanks for the offer. I appreciate it."

"Just paying for the ice," I said nonchalantly.

I wanted to keep the talk going. It wasn't hard. He was a witty raconteur with a seemingly endless supply of anecdotes about horse racing, poker games, the casinos of Las Vegas. He had a wry self-mockery that I thought might disguise a kind of self-hatred.

"Married?" I asked him.

"Yeah," he confessed. "Still am. She waltzed out on me when the gambling got too much for her. Caviar one day, beans the next."

"Did she know it before you were married?"

"Hell, yes. I never tried to hide it. I guess she thought she could change me. What did your boyfriend do?" he asked suddenly. "The one who died?"

I thought a moment, then decided to follow the script. If it scared him, it was better to know now so I wouldn't be wasting my time.

"He was in the rackets."

Donohue didn't seem surprised.

"Uh-huh. What was his game?"

"Jewelry stores. He worked alone most of the time or picked up local talent for a big job. He did all right —until the last one."

"Yeah," he said, sighing. "Always the last one. How did he get snuffed?"

"I didn't say he got snuffed."

"I know you didn't. I guessed."

"You guessed right. It was a jeweler with more balls than brains."

"Wasn't your man carrying a piece?"

"Of course. The other guy was faster, that's all. Bang, bang. Like that."

"Were you there?"

"No. I was waiting for him back in the hotel. Bags packed and two airline tickets to New York. Ready to take off. When he didn't show, I knew it had gone sour. So I came east just like we planned. Only I came alone. Jesus, I'm running off at the mouth. The vodka, I guess. I hope I can trust you, Jack."

"I haven't heard a word you've said."

"Good. Keep it that way."

"Freshen your drink?"

"Why not?"

When I reached for the drink he had poured, he didn't release the glass. My fingers were around his. He looked into my eyes.

"Were you in love with him? The guy who got burned?"

"He was all right," I said, shrugging. "He treated me fine. But love? What's that?"

"A four-letter word," Jack Donohue said with one of his brilliant grins. "You're my kind of woman: no sentiment, no regrets, hard as nails."

"That's me," I said.

"Let's fuck," he said.

"Okay," I said.

He was as good as I hoped he'd be. It was far from the adolescent tumbling of Dick Fleming and the earnest ministrations of J. Mark Hamilton. Jack Donohue was a sword, as hard and as sharp, with demonic energy. He was a one-way lover, doing exactly what *he* wanted, what gave *him* the most pleasure. Which happens to be the kind I like.

Later, much later, we had a final drink in bed, talking nonsense in drowsy voices. He fell asleep before I did. I turned on my side to hold his long, slim, smooth weight in my arms. My forearm slid beneath his neck, my hand under his pillow.

I felt the gun.

The Lord's Day

~~~~~~

I awoke Sunday morning in my own bed in Room 703 at the Hotel Harding. Awoke staring at that cracked and peeling ceiling, wondering if it might fall and crush me where I lay, a victim of too much realism.

Up, showered (cold, no hot water available), and into my tart's uniform again. Reflected that Jack Donohue had been gentleman enough not to crack wise when I divested myself of wig and fore-and-aft falsies before climbing between his sheets. There were plenty of old, and bad, jokes he could have made but didn't. He seemed satisfied with my performance. I know I was with his.

I ventured out into a rainy, bedraggled Sunday morning on upper Broadway—not one of life's more exhilarating experiences. I had a small breakfast in a fast-food joint where both customers and the staff seemed to be sharing the same large, economy-size hangover. Then I found a supermarket that was open and bought myself some drinking glasses, canned soda and tonic, a few dishtowels, paper towels, toilet paper.

I could have brought all that stuff over from my East Side apartment, but I was being careful to carry nothing on my person or keep anything in my room that might connect Bea Flanders of the Hotel Harding with Jannie Shean of East 71st Street. My driver's license and credit cards were hidden under the front seat of the rented Ford. Other than that, there were no papers, letters, clothing labels, or possessions that might betray me. If Blanche wanted to toss my belongings, or even Jack Donohue, they'd find nothing.

Back to the hotel with my new purchases. Even though the room clerk at the Harding had warned "No cooking," Jack Donohue had assured me I could get away with a small hotplate, so I had also bought two cups and saucers, spoons, and a jar of instant coffee. When hardware stores opened on Monday, I'd pick up a hotplate or one of those immersion heaters for making a quick cup of coffee or soup.

Then I went back down to the rented Ford and drove home to civilization. On the way, I stripped off the blond wig, wiped most of the guck from my face, and changed into the pair of comfortable loafers I had squirreled in the car. By the time I arrived on East 71st Street, I was a reasonable facsimile of myself. With my trenchcoat buttoned up to my chin, I was able to sail by the doorman with no trouble at all, and even chatted with a neighbor (female) in the elevator with no embarrassing questions asked as to how modest-bosomed Jannie Shean had suddenly become Wonder Woman.

Upstairs, alone, door locked, I treated myself to a hot, sudsy bath, a big glass of chilled chablis and, later, a decent breakfast: a sardine sandwich with sliced onion, half a pint of strawberries, and a cup of yogurt.

Then I called my sister and chatted awhile. Or rather, she chatted and I listened, saying "Oh?" and "Really?" and "Fantastic!" at the right moments. Finally, when she ran down, I mentioned casually that I might be going out of town for a few weeks, doing research for a new book with a St. Louis background, and if she didn't hear from me for a while, not to worry.

"I'll call you when I get back," I told her.

"Call me when you get back," she said.

That's my sister.

I made a few additional calls of a similar nature to friends, and told all of them the same "may be going to St. Louis" story. Their interest was underwhelming. Then, having accounted for my absence, I got down to business.

When I told Dick Fleming that I would be coming back to the East 71st Street apartment occasionally to pick up my mail, pay bills, etc., it was the truth. But it wasn't the *whole* truth. I came back to keep my journal, Project X, up to date.

That diary was the *raison d'être,* the only justification for enduring the discomfort of the Hotel Hard-On and the danger of conning the likes of Jack Donohue. I referred to him as "Black Jack" in my account. I thought it was an apt description of his physical appearance. And not a bad label for his *membrum virile* either.

I wrote steadily for almost three hours, then locked the ms. in my top desk drawer. Answered two fan letters, sent Con Edison their monthly ransom, and scrawled a few lines to mother Matty in Spain. Then back into my floozy's costume again, and I sallied forth to resume the life of Bea Flanders, Master Criminal.

I discovered that getting *out* of a disguise is a lot faster and easier than getting into it. I had to pull into a parking area in Central Park for about half an hour before I had the wig adjusted and the heavy makeup applied to my satisfaction, a process watched with some amusement by a young couple parked in a nearby car. The hell with them.

I couldn't have been back in Room 703 for more than three minutes when there was a knock on the door.

"Bea? Jack."

I let him in. We were both very cool. No reference to our acrobatics of the night before. No passionate kiss, not even an intimate hug. We were both casual acquaintances. Maybe I was a bit hurt and disappointed. I don't think I was, but *maybe* I was.

"Been out?"

"Yeah," I said. "Buying a few things I need. Like drinking glasses. Now I won't have to bother you."

"Uh-huh. Hungry? Want to grab something to eat?"

"Sure. We'll go Dutch—okay?"

"What else?"

We walked through the drizzle, two blocks south to a side-street bar-restaurant called Fangio's. It advertised "Oriental and Puerto Rican Food." If that sounds odd to you, you haven't been in New York lately.

Fangio's was a basement joint, three steps down from the sidewalk. In the rear was a squarish dining area lined with booths. That's where we went, to a booth against the far wall where we could see everyone who entered and everything going on.

I wanted a glass of white wine. I ordered a vodka on the rocks instead. Donohue asked for a double bourbon and grabbed the waitress' wrist before she could get away.

"Ribs okay for you?" he asked me.

"Fine."

"Two on the ribs," he told the waitress, releasing her. "And heavy on the sauce."

I looked around. The bar was crowded. Most of the customers were watching a football game. It was noisy, smoky, more a drinking than an eating place. The smell of stale beer and old cigars, a few framed photographs of horse races and ballplayers. Realism.

Donohue seemed distracted.

"Waiting for someone?" I asked him.

"Sharp gal," he said, smiling bleakly. "As a matter of fact, I am."

"Sure you want me here? I can take off."

"No, no," he said hurriedly. "It won't take long. A minute or two. You stay right where you are."

I may have been imagining it, but I didn't think so. I thought he was using me, that my presence was needed and wanted. I stared at him as he kept his eyes on the front door, inspecting everyone who came in. I didn't think he was frightened exactly, but he was tensed, coiled. He sure didn't look like a man expecting good news.

We were on our second round of drinks when Donohue said, "There he is." He slid out of the booth, then smiled tightly and patted my cheek. "This won't take long, Bea," he said. "I'll be right back."

He moved toward the bar to meet a man who had just entered. If they shook hands, I didn't see it. The other man was short, squat, and smiling. My God, did he smile! Donohue grinned frequently, but this man smiled constantly. But it was more grimace than smile: a stretching of his mouth, a squinching of his eyes. It looked painful: a contortion of his features.

You kept waiting for that frog face to relax, to melt into something easier and more natural. It never did; that smile was frozen.

They spoke for a few moments, both standing away from the bar, heads close together. Once the smiling man struck Donohue's shoulder with his knuckles, a little harder than just a friendly tap. Then Donohue jerked his thumb toward me, and the short, squat man stepped clear to glance in my direction. I saw he was wearing a sweater under his suit jacket, no raincoat or topcoat. He had on a black leather cap, rakish as a beret. I thought he tipped the cap to me, but he may have been merely adjusting it.

Donohue put a hand on the other's shoulder, patted him a few times. Then he turned, came back to our booth. He arrived just as the waitress brought our ribs.

"Pleasant fellow, your friend," I said casually. "Always smiling."

"Yeah," Donohue said. "That's what they call him —Smiley."

"A close friend?"

"Not exactly."

"What does he do?"

He didn't look at me. He finished a rib, put the naked, gleaming bone carefully aside, wiped his fingers delicately on a paper napkin.

"Smiley?" he said. "Smiley is a villain."

I was about to quote Shakespeare on the same subject and clicked my mouth shut just in time. To cover my fluster I made a long guess.

"You owe him?" I asked.

He nodded. Stolid expression. "Almost five big ones."

"What will happen to you if you don't pay?"

"At best? Two busted kneecaps."

"And at worst?"

"They'll squash me," he said with a flimsy grin. "Don't happen to be carrying that kind of loot, do you?"

I shook my head.

He grinned, this time with genuine mirth.

"Just a joke," he said. "Not to worry. I'll work it out."

"Can't you just take off?"

"Not really. They'd find me. Eventually. As somebody said, 'You can run, but you can't hide.' "

"Is it worth all that to them? Five thousand? To go to that much trouble?"

"It's not the gelt," he explained patiently, "it's the principle of the thing. They let a small fish like me welch, the word gets around. Next time it might be a big fish. They can't afford that. So they run a tight ship. You said you had an idea for a campaign?"

The sudden question stopped me. I put the half-gnawed rib back on my plate. Jack Donohue was staring at me with stony eyes. I began to understand his pride. He wouldn't show his hope. It would be weakness.

"I have something going, yes," I told him. "It looks good."

"How much?" he said hoarsely.

"Plenty," I said. "Your five thousand is chicken feed. This means big money. *Big.*"

"So? Tell me."

I shook my head. "Can't," I said, "without getting the okay from my friend."

"Your friend? The Tooth Fairy? Why him?"

"I owe him."

It was language he could understand.

"All right. Let's meet and talk about it. Set it up."

"Finish your ribs. Have another drink. On me."

"Sure," he said, flashing his teeth. "Why not?"

"I'm sleeping alone tonight," I said, staring into his eyes.

He shrugged. "You're the boss, Bea."

I actually believed it.

Busy, Busy, Busy

~~~~~~

Writing is a lonely business. Hardly an original observation, but true. I mean, it's you, a typewriter, and a blank sheet of paper. I'm not talking about plays or movie scripts. Those are communal endeavors, writing by committee. But novelists and poets are recluses. And after you spend a few years at this anchoritic occupation, you lose the sense of the great big world out there. You forget how to act, how to *do*. The universe is condensed on that blank sheet of paper.

That was the way I had been living, like a goddamned hermit. A few friends, a little sex now and then to reassure myself that I was still alive. But generally I had been living an inactive life, sedentary, chained to the secondhand oak swivel chair.

But now—presto!—I found myself living not only one, but *two* full lives. I was Jannie Shean, crafty girl-novelist, plotting a cockamamie scheme to get more realism in my writing. And I was Beatrice Flanders, the big-titted doxy, flaunting her padded ass and planning to rip off a swanky midtown jewelry store.

And you know what? I loved every minute of it!

The best thing was that I wasn't flummoxed or reduced to gibbering ineptitude. I handled both identities, adroitly I thought, and did everything that had to be done. Take that Monday for instance . . .

It occurred to me that as Bea Flanders, driving a rented car, I could continue my surveillance of Brandenburg & Sons with lessened risk. I could double-park a "new" car on East 55th Street, and I could spend more time at my observation post in the luncheonette across the street, a stranger to the staff.

So I did exactly that early Monday morning. The routine was what I had learned to expect: Brandenberg employees arrived about 8:45 A.M., the commercial cleaning truck and crew showed up around 9:00, departed at 9:45, and the store opened for business at 10:00 A.M. It was comforting to know that the daily routine appeared to be unchanging.

I drove slowly around the neighborhood for almost an hour. Dick Fleming had reported that he could spot no definite schedule for police patrol cars or foot patrolmen. They seemed to wander by at irregular intervals, and we guessed that was deliberately planned.

When I returned to East 55th Street to pass the jewelry store a final time, I saw one of those slick-looking gents exiting. He was carrying the usual black attaché case, and manager Jarvis escorted him to the door to shake hands and bid him farewell.

Just for the hell of it I trailed the tall, somberly clad messenger, but not for very long. On Fifth Avenue he slid into the back seat of a chauffeur-driven black Mercedes. They pulled away from the curb and headed southward. I watched them go. It was, I thought, a nice way for a jewelry salesman to make his rounds.

In Jannie Shean's apartment I brought my journal up to the minute, including the significant dinner with

Jack Donohue at Fangio's the night before. Then into the shower, followed by the careful donning of my favorite Halston, a black crepe cocktail dress that suggested there was more underneath than actually existed. God bless Halston!

I took a cab down to Park Avenue and 54th. I was a few minutes early, and watched from across the avenue. I didn't have long to wait; in a few moments manager Jarvis and escort came striding around the corner from 55th Street. I went darting across Park Avenue, through the traffic, against the lights. Horns blasted, tires squealed, cabdrivers shouted two words at me. They were not Happy Brithday.

I watched Jarvis make his night deposit. The two men talked a moment, then separated. Jarvis came toward me. I started walking purposefully, directly toward him, eyes down.

"Why, Miss Shean!" he said, smiling, taking off his bowler. "This *is* a pleasant surprise. Noel Jarvis, manager of Brandenberg and Sons."

"Oh?" I said, puzzled. "Oh, of course! How are you, Mr. Jarvis? Nice to see you again. Finished for the day, are you?"

"Ah, yes," he said blithely. "Ready to relax after the chores are done. I must say you do look smashing. Big evening ahead?"

"I hope so," I said. "Eventually."

We had been exchanging these civilities in the middle of sidewalk traffic, buffeted by pedestrians rushing homeward. Noel Jarvis took my elbow lightly, politely, and drew me back to the building line, out of the scurrying stream.

"I can't *tell* you what a pleasure it is," he said, "meeting you like this. I was hoping against *hope* I might see you again."

He did have a tendency to speak in italics, but the

effect wasn't as phony as you might think. Probably because the man was physically impressive and unmistakably masculine. He might have had a paunch, but the shoulders were wide, the chest admirable.

It was the first time I had really looked at him, close up. He had the ruins of a very handsome face, gone to seed a bit now but still showing what had been hard, craggy features. I estimated his age at fifty-two to fifty-five, in that range, and I guessed that thirty years ago he had been a very sexy lad indeed. Now there were burst capillaries in the meaty cheeks and nose, but the mouth was still tight, teeth his own and good, the smile secret and knowing.

The only thing about him I disliked, I decided, were the small eyes of a washed-out blue. Too innocent to be true, those eyes.

". . . a little fun bar across the avenue," he was saying. "Just to relax for a few moments. If you have the time, of course."

"What?" I said, confused. "Oh. Well . . . yes, just one. Then I'll have to run."

"Of course," he said. "Understood."

So there we were, three minutes later, tucked into a cozy booth in a Park Avenue bar-restaurant. I remembered it vaguely as having five different names in as many years. On the evening I had my first fatal drink with Noel Jarvis, it was called Lucifer's. Was fate trying to tell me something?

It didn't take long to realize I was in the presence of a very, very heavy drinker. I was just finishing my first glass of white wine when he was sipping on his third martini, straight-up with a twist of lemon. As far as I could see, though, he could have been drinking ice water for all the difference it made in his speech and deportment.

He was good company too. Glib, witty, intelligent

and informed, and very fast with a gold Dunhill to light my cigarettes. He recognized my dress as a Halston. He told me scandalous stories of a few of his more famous customers. And he made me feel that at that moment he wanted nothing more from life than to be sharing a comfy, after-work drink with little ol' me.

I don't mean he came on heavy. There was no knee-rubbing, no hand-grabbing, no "accidental" touches, no leers—nothing like that. He just made me feel I was important to his happiness.

Doing my Mata Hari number, I got him talking about his trade. It wasn't hard at all; he was delighted to jabber on about diamonds, the controlling cartels, how price was determined, where the main cutting centers were located, how important the Israelis were to the business, how an increasing percentage of the sales of Brandenberg & Sons was now in unset diamonds, sapphires, emeralds, and rubies. For investment.

"Oh yes," Noel Jarvis said. "Investment. At the moment, I can assure you, diamonds are generally overpriced. But if you believe, as I do, in a continued inflation rate of seven to eight percent, I suggest you put all your loose change in gemstones. You do have some loose change, don't you, Jannie? I may call you Jannie, may I not?"

"Of course," I said automatically. "Yes, I have a few odd pennies. But wouldn't I do better to buy set pieces, especially antique necklaces and chokers and things of that sort? I've been reading stories of the fabulous prices they bring at auctions."

"Um . . . well," he said thoughtfully. "Not necessarily. Some pieces have an antique value, an historical value. Tiaras and brooches owned by this queen, this and that duchess, and so forth. If you're a collector, that might be of some interest. But what you must look for, beyond the provenance of a particular item, is its intrinsic worth. The cut of the stones, their color, weight, brillance, and so on. I *really* think you'd do better with individual stones. So small, so easy to conceal—for safety's sake, of course. So easy to take across the borders in case—God forbid—you might have to travel suddenly with a good portion of your wealth. In addition to the sale of cut but unset gems for investment, there is another trend these days, and that is to have very valuable stones mounted in extremely simple settings. For instance, just the other day we designed and produced a pendant for a movie star whose name I shall not mention. The white gold chain was worth three hundred. The eighteen-carat, pear-shaped diamond suspended from it was worth half a million."

"My God!" I gasped. "What's the point—a rock like that hanging from a little chain?"

"Several points," he said, smiling benignly. "The finished item is very simple, very elegant. Can be worn with a variety of gowns at a variety of functions. Marvelous with Halstons, for instance. Nothing ostentatious about it. And, most important perhaps, it never seems to occur to thieves that a simple chain-and-stone-necklace could be so valuable. So in addition to selling individual stones for investment, we also do a very good business indeed in valuable gems in quiet settings. Something you might care to keep in mind. Can you have dinner with me?"

The sudden question caught me off-balance.

"Uh," I said. "Well . . . no. I'm sorry. I do have plans."

"Of *course* you do," he said. "I wouldn't have thought otherwise. Do you suggest I ask again—or is the hope hopeless?"

He looked at me with such quizzical charm, with such a graceful shrug, that I couldn't resist him.

"I hope you do ask me again," I said firmly. "Do call me. I'm in the book."

"I know," he said gently. "I looked."

I thanked him, shook his hand, prepared to leave Lucifer's. Noel Jarvis wanted to go with me, to deliver me by cab to wherever I was going. But I insisted he stay, and he agreed, ordering his fifth martini.

When, at the doorway, I glanced back, he was still sitting upright in the booth, still smiling, very steady, a hand raised in farewell.

The Duel

~~~~~~

"I understand you're getting hairy around the heels," Dick Fleming said.

Jack Donohue shrugged. "When you're hot, you're hot; when you're not, you're not. Where did you say you were from?"

"I didn't," Fleming said. "Does it matter?"

"Oh . . ." Donohue said vaguely.

"Kansas City," Dick told him, "Originally. A little here and a little there since then."

"And what are you doing now?"

"Anyone I can," Fleming said, and the answer seemed to satisfy Donohue.

We were sitting in a back booth at Fangio's. The pleasing thought occurred to me that maybe I was the bone of contention. These two dogs were sniffing around what they considered to be a bitch in heat. No wonder there were snarls, snaps, and growls. It had gone on all during dinner.

"I can't work with the Tooth Fairy here," Donohue said finally, glowering at me. "I've got to have guys at my back I can trust. No insult intended, Fleming, but the chemistry is wrong."

"Suits me," Dick said. "You don't impress me as being the kind of brainy pro we're looking for. Let's split, Bea."

I decided to crack the whip.

"You shitheads," I said coldly to both of them. "I've spent too much time on this campaign to blow it because you two can't get along. I don't expect you to like or trust each other. All I'm asking is that you work together just long enough to pull this off. Then you can go at each other with icepicks for all I care. But either you work together, or consider yourselves out, and I'll find myself some other boys."

The two men stared stonily at each other.

"I'll go along," Fleming said.

"Strictly business," Donohue said.

"All right," I said. "Remember that. I'm the boss lady, but we're all in it together. One goes down, we all go down. So we work as a team. Agreed?"

They both nodded.

"Jack," I said, leaning toward Donahue, "this is what I've got. . . ."

I spelled it out for him: all about Brandenberg & Sons, the address, size, number of employees, daily schedule—everything Dick and I had been able to learn.

Black Jack listened intently, occasionally interrupting to ask sharp, one-word questions: "Cops?" "Alarms?" "TV?" "Customers?" I answered as fully as I could. I thought he was impressed but was trying not to show it.

"When do you figure on hitting?" he asked.

"About two weeks before Christmas," Fleming said. "Early in the morning. Right after it opens. No customers in the store."

"Still," Donohue said, "we can't handle it, just the three of us. Need a wheelman. Maybe a peteman if that safe is locked. Also, you're talking about six or seven workers in the place. Too many for us to keep an eye on and sweep the joint at the same time."

"Right," I said, nodding. "I figure at least two more, maybe three."

"What take do you figure?"

"A million," I said. "At least. That means two, three hundred thousand from the fences or insurance company, depending on how we want to handle it. We can decide that later. What's important right now is to get this thing rolling. Get it planned down to the last detail. Recruit the help we'll need."

"How do you figure on splitting?"

"We can work out the fine print later," I told him. "But right now I'm planning a flat fee for the hired hands. As little as they'll take. Their pay and expenses come off the top. The net we split forty-thirty-thirty. Me, you, and Dick."

"Mmmmm," he said. "Well," he said. "I'll tell you," he said, "I know you don't expect a yes-no answer right here, now, this minute."

"Why not?" Fleming said hotly. "It's a good deal."

"Who for?" Donohue said. "Let me decide. It's my cock on the block. I'll take a look at the place, Bea. Mosey around. See how it feels. There's a lot I like about it, and a lot I don't like."

"Such as?" I said.

"Such as early-morning customers wandering in or street cops strolling by. Such as hidden alarms you don't know about. Such as those two repair guys in the back room slamming and locking the door the minute we come barreling in from the street. A lot to think about. Let me look the place over. Give me a couple of days. Then I'll get back to you. Okay?"

I looked at Dick. He looked at me.

"A couple of days," I agreed. "Then if you're in, you're in. If you're out, you're out, and no hard feelings. But don't stall. I want to get this show on the road. I want it so bad I can taste it."

Black Jack looked at me admiringly.

"You're something else again," he said. "I won't stall. Two days, three at the most. If it's as good as you make it sound, then we can go right ahead. I know a couple of heavies who might be just right for a job like this. Smart—but not too smart. And all the balls in the world."

"Sounds good," I said. "Let's see—you figure two, three days to make up your mind? How about Friday night in my place at the Harding?"

"Friday night is fine," Donohue said, grinning. "But why not make it my place? More chairs. And ice."

We stood up to leave. I paid the tab. Neither of the men objected. Being a mob boss was becoming an expensive proposition.

Jack and I walked Fleming over to Broadway.

"Where you kipping?" Donohue asked casually.

"The Village," Dick said, just as casually. "A crummy hotel. If this thing clicks, I figure on moving up."

"It'll click," I assured him. "You can take that to the bank."

"We shall see what we shall see," Jack Donohue said.

We put Fleming in a cab. He wasn't too happy at leaving the two of us together.

Donohue and I strolled. It was getting on to twelve, but that raunchy neighborhood was alive. The night people were out: the pimps and prosties, the pushers and hooked, the drunks and the loonies. The streets were thronged with the pushing, noisy, brawling mob.

"You trust him?" Donohue asked.

"As much as I trust you," I said.

He gave me another of his scintillating grins.

"Fair enough. I'm just wondering if he'll be there if push comes to shove."

"Sure he will," I told him. "He's not a paper doll. He won't fold."

"If you say so."

Upstairs at the Harding, we went to his room. He fixed us drinks. We kicked off our shoes.

"Where you from, Jack?" I asked him.

"Originally?" he said. "You wouldn't believe."

"Sure I would."

"How about a good Irish-American family in Boston? Sister a nun and both brothers priests. Father and uncles in city politics. Plenty of cops in the family, too. How does that grab you?"

"You're the black sheep?"

"Blacker than black."

"Ever go back?"

"To the family? Now and then. The prodigal son returns. They kill the fatted calf. Always glad to see me. No questions asked. We have a ball."

"I can imagine."

"They think I'm going to hit it big one of these days."

"Sure you are," I said. "On Friday night."

"Maybe," he said. "We'll see."

He seemed vulnerable, sapped by the memories. Failure dogged him. Suddenly I felt guilty.

"Let's go to bed," I said.

"Let's go," he said.

Something Fishy Going on Here

~~~~~~~~~~~~~~~~~~~~~~~~~~~~~~~~~~~~~~

I had a large-scale map of Manhattan and a hand-drawn map of East 55th Street between Fifth and Madison avenues. The homemade one showed every store and hotel front on the block. I included taxi stops, a construction site, and the location of traffic lights, no-parking zones, etc.

Then I began drawing up a schedule: What time the car should start from the Hotel Harding. How long it would take to drive south to East 55th Street. Where the car should be parked. How long the robbery itself would take. The getaway.

I knew that Brandenberg & Sons should be invaded the moment the front door was opened for business at 10:00 A.M. With that as my start, I scheduled time for parking the car, time for getting downtown from West 94th Street, time for the mob to assemble at a pre-determined point. I allowed for plenty of slippage in case of late arrivals or unexpected traffic jams.

Gradually, over those two days, I evolved what I thought was a reasonable and efficient plan of action: preparation, advance on the target, assault, and withdrawal. I plotted the most efficient routes.

I also planned personnel deployment. I would drive the getaway car. I would stay outside, double-parked, motor running, while Fleming, Donohue, and the other two thugs we recruited would pull the actual job. Mask or no mask, I thought I might be recognized by Noel Jarvis. And he had my real name and address. The others would be strangers to him. He had seen Dick Fleming once, briefly, but I doubted if he'd recognize him in a mask.

I went over my marvelously detailed scheme again and again, eliminating, adding, refining. I thought it took every possible eventuality into account, and, as written, was ready for word-for-word transferral to the next Big Caper novel I'd write.

Most of this literary work was done in my East 71st Street apartment. When the details of the Brandenberg & Sons ripoff were complete, I transcribed the entire thing into my journal, the Project X that was fattening into a full-length manuscript.

Then, on Thursday night, I prepared for my dinner date with Noel Jarvis. He had called, and I had accepted. The femme fatale of East 71st Street—and points west!

That dinner turned out to be something special. We went to an Italian restaurant way over between Ninth and Tenth avenues. The walls were white tile and there were paper flowers in plastic vases on the tables. But the food was scrumptious.

Noel Jarvis was treated like he owned the joint. I mean, the staff *hovered*. The spiffy headwaiter spent at least ten minutes suggesting this and that. What I finally ended up with was a huge, succulent double veal chop, charred on the outside, pink on the inside, doused with a pizzaiola sauce. I could have married that veal chop.

Two hours and two bottles of wine later, I sat back

groaning, staring at the remnants of my warm zabaglione with glazed eyes.

"You eat like this every night?" I asked Jarvis. "Don't answer that. If you said yes, I might move in with you."

"Yes," he said promptly, beaming. He had demolished most of the wine, but seemed reasonably lucid and steady. As a matter of fact, I was sipping delicately at a small Strega while he was working on his second brandy stinger.

He wasn't paying for all this; other diners had sent over the wine and after-dinner drinks. And when Jarvis asked for our bill, the headwaiter assured us it had been taken care of.

"Courtesy of Mr. Smith," he said.

"God bless Mr. Smith," I said. "Long may he wave. Friend of yours, Noel?"

"In a manner of speaking," he said. "A good customer. It was very kind of him. I must reciprocate. Well, my dear, it's time for us to move on. What would you like? A disco? A piano bar? A nightcap somewhere?"

"You're the working man," I said, "who has to get up early in the morning. Let's save the disco and piano bar for a weekend. A nightcap in some quiet place would suit me fine. Anyplace I can kick off my shoes."

"Excellent," he said. "I knew you were a woman of discernment the moment I saw you. If I make a suggestion, I hope you won't be offended."

"Your apartment?"

His ruddy face positively glowed.

So we rose to depart. Noel Jarvis passed out the green stuff to maitre d', headwaiter, waiters, busboy, and then excused himself to dart into the kitchen where, I presumed, he rewarded the chef. His largesse no longer surprised me.

He lived on East 21st Street, near Gramercy Park. His apartment turned out to be a somewhat seedy palace. Two bedrooms, two baths, and a living room that looked like the lounge on the QE2. The furnishings were heavily baroque: lots of crystal, porcelain, velvet sofas and armchairs, gilt-framed paintings, marble cupids. It didn't look exactly like an auction gallery, but almost.

The place threw me. I had figured him for a man of some taste. This overstuffed apartment was out of character. It came awfully close to what a longshoreman might buy after winning the New York State lottery. Everything was expensive and everything was awful: The colors were a bedlam, the paintings atrocious. There was a floor lamp in the shape of a giant striking cobra.

I murmured the expected compliments, and Jarvis seemed pleased. He showed me through the entire museum. The bedrooms were visions in glimmered pink and purple satin. The bathrooms had little guest towels that had never been touched. The kitchen was the best, all business with stainless steel copper pots and pans.

"You like to cook?" I asked him.

"Love it," he said, coming alive. "I hope you'll come for dinner some night. I'd like to show you what I can do."

I said I'd like that.

We went back into the living room and I kicked off my shoes. It was pleasant scrubbing my toes into those buttery Oriental rugs. He had told the chauffeur to wait for me, I wouldn't be long, and to drive me to my door and make certain I was safely inside. So I really had no fears of a heavy come-on. He was a per-

fect host, and a fascinating conversationalist—until
he passed out.

It happened so quickly that at first I wasn't aware
of what was going on. I was nursing a brandy. He had
slugged down two, and was chattering away like a
magpie, working on his third, when he suddenly
stood up and excused himself. Minutes passed, and
I wondered how long it took him to pee. Then more
minutes, and I heard no sounds at all. I began to get
concerned. Fainting spell? Heart attack?

"Noel," I called softly. Then, louder: "Noel! I really
do have to get going. And I'm sure you have to get
up early."

No answer.

I sat there a moment. Then I finished my brandy,
rose, wandered toward the bedroom, having first put
on my shoes. If I found him naked, waiting with a
leer, I was prepared to make a fast withdrawal.

I found him fully dressed and prone on the satin
coverlet of the king-sized bed in the master bedroom.
His head was on the pillow, face turned to one side.
He was snoring gently.

He hadn't managed to get his feet off the floor when
he collapsed onto the bed, so I lifted them up and took
off his shoes. I also loosened his tie, unbuttoned his
collar, unbuckled his belt. During these ministrations,
he didn't stir. He was out cold, a not unpleasant reek
of wine, garlic, and brandy rising from his burbling
lips.

I thought I went about it very cleverly. I went back
into the foyer, double-locked the door and put on
the chain. Drew all the curtains and shades. When I
went back into the master bedroom, Noel Jarvis hadn't
changed position. He was still snoring gently.

I went into the main bathroom and took a look

in the medicine cabinet. Jarvis had an eye-widening selection of vitamins and minerals in there, plus Librium and Valium and several other pill and capsule containers without labels. Just clear plastic containers of pills and capsules. All colors and shapes.

I came back into the bedroom. Still no movement from Jarvis. I went through the big walk-in closet first. Nothing in there but an enormous and costly wardrobe of suits, jackets, coats, hats, shoes, ties. Good labels, too. Italian and English designers. In the first of the twin dressers, in cream-colored French provincial, were enough shirts, drawers, socks, and scarves for a regiment. Plenty of pure silk, and lots of pure cotton, which these days is almost as expensive as silk. Linen handkerchiefs. Foulard squares. Ascots. Monogrammed undershirts.

The top drawer of the second dresser was filled with jewelry: cufflinks, and studs and rings, bracelets and neck chains. At least a half-dozen wristwatches. Stickpins.

The bottom drawers held his winter and sports stuff: heavy flannel shirts, sweaters, waistcoats—things like that. Plenty of suede and good glove leather.

I had taken care, with all the drawers I opened and inspected, to leave things just the way I found them. I turned nothing over. I rearranged no stacks. I just thrust my fingers down between the piles of fabric and groped around on the bottom of each drawer. Nothing.

Until I came to the last drawer of the second dresser. Heavy knitted sweaters in there, each in its own plastic bag. I should be so neat! I was prying down at the bottom when I felt it. Something.

I glanced toward Noel Jarvis, still sleeping, his face turned away from me, I gripped what I had discovered and slowly, carefully, drew out a passport.

I took it to the bedside lamp and flipped through it quickly. It was undoubtedly a photograph of Noel Jarvis: the heavy jowls, meaty nose, flinty eyes, smiling mouth. The passport showed three overseas trips in the past two years: to Holland, Italy, Israel. Everything seemed in order.

Except for one thing.

The name in the passport was Antonio Rossi. I stood staring at the signature, a little ashamed at myself for prying. If an Italian wished to use an English name, it was really none of my business. I could understand it; he was the manager of a shop with a clientele that might be impressed that way.

That left only a small bedside table, a taboret covered with antiqued gold leaf, stamped with a colored, vaguely Persian design. Jarvis' head, on the pillow, was awfully close to that table, and I debated a moment as to whether I really wanted to risk opening the top drawer. Finally, watching the face of the sleeping man constantly, I softly pulled the drawer out, just far enough to take a quick look inside.

It wasn't finding a revolver that surprised me so much. The manager of a jewelry store would have little trouble getting a gun permit. But this gun was shockingly big. I don't know make or caliber, but it looked like a cannon without wheels. The black leather half-holster seemed old and worn.

Then I turned off all the lights and got out of there, making certain the front door locked on the spring latch. I rode home grandly in the limousine, and the uniformed chauffeur insisted on seeing me to my door.

"Mr. Jarvis ordered it, miss," he said firmly, so I let him do his job.

Later, safely locked within my own apartment, I undressed swiftly, got into bed, and tried to ponder the contradictions in the character of Mr. Jarvis-Rossi.

But I fell asleep thinking of a broiled veal chop and warm zabaglione, and smiling happily.

A Meeting of Minds

~~~~~~

At 9:00 that Friday night we were seated in Donohue's room at the Hotel Harding. I was Bea Flanders in blond wig and tight turtleneck. Jack looked like Hialeah; knife-creased silk slacks, nubby gold sports jacket, white moccasins decorated with brass trim. Dick Fleming, by contrast, looked pretty drab.

Donohue was polite, unsmiling, and very, very cool. He got us comfortable, locked the door, and supplied us with vodkas on ice. The glasses were clean.

"Well?" I demanded in my gunmoll voice, having decided to come on strong. "Are you in or out?"

"I took a look at the place," Donohue said, staring at me. "I've practically lived on that block for the last two days. I was into the store twice, and I checked out the daily routine. Before I tell you what I think, spell it out for me in more detail. Just how do you plan to hit it?"

I had brought along my schedules and maps. I went over it once more:

The precise time the three of us plus the two added recruits would meet.

The route the five of us would take south, me at the wheel.

I would stay with the car, double-parked near the construction site at the corner of East 55th Street and Madison Avenue.

The four men, masked, would go into Brandenberg & Sons at 10:00 A.M., the moment the door was unlocked for business.

Two men would race to the rear, to the vault room, before the repairmen had a chance to slam the door or lock the safe.

The other two would cover the manager and clerks in the front room, force them to lie down, gag and tape them. The two repairmen would be treated similarly, and the aged porter if he was present.

Then the safe and showcases would be rifled as rapidly as possible. Obvious pressure alarms would be avoided; the glass cases would be smashed from the top rather than the sliding doors forced.

"Then everyone piles out," I finished, "and gets in the car. By this time I'll have pulled up in front of the store. The best route for a getaway, I figure, is to—"

"Bullshit," Jack Donohue interrupted harshly. "Pure, unadulterated bullshit! It sucks. Do it your way and we'll all be in the slammer within an hour. If we're not in the morgue with tags on our big toes."

I looked at Fleming. He looked at me.

"All right," Dick said. "Let's go."

"Right," I said, preparing to rise and depart. "You say you don't want in. That's okay if—"

"Shut up and sit down!" Donohue snapped. "You too, Fleming. I didn't say I didn't want it. I just said you got a lousy plan. I thought you told me your old man was a whiz at jewelry jobs? If this is an example of how he did it, no wonder he got squashed."

"What the hell's wrong with my plan?" I said hotly. "I worked weeks on this. It's got—"

"Shh, shh," Donohue said, relaxing and giving me one of his brilliant grins. "Just keep your voice down, Bea. Take it easy and I'll tell you what's wrong."

"First of all," he started, "I like the place. For a target, I mean. Big enough but not too big. Not too many clerks. And lots of lovely, lovely rocks—"

"Bea told you," Fleming broke in. "At least a million."

Donohue turned to him, flashed one of his high-powered grins.

"I agree," he said. "A minimum of a mil. Probably more. And I'm just talking about the stuff up front, in the cases. What's in that safe in the back room—well, who the hell knows? But it must be beautiful. Okay, that's agreed. The place is worth the risk. And it's ripe for plucking. No armed guard. No TV cameras that I could spot."

"So you want in?" I asked him.

"I want in," he said, nodding, "but not if I have to follow your script. First of all, with a gang of five you want *two* cars, not one. On the getaway, they split up. That confuses witnesses and the cops, and doubles your chances of at least one car making it with half the take."

"Well . . . all right," I said grudgingly, "I'll buy that. But that means more people. At least another wheelman."

"Correct," Black Jack said. "But more than just another driver. Bea, we just can't go busting in there when the store opens at 10:00. What if a street cop or a squad car comes wandering by?"

"Chances are slim," Fleming said. "They work on a—"

"I know how they work," Donohue said sharply.

"No regular schedule. I'm just saying *what if?* A cop comes rumbling by while we're inside, and you've got the Shootout at the O.K. Corral. Or a couple of early-morning customers stroll in. Then what? That place could begin to look like Grand Central Station. With only four of us to truss them all up and cover them and empty out the place at the same time? No way! Bea, it just won't work. We need more people and we need a better scam."

"Like what?" I said.

"Like this," he said. He leaned forward, elbows on knees. "I checked out that place for two days running. The key to the whole thing is that cleaning truck that comes an hour before the store opens. You spotted that?"

"Sure," I said. "Every morning. At 9:00. They spend about thirty to forty-five minutes in there. The manager unlocks the door to let them in, then locks it again after they leave."

"Every morning?" Donohue asked.

"Every morning," I told him again. "Like clockwork. I watched."

"Good," he said with a satisfied grin. "That's what I figured. The key is this: That truck is from the Bonomo Cleaning Service. It double-parks right outside the store. On both mornings I watched, the manager was waiting inside the door. When he saw the truck pull up, he unlocked the door. Get it? All he's looking for is the truck, he doesn't even wait to see if the guys getting out are his regular cleaning crew or a gang of pirates. He sees the truck; he unlocks the door."

"Hijack the truck!" Fleming burst out.

"Right!" Donohue said, looking at Dick with new respect. "Now we've got our second vehicle. And that cleaning van can hold a football team. And if we work fast enough, we can pile through that unlocked door before the manager realizes it's not his usual cleaning crew. Four, or six, or even a dozen guys inside, and the door locked, the shutters down, one hour *before* the store opens for business. My God, in an hour, with enough outlaws, we can take the paper off the walls!"

I had an objection. "What if the manager doesn't unlock until he makes sure it's his regular cleaning crew?"

"That's what he *should* do," Donohue said, "but it's not what he does. He's waiting for the cleaning truck, he sees it park in front of the store, he unlocks the door. If he looks at the guys on the sidewalk, all he sees are the uniforms they wear. I'll bet ten to one on it. A guy in a uniform or any kind of unusual clothes, you don't look at his face, you look at what he's wearing."

"So then?" I said, beginning to get excited by his idea.

"So then the moment that door is open, the guys in the front of the van rush it, and the guys in back push in right after them. I don't mean it can be a stampede, but they don't mosey either. Listen, it'll be 9:00 in the morning; a lot of people on the streets. But all they'll see is guys in uniforms—you know, those coveralls they wear—piling out of a truck and hurrying into a store to clean it up before it opens for business. Who's going to figure a heist is coming down? If it's timed right, there won't be a squeal. And cleaning guys always take tools and bags along with them— right? So we go inside with everything we need to take the place apart. We've got a whole hour and enough guys to make sure none of the clerks makes like a hero. When we've got what we came for, we leave everyone tied and gagged. We split the loot. Half the guys and half the take go in the cleaning van. You take the rest, Bea. We go by different routes. We meet later for the split. How does that sound?"

Fleming and I stared at each other again.

"What do you think, Dick?" I asked him.

"How do we get the truck?" he wanted to know.

"Easy," Donohue said. "It's from the Bonomo Cleaning Service. Sign painted on the side. But it's also got a number painted on the cab door. It's a truck number 14. So we find out where this Bonomo Cleaning Service is located. We stake the place, find out when the trucks start on their rounds. We follow truck number 14. We learn its routine. It'll take time, but it can be done. Then, on the day we decide to hit, we hijack Bonomo truck number 14 just before it gets to Brandenberg."

"What about the driver?" I asked. "And his helper? They find their truck gone, they're going to scream to the cops. Then there's a bulletin out and we're sitting ducks."

Donohue snapped his fingers. "Right," he said briskly. "You're thinking smart, Bea. So we take the truck *and* the crew. We tie 'em, gag 'em, and toss 'em in the back of the van. When we're finished, we ditch the van and cut the guys loose."

"One thing still bothers me," I said. "Are you *sure* the manager is going to open that door as soon as the truck pulls up? Before he inspects the cleaning crew to make certain they're his regulars?"

"Sure, I'm sure," Black Jack said. "He did it both mornings I watched."

"Two mornings," I said. "Not enough to bet everything on a habit pattern."

"All right," Donohue said, frowning at me. "Suppose he does look through the glass door before he unlocks it. So he sees two cleaning guys he's never seen before. What's he going to do—ask them through a locked door what they're doing there and where are his regular cleaners? No, he's going to unlock that door to talk to them. After all, the regular truck is there, and these guys are wearing Bonomo coveralls and carrying mops. He's not going to be so suspicious that he'll keep the door locked while he calls Bonomo to find out what's going on."

"Maybe he will," I said, "and maybe he won't. But I don't want this whole job to hinge on that—how the manager will react if he spots two strange cleaning men. Too chancy."

The three of us sat staring at the worn linoleum.

"Look, Jack," I said finally, "we're planning this for a week or two before Christmas, so we've got some time to get it right. Let's do this: Next week Dick and I will cover Brandenberg and Sons every morning at 9:00. We'll watch the exact sequence: when the cleaning truck pulls up, when the crew gets out, when the manager unlocks the door. If it happens the way you say it does—he unlocks the door the moment the truck appears—then we'll go with it the way you said. If he inspects the crew *before* he unlocks the door, then *we*'ll have to think of something else. Okay?"

"Jesus," Donohue said disgustedly. "You're acting like an old woman. We've got to take *some* chances."

"We're taking plenty," I assured him. "I just don't want to take any unnecessary ones."

"All right." He sighed. "You check it out. And what will I be doing meanwhile?"

"You can locate the Bonomo Cleaning Service," I told him. "Find out when their trucks start going out. Try to get the schedule for truck number 14. Also, maybe you can ask around about fences. Guys big enough to handle a haul like this. You know this town better than I do; you'll know where and who to ask. Can you do that?"

"Sure," Donohue said promptly, mollified. "No problem. . . . You want to work through fences rather than the insurance company?"

"Depends," I said. "On what we get and what we're offered. But we've got to start somewhere, so we better have some names when the stuff is in our hands. Now what about those two heavies you said you could recruit?"

"I can get them," he promised. "I asked them, casual-like you understand, without telling them exactly what it was, and they're ready for a fight or a frolic. Look, these guys are mutts. Great brains, they're not. But they'll do what they're told to do and not cry."

"We'll need more," Fleming said, "if we go along with the cleaning truck gimmick. Another driver there. And another two or three to go inside."

"Not to worry," Black Jack said. "This town is crawling with out-of-work bentnoses. We'll have our pick. How we'll pay them—flat fee or a split—is something we'll have to decide after we get the ball rolling."

He rose, poured us more vodka. We raised our glasses to one another.

"Success," Dick Fleming said.

"Luck," Jack Donohue said.

I didn't say anything. Donohue too fell silent, looking pointedly at Fleming. Dick got to his feet, muttered something about having to see someone, and left us. But not without a reproachful glance at me. I was certain he knew how my evening would end.

"He's okay," Donohue said, moving about, mixing us fresh drinks. "Not a bad asshole after you get to know him. And he's no dummy. He knew right away about hijacking the cleaning truck. Not the kind of man I'd want for a close friend, but I can work with him. I just hope he's a stand-up guy if things get rough."

"He will be," I said. "I trust him."

"I hope you're right, Bea. You want to go to bed now?"

"Sure," I said.

I did everything for him. Guilt racked me.

The Plot Thickens

So, for five days I spent my early mornings on East 55th Street, watching closely as the Bonomo Cleaning Service van arrived in front of Brandenberg & Sons. On Monday, Wednesday, and Friday, I was Beatrice Flanders. On Tuesday and Thursday, I was Jannie Shean. Schizophrenia, where is they sting?

I watched from the luncheonette across the street, from the rented Ford, and from my own XKE. I even took notes, marking down the precise times of the arrival of the cleaning van, the unlocking of the front door of the jewelry store, the entrance of the cleaning crew, and their departure.

This is what I found:

On the first four mornings of the week, things went just as Donohue had reported: The truck double-parked in front of Brandenberg, and almost immediately the door was unlocked and opened. Obviously Noel Jarvis had been awaiting its arrival.

But on Friday morning, something different and disconcerting happened. The truck parked, the crew got out carrying their mops and vacuum cleaner. They

crossed the sidewalk. But the door of Brandenberg &
Sons remained closed and locked. The cleaners banged
on the door. It was almost a minute before Jarvis appeared to let them in. Maybe he'd been busy in the
back room, maybe he'd been in the can. Who knows?
But meanwhile the Bonomo cleaning crew cooled their
heels outside.

I know it sounds like a ridiculously small detail, but
our whole scheme of barreling into the store from the
cleaning truck was based on the door being unlocked
and open. On such tiny details the entire Big Caper
depended. A good lesson for me. I had never realized
that a major crime must be as precisely timed as a
military operation.

I made copious notes, and included everything in
the Project X manuscript. I also found time to call
Sol Faber—remember him? my agent—and reported
that the new book was coming along famously. I
hoped to have the ms. in his hands by late January.

He was delighted.

"Jannie, dolll," he said anxiously, "is it realistic, like
Aldo Binder wants?"

"Completely realistic," I assured him.

"And it's got a real ending? I mean, it just doesn't
stop? Everything gets tied up neat and tidy?"

"You wouldn't believe," I told him.

On Friday night, Donohue, Fleming, and I met
again. This time in the back room of Fangio's. Dick
and I had dined at Tommy Yu's. I don't know where
Jack Donohue ate his dinner, but he was waiting alone
in a booth when we arrived. He looked tired. And not
too happy.

"Been up every night since Sunday," he grumbled,
after our vodka-rocks were served. "From like midnight to ten. I try to sleep during the day. I'm dead."

"So?" I said coldly. "How did you make out?"

"I found the Bonomo Cleaning Service garage. It's on Eleventh near 54th. Most of the trucks go out at one in the morning when a new shift of cleaners comes on. That outfit must have fifty trucks. Took me two nights to spot truck number 14. I mean, suddenly they all come pouring out of the garage, and at that hour it's tough to spot the numbers."

"You followed it?" Dick asked.

Black Jack sighed. "That's where it gets screwy. You'd think they'd have a regular schedule of places to clean, a regular route to follow. But they don't. On each of those three nights I tailed truck 14, they went to different places. All over Manhattan. They always ended up on East 55th Street, but there was no way of knowing where they'd be before that or where we could be certain of hitting them."

Depressing news. The three of us sat hunched over our drinks, trying to figure it out.

"It doesn't make sense," I said. "The cleaning service has X-number of customers. You'd think each truck would be assigned to the same places every night."

"You'd think so," Donohue said mournfully, "but that ain't the way it is."

It was Dick Fleming who came up with the answer. He raised his head and looked at Jack and me, back and forth.

"Sure, they work a regular route," he said, smiling. "But on the same days each week. Get it? Brandenberg is an expensive shop. It's got to be spotless. So it gets cleaned every morning. But the other places truck 14 goes to, maybe they get cleaned three times a week, or twice, or only once a week. So each morning's route would be different. But I imagine if you followed truck 14 for a month, you'd find their route on Monday is the same every Monday, and every Tuesday is the same, and so on."

Black Jack reached across the table and patted Dick's cheek. "Brains," he said. "The kid's got brains. I'll lay five to three he's exactly right. Now why the hell didn't *I* think of that?"

"So all we have to do," I said, "is decide what day of the week we want to hit, and chart the route of truck number 14 for that morning."

"Let's make it a Friday," Donohue said. "Fridays have always been lucky for me."

"Friday is good," Fleming said. "Around Christmastime most New York stores stay open on Saturdays. That means that on Friday morning Brandenberg and Sons will probably have a big stock on hand for Friday *and* Saturday."

"Beautiful," I said. "I'll drink to that. Friday it is. We'll decide the exact date later."

We ordered another round. After it was brought, I gave Donohue the bad news of how, that morning, the cleaning crew had to wait at least a minute on the sidewalk before the manager unlocked the door.

"Dick and I came up with an answer," I said. "See what you think of it. We hijack the truck and cleaning crews as planned. But only *one* of them, the helper, gets tied up and tossed in the back of the van. The other guy, the driver, keeps his coveralls on, and he really does the driving, with a gun in his ribs. The guy holding the gun is wearing the helper's coveralls. They pull up outside Brandenberg and Sons. The driver gets out because he knows that piece is pressed into his spine. He collects a few mops and buckets and walks up to the door. Our guy is right behind him, prodding him with—"

"I get it, I get it!" Donohue said excitedly. "If the manager has already unlocked the door, all well and good. The rest of the guys pile out and in. But if they have to wait, or the manager looks through the door before he unlocks it, he sees his regular cleaning man with a new helper. Naturally he's going to unlock."

"You think it'll work?" Fleming asked.

"Money in the bank," Black Jack assured him. "Can't miss. I got to hand it to you two; you come up with the answers. Jesus. All right, now I can tell you. Our two heavies are waiting at the bar, right over there. I wasn't going to say anything to them until I was sure we had a workable plan. Now I think we better bring them in. We got a lot to do. Should I call them over?"

"Sure," I said, craning toward the bar area up front. "Which two are they?"

"See there in the middle? Near the beer taps? The big guy is Hymie Gore. All muscle. Even between the ears. But he moves fast. The thin, twitchy guy they call the Holy Ghost. Nobody knows his real name. Just the Holy Ghost. He's a shadow; now you see him, now you don't. Both of them have sheets, but nothing recent. I'll go get 'em."

He slid out of the booth, headed toward the bar.

"Hymie Gore and the Holy Ghost," Dick Fleming said. "Enough realism for you, Jannie?"

"I'd never use it in a book," I said. "Who'd believe it?"

Donohue brought the two men back to our booth. They were both carrying their beers. The Holy Ghost slid in next to Black Jack. Hymie Gore pulled up a chair and sat at the end of the table. He slopped over the seat. No introductions were made. We all smiled at one another and made polite small talk: the weather, the crime rate in New York, where to get a really decent plate of ribs. The waitress came over and Donohue ordered vodkas for all of us. I knew who'd bounce for the drinks.

Hymie Gore—a name so improbable that even Brick Wall would never use it—was a tell-me-about-the-rabbits-George type of guy: big, hulking, with a forehead so low that his bristly hair seemed to end in eyebrows. When his drink came, he folded his fist around the glass and it disappeared. He had a surprisingly high-pitched, wispy voice, like a tuppenny whistle, and he belched continually—little rumbling burps after which he'd tap his lips with a huge, broken knuckle and say, " 'Scuse."

The Holy Ghost grinned, grinned, grinned. Either he was growing a beard or he hadn't shaved in three days. His face looked like those fuzzy photographs you see with the captions "Is this the true shroud of Christ?" He couldn't keep his hands or feet still: always tapping, tapping. I thought he was on something. He was, but I didn't find out until later what it was. Relatively innocent—he drank about twenty cups of black coffee a day.

Dononue waited until the waitress was out of earshot. Then he said to the two men:

"What we got here is a jewelry store. Very fancy. Mucho dinero. We got it worked out how to get it before it opens. Like nine in the morning. No B and E. Legit. No customers. The manager, three salesmen, two guys who do repairs. Maybe a porter, an old geezer."

"Silent alarms?" the Holy Ghost asked in his hoarse voice. He was half Hymie Gore's heft, and had a voice twice as low.

"Sure," Donohue said. "What else? But no armed guard, no TV cameras. We go in when the shutters are still down. Dig? The place hasn't opened for business yet. So what cop is going to look in? The stones are up front in showcases and in a back room where the safe is. A piece of cake."

"Yeah," Hymie Gore squeaked. "The last piece of cake I went for cost me three-to-five."

"I'm telling you," Donohue said. "Can't miss."

"The five of us?" the Holy Ghost wanted to know.

"No," I said. "Two more. Maybe three. But not right away. Pick up help when we're ready to hit. But we got a lot to do, and a month to do it in."

"What's the split?" the Holy Ghost rasped.

"To be negotiated," Donohue said, "if you decide to come in."

"Negotiated," Hymie Gore said wonderingly. "What does that mean?"

"I want ten," the Holy Ghost said.

"Ten what?" Fleming asked.

"Percent—of the take."

I looked at Donohue. He gave me a brief nod.

"All right," I said. "Ten percent. For each of you. But off the net. Expenses come off the top."

"That's fair," Donohue said.

"Yeah," the Holy Ghost said hoarsely. "Who's running the show?"

"I am," I said.

"You? A lady?"

"That's right."

"She's okay," Donohue told the heavies. "I'm with her."

"Want to think it over?" Fleming asked them.

"I already did," the Holy Ghost said. "It's before Christmas?"

"About two weeks before," Fleming said.

"Good. I got a lot of gifts to buy. I'm in. You, Hyme?"

"What?" the big man said dazedly. "Oh. Yeah. Sure. We should carry things?"

"Of course," Donohue said. "You got one?"

The giant considered carefully.

"I can get," he said finally.

"Good," I said. "Now here's what we've got. . . ."

"I like it," the Ghost said after I finished. "Especially the cleaning truck angle. That's cute."

"Yeah," Gore said. "That's cute."

"Like Bea said," Donohue told them, "we'll need maybe two, three more guys, so keep your eyes peeled for some hard cases. Maybe we'll pick up a car the night before we hit. Nothing flashy. We'll ditch it right after the take. It should be a four-door with some power under the hood. Also, we'll need a place we can go to later. A garage would be best. Where we can pull in, unload, switch cars. We'll leave the stolen heap and the van there. We can end up at the Harding. You could waltz into that place carrying the White House and no one would say 'Boo.' Also, we got to figure how to get coveralls for all of us from the cleaning service. I got an idea on that. Also, we should think of maybe like a diversion. Something happening, say, five blocks away the time we hit. Maybe a call to the cops that a bomb's been planted. Or maybe a real smoke bomb. Hell, we could blow up a mailbox. Some such shit. Just to keep the local blues busy."

I looked at him in admiration. I hadn't even *thought* of a diversion.

"Also," I said, trying to prove I really was the boss lady, "we'll need masks or stockings. Something to hide our faces. Tape, rope, gags for the cleaning helper and the people inside the store."

"A peteman?" the Holy Ghost said. "In case that safe is locked?"

Donohue looked at me.

"No," I said definitely. "If it's locked we won't have time to blow it. Or drill. And we don't want the noise and can't carry the equipment it'd take. There's plenty in those showcases. All we'll need is a hammer and a bag."

"That's lovely," the Holy Ghost said, tapping away frantically with fingers and feet. "A hammer and a bag. I love that."

"Yeah," Hymie Gore said. "Lovely."

"Will you take your share in rocks?" Donohue asked them.

"What?" Fleming said quickly. "I don't follow."

"We'll have to fence the stuff," Donohue explained. "Or make a deal with the insurance company. That'll take time. Weeks probably. Maybe longer. And the boys want the cash for Christmas. Will you guys take some of the ice as your cut? Fence it yourselves? Faster bucks. You take, say, a couple of nice rings, a necklace. Whatever. Then you don't have to wait until the whole shmear is sold. You got your split right away."

"Yeah," the Holy Ghost croaked. "That sounds good. I'll take some of the rocks."

"Yeah," Hymie Gore said, nodding violently. "That sounds good. Me too."

"Fine," Black Jack said. "This is going to be a big one. Glad you boys will be with us. I'll be in touch."

As if he had given them a command, they drained their glasses, rose to their feet and, nodding to me, shambled out of Fangio's. We watched them go.

"What do you think?" Donohue asked.

"They'll do," Dick Fleming said in what I now recognized as his Big Caper voice.

"Jack," I said, "what was that business of paying them off with part of the loot? With actual stones?"

He stared at me.

"Don't you get it?" he said. "I told you these guys were mutts. Pay them off in stolen property, and before you know it they'll be trying to hock it or peddling the stuff in every bar on Broadway, including right here in Fangio's. No self-respecting fence would touch them. They're wingdings. So they peddle the stuff, and right away the blues pick them up. The rocks are identified as part of the Brandenberg heist, and the fuzz get big headlines about how they broke the case so quick. You think they're going to look for anyone else? No way! File closed. And we're home free."

"Hey, wait a minute," Dick Fleming said. "Won't they talk if they're picked up? Identify us? Cop a plea?"

"Oh sure," Donohue said cheerfully. "They'll sing their little hearts out. What do you expect? But I'll be long gone by then. Won't you?"

"Of course," I said hastily. "Long gone."

"Naturally," Black Jack said. "The survival of the fittest. Wow, we're really rolling now! Let's have another round. This one is on me."

So we had one more drink. Then Donohue said he was going back to the Hotel Harding and get to bed early.

I said I was going to drive Dick Fleming home, down to the Village. So we all shook hands and parted. I paid the check, including that last drink Donohue had grandly offered.

The Confidence Man

For the next three weeks, I spent most of my time in the guise of Beatrice Flanders, with Black Jack Donohue. He seemed to have no objection to my tagging along. In fact, I think he enjoyed the opportunity to display his expertise.

As we came closer and closer to that fatal Friday, his eyes sparkled, the brilliant grin became more frequent. "My luck has changed, babe," he said to me, laughing and snapping his fingers. "It's coming my way now. And I owe it all to you."

"Sure, Jack," I said.

The way he handled the problem of getting enough Bonomo Cleaning Service coveralls for the entire gang was very cute.

Donohue had a dozen business cards made up showing that he was sales manager of the Big Apple Laundry and Drycleaning Co., at a fictitious address. Then he dressed in a conservative suit of dark-gray flannel and donned a pair of horn-rimmed spectacles fitted with window glass. The business cards bore a telephone number—the phone booth at Fangio's.

Thus prepared and accoutred, Black Jack paid a visit to the office of the Bonomo Cleaning Service. He claimed to be sales manager of a new company specializing in industrial laundry and drycleaning.

"We are brand-new, sir," he said to the boss of Bonomo. "Just started operations a month ago. Not yet listed in the telephone directory. But if you'll just phone the number on my card, you can verify what I'm saying."

I was stationed near the phone booth at Fangio's at the time Donohue told me to be there. When the phone rang, I grabbed it and said, "Big Apple Laundry and Drycleaning Company. Good morning." A harsh voice asked if we had a man named Sam Harrison working for us.

"Yes, sir," I said briskly, as rehearsed by Donohue. "Mr. Harrison is our sales manager. He's out of the office at present, calling on customers, but if you'd care to leave a message or a number he can call . . . ?"

"No," harsh-voice said, "that's okay."

So Donohue-Harrison made Bonomo a generous offer. He would take a dozen pair of dirty coveralls, have them back the following day, cleaned and pressed, at absolutely no cost to Bonomo. Just to prove the speed and efficiency of Big Apple's service. And the cost for a regular contract with Big Apple would be a guaranteed 10 percent less than what Bonomo was currently paying.

What did the harsh-voiced boss at Bonomo have to lose? At worst he'd never get back his dozen coveralls. Peanuts. At best, he'd get the dozen coveralls cleaned for free and could cut his laundry costs by 10 percent.

So harsh-voice handed over twelve soiled, light-blue coveralls with "Bonomo Cleaning Service" stitched across the back. They ended up in Jack Donohue's room at the Hotel Harding.

"See how easy it is?" he said to me, laughing like a maniac. "Some fake paper, an earnest manner, lots of balls, and you're in like Flynn. All life is a scam, babe. Some small, some big."

We didn't score such a complete success with the fence, but it wasn't a failure either. Donohue came up with the name of a man with a Wall Street address. He called, mentioned his contact, and set up an appointment for 4:00 P.M.

I couldn't believe a receiver of stolen property would be working out of an office in the financial district, but Donohue didn't think it strange.

"This is a big man," he assured me. "Deals in millions. I mean hijacked truckloads, traveler's checks, crates of transistor radios, airline tickets, computers, stock certificates, machine tools, bearer bonds—stuff like that. You think a man with the cash to handle deals like that would be working out of a phone booth? Bea, this guy is *class*."

I drove Jack down to Wall Street. The office we were looking for was in one of those buildings so high that it turned your stomach just looking up at it.

But the office itself wasn't much. Down at the far end of a marble corridor. The legend on the door read "Merchants Provisions, Inc. Asa Coe, President." There was a small outer office where a pouty, middle-aged lady sat at a typewriter. She had an enormous beehive hairdo of glossy black curls, earrings just slightly smaller than barrel hoops, and rings on every finger. A gypsy. If she had shaken a tambourine, shoved a hand at us and said, "Cross my palm with silver and I will tell you secrets of your past, present, and future," I wouldn't have been a bit surprised.

She looked up slowly as we came in.

"Yes?" she said coldly, eyeing Jack.

"Mr. Morrison," Donohue said. "To see Mr. Coe. I called for an appointment."

"I'll tell," the gypsy said.

She stood to go into the inner office. She had a bosom that looked like it was stuffed with goose down. But there was no doubt about it; it was hers.

She was out in a few seconds.

"He'll see," she said, giving Jack Donohue a slow, calculating up-and-down stare.

The man in the inner office was, I guessed, about 342 years old. I thought it was hot as hell in there, but he had on a wool plaid shirt (buttoned to the neck; no tie), a cardigan under his suit jacket, and a wool scarf pulled across his scrawny shoulders. He was also slurping from a big mug of steaming tea.

He was seated behind a beat-up wooden desk, and there was nothing else in his private office. I mean *nothing*. There was his scarred desk, his wooden swivel chair, and four dark-brown walls. No file cabinets, no chairs for visitors, no pictures, no papers on his desk, no coat rack. It looked as though he had just moved in five minutes ago and was waiting for the rest of his furniture. Or maybe he was moving out, waiting for the brawny guys to wheel out desk, chair, and him.

"Mr. Coe?" Donohue said.

The mummy looked at him. His face was a road map of wrinkles, and his complexion matched the walls. He faded into the background. All you saw were bright eyes and brown-stained teeth.

Then Coe nodded. That was some nod. It started slowly and then grew faster. For one horrible moment I wondered if he'd be able to stop, or if the nod would become more violent until the shriveled head snapped off the shrunken neck and bounded across the floor.

But gradually the nod slowed, then stopped. The glittering eyes stared.

"Yes?" he said. A whisper.

"My name is Sam Morrison," Jack Donohue said loudly. "This lady is my associate, Miss August."

"Yes?" Coe whispered.

"As I mentioned on the phone, sir," Donohue went on bravely, "Mr. Winowitz gave me your name and suggested I call. I presume you checked with him?"

"Yes?" Coe said.

I think he said "Yes." It was so faint, all I heard was "Ssss."

"I'm expecting a shipment," Donohue went on confidently. "About the middle of December. I wanted to explore the possibility of converting the merchandise to ready cash. As soon as possible after delivery."

We were both standing before that battered desk, two naughty students brought to the principal's office. Mr. Asa Coe slurped his tea, watching us over the rim of his mug.

"What?" he said.

"Uh, precious gems," Donohue said. "Set and unset. A large shipment."

"Large?"

"Yes, sir. Very large."

"Ten," Mr. Coe whispered.

"No, sir," Black Jack said. "Thirty percent. Best quality. Top-notch."

The ancient sighed. Or maybe he was just blowing on his brew to cool it.

"We'll see," he said.

"But you're interested?" Donohue persisted.

"We'll see," Coe repeated. "When you got, you call."

"All right, sir," Jack said. "That's good enough for me. We'll be in touch."

So far I hadn't said a word. I didn't think Asa Coe had even glanced at me since we entered his office. But as we were leaving, at the door, he called softly, "Girlie." I turned back.

"Girlie," he asked in his breathy voice. "The titties —they're yours?"

"No," I said.

"Didn't think so," he whispered, and put his shiny beak back down into his tea cup.

I thought the whole interview had been a disaster, but Jack didn't agree. On the drive back uptown, he explained:

"The guy's interested. That's the important thing; he didn't say no. Naturally he's not going to say yes and set a final price until he sees what we've got. Winowitz told me what to expect."

"But that office! Empty. Hardly looks like a guy with enough bucks to swing a big deal."

"You expect him to keep records, Bea? It's all in his head. When we've got the stuff, I'll call again and he'll set up a meet. I tell you, he's interested."

We had other things to do. Hymie Gore and the Holy Ghost had been touring midtown Manhattan in Hymie's battered Dodge, looking for a place where the car switch could be made after the robbery. They had located a padlocked garage in a row of abandoned tenements, stores, and small warehouses west of Ninth Avenue on 47th Street. The entire blockfront was empty, sheet metal nailed over the windows. It was scheduled for demolition, to be replaced by a high-rise apartment house. "No Trespassing" signs were everywhere, and at night the area was patrolled by a security guard with an attack dog.

"We timed him," the Holy Ghost said. "He makes his rounds on the hour. Takes him ten, twelve minutes. Then back to this storefront that's still open.

They're using it like for an office. He sits in there watching this little TV set he's got. Then, on the hour, he makes his walk again."

"Yeah," Hymie Gore said. "On the hour."

We drove slowly down the block, the two heavies in the back seat of my rented Ford.

"There it is," the Ghost said. "On your right. See? Two steel doors. They're padlocked. A five-and-ten lock. I could spring that with a toothpick."

"Looks good to me," Donohue said. "But across the street, on the left, people still living in those slums?"

"Oh sure," the Holy Ghost said. "But this time of year they ain't hanging out their windows. And they see us at the garage, who's going to scream? A garage door opens, a car pulls in. At night this is. Or early in the morning. So it's a car going into a garage. Big deal. No one's going to panic. They figure it's done so openly, the watchman's got to know—right? And after we hit, we come back in broad daylight to make the switch. So if anyone sees, so what? Even if they call the blues, we'll be in and out so slick, what can they tell?"

"Mud on the license plates," Donohue said.

"Of course," the Ghost said. "What else? Well? What do you think?"

"The location's good," I said. "With luck, maybe ten minutes from the hit."

"Fifteen tops," Donohue said, nodding.

During dinner at Dick's apartment that night, I gave Dick a report on the Great Coverall Scam, the meeting with the Wall Street fence, and the discovery of the abandoned garage on West 47th Street. He listened closely.

"You kow, Jannie," he said slowly, poking at his bowl of stew, "I really think this thing could come off. I mean, if we were actually going to pull it, I think it would have a very, very good chance of succeeding. Don't you?"

"Damned right!" I said emphatically.

"Yes," he said thoughtfully. "Jannie, have you given any thought to how we're going to get out of this? I mean, when do we disappear?"

"I want to stay in until the last minute. We'll have like a final briefing the night before. Then you and I will just fade away. I can leave my Bea Flanders junk at the Hard-On—I'll never be using it again. We just won't be there when the show is supposed to get on the road that Friday morning."

"And what happens then? Jan, you don't suppose they'll try to pull it without us?"

"No way!" I say. "First of all, they'll be spooked by our nonappearance on Friday morning. They'll think we've chickened out, and they'll start wondering if maybe we've gone to the cops. Also, they're counting on my rented Ford and your VW in that 47th Street garage to make the switch of the loot. No, I don't think we have to worry about them trying it on their own. The whole plan will be destroyed when we don't show up."

He nodded. He shoved his half-finished plate of stew away. He drained his glass of burgundy, then refilled it and topped mine off.

"I'm sorry," he said. "In a way. Aren't you, Jannie?"

"That we're not going through with it?"

"Yes."

"Sure, I'm sorry. In a way."

Something to Think About

~~~~~~

"Bea, there's something you and me have got to talk about," Jack said. "We been putting it off, but we're getting close now, and we should get it settled."

"The split?" I said.

"Right," he said. "The split."

We had been trailing the Bonomo van all night, doing a final check on its Friday route and timing.

"You've had expenses," Jack said. "Picking up our drinking tabs, the gas for your car. The masks, tape, rope, and so forth. So all that comes off the top."

"Forget it," I said. "It doesn't amount to that much."

"No, I won't forget it," he said stubbornly. "I figure a couple of C's should cover you. Right?"

"More than enough," I said. "Too much."

"Let's call it two C's. That comes off first. Then I figure the two muscles we bring in at the last minute, we can get them for five big ones each."

"They'll sign on for that?"

"Sure they will," Donohue said. "And be happy to get it. So that's another ten thousand off the top.

Now, out of what's left, Hymie Gore and the Holy Ghost get ten percent each."

"In rocks," I reminded him.

"Correct. In rocks. So their share will be approximate. But that leaves like eighty percent for you, me, and Fleming. I figure thirty-five percent for you— after all, it was your idea—and twenty-five for me, and twenty for Fleming. How does that sound, Bea?"

I sat awhile in silence, as if I were giving his proposal careful consideration.

"It's fine with me," I told him. "You're the boys who are actually going in, while I sit outside in the car. So I figure my thirty-five percent is generous. But I'm not sure Dick will be happy with twenty."

"Why the hell not?" Donohue demanded. "I can't see where he's contributed much to this caper."

"Jack, he was in from the beginning on all the planning. You've got to admit he came up with some good ideas. Like this truck route business tonight."

"Well, maybe," he said grudgingly. "But you and me have been doing most of the work."

"I'll talk to him. I think I'll be able to get him to take the twenty without screaming too much."

"You do that," Donohue said. "Talk to him. How close are you to this guy, Bea?"

"What do you mean—how close?"

"I mean, I can't figure out what's between you two. He's not your brother, is he?"

"Of course not. What gave you that idea?"

"I don't know. Sometimes you act alike. Talk alike. Even look alike, in a way. Is it a sex thing? I mean, between the two of you?"

"Jack, he's just a friend. I knew him out west, then looked him up when I came to New York."

"A close friend?"

"So-so. I like him. I get along with him."

"Bea," Donohue said softly, "we could cut him out. Easy as pie. Make the sale to Asa Coe and take off. Fleming could never find us."

"No," I said instantly. "I couldn't do that."

"Or a fake count," Black Jack said gently. "Con him out of coming to meet with the fence. Then he has to take our word for how much we get for the stones. You and me could be big winners, babe."

I turned my head away, looked out the window. Or tried to. But it gave me my reflection back. And behind me was the dim, wavery image of Black Jack Donohue staring at me steadily, his face stony. I turned back to him.

"I'll think about it."

"You do that," Donohue said. "You think—Oh-oh, here they come! Two more stops before they get to Brandenberg's."

We followed right along, keeping at a cautious distance, and Donohue said nothing more about the split. But I did think about it. I thought how Jack was ready to deceive Hymie Gore, the Holy Ghost, Dick Fleming, and for all I knew, me.

If I had ever felt guilty about betraying his hopes and dreams by this make-believe Big Caper, I felt it no longer. He really, I told myself, was not a very nice man.

"All right," Donohue said, as truck 14 pulled away from a rug store on 50th Street and Madison. "Now they're heading for the last stop before Brandenberg. How we doing?"

"Right on schedule," I said, consulting the clipboard. "A few minutes off here and there, but all the stops check out."

"Good. Now they're pulling up. It's that antique store."

It was on Madison, between 53rd and 54th streets.

We parked across the street, down the block, and watched. It was 8:15 A.M.; the sidewalks were filling up with people. Sunlight came shafting through the slots between buildings. It promised to be a sharp, clear day. The morning rain had vanished, leaving the pavements clean and glistening.

"They'll leave here in about forty minutes," Donohue said. "Go north on Madison. Turn west on 55th. Pull up in front of Brandenberg's. So we've got to take them sometime between the two stops."

"When they come out of the antique shop," I said. "It's the only way. Jack, you notice when they double-park and go into the place they're cleaning, they don't lock the truck? I mean, they probably take the ignition key, but I haven't seen them lock the rear doors of the van after they take their cleaning gear out."

He turned sideways on the seat to stare at me.

"Bea," he asked dubiously, "are you sure of that?"

"Absolutely. I've been watching them all morning. They probably figure they've got nothing in there worth stealing. But you just wait until they come out. You'll see them go to the rear of the van, open the unlocked doors, and put their cleaning gear inside."

We waited. At 8:53, the two Bonomo employees came out of the antique shop. They were carrying a canister vacuum cleaner, mops, buckets, rags, and a feather duster on a long, jointed pole. They went to the rear of the van, opened the unlocked doors, began to stow their gear inside.

"Babe," Donohue breathed, "you're a whiz. A *whiz!* That's it; they don't lock those back doors."

"So while they're inside the shop," I said, "we can be putting our guys inside the van."

"They'll be wearing the Bonomo coveralls," Jack said. "No one on the street will look twice."

"Right," I said. "Then the real Bonomo guys come out of the antique shop, open the back doors of the van, and—"

"And they're staring down the muzzle of a piece that'll look as big as the Brooklyn-Manhattan tunnel. I love you!"

Laughing, he grabbed me, pulled me close, gave me a hard kiss on the lips. I resisted. Oh, maybe a second or two.

Then I pulled away.

"Hey," I gasped. "Early in the morning for fun and games. They're taking off. Don't you want to follow them?"

"What for?" he said. "I know where they're going. To Brandenberg and Sons. To fame and fortune. Just where we'll be going a week from right now. Kee-rect?"

"Kee-rect,' I said.

It was a hard, cold morning, but suddenly I was covered with sweat. Not perspiration. Sweat. I had never been so scared in my life. I think, at that moment, I finally realized exactly what I had done, was doing. I knew I was going to walk away from it, but even that didn't help. I felt I had set an avalanche in motion, rumbling down. How do you stop an avalanche?

"My God," Jack Donohue said. "You're shaking. Cold?"

I nodded, teeth making like castanets.

"Let's stop for some hot coffee," he said solicitously. "Can't have you coming down with the flu. Not now. When we're so close."

Alarming News

~~~~~~~~~~~~~~~~~~~~~~~~~~~~~~~~

The city was girding up for Christmas. Scrawny Santa Clauses on every corner, ringing bells and tugging at false beards. Wet weather, snappish, with freezing rain and dirty slush hinting at worse to come.

Still, it was *Christmas*. You remember that, don't you? Peace on earth, goodwill toward men, and all that jazz? Suddenly midtown Manhattan was invaded by a determined army of shoppers, all with a fistful of cash in one hand and a Bloomingdale's shopping bag slung in the other. They had buying mania in their eyes, and seemed determined to strip every store bare of everything that could be wrapped in cutesy paper, tied with a red ribbon, and stamped "Do Not Open Until Xmas."

That was all okay with me. Mobs on the street as early as 8:00 A.M. Hustle and bustle, shoving and confusion. In all that scurrying throng, who would have time to notice a bunch of guys in cleaners' coveralls doing their own brand of Christmas shopping in one of the city's prestigious jewelry stores? 'Tis the

145

season to be jolly, ho-ho-ho, and so forth. It would make a great novel.

I slept until late Friday afternoon at the Hotel Harding. Then, Blanche coming in to clean, I had a quick vodka, then got out of there and drove through heavy Christmas traffic over to my East 71st Street pad. It was a relief to peel off the sponge rubber, soak in a hot tub, enjoy a few more vodkas in the rough, and forget everything. For a while.

But work habits die hard. So there I was, early in the evening, slaving away at the typewriter in my cluttered office, working on my private manuscript, Project X. I wrote down everything that had been happening to me, including my very, very secret musings on the character of one Black Jack Donohue. I must admit, he didn't come across on paper. I mean, I couldn't figure him, couldn't pin him down, couldn't fit him into any neat personality slot. Sometimes I thought him a shallow, two-dimensional cutout, a cartoon of the cheap, criminal hustler. Other times I thought I glimpsed something deeper and more complicated there, a man who was nervy and frightened, brave and scared, laughing and peevish. In short, human.

That night I wanted to be alone. I have a highly developed taste for solitude, and had few recent opportunities to enjoy that pleasure. So that Friday night, locked safely in my East Side burrow, I devoted all my time to what I call "schlumpfing." Men might not understand it, but women will.

I washed my hair. Did a few stretching exercises. Cut and painted my toenails. Tried a new moisturizer I had bought. Ate some odds and ends I found in the refrigerator. Mixed a few crazy drinks, like a grasshopper and a black Russian. Wrote a letter of progress to Aldo Binder and tore it up. Put some Cole

Porter on the turntable and danced naked around my living room, Ginger Rogers without Fred Astaire. In other words, I just schlumpfed around, spending time as though it would never run out.

I was half-listening to the midnight news on an FM radio station when I became aware of what the announcer was saying. I dropped what I was doing and listened to every word.

The newscaster was reporting a jewel robbery in San Francisco. A well-known, exclusive shop called Devolte Bros. Five or six masked gunmen. In broad daylight. Held up clerks and customers. Ransacked the store, taking only the most expensive items. In and out before police could respond to the alarms. Loot was estimated at more than two million dollars.

I turned off the radio. Two million dollars. Six masked gunmen. In and out so fast that the silent alarms were worthless.

As they say in novels, it gave one pause. The whole caper sounded like a rehearsal for our Brandenberg & Sons hit. And apparently it had gone down as planned: no one hurt, a clean getaway. I was sure Jack Donohue would hear of it, or read of it, and now I wasn't so certain of what I had told Fleming—that the gang wouldn't dare pull it without us.

Suppose they did? And suppose they got caught and warbled like canaries? I could see the headlines now: "Thieves Blame Blond Boss. Cops Seek Femme Brain of Gem Heist. Bea Flanders Sought by FBI. Where Is the Sexy Crime Czar?" And so on. Nice thoughts. Two hours later I got out of bed and popped a sleeping pill.

On Saturday morning I went out for the papers and read everything I could find on the robbery in San Francisco. Details were scant, but apparently six masked and armed robbers suddenly invaded the jewelry store during the lunch hour. Two of the crooks cowed clerks and customers at gunpoint while the other four did a quick and efficient job of cleaning out the display cases and the back room safe, taking the loot away in what appeared to be pillowcases.

One lovely touch was noted. When the last crook ran out the front door, he paused long enough to insert a rubber wedge-shaped stopper under the door, which opened outward. It effectively delayed pursuit long enough for the thieves to escape unscathed in two cars, one of which had been identified as a stolen taxi.

That rubber doorstopper was a neat gimmick. The front door of Brandenberg & Sons also opened outward. I would have bet my bottom buck that right then, at that moment, Black Jack Donohue was out shopping for wedge-shaped rubber doorstoppers.

I spent the next night at the Hotel Harding, but there was no sign of Donohue. I was disappointed. I had had enough solitude the night before. How many nights in a row can one schlumpf? I stopped in at Fangio's for a drink at the bar, but didn't see Black Jack, Hymie Gore, or the Holy Ghost.

On Sunday, Donohue still absent, I went back to East 71st Street. I called Dick Fleming at home. No answer. I called my sister. No answer. I called Sol Faber. No answer. It was that kind of day. Where *was* everyone? So I went to a lousy French movie and had dinner alone a Chez Morris. *That* didn't improve my disposition. Or my digestion either.

Went back to my apartment to put on my doxy's costume, preparing to return to the Hotel Harding. Then *my* phone rang. At last! I was beginning to think Manhattan had become a desert island.

It was Noel Jarvis, and he said he had been trying to reach me for three or four days. I mumbled something about being busy with Christmas shopping, and he said he had been busy too; the store was doing an "absolutely fabulous" trade. I told him how happy I was to hear it, and what else was new?

What was new, he said, was that he hoped, I might be free the following night, Monday, to have dinner at his apartment. Told him I'd be delighted. He said to show up around "eightish," very informal, wear jeans if I liked. He promised a special banquet, and he was going to get started on the sauce the moment I hung up.

So I hung up.

Monday. A lonely day mooning around the Hotel Hard-On and environs. I had heard Jack Donohue come in about 2:00 A.M. But he hadn't knocked on my door, and when I awoke, he was gone again. I know; I knocked on his door.

Back to the East 71st Street apartment to prepare for my dinner with Noel Jarvis. The phone rang a little after 6:00. He couldn't have been more apologetic. He had to ask me to postpone our dinner date. He was tied up at the store. They were taking inventory and he was afraid he wouldn't be able to get away in time to do the dinner justice. Would I ever forgive him? Would I give him another chance? Would I come to dinner the following night, Tuesday?

Yes, yes, and yes.

So I called Dick Fleming. I wanted to hear his voice. I wanted to tell him how uneasy I felt. How, after three days with no contact with Jack Donohue, I was beginning to wonder if something was going on. I didn't know about—and should. I wanted to tell him about the Devolte Bros. robbery in San Francisco, if he hadn't heard about it. Tell him about the door-stopper. Tell him to rush over to my place for a quick roll in the hay.

His phone rang and rang. No answer. Where *was* everyone? What was going on?

Finally, on Tuesday, I reentered the land of the living. Had a hamburger lunch with Jack Donohue at a nausea noshery on Broadway. As I had guessed, he had read all the newspaper stories on the Devolte heist and thought the doorstopper gimmick was pure genius. He had already bought two of them. He had also slipped the lock of the Hotel Harding linen closet and had waltzed away with a dozen reasonably clean pillowcases. To carry off the Brandenberg loot. He was full of piss and vinegar, looking forward to our dress rehearsal on Thursday night. We made plans for the five of us—me, him, Fleming, Gore, and the Ghost —to meet at the West 47th Street garage at 12:30.

"What about the stolen car?" I asked sharply.

"Not to worry," he said. "Our two heavies have a good one spotted. Parked in the same place every night. They've got the right keys for it. A seventy-six Chevy four-door. They'll bring it to the garage on Thursday. We've done time trials in traffic from East 55th to the garage. Not over fifteen minutes."

"Good," I said. "Now what about the two other guys, the pickup help?"

"On standby," he assured me. "They agreed to the five grand each. They don't know what or where or when we're going to hit, but they're ready for anything. You and Fleming will bring your cars to the garage at 7:00 on Friday morning. Leave them there. The three of us will take the stolen Chevy to Madison Avenue, with the masks, rope, tape, stoppers, coveralls, pillowcases and so forth. Meanwhile, Hymie Gore, the Holy Ghost, and the two standby muscles will get over to 54th any way they can. Don't worry; they'll make it. They'll come into the Chevy, one at a time to pull on the Bonomo coveralls. We wait for the cleaning truck to show up at that antique shop. Then all the men, including me and Fleming, will take the van. You follow us up to Brandenberg's in the Chevy. And that's it. We'll go over all this in more detail on Thursday night so everyone knows his job and the timing."

"You've got it all figured out," I said.

"You better believe it," he said, smiling at me.

I went back to East 71st Street. I took along some personal belongings from the Hotel Harding, preparing for the final break on Thursday night. I wasn't sure how I felt about the final split. Half-relief, half-disappointment. Dichotomous. There's a word for you. I had never used it in a novel. I made a mental note to use it in my novel about the Brandenberg ripoff.

I took Noel Jarvis at his word and dressed informally. When I bopped into his museum-apartment, it was apparent he had spent much time building the appearance of casual elegance. Hound's-tooth jacket, gray-flannel slacks, fringe-tongued black moccasins, a paisley ascot around his neck—and a rubicund complexion that signaled two double martinis. He was bubbling.

"Beautiful," he said, taking my mink and dropping it on the floor. "You, me, the dinner. Everything. Listen, hon, I mixed this shaker to keep me company while I've been cooking. How about—"

He held up a crystal shaker and peered at a few inches of liquid and chips of ice in the bottom.

"Dregs," he said sadly. "I better stir up another batch."

I followed him into that stainless steel workshop. He had a zillion dishes, bowls, pots, and pans going. And if he was weaving slightly, he seemed to know exactly what he was doing: beat this, whisk that, stir here, chop there, cans opened, jars stirred. He was busy as hell, pausing only occasionally to take a delicate sip from his martini. I perched on a kitchen stool and watched the nut work.

"Inventory all finished?" I asked casually.

"What?"

"The inventory. Last night. At the store."

"Oh," he said, not looking at me. "Oh yes. All finished. Perfect. Everything checked out."

"It's unusual, isn't it? Taking inventory two weeks before Christmas?"

"Oh no," he said. "No no no. Take them all the time. Once a month, at least."

"Shoplifting?" I guessed.

"My God, no!" he said, busy at the stove. "Our losses are minimal. We do have a foolproof system of showing the merchandise, you know. One item at a time. You don't see item two until item one is stowed safely away. No, the inventory is, for us, internal security."

"Internal?" I said, figuring that out. "You mean you don't trust your help?"

He laughed. A hard, toneless laugh.

"Of course," he said. "Trust 'em. Have to. What? But still . . . temptation, you know. A lot of small, very valuable items."

What he said made sense. But I had the oddest impression that he was conning me, an eerie feeling that he was reciting a prepared speech.

That dinner was something. Blue point oysters on a bed of shaved ice. Each succulent blob topped with a spoonful of Beluga caviar. Don't knock it. A salad of tiny cherry tomatoes on romaine leaves with an anchovy dressing. A pasta dish that was a mixture of noodles, elbows, gnocchi, and God knows what else, all in a sort of Alfredo sauce, rich enough to put two inches on your hips instantaneously.

What else . . . let me remember. The main dish was

braciole—slices of rare steak spread with a paste of parsley, cheese, garlic, salt, pepper, oil. Thin slices of salami and bacon atop that. Crowned with a tomato sauce. Your gastric juices flowing? You should have tasted it. I wanted to put a dab behind my ears and, possibly, just a touch in the armpits.

And then minor things like french-fried zucchini, balls of rice molded with ground steak and Parmesan cheese. And Key lime pie made from grated lime peel. Espresso. Some kind of liqueur that tasted of burnt almonds and burst into flame when Noel Jarvis carefully put a match to the surface of each glass.

And, of course, wine during the meal. A dry white to begin. A rich, heavy chianti classico to finish.

"Marry me," I said to him.

"Dee-lighted," he said, giggling. And I wondered how long it would be before he was once again prone in the master bedroom. In all honesty, I was feeling no pain myself. But it was obvious he had a head start on me. And was keeping ahead. With no urging on my part.

By this time we had wandered back into the lush living room, carrying our coffee and brandies, belching gently.

"Help you clean up?" I offered halfheartedly.

"Nonsense," he said stoutly. "Someone will come in tomorrow morning. Go through the place."

"Who?" I said idly. "The FBI?"

It was a joke; that's all it was: a silly joke. It made no sense whatsoever—I admit it. But I was bombed enough so that I had a good excuse for not making sense. I admit that "Who? The FBI?" was just nonsensical, just something to say. No reason for it. But Noel Jarvis' reaction was incredible.

He jerked to his feet, spilling most of his drink down his shirtfront. I didn't like the look in his eyes.

"Why did you say that?"

"My God, Noel," I said. "Take it easy. It was just a joke. A lousy joke, I admit. I didn't mean anything by it. Just something to say."

He collapsed as quickly as he had pounced on me.

"Of course, my dear," he said lolling back. "A joke. No, no, not the FBI. Just the cleaning lady. Take care of everything, she will. Enjoy the dinner?"

"I told you," I said. "The best. The very best. You don't eat like that every night, do you?"

He was sitting in a velvet armchair. Suddenly he slid down until he was hung on the end of his spine, legs stretched out in front of him. All of him was limp, beamy, and relaxed. Another inch down and he'd have crumpled onto the floor.

"You know," he mumbled, "let me tell you something, luv."

"Tell me something."

I don't apologize for this drunken conversation. I'm just trying to report it as accurately as I can.

"What I'd really like to do," he said slowly. "What I'd really, *really* like to do. All my life. Is run a restaurant. That's what I'd really like to do. Yes. But who of us can do what we . . ."

He left that sentence unfinished. I knew what he meant. It was sad; he would have made a hell of a chef.

"Hey," I said brightly. "Noel, did you read about that robbery? In San Francisco? Last Saturday, I think it was."

"Friday," he said, looking at me blearily. "Afternoon. Heard. About it. Devolte Brothers. San Fran."

I realized he wouldn't be with me much longer.

"How about a nightcap?" I suggested. "A brandy? Settle all that marvy food. I'll get it for you."

He grinned at me.

I went into the kitchen, found a bottle of Remy Martin. I didn't slug him, honest I didn't. I poured him exactly as much as I poured for myself. An ounce each, being very drunkenly exact with a little measured jigger he had.

He was still conscious when I came back into the living room. He took the brandy snifter from me with a glassy smile. I pressed his fingers around it.

"Cheers," he said, missing his mouth on the first try. But he finally made it.

"You bet," I said, standing near him so maybe I could catch him when he collapsed. "Listen, Noel, aren't you afraid that your place could be ripped off like Devolte? In San Francisco?"

He straightened up, pulling in his legs. His eyes rolled up to me. I could almost hear the rumble.

"No way," he said, shaking his big head. "No way."

"They had alarms," I reminded him. "The newspaper stories said so. But by the time the cops got there, the place was cleaned out and the crooks were gone. With all the jewelry."

"Silent alarms," he said drowsily. "Bullshit. I beg your pardon, dear lady. The theory is, with silent alarms, you see, the police or a private agency are alerted and come running. No danger to people in the store. Like me. Who sounds the alarm. You see? Right? You press an ordinary button in the store, a bell goes off, a siren, whatever, gas, smoke, and a cheap crook panics and shoots. You understand? Like if Brandenberg got held up, I press a button, bells ring, and they shoot me. Could happen."

"Sure," I said. "Of course. I understand. That's why they call them silent alarms. You press a button, nothing happens in the store. But the cops in the precinct house or guards in a private security agency, they're alerted. But no one in the store gets hurt."

"Right," he said, nodding wisely. "No one gets hurt."

"I hope you've got silent alarms in your place," I said, trying to yawn. "I wouldn't want you hurt."

"Bless you, my child," he said, taking a sip of his brandy. "Bless you. Better than that. Much better."

"Better?"

"Oh yes," he said, bobbing his hand up and down like an idiot. "Much better. You know our store—the chair rail that runs around the wall? Right around the wall, behind the display cases?"

"Sure. I've seen it."

"Seen it," he said, smirking. "It's all pressure. We stay away from it. The whole rail. Waist-high. On the wall. It's pressure. In sections. Back into it, it goes off. You know? We're held up. Our hands in the air. We back up. Our ass—I beg your pardon, dear lady—our ass presses against the chair rail. It activates the alarm."

Puzzling. I was puzzled.

"So?" I said. "Nole, you back into that railing, and it activates a silent alarm. Then? In another ten or fifteen minutes cops or private security guards could be swarming all over the place. But by then the crooks could be long gone. That's what happened in Frisco. So what's the point?"

"The point," he said. "What's the point. Ho-ho!"

The empty brandy snifter slipped from his limp fingers, thumped to that thick, buttery rug. His head began to loll, bobbing on his thick neck. I was still standing alongside him. I should have been kind. After that magnificent dinner, I should have let the cook drift off to a deep, drunken, well-deserved rest. But I had to know.

"Noel," I said loudly, bending down so my lips were near his ear, "what's the point? The point, Noel? If you or any of the clerks back into the railing, the silent alarm goes off. So?"

"You see," he muttered, chin on chest. "Silent alarm. They come right away. Five, ten, fifteen minutes."

"Yes, yes," I said desperately, "but by then the crooks are gone. With everything in the store."

He heaved suddenly. I thought he might be about to throw up, to crack his cookies, and I stepped back hurriedly. But no, it was just a spasm of mirth.

"Nonononono," he mumbled, settling back. "Not going. Anyplace. The crooks. You back into the railing. It sounds silent alarm. Cops come. But also, it locks the door. Electrical. Front door. Locks. Only way out. Heavy double-glass. Take 'em an hour to smash through that. See? Silent alarm. Door locks. Can't get out. No back way. Trapped."

"Noel," I breathed, "that's beautiful!"

But he didn't hear me. He was gone. Head tilted to one side. Face flushed and smiling. I went into the kitchen, made some efforts at cleaning up. I mean, I rinsed and stacked the dishes in the sink. Emptied ashtrays. I figured I owed him all that. I didn't think I'd be seeing Noel Jarvis again.

I got home without being molested, raped, or murdered. The cabdriver told me all about his kidney stones, and I said things like "Really?" and "No fooling?" When I was safe inside my own apartment, the first thing I wanted to do was to call Dick Fleming and tell him about those crazy pressure alarms that locked the front door at Brandenberg & Sons.

But then I had just sense enough left to note that it was past midnight. And sense enough to realize that, while not exactly zonked, I was spending an inordinate amount of time thinking about that cabdriver's kidney stones. So I undressed and fell into bed, laughing like a maniac.

I awoke Wednesday morning with an awful hangover. I did what I could: popped aspirin, drank a quart of water, and rubbed my temples with ice cubes. Then ate the cubes. After a while the shakes stopped and I was able to make a cup of instant coffee and toast a frozen bagel. I was getting along all right, recovering slowly, when the phone rang, and I thought that shrill bell would cleave my skull.

"Noel Jarvis here," he said briskly. "Just wanted to make certain you arrived home safely."

"I hate you," I told him. "You forced me to eat all that divine food. You practically poured all that beautiful wine down my throat. It's all your fault."

"Ah," he said, "we have the whimwhams this morning, do we?"

"*I* do," I said grumpily. "You sound in offensively good shape."

"Listen, Jannie," he said, suddenly serious, "if you're really suffering, I know exactly what you need. Do you have any cognac in the house? Or any kind of brandy?

"Do as I say," he said sternly. "Exactly one ounce. No more, no less. Take it straight. No ice, no water. In twenty minutes you'll be leaping into the air and clicking your heels."

"Promise?"

"I promise."

I thanked him for a marvelous dinner and he said he'd be in touch. As soon as I hung up, I dug out a half-full bottle of Courvoisier and measured out a precise ounce. I held on to the kitchen counter, closed my eyes, and downed the shot in three determined gulps. Murder. Then I looked at my watch.

You know, he was right? In almost exactly twenty minutes that Mt. Vesuvius in my stomach stopped erupting, and I thought I might live to play the harpsichord again. In fact, I was feeling so chipper, I took a second brandy into my office and set to work on my secret manuscript, describing all the events of the preceeding evening, including that business about the pressure alarms in the chair rail at Brandenberg & Sons.

That chore completed, I showered, shaved my legs with a steady hand, put on my trollop's togs, and set out for the Hotel Harding, happy that I wouldn't have to be making the Beatrice Flanders transformation many more times. It had started as a lark and was becoming a drag.

I knocked on Jack Donohue's door. He wasn't in, which was fine with me.

Anyway, I didn't see him. I carried out the hotplate and some personal junk in a shopping bag, so fatso behind the lobby desk wouldn't think I was skipping. I reckoned that Fleming and I could handle the suitcases and the rest of my stuff on Thursday night. That was when I figured to split. And even if I had to leave everything behind, it would be no great loss. I had made certain there was nothing in the room to connect Beatrice Flanders with Jannie Shean.

As a matter of fact, the room clerk wasn't behind the desk when I came downstairs. So I unloaded the shopping bag into the trunk of the rented Ford and went back upstairs for a second load. This time I took Bea's black wig, extra sets of falsies (front and back), and most of her clothes. Who knows—someday I might be invited to a masquerade party.

I got back to East 71st Street late in the afternoon. One of the things I had brought back with me was my trusty, handy-dandy pistol. That I carefully stowed away in the bottom drawer of my desk. Then I called

Dick Fleming at his office, and suggested we meet for dinner at Chez Morris. He groaned.

"Jannie," he said, "can't we go someplace for a decent meal?"

"I had a decent meal last night," I told him. "Tonight I want food I can't eat. I've got to drop at least three pounds. Please, Dick, humor me. I've got a lot to tell you."

"Well . . . all right," he said grudgingly.

"That's a love," I said. "Afterwards we can come back to my place for a sweet, rich, wonderful dessert."

"Oh?" he said, interested. "What?"

"Me," I said.

The dinner was just as lousy as I hoped it would be. I ate three mouthfuls, and Dick, trying hard, finished only half his fried sole.

One of the reasons I ate so little, aside from the loathsomeness of the food, was that I was talking so much. First of all I told Dick about the final meeting at the West 47th Street garage on Thursday night.

"Can you make it?" I asked him.

"Wouldn't miss it for the world," he promised.

I gave him all the details of Donahue's plan. Dick put his elbows on the table, began rubbing his eyebrows back and forth.

"Something wrong?" I asked him.

"Too loose, Lautrec," he said. "How are the other guys going to get to the antique shop on time?"

"Beats me," I said, shrugging. "Donohue was vague about it. Maybe they'll take cabs. Maybe they'll steal another car. Maybe one of them will use his own car."

"Maybe, maybe, maybe," he repeated. "I just don't like it. It's not well planned. Doesn't sound like Donohue. He's usually so careful about details. And that business of them coming into the car one at a time to put on the coveralls—that's crazy."

I thought about it for a moment.

"You know," I said, "you're right. The rest of the caper took a lot of work, a lot of planning, a lot of thought. I admit the part you mentioned just doesn't hang together. It's sloppy. But it's Donohue's idea, so I guess he figures it'll work."

"Well . . . it's not our worry, is it, Jannie? We take off Thursday night and the whole thing stops dead. Isn't that right?"

We stared at each other across the table with blank eyes.

"Sure," I said finally. "Stops dead. But I did want the whole thing to be foolproof."

I told him about the dinner with Noel Jarvis, and he practically slavered when I described the oysters, the beef braciole, the Key lime pie. Then I related Jarvis' reaction to the Devolte Bros. holdup in San Francisco, and how the chair rail at Brandenberg sounded a silent alarm and locked the front door.

"So?" Dick said, smiling. "A great detail for your book. I told you that you should, ah, cultivate his acquaintance. How else would you have found out about that cute gimmick?"

"That's not the point. The point is, do I tell Jack Donohue about that chair rail and the locked door?"

Fleming looked at me, blinking a few times, thinking. . . .

"No," he said at last, "you can't tell him. Because then he'd want to know how you found out. Then what would you say?"

"But if they try the heist without us, Dick, they'll all be trapped."

"So?" he said coldly. "Their problem, not ours."

"I suppose so," I said slowly. "Still . . ."

He reached across the table, took up my hand.

"Jannie, I know you feel a kind of—of responsibility for Donohue, Hymie Gore, the Holy Ghost, and the other guys they're recruiting. But it's *their* choice. Don't you understand? Sure, you gave them a target and a plan. Or we both did. But we're not forcing them to go through with it at the point of a gun. They can pull out of it anytime they want to. Just as we can, and will. So if they try it by themselves and get caught, it's their own fault. It has nothing to do with us."

I shook my head bewildered.

"Dick, I can't figure the morality of this. What you say makes sense. In a way. But if those nuts try it on their own and get picked up or someone gets hurt, I'm going to feel partly to blame. Besides being scared out of my wits that they'll tell the cops about us."

"What's to tell?" he argued. "They know you as Bea Flanders. Her description and address are nothing like Jannie Shean, who lives on the East Side. And I look a million other guys in New York and they don't even know where *I* live. So we've got nothing to worry about, Jannie."

He kept talking like that all the way back to my apartment. Even after we were naked in bed together, he kept reassuring me, telling me it was going to be all right, we'd make a clean split the following night, and Donohue & Co. wouldn't be fools enough to try it on their own. It all sounded so logical.

So why did I cling to him so frantically, hug him so tightly, and insist he spend the entire night to help warm my bed? Because I had a chill that wouldn't end, and I didn't want to be alone.

Dress Rehearsal

~~~~~~

I'll never forget Jack Donohue's mood that Thursday. He was flying high—but not on alcohol or drugs. He spoke rapidly, almost spluttering in his haste to get the words out. His eyes sparkled. The brilliant grin came and went. He snapped his fingers frequently and occasionally broke into a little tap dance.

He came to room 703 to coordinate our moves that evening, when we were all to meet at the 47th Street garage.

"Park your car a few blocks away," he instructed me. "If Fleming drives his heap, tell him to do the same. Then both of you walk over to the garage. Figure to get there about 12:30. Around then. The night watchman will have made his rounds and be back in his storefront, watching TV. We'll get there ahead of you—me and the others. The door will be opened for you. Then we'll go over the timing again for Friday morning. Okay? Okay?"

"Jack," I said, "for God's sake, will you have a drink and calm down? You've got the jits."

"No booze for me," he said, flashing the grin.

"Plenty of time for that after we've got the rocks. By God, Bea, do you realize that at this time tomorrow I'll be rich? We'll all be rich!"

"Sure," I said, "but I'd rather see you play it cool. Come on, sit down for a minute, dip your nose in the vodka. I got my daily delivery of ice from Blanche."

"Well . . . all right. But just one. Then I've got to run. I've got a million things to do."

"Yeah?" I said, pouring us each a vodka in the rough. "Like what?"

"I've got to locate our two muscles and give them their marching orders. Find an iron for Hymie; his source didn't come through. Make sure those coveralls are the right size for our guys. Make a checklist of the stuff we'll be carrying: coveralls, masks, tape, rope, pillowcases, and so forth. I want this to go down just right, Bea. We'll be in and out of there so slick, they won't know what hit them. And no rough stuff. No-body get hurt. This'll be bigger than the Devolte heist in Frisco. Don't you think so?"

"Could be."

He looked at me shrewdly for a long moment.

"What are you going to do with your share, babe?"

"Take off."

"With Fleming?"

"Could be," I said again, shrugging. "I've been moving some of my stuff over to his pad."

"I know," he said, watching me. "Blanche told me you were emptying out your room."

I don't think I showed dismay.

"It makes sense. Every rat has another hole. If someone at Brandenberg makes me, it won't take long for someone here at the hotel or at Fangio's to tie me up with you, Hymie Gore, and the Holy Ghost. So I figured I'd move before we cash in. Just being super-careful."

"I always said you've got a brain," he said admiringly. "As a matter of fact, I'm figuring on doing the same thing. We can each take a part of the loot so there's no possibility of a cross."

"Just what I was thinking."

He laughed heartily, slapping his knee.

"I'd never cross you, Bea. You know that. You're too smart for me."

"Just keep thinking that way," I told him coldly. "Right now we both need each other. A marriage of convenience."

"I couldn't agree more," he said warmly. "This whole shmear wouldn't have been possible without you, babe. Well, I've got to run. Sticking around?"

"For a while." I hesitated a moment. Since he knew I was moving out, there didn't seem any harm in completing the split. "I'll probably take my suitcases and the rest of my stuff to Fleming's place. I'll give them notice here, tell them I'll be out by Saturday."

"Good enough," he said, nodding. "It'll be a pleasure to get out of this fleabag, won't it, babe?"

I agreed. Wholeheartedly.

"Sure," he said. "You're used to better than this; I can tell. What are you going to do with your share? Europe? South America?"

"Maybe. But I figure the blues will be watching overseas flights after the heist. I may just hole up in a small town somewhere. Vermont. Maine. Like that. Until the heat dies down."

"But not too small," he warned. "Not someplace where people ask questions about strangers. Me, I'm heading for Miami. A hustler like me can get lost in the crowd down there. Want to come along?"

I looked at him a moment, not certain he was serious. He seemed to be; he wasn't grinning and his eyes were steady.

"One thing at a time," I said finally. "I'll decide after we've got the money in our hot little fists. If we ever do."

"Can't miss," he assured me. "Call it gambler's hunch or whatever, but I *know* it. This is going down, Bea."

After he left, I finished packing. Then I carried my two practically empty suitcases downstairs and told Godzilla behind the desk that I was checking out Saturday.

"Before noon," he growled. "Stay a minute over, you get charged another day."

"I'll remember that."

"Leavin' kinda sudden, ain't'cha?" he said, leering. "Wassa matta, business been lousy?"

"I'm going back to Chicago," I said, figuring it would be smart to give him a bum steer.

"Yeah? What's so great about Chicago?"

"The desk clerks there take baths."

It wasn't history's wittiest insult. I reflected that the demise of Beatrice Flanders was coming none too soon.

Back at the East 71st Street apartment, I called Dick Fleming at his office and we synchronized watches. He said he had to work late, a few hours, but would be finished in plenty of time to make the 12:30 P.M. meeting. We agreed that I'd pick him up at his apartment and we'd drive over to the garage in my rented Ford. Later, we'd have a few drinks together and celebrate the finish of the Great Literary Caper.

"And that'll be the end of it," I said.

"I suppose so," he said. He sounded forlorn.

I picked Dick up at his apartment at 11:30, as agreed upon. He got behind the wheel while I applied wig and makeup, completing the doxy transformation. By 12:15 we had found a parking space on

West 49th Street. About 12:25 we locked the car and started walking down to 47th Street.

At that hour, it was a ghostly neighborhood, all shadows and dark windows. Dick took my arm and I was just as happy.

"I should have brought the gun," I said, trying to laugh

"What for? Jesus, I hope they're there! I don't want to go wandering around these streets any longer than we have to."

It went like silk, as Donohue would say. We came abreast of the garage on the abandoned block, turned in, the door opened, and there was Hymie Gore, grinning.

"Ain't this grand?" he said.

We stepped inside and Hymie closed the door behind us. Then we were in blackness, with just the merest glow coming through brown paper that had been taped over the garage door windows.

"Okay, Hymie?" It was Donohue's voice calling, very hard.

"Sure, Jack. They're here."

"Fine. You stay at the door, Hymie. Keep a sharp eye."

"I'll keep a sharp eye, Jack."

A match flickered, dimmed. Then a kerosene lantern flared. It was impossible to see the corners, but the place looked big enough to hold six cars. Two grease pits, two lifts. A back office, glass inclosed. Those windows had also been covered with taped-on brown paper.

"I'm here," Donohue said. "Watch your step—the floor's greasy. We checked the light from the street. We don't show a glimmer."

We moved cautiously into the inner office, following the lantern carried by Black Jack. The place was maybe ten-by-ten. No chairs. A lot of filth: old news-papers, sodden cartons of discarded business records, one ripped truck tire.

I shivered, imagining I heard the scuttle of rats.

"The Waldorf it ain't," Donohue said, laughing. "But we're not going to live here. You know the Holy Ghost. Now I want you to meet these two despera-does, our new recruits. This dusky gentleman is Clement. Clement, this is Bea Flanders and Dick Fleming."

He held the lantern close to the man he was in-troducing: a tall, slender black man wearing horn-rimmed glasses. He was clad in a gray-flannel suit, button-down shirt, regimental-striped tie. He gave a little bow and flashed a mouthful of teeth.

"My confreres," he said in a rich, rolling baritone. "So pleased to make your acquaintance."

"And this gorilla," Donohue said, moving the lan-tern, "goes by the name of Smiley."

There he was: short, squat, and smiling. Just the way I had seen him before, wearing a sweater under his jacket, no topcoat or raincoat. And the black leather cap, rakish as a beret.

"Nice," he said. Whatever that meant.

"Okay," Jack Donohue said. "This won't take long. We've got maybe forty-five minutes, an hour, before we can leave. After the watchman makes his mid-night rounds. I'll go over it once. If you got any ques-tions, speak up. Now you'll notice the garage is big enough for five, six cars. No problem. So here's how we'll work it . . ."

He went over it once again: how Dick would bring his VW and I'd bring my rented Ford. Donohue would be waiting for us in the stolen car, inside the garage. We'd all transfer to the Chevy and drive over to the antique shop on Madison Avenue. We'd arrive there in plenty of time to find a parking space before the arrival of the Bonomo cleaning van. The four heavies would find us, come into our car one at a time to don Bonomo coveralls. The cleaning truck would be hijacked. The helper would be tied up, left on the floor of the van. The regular driver, at gunpoint, would be forced to drive up to Brandenberg & Sons. All the men, in coveralls, would be in the van. I'd follow in the stolen Chevy. Donohue would be right behind the driver, gun in his ribs, when the Brandenberg door was opened. Then all the men would pile in, locking the door behind them. I'd pull up directly behind the parked cleaning truck. When the place was stripped, and they came out with the loot in pillowcases, Donohue would jam the door closed with a rubber stopper. Then he and Fleming would come back to my car with approximately half the take. Gore, the Ghost, Smiley, and Clement would take the van with the rest of the loot. The regular Bonomo truck driver would be left trussed-up on the floor of Brandenberg's, with the employees. We'd all rendezvous right here, in the 47th Street garage. The men would take off the coveralls and ditch the van and stolen Chevy, after wiping both clean of fingerprints. Then we'd all pile into Dick's VW and my rented Ford and go back to Donohue's room at the Hotel Harding to count and split the take. A few hours later we'd make a call to the cops, telling them where to find the tied and gagged helper in the Bonomo van in the 47th Street garage. Just so the poor guy didn't suffocate or die of starvation.

"Any questions?" Black Jack asked when he had finished.

"A lot of questions," Dick Fleming said boldly. "You mean, after the heist, seven of us are going to go walking through the lobby of the Hotel Harding carrying bulging pillowcases?"

"Not to worry," Donohue said, and I could see his grin in the yellowish lantern light. "I'm bringing along some cheap suitcases, shopping bags, boxes, plastic garbage bags—like that. We'll go into the Harding two or three at a time, just strolling. That desk clerk won't see a thing, believe me. He's greased."

"Another thing," I said. "When do you guys pick up the tape, masks, rope, and pillowcases you'll need for the hijack and heist?"

"When we get out of the stolen Chevy on Madison," Donohue explained patiently. "Those coveralls have a million pockets. Plenty of room for all the shit."

"How are the four guys going to get over to Madison?" I demanded. "How do we know they'll get there on time?"

"I guarantee it," Jack said. "They'll be there."

"No doubt about it," Clement said. "We'll be there."

Smiley smiled.

I looked at Dick Fleming. He looked at me. I think we had the same idea: that we had pushed our legitimate questions as far as we could. We had sounded like concerned participants. We had played out the charade. I made one final effort to prove myself the professional thief.

"What about those diversions you mentioned?" I asked.

"All laid on," Donohue assured me. "A friend of mind will make the calls to the cops and newspapers at exactly a quarter to nine tomorrow morning. He'll report bombs planted in all the airline ticket offices and travel agencies in Rockefeller Center. Courtesy of some goddam Puerto Rican bunch. Fuck 'em.

What a beautiful mess that'll be, with cops cars, the bomb squad, and all those people trying to get to work. The buttons won't have any time to worry about what's going down on East 55th Street."

I couldn't think of anything else to say. Apparently Dick Fleming couldn't either. We stood there in silence. I remember that Jack Donohue had placed the kerosene lantern on the floor. We were all standing around it, a circle of ghastly, deeply shadowed faces: eyes sunk in black sockets; chins, noses, and brows highlighted in ocher, but all else in wavery gloom. Everyone seemed to be looking at me. I felt like head witch in a coven, expected to produce the human sacrifice for the evening's festivities.

"Well" I said lamely, "I guess that takes care of everything. See you all in the morning."

"You bet!" Donohue said enthusiastically. He held his wrist down near the lantern to read his watch. "Another five minutes or so and we can take off. We better not all leave at once. Bea, you and Fleming slip out first. Then the rest of us will split at intervals. That's so no one in the tenements across the street sees a mob coming out of here at one time and begins to wonder what the hell's going on."

That was fine with me. The faster I got out of that bone-chilling place, the better. It smelled of grease, damp, and dead things.

"See you soon," Black Jack Donohue said with a smile as Fleming and I departed.

I flipped a hand at him and didn't look back.

An hour later I was back into my old comfortable Jannie Shean clothes. Dick and I were sitting at one end of the crowded bar at Chez Morris, celebrating our deliverance with vodka stingers. Everyone was watching the TV set behind the bar, yelling at a rerun of football highlights of the week before. Morris was down at the other end of the bar, chatting up a bird who looked so much like Beatrice Flanders that I thought she had swiped my falsies.

"You notice?" I asked Dick. "Donohue sure slurred over how the four heavies are going to find us wherever we've been able to find a parking space on Madison."

"Right," Dick said. "And then having us all walk into the Harding carrying the loot. I don't care if it's in shopping bags, *someone's* going to notice that parade."

"Well, it's not our problem anymore, is it?"

"Still, it offends my sense of artistic integrity. You know what I mean. We had a perfect plan going. Every detail thought out. Now he's got a gang of bentnoses climbing in and out of a car parked on Madison Avenue, putting on coveralls at 8:30 in the morning."

"You're right," I agreed. "I guess Jack isn't the slick operator I thought he was. Screw it. Let's get drunk."

"I'm game," he said.

We tried, but it didn't take. Vodka stingers, brandy stingers, straight brandy, nothing helped. By the time the bar was emptying out, Morris was looking at us anxiously.

"You going to make it, Jannie?"

"You bet your sweet patootie," I said. "I dare you to refuse us another drink."

"I refuse you another drink," he shot back promptly.

I leaned across the bar and kissed him.

"In that case," I said loftily, "we shall take our business elsewhere. Home."

On the walk across the street to my apartment,

Dick Fleming hung on to my arm and I hung on to his. A dizzy waltz.

"I thought I'd feel a kind of—you know—triumph," I said. "But I don't."

"I know," Dick said, nodding sadly. "I thought there'd be risk and danger. Ridiculous. A bunch of rumdums."

"Stupid rumdums," I said. "Jesus. Black Jack Donohue. The Rockettes dancing in and out of the car, putting on coveralls."

"Hymie Gore! The Holy Ghost! Can you imagine?"

"Smiley," I added. "Clement in his—executive suit. I tell you, crime in America has come to a pretty prass."

"Pretty pass," he corrected me with great dignity.

"That's what I said, diddle I? Now, when I write it, I've got to improve it. Fuck reality. Fuck Aldo Binder. It's all imagination, Dick m'lad. Better than reality. What do all these wet-brains know about planning a Big Caper? Master criminals, my ass. We did all the planning. The best parts were ours."

"Right," Dick said stoutly. "All ours."

We went up in the elevator, assuring each other we were the Einsteins of crime. I had a little trouble with the lock to my apartment. I kept stabbing the door. Finally Dick took the key from me and, using both hands, finally got the key in, the door opened.

I was very careful. Closed and locked the door behind us. Put on the chain. We went stumbling down the dark hallway. I fumbled around, found the wall switch, lighted the living room.

There was a crowd sitting around.

"Hi there!" Jack Donohue said brightly.

It All Goes Down

⌇⌇⌇⌇⌇⌇⌇⌇⌇⌇⌇⌇⌇⌇⌇⌇⌇⌇⌇⌇⌇⌇⌇⌇⌇⌇⌇⌇⌇⌇⌇⌇

Talk about instant sobriety!

Being a professional writer, I am familiar with, and have used, the entire lexicon of literary clichés. Like: "He grew red with rage." "She turned green with envy." "Their jaws dropped in shock and disbelief." I had always thought they were just motheaten expressions, exaggerated descriptions of ordinary emotions. But I discovered they were clichés because they were true. At least that last one was, because when I looked at Dick Fleming, his mouth was wide open, and I suddenly became conscious of my own unhinged jaw. Shock and disbelief? You know it! I was fish-mouthed.

"Come on in," Donohue said genially. "Take a seat. Sample a bite of this nice brandy. Smiley, why don't you pour the folks a shot? Looks like they could use it."

I watched in silence as the smiling man poured *my* Courvoisier into *my* brandy snifters and handed them to Dick and me. I took a jolt, then looked around at all those grinning faces: Donohue, Smiley, Hymie

Gore, the Holy Ghost, Clement, and a small, tight-faced woman I had never seen before. All lounging in *my* chairs and sofa, drinking *my* booze.

Donohue saw me staring at the dark woman.

"Angela," he told me. "A special friend of the Holy Ghost. Right, Angela?"

She shrugged. There was plenty of heat in the apartment, but Angela was wearing a ratty sweater-coat that came to her ankles, plus another cardigan under that, plus a knitted cloche that came down over her ears, plus a woolen scarf that went around her neck three times. That woman was all yarn.

"Angela has special talents," Black Jack said, still low-voiced, still pleasant. "Show them, Angela."

I don't know how she did it, I don't know where it came from, but suddenly her wrist flicked and there was an open knife in her hand. Either a gravity knife, the blade sliding out of the handle and locking, or a flick knife, the blade swinging out and locking. Whatever it was, the four-inch steel was suddenly there, sharp and gleaming.

"Wasn't that beautiful?" Donohue asked me. "Never saw where it came from, did you? A real artist, our Angela is."

I took my eyes away from the shiny blade with a conscious effort of will. What I saw next wasn't any better. The black man, Clement, was holding my beautiful little Beretta automatic pistol. Not pointing it at anyone. It was just dangling casually, his fore-finger through the trigger guard.

But what was even worse was what I saw on the floor, stacked neatly at Donohue's feet. Project X. My secret manuscript. The complete record of my Big Caper.

He saw me staring.

"Black Jack?" he said, laughing. "What a name!

Jannie, you could have done me better than that."

Dick Fleming recovered before I did. "What do you want?" he said hoarsely.

Donohue turned his head slowly to look at him.

"What do we want?" he said. "That's obvious, isn't it? We want *you*. Both of you. But before we get into the whys and wherefores, let's get some ground rules straight. Either of you get any ideas of suddenly shouting, screaming, making a fuss—don't. You saw how fast Angela is with her sticker. Clement can be even faster with that nice piece of yours, Jannie. Make a peep, you're dead; it's that simple. No joke. No threat. Just the truth. You try to fuck us up, you're dead and gone."

As he said this, his face seemed to grow thinner. It certainly became bleaker. I had no doubt he meant what he said. I don't think Dick Fleming had any doubts either.

"How long have you known?" I asked Donohue.

Everyone had a merry laugh.

"From the start," Donohue said. "From the very start. Never try to hustle a hustler, Jannie. You know, you're one lousy actress."

That hurt.

"What did I do wrong?" I asked angrily.

"Everything," he said. "No way could you hide that finishing school accent of yours. And the words you used. Crook slang from the nineteen-twenties. You kept flipping back and forth, Beatrice Flanders to Jannie Shean. And where would a cocktail waitress from Chicago get a bikini suntan like you got? Mannerisms. Even the way you walked. I spotted you for a phony the first time I saw you. You didn't wiggle right. So I asked myself, why? What was your game? Undercover cop? No way. You were too clumsy. And you," he said, turning to Fleming, "you were no better. A couple of fucking amateurs. I suggested we throw Hymie Gore and the Holy Ghost to the cops, and the blues would stop looking for anyone else. You went right along with it. As if the cops would be satisfied with Hymie and the Ghost. They'd know a couple of dummies like them couldn't plan and pull a first-class heist like this."

I looked at the two men he was talking about. His description hadn't bothered them in the least. They were grinning and nodding like idiots.

"So why did you play us for suckers?" I said furiously. "Why did you agree to go along? You could have just walked away."

"Ahh, Jannie, Jannie," he said, shaking his head sorrowfully. "You know the answer to that. You and Fleming are a pair of lousy crooks, true, but you've got imagination, babe, and you've got a knack. Between the two of you, you came up with a perfect campaign. You cased Brandenberg and Sons just right. You did all the work for us. Walk away from it? Are you kidding? It's too good."

"You're going through with it?" Fleming said incredulously.

"We're going through with it," Donohue said. "You and Jannie. All of us. As planned. With a few minor changes."

"The hell you say!" Dick said hotly.

"Angela," Black Jack said, sighing. "Clement."

The knife was there again, blade shining, the point aimed at me, moving gently back and forth, a snake's head. And suddenly Clement was gripping the automatic hard, holding it at arm's length, the muzzle not far from Dick's temple.

"All of us," Donohue repeated, nodding. "You're in this as deep as we are. You'll come along. Try to run, try to yell, and—blotto! Think I'm not serious?

Go ahead—yell. Scream the place down. Call my bluff."

Looking at those cold eyes, that drawn face, thinned lips and jutted jaw, I had no desire to call his bluff. And apparently Dick Fleming didn't either. But he did try a way out.

"Keep me," he told Donohue. "I'll do everything you want. No trouble. But let Jannie go. She won't talk. Not while you've got me. You don't need both of us."

Black Jack flashed a brilliant grin around the circle of his mob.

"How about this guy?" he said. "The last of the red-hot lovers. Noble, Fleming, noble as hell—but no cigar. We'll take both of you. Safer that way. What if we took only you, and you get burned in the heist? Then she spills. Can't have that."

I moved to take Dick's hand and press it. "Thank you," I whispered to him.

"All right," Donohue said, bending to pick up my manuscript, "enough of this lovey-dovey bullshit; let's get down to the nitty-gritty. We haven't got all that much time."

"Wait a minute," I said. "Before you start, answer a few questions. Like how did you know I lived here?"

He looked at me.

"How did I know?" he said. "Come on, Jannie. Easiest thing in the world. I followed you. All those trips back and forth; it wasn't hard. The Holy Ghost got into your rented Ford and found your license under the seat. That gave me your name. And Blanche told me all your clothes were brand new, no cleaners' tags or marks. Everything fitted: You were a phonus-balonus."

"All right." I said, gritting my teeth with shame,

frustration, rage. "But how did you get into this apartment?"

"Made copies of your keys," he said blithely. "Came up through the garage."

"Copies of my keys?" I said furiously. "When? When did you ever have my keys?"

He looked at me, smiling gently. Then I knew. The nights I had slept over in his room. While I slept, he had taken my keys, slipped them to Hymie Gore or the Holy Ghost waiting outside in the corridor. Those gonifs could have had copies made at three in the morning and the originals passed back to Donohue before I awoke.

"You really want me to tell you when I got your keys, Jannie?" Donohue asked.

"No," I said shortly. "I can guess."

"I'll bet you can. Anyway, I've been dropping up here almost every day. Bet you never noticed a thing out of place, did you?"

"No," I said honestly, "I never did."

"Didn't cop a thing," he assured me. "Didn't even sample your booze. I just wanted to keep track of the latest developments. In this . . ." He tapped my manuscript.

I hated him. God, how I hated him. Not so much for making a fool of me; I guess I deserved that. But I couldn't stand the thought of his getting into my apartment, my secret place, my *home*, and rummaging around. Looking through all the drawers in my dressers and desk. Probably fingering my lingerie. It was rape.

But then he said something that dissolved my hate.

"You know, Jannie," he said, flipping the pages of my manuscript, "you're really a very good writer."

"Thank you," I said faintly.

I loved him.

Don't try to figure writers; we're all nuts.

"Very good," Donohue went on, nodding. "Make a hell of a novel. Too bad you can never publish it."

"Yes," I said miserably, "isn't it?"

He turned suddenly to Dick Fleming.

"Thank God you talked her into dating that manager, Noel Jarvis. How else would we have known about the pressure alarms in that chair rail and the door locking automatically? Weren't going to tell us about that, were you? But that's okay; I understand. You figured you were out of it, and we'd never try it on our own after you didn't show up. Well, here we are, all together, and this Big Caper—Jesus, what a cornball name that is!—your Big Caper is going down right on schedule. Here's what's going to happen . . ."

The others must have heard it all before, because no one interrupted. And Dick and I were too stunned to object. He had it all worked out, down to the fine details, and I realized where he had been and what he had been doing those afternoons and evenings I couldn't find him at the Hotel Harding. He had started with the Big Caper that Dick and I had planned. And then, consulting my Project X as I kept it up to date, he had refined the scheme and made the changes necessary to ensure our unwilling cooperation.

Here's how he planned it . . .

We would all stay right there in my apartment until 8:00 A.M. Dick and I could sleep if we wished, sitting up in living room chairs or sharing my bed, if that was our inclination. If we wanted to use the toilet, Angela would accompany me, Clement would go along with Dick. The bathroom door would remain open at all times.

The others might catch a few winks, too. But there would always be three of the six awake, watching us. Angela had her knife; all the men were armed with pistols or revolvers. Smiley also carried a leather-covered, flexible sap, which he proudly displayed, swishing it through the air with great enjoyment.

In the morning, everyone would be up and about, readying for a busy day. I would prepare a pot of instant coffee. If I refused, Angela would make it. A morning eye-opener (brandy, scotch, whatever) would also be provided to those who requested it. At precisely 8:00, we would all depart. Angela would be directly behind me, knife ready. Clement would be on Fleming's heels, prodding him along with my spiffy Beretta. We would take the elevator down to the basement and exit through the garage.

"Now here's how the cars will work," Donohue explained. "Jannie, Angela, me, Hymie, and the Ghost go in Jannie's rented Ford. Fleming, Clement, and Smiley go in Fleming's VW."

"My car?" Dick said, astonished. "It's parked five blocks away."

"The hell it is." Black Jack grinned. "It's right around the corner. Jannie isn't the only one we tailed, you know. We know where you live, where you work, where you stash your Bug."

Dick sighed, "All right," he said. "Don't tell me how you got in with a coat hanger and started it. You jumped it—right?"

"*I* didn't," Donohue said. "The Holy Ghost did. A genius with cars, that clod is."

The Ghost twitched in appreciation.

"All right," Jack went on. "Now the eight of us are in two cars. Five in the Ford, three in the VW. Over we go to the garage on West 47th Street, where we've parked the stolen Chevy. All our gear is in the garage. The men put on the Bonomo coveralls there. Oh, another detail you might be interested in, Jannie. As a writer. That's where we also put on gloves. Thin cotton gloves. Black. The kind undertakers use."

This amused everyone. Don't ask me why.

Then the five passengers in my rented Ford would transfer to the stolen Chevy and drive over to Madison Avenue for the rendezvous with the Bonomo cleaning van in front of the antique shop. The three passengers in Dick's VW would also drive over. Black Jack paused and looked at me.

"That seemed to bother you, Jannie," he said with real enjoyment. "I wasn't sure I could con you about that. I mean, how the heavies were going to get over to Madison Avenue in time for the hijack of the truck. Now if they leave the VW in the garage, you want to guess how they'll do it?"

I shrugged. "Another stolen car, I suppose."

"Right," Donohue said, nodding approvingly. "Another hot car. And guess what it is? A beautiful bottle-green Jaguar XKE. Ain't dot nize?"

"You bastard!"

"I had your keys," he said innocently. "Seemed a shame not to use them."

The two cars would then proceed to Madison Avenue, staying close together. We would not stop, but would circle the block until we saw the Bonomo van double-parked in front of the antique shop. Then the Chevy would pull up in front of it, the XKE behind it, boxing him in. The coveralled men would get into the back of the van, pulling on their stocking masks when they were inside. Including poor Dick Fleming, prodded along at gunpoint.

But no mask for Donohue. As he said, he'd go naked. Except for a paste-on mustache and a Band-Aid taped across his forehead.

"Sure they're phony," he admitted cheerfully. "But they're what witnesses will remember."

When the Bonomo cleaning crew came out of the antique shop and opened the back doors, they'd be yanked into the van at the muzzle of Smiley's cannon. The helper would be blindfolded, trussed, gagged, pushed to the floor of the van. The driver and Donohue would get into the cab. Black Jack armed, of course.

"It'll never work," I told him. "Someone on the street will see. The sidewalks will be crowded."

"It'll go like silk," he assured me. "The boys will be inside the van with their shooters. I won't pop out of the Chevy until the last minute, until the real Bonomo guys are at the rear doors of the van. Get it? With me behind them, nudging their asses, and the boys inside pulling them in, what are they going to do —except maybe faint? It'll work; you'll see."

Once the truck was taken, we'd start off for Brandenberg & Sons on East 55th Street. Right about then, Donohue's friend would be making the diversionary calls to the New York cops and newspapers, reporting bombs planted in Rockefeller Center.

The van would pull up in front of Brandenberg's, double-parking. The driver and Donohue would get out, taking some cleaning gear from the truck to make it look legit. The Chevy, me driving, Angela and knife alongside, would pull up behind the truck.

Once the door was opened, the rest of the gang (and Dick Fleming) would pile out of the van and into the store. This time the famous rubber doorstopper, inspired by the Devolte Bros. holdup in San Francisco, would be used for a different purpose; it would be wedged between door and jamb so the door couldn't be electrically locked in case the chair rail alarm was pressed.

"A risk," Donohue said. "I admit it. I would prefer to keep that door locked while we're inside, gathering the goodies. But I can't take the chance of it being jammed electrically. Then we'd really be in the stew. So we'll keep it wedged open just an inch or so."

When the robbery was completed, they'd come out with their full pillowcases, leaving all the employees of Brandenberg & Sons, plus the Bonomo driver, gagged and tied on the floor. After everyone was out, Donohue would use the rubber stopper to wedge the door tightly closed, just for an added safety factor in case someone got loose in time to start pursuit.

When they came out, Donohue, the Holy Ghost, and Hymie Gore would race to the stolen Chevy with their share of the loot. I'd push over (closer to Angela's knife!), and Donohue would get behind the wheel. Smiley, Clement, and Dick Fleming would take their part of the Brandenberg treasure into the van.

We'd all meet at the West 47th Street garage and transfer to my rented Ford and Fleming's VW.

"And then we all waltz up to your room at the Hotel Harding?" Dick asked. "And divvy up?"

"Oh no," Donohue said, flashing his eighteen-carat grin. "I never planned a stupid move like that. We've got a better hidey-hole. You'll find out when the time comes."

"And what about my XKE?" I demanded. "You're going to leave it parked in front of that antique shop on Madison Avenue? It'll take the cops about ten minutes to find out where the Bonomo truck was hijacked, to find the double-parked Jaguar, and trace it back to me."

Smiley spoke for the first time.

"Yeah," he rasped, showing his teeth. "Ain't that a shame?"

There didn't seem much more to say. I moved closer on the sofa to Dick Fleming. Donohue made no objection. Gore, the Ghost, and Clement stretched out their legs, closed their eyes, determined to sleep. Smiley, Angela, and Black Jack remained awake and alert. Smiley was demolishing what was left in the bottle of Courvoisier, but it didn't seem to affect him. He just kept smiling. The least he could have done, drinking *my* cognac, was to take off that ridiculous black leather cap.

" 'O what a tangled web we weave . . . ,' " Dick said wryly.

I nodded.

"Jannie, why in God's name did you put it all down on paper?"

"I thought it would make a good novel," I said miserably.

"Lousy ending," he growled. "See any way out?"

"Possibly," I said. "The weak part is—"

Jack Donohue had been watching us whispering, making no effort to separate us. But now he interrupted.

"Jannie," he said, "you didn't know I was a mind-reader, did you?"

I looked at him.

"I know what you're thinking right now," he said. "Looking for a way out. A kid like you, with the imagination you got, it figures. So you see right away where your best chance is. After that Bonomo truck is hijacked in front of the antique store. From then until the finish of the heist, you're alone in the Chevy with Angela. Just the two of you. That's when you figure you'll make your move. Right? Scream or try to jump Angela. Jannie, don't try it. I beg you, don't try it. She'll cut you to ribbons. Angela?"

He looked at the small, dark, tight woman, swathed in yards and yards of knitted wool. She looked at me, eyes black and tiny as raisins.

"I keel you," she said. Her voice was a whisper.

"Listen to her, Jannie," Donohue urged. "She ain't kidding. It wouldn't be the first time, believe me. Besides, what if you did bust this caper wide open— what good would it do? I'm taking all your writing along with me. You scream down the cops and there's the evidence you planned the whole thing. You and Fleming. Think you can talk your way out of that?"

"Snookered," Dick said softly, closing his eyes.

I may have dozed off myself. Shock, booze, fear. I know I went over Donohue's scenario again and again, looking for a way out, a weakness Dick and I could exploit, something to throw the bad guys off guard long enough to escape. I couldn't see anything in our favor but chance and accident. I fell asleep hoping they wouldn't hurt Noel Jarvis, and wondering if I should ask Donohue about that passport, and whether he thought the real name of the manager, Antonio Rossi, had any particular significance. Black Jack would know all about fake names and assumed identities. He was a professional thief. I knew what I was: a professional klutz.

My eyes opened, I glanced at my watch. About 7:00 A.M., the morning light beginning to creep through my east windows. There was a dull weight on my left shoulder: Dick's head; he was sound asleep. So were Angela, the Holy Ghost, Smiley. But Hymie Gore was awake, cleaning his fingernails slowly and meticulously with a pocket nailfile. Clement was awake, holding my Beretta in his lap, looking at me gravely. Donohue was awake—or was he? His eyes were hooded, half-closed. But I had the feeling that if I made a sudden movement, his eyelids would fly up like roller shutters and he'd be at my throat before I took a stop.

So I looked at Clement, returned his stare boldly, wondered if there were some way I could grab that pistol. He was a dapper black man in his establishment clothes. Still unwrinkled, calm. He seemed carved, a basalt statue.

I jerked my chin toward him.

"What's with the IBM suit?" I asked in a low voice.

He looked down at his wingtip shoes, black hose, precisely pressed dark flannel suit. Button-down collar and regimental striped tie.

"Cool chic," he said. "You go into the lion's den and want to come out alive, you dress like a lion. You dig?"

"You're full of shit," I said flatly. "It's envy. Jealousy. Imitation. Your lousy try at upward mobility. Forget it. It won't work. You look like a clown."

"You think?" he said, looking down at his clothes.

"I *know*," I said. "I tried a disguise. It didn't work for me."

"You weren't so hot at it. Me, I got it down right. The threads, the walk, the talk; I can pass. I could stroll into the *Pru*-dential and be greeted like a brother."

"If you chalked your face maybe," I said cruelly.

His eyes lifted slowly. As slowly as the muzzle of the gun lifted.

"Easy, Clement," Jack Donohue murmured, his eyes still half-closed. "She's just trying to rile you into making a stupid move. Can't you see that?"

"Yeah," Clement said, relaxing, the gun drooping again. "Yeah, that's what it was. The little lady was getting to me."

Donohue opened his eyes wide, yawned, stretched.

"Let's you and me go into the kitchen, little lady," he said to me. "Put some coffee on."

I was tempted to refuse. Why the hell should I wait on those bastards? But if I didn't make the coffee, Angela or someone else would. And I might not get any. So I slid carefully from under Dick Fleming's head, propped him against a soft pillow, and preceded Black Jack into the kitchen.

He leaned against the counter, watching me put water on to boil, set out cups and saucers.

"Nice place you got here," he offered.

I didn't answer.

"Still trying to figure out how to beat me?" he said. "Like maybe throwing boiling water in my face? Forget it. When I have to, I can move so fast you wouldn't believe it. That was a nice try with Clement, but I was awake, I was listening."

"I'll find something else," I said, not looking at him.

"Maybe," he said. "You or Fleming. I still don't know what's between you two, but if one of you sees an opening, maybe you can queer this whole deal and take your chances with the cops. But if you do, just remember we still got the other one. That's why I'm keeping you in separate cars. One of you fucks up, the other one gets it. Remember that."

Lovely phrase: "gets it." I didn't want it. But I realized what a smart apple this Black Jack Donohue was. He didn't know what the relationship was between Dick and me. And if he had known, he wouldn't have understood. But he was shrewd enough to know that I wouldn't endanger Dick, or Dick me. Donohue's entire plan was based on that perception. Checkmate.

The coffee was ready; Jack called into the other room. They came straggling in, two at a time, to get their cups. I brought Dick's to him. We sat side by side on the sofa, sipping the hot brew, listening to the Donohue Gang.

Donohue let them go on until the coffee was finished. Then he glanced at his watch.

"All right," he said, "let's put this show on the road. Sorry we can't help you wash up, Jannie, but first things first! Now you all know how we're going to move out. Not fast, not running, but brisk. Like we've all got jobs to get to. We meet anyone in the hall or on the elevator, and it's smiles all around, and 'Good morning' and 'How are you?' Everyone pleasant, everyone easy. No strain, no pain. We get any questions, let me handle it. Down to the garage where we split up. We meet again in the 47th Street garage. All set? Everyone ready? Let's go!"

I had hoped that Donohue might forget my manuscript. But no, he went into my office for a big manila envelope, tucked Project X inside, and put it under his arm. He saw me watching him, and winked at me. That son of a bitch!

Then, hatted and coated, we all filed out. My legs were trembling, heart pumping, and I felt as though I might throw up any minute.

If that was realism, I wanted no part of it.

The Big Caper

~~~~~~

I was participant. I was observer.

I went stumbling along, conscious of Angela close behind me, snickersnee at the ready. Felt watery knees, faintness, a looseness of the bowels. I did what I was told, allowed myself to be herded, pulled, pushed into the car.

I wasn't thinking straight; I admit it. I couldn't concentrate on my plight or how to escape it. Images and notions appeared, flashed by, disappeared: a speeded-up film. It all went so fast. I saw the familiar scenes of midtown Manhattan: streets, traffic, storefronts, pedestrians. But I was not part of it; it was all strange to me. I was a traveler in a foreign land. As participant, I played my role like a zombie. I could have been drugged. I remember making weird, squealing sounds until, in the car, Jack Donohue gripped my arm fiercely. Then I was still.

And all the time, acting, I'm sure, like a goddamned somnambulist, I was observing Donohue and the others. I was watching their reactions, making mental notes, telling myself to remember. Everything.

Every detail. The writer at work. So, at the moment of my own death, I might note: "Now I am weakening. Everything growing dim. Darkness closing in. There. That's it."

Now the thieves were all business, sober and intent. In the rented Ford with me were Donohue, Angela, Hymie Gore, and the Holy Ghost. Angela watched only me, but the heads of the others swiveled constantly, a slow wagging back and forth. They were only watching the traffic about us, but those oscillations had a sinister, mesmeric effect, the deliberate movements of snakes about to strike.

I saw that, noted it, and marveled at their nerve and resolve. All the crimes I had plotted in those sad, *fictional* novels of mine were as nothing compared to this. I could imagine criminal projects, but this was the real thing. I began to grasp the purpose it required, the resolution to take step A, which led to step B, which led to step C, and so on.

I had another vagrant thought on that trip to the West 47th Street garage. It will probably make me sound like a snob, a prig, an elitist, whatever, but if this is to be a true and honest account, I must record it.

I thought that Dick Fleming and I were superior to these creatures. We were better informed, better educated, more intelligent, more sensitive. It was a matter of breeding, of class; yes, it was. We would never have chosen to associate with any one of them if it hadn't been for our harebrained scheme. Quite simply, they were beneath us.

Yet there we were, in the power of those inferior beings. Because they had shrewdness, strength, vigor, and determination that could not be denied. Most important, they were not daunted by action. I tried to recall an instance in my life in which I had planned and carried out a project of moment. I could not think of a single one. A fitting irony that the superior, well-bred, upper-class Jannie Shean should find the first significant act of her life to be a criminal enterprise controlled by denizens of the deep with few brains, fewer social graces, but with the desperate courage to challenge fate and defy society. It was a depressing, humbling thought.

The other car arrived at the garage before we did. The doors were opened for us by Clement, and quickly closed. Inside were now Dick Fleming's VW, my XKE, the rented Ford, and the stolen Chevy.

Everyone went about the assigned tasks with a minimum of talk and confusion. The men donned the Bonomo coveralls, including poor Dick, who was urged on by either Clement or Smiley, their guns prominently displayed. I admired Black Jack's attention to detail, for each man had been issued a pair of coveralls that fitted reasonably well, from the skinny Holy Ghost to the squat Smiley and mountainous Hymie Gore.

Grease was smeared on the license plates of the VW and the rented Ford, the final getaway cars.

"Not too thick," Donohue cautioned. "We don't want to get stopped by some hot-rock cop. Just cover one or two of the numbers, enough to confuse witnesses."

Then he ran through a checklist, making certain each man carried stocking mask, tape, a few lengths of rope. Gore, the Ghost, Smiley, and Clement carried short crowbars or pieces of pipe. Donohue also had two doorstoppers. And everyone carried at least three folded pillowcases. All were armed, of course.

Donohue inspected each member of his gang, looking for all the world like a sergeant preparing his squad for parade. Then he took a black mustache from a small paper sack, licked the pad on the back, and stuck it on his upper lip, pressing it firmly in place. He unwrapped a Band-Aid, placed it across his forehead. He inspected his reflection in a car window, not smiling. He should have looked ridiculous but he didn't. I remember thinking that black mustache did something for him, gave him dash, and he should grow one.

He looked at his watch, then took a final glance around. The VW and my rented Ford had been backed into the garage, ready for a quick exit. The keys were left under the floor mats.

"All right," Black Jack said. "Put on your gloves. Wipe down the Chevy and the XKE, and I mean really scrub them."

They worked swiftly, rubbing door handles, steering wheels, door frames, interior armrests.

"That's enough," Donohue said. "Time to get going. Me, Jannie, Angela, Hymie, and the Ghost in the Chevy. Jannie, here's a pair of gloves for you; you'll be driving. You other guys travel in style in the Jag. Let's go."

His commands were terse, hard, toneless. No joking. No banter. It was all business, strictly business.

We rolled out. I drove the Chevy, Angela sitting beside me, her knife a few inches from my ribs. Donohue sat next to her, on the outside. Hymie Gore and the Holy Ghost were in the back seat. I glanced in the rearview mirror long enough to see my bottle-green Jaguar follow us out, Dick Fleming driving. The XKE paused just long enough for Clement to hop out and close the garage doors.

Then we were on our way. My Big Caper was going down.

On the drive over to Madison Avenue, I wondered if Jack Donohue hadn't been right. He had told me he felt his luck had finally changed, that this robbery would go off exactly as planned, an enormous success. So far it had certainly gone smoothly. No hitches, no accidents. There hadn't even been any witnesses in the elevators or garage of my apartment house to note our departure. Perhaps, I thought, gamblers and thieves had an instinct for these things, the way hunters sense game in the vicinity or experienced soldiers sense an opportunity for a kill.

The trip to the antique shop was uneventful. That knife point held unwaveringly near my ribs was a constant reminder not to try anything foolish, like a contrived stall or a deliberate crash.

"Slow down a bit," Donohue commanded. "Let the Jag catch up."

I obeyed. I slowed until the XKE was directly behind us. Then, in tandem, we went crosstown to Madison, made a left, and headed uptown. I drove carefully, heeding every stoplight.

"Smart girl," Black Jack said tensely. "Keep it up; you're doing fine."

We came to 53rd Street and glanced ahead. No Bonomo truck parked in front of the antique shop.

"No sweat," Donohue said. "A slow turn around the block."

I went over to Park Avenue on 54th Street, drove south, came back to Madison on 53rd, then turned north again. The Jaguar was right behind us.

Still no truck.

Donohue glanced at his watch. "They're a few minutes late," he said lightly, and I admired his nerve. I was ready to pee, aching to pee. "Another turn around the block, Jannie."

We made the circuit once more. The streets were heavy with early-morning traffic. The sidewalks were clogged with workers hurrying to offices and stores. It took us almost five minutes to work our way around the block onto Madison Avenue again.

And there was the Bonomo van, double-parked near the antique shop.

"Bingo," Jack Donohue said with great satisfaction. "And look—how's that for luck? They're parked a door down so they won't be able to look out the windows and see what we're doing."

He was right: The Bonomo truck wasn't double-parked directly in front of the antique shop. I began to wonder if the gods of crooks, if there are such, hadn't decided to throw in with Black Jack Donohue.

"Pull up in front of him," he directed me. "Back up until you're about five feet away. Keep the motor running."

I did as I was told. I watched in the mirror as Dick Fleming pulled up behind the van. The three vehicles were in a tight group.

"Good, good," Donohue murmured. "Doing fine, doing fine. Now we wait . . ."

We waited, silent and motionless, for almost ten minutes. A squad car rolled by on the other side of the avenue, but the two cops didn't even give us a glance. I didn't see any foot patrolmen.

Donohue turned to the men in the back seat.

"It's time," he said.

They nodded, got out of the car slowly. Went to the back of the van, walking in the street, not on the sidewalk, keeping parked cars between them and the Bonomo cleaning crew inside the antique shop.

I watched in my rearview mirror as Dick Fleming, Smiley, and Clement got out of the XKE, moving leisurely. As far as I could observe, none of the hurrying pedestrians noticed a thing. The five coveralled men disappeared inside the van and closed the rear doors.

'Beautiful," Donohue breathed. "Isn't that beautiful, Jannie?"

I didn't answer.

"Just like you planned it," he said. "You should be proud."

I wasn't proud; I was numb. I knew what was going on inside the van: The five men were pulling on their stocking masks, poor Dick Fleming being urged on by the prodding of Clement's gun. *My* gun.

"Here they come," Donohue said suddenly.

I looked up. The Bonomo cleaning crew was coming out of the antique shop.

"My turn," Black Jack said. He opened the door on his side. "If she gives you any trouble," he said, "kill her."

He was speaking to Angela, but he was looking at me when he said it.

I hope I never see eyes like that again. Holes. Empty. Deep, deep pits.

I watched him go. He timed it just right, hesitating on the traffic side of the double-parked cars until the Bonomo cleaning crew had gone to the rear of their van and opened the doors.

They stood frozen. Then Donohue was behind them, hands at their backs, shoving them forward. Other hands from inside the van reached out, yanked them in. No shouts. No screams. No shots. It had been done.

I let out a long, quavering sigh. Angela hadn't been watching the action. She had been watching me. And that knife blade never wavered, never drooped.

"Angela," I said desperately, "why don't we—"

"Shut up your mout'," she said tonelessly. "You jus' do like you was tole. You jus' drive, that's all you do. You say nuttin. You unnerstan'? Nuttin. Ever' word you say, I cut you a leetle."

So I said nuttin. I want this clearly understood: At that moment, and during what followed, I was absolutely certain that she meant what she said, that she was capable of cutting me and killing me. That's why I did what I did. I was in fear of my life. I want everyone to know that. I acted under duress. I am not legally responsible for what happened.

I watched again in the rearview mirror. I saw the Bonomo driver climb out of the rear of the van. Jack Donohue was close behind him, a hand in his coverall pocket. The two men, walking almost in lockstep, moved to the passenger side of the van's cab. The Bonomo driver got in first and slid across the seat. Donohue followed him inside and slammed the door.

Nothing happened. I glanced at my watch. About 8:53. A few minutes early. We waited. Then, at 8:57 the motor of the cleaning truck was started. It slowly, carefully, pulled out around us into the northbound traffic. I got a glimpse of the driver as they passed. His face was white. He looked like he was about to weep. Then I felt a light prick from Angela's knife. The tip sliced through cloth coat, dress, and touched my flesh. Just touched. It was enough. I pulled out after the cleaning truck, not tailgaiting but close enough so no other car could cut between us.

That's when I heard the sirens, a lot of sirens and buffalo whistles. They were coming from the west and south. I knew what they were: squad cars, fire engines, and the bomb disposal truck, all converging on Rockefeller Center in answer to those diversionary phone calls Jack Donohue had set up. That son of a bitch!

We turned west on 55th Street. The cleaning truck pulled to a stop in front of Brandenberg & Sons. I pulled up behind it. There was no parking allowed on this street, so the van was able to angle in to the curb. I was farther back, double-parked outside a truck apparently unloading material for the construction site on the Madison Avenue corner.

The Bonomo driver and Donohue got out of the cab. They went to the rear of the van. The driver pulled out a mop and a small, canister-type vacuum cleaner. Then he marched up to Brandenberg's. Donohue was close behind him. He was carrying a pail in one hand. The other hand was still in his coverall pocket.

They stood an instant outside the door. It was unlocked almost immediately.

Then the rear doors of the van swung wide again. Five men, stockinged heads lowered, moved swiftly the few steps across the sidewalk. They pushed into the opened door on Donohue's heels.

The door was closed behind them.

They were inside.

So far, everything I have related I saw and heard with my own eyes and ears. What follows next I learned later from Dick Fleming and Jack Donohue . . .

The moment the door to Brandenberg & Sons is opened, Donohue shoves the Bonomo driver through. Shoves him so hard that the man stumbles forward, falls to his knees before a startled Noel Jarvis.

Jack whips out his gun, points it directly at the manager's face, a few inches away. The masked thieves come rushing in, drawing their guns. Nothing is said. Nothing has to be said.

Hymie Gore and the Holy Ghost dash directly to the vault room. They are in before the outer door or the safe door can be locked. The two repairmen are herded into the main showroom. All employees are told to stand in the center of the floor, away from the silent alarms and the chair rail around the walls.

Noel Jarvis says—both Donohue and Dick Fleming remembered this later—"You're making a mistake. A terrible mistake."

All the employees are patted down. One of the clerks and one of the repairmen are carrying pocket transmitter alarms. More surprising, all three clerks are armed with short, blunt pistols in hip holsters. Transmitter alarms and weapons are confiscated.

All employees and the Bonomo driver are made to lie prone in the center of the showroom. Their wrists are tied behind them. Their ankles are roped. Just before their mouths are taped, Noel Jarvis repeats, "You don't know what you're doing. You're making a terrible mistake." Then he, like the others, has his mouth and eyes taped shut.

The thieves remove their stocking masks and set to work.

The Holy Ghost watches over the fettered men. The others start smashing showcases and removing small leather packets from the safe. Everything goes into the pillowcases. There is no time for selection; everything is taken: rings, necklaces, watches, tiaras, earrings, cufflinks, unset gems, chokers, emeralds, bracelets, diamonds, gold sapphires, silver, rubies—the works.

Dick Fleming is put to work closing the mouths of full pillowcases with strips of tape. He is under the gun of the Ghost.

The others empty all the showcases, the big safe in the vault room. They work swiftly, sweeping their loot into the pillowcases with the edges of their gloved hands. Very little talk. Very little confusion.

Donohue works as hard as the others, glancing at his watch occasionally.

"Fifteen minutes," he says.

"Another ten minutes," he says.

"Five minutes left," he says.

They redouble their efforts, digging into bottom drawers in the display cases, cleaning out the show windows behind the drawn steel shutters, reaching deep into the big safe to pull out more of the black leather packets.

"One more minute," Donohue says.

They drag their full pillowcases to the door. Fleming tapes up the mouths. There are fourteen bags of loot for the six men to carry.

"We can't manage," Clement says. "Too heavy."

"We can manage," Donohue says. "Hymie, take four."

"Sure, Jack," Hymie says.

Donohue says: "Smiley, Clement, Fleming go out first to the van. Hymie and the Ghost go next to the Chevy. I'll be along as soon as I wedge the door shut. No wild running, but move quick. Let's go."

From then on, I saw what happened.

Clement came out first, carrying a taped pillowcase in each hand. After him came Dick Fleming, also carrying two cases. He was closely followed by Smiley, who was lugging two pillowcases in one hand. The other hand was in his coverall pocket.

The three burdened men took a few swift steps to the rear of the Bonomo van. They opened the rear doors, threw their stuffed pillowcases inside. Clement and Fleming climbed in, closed the doors. Smiley went around to the driver's side of the cab.

All this had been done in full view of a score of passing pedestrians. No one noted a thing. No one shouted or raised an alarm. Why should they? Three coveralled cleaning men were returning to their van, that's all.

Then came Hymie Gore carrying four pillowcases in his big hands, and the Holy Ghost carrying two.

They walked rapidly, purposefully, to where I was parked, threw their loot in the back seat, and climbed in.

"Start up," the Holy Ghost said hoarsely. "He's coming out in a minute."

I started the engine. We all looked toward the front door of Brandenberg & Sons. Jack Donohue came out casually. He calmly put his two pillowcases down on the sidewalk, then bent as if to tie his shoelace. I saw him slip the rubber wedge under the door, jamming it shut.

He picked up his two pillowcases, straightened, started to move toward us.

As he swung around, he bumped full-tilt into a man turning into the entrance. The man was one of those soberly clad jewelry salesmen we had noted making frequent visits to Brandenberg & Sons, attaché case handcuffed to the left wrist. I saw Jack Donohue smile, saw his lips move, imagined him aplogizing for the collision.

Donohue came back to the Chevy, circled to the street side. Hymie Gore opened the back door, took the pillowcases, slammed the door. Then Black Jack opened the front door on the driver's side.

"Shove over," he said.

Angela slid to the door, I moved closer to her (and her knife), and Jack got behind the wheel.

I was conscious of all this happening. But I was watching that jewelry salesman. After bumping into Donohue, he had stopped right where he was. He just stood there, watching Black Jack walk away, come back to our Chevy with the pillowcases, toss them to Hymie Gore in the back seat, then get behind the wheel.

The salesman saw all this. He turned suddenly to the front door of Brandenberg's, shielded his eyes, peered within. Then he turned back to the street, went down on one knee. His right hand went into the left side of his topcoat and jacket, reaching.

At the same time this was happening, the Bonomo Cleaning Service van began moving. Donohue started the Chevy rolling. The light at the corner of East 55th Street and Fifth Avenue turned green; traffic began moving across the avenue.

It all happened at once. No sequence that I could remember.

"Move it, move it, move it!" the Holy Ghost howled.

The jewelry salesman pulled a gun from inside his jacket and slowly, carefully, sighted it at me as we accelerated past him. Later, of course, I realized he didn't especially want to kill *me*. But at the time I saw the muzzle of his revolver tracking us, and it seemed that big eye was looking only for Jannie Shean.

Then the rear door of the Bonomo van ahead of us opened slightly. A black hand with a gun came out. A shot was fired. The glass door of Brandenberg & Sons shattered, not far above the head of the man kneeling on the sidewalk. Shards came crashing down.

"You fucking idiot!" Donohue screamed.

The salesman flattened after the shot was fired and began to aim again, propping his elbow on the concrete. This time his gun was pointed toward the van ahead of us. I heard at least three shots, and saw the revolver jump in his hand.

Now there were yells, shouts. Pedestrians scattered. Squeal of brakes as cars pulled up, drivers ducked down out of sight. There was a great blaring of horns, a momentary traffic jam at the corner, then more screams and shrieked curses.

The van sideswiped a parked taxi, bounced back into the street, jammed ahead. The back door was

opened wide. Clement was firing at the prone salesman.

Then, unaccountably, there was a man on the sidewalk in front of the Hotel St. Regis. All the other
pedestrians had run for cover. But this man, conservatively clad in gray topcoat and gray fedora, had fallen
into a low crouch, knees bent. He was holding a large
revolver in his two hands, calmly squeezing off shots at
the fleeing van as if he were on the firing range.

(Later newspaper reports said he was an FBI man,
assigned to the Manhattan office, who had gone to the
St. Regis in hopes of effecting a reconciliation with his
estranged wife.)

The Bonomo van accelerated across Fifth Avenue,
heading straight west on 55th Street. We went hurtling
right behind, Jack Donohue cursing and wrestling the
wheel. I wondered why we hadn't turned south on
Fifth, then realized it would be jammed by the police
response to those bomb-scare calls.

So we went speeding west on 55th Street, as fast as
we could. Traffic was heavy, but we were moving, and
once we were across Sixth Avenue, I began to think
we might make it.

"Anyone hurt?" Donohue asked. He was driving
like a maniac, scraping fenders, shooting through
openings, jumping lights.

No one in our car was hurt. But when I turned to
look back, I saw a hole in our rear window with cracks
radiating from it like a star.

Hymie Gore saw me looking, and stuck one of his
thick fingers through the hole.

"Ain't that cute?" he said, grinning.

A Bloody Mess

~~~~~~~~~~~~~~~~~~~~~~~~~~~~~~~~~~~

The van arrived at the West 47th Street garage before we did. As we pulled up, Smiley opened the outside doors, then closed them behind us.

"Trouble," he said as Donohue got out of the
Chevy.

Jack stripped away his fake mustache and the
Band-Aid stuck to his forehead. Then he stood, hands
on hips, staring at the back of the Bonomo truck. One
of the rear door windows was shattered. There were a
half-dozen bullet holes puckering the back doors and
body of the truck.

"Nice shooting," Donohue said sourly. "Who caught
it?"

"The helper," Smiley said. "Flat on the floor,
trussed like a chicken, you'd think he'd be safe. He
took one through the top of his head. One pill and he's
a clunk. Clement caught two, one bad. He's going."

"Let's take a look," Donhue said.

He opened the rear van doors. I stood at his shoulder, peering in. It looked like a slaughterhouse in
there. The roped, gagged, and taped Bonomo helper

lay motionless in one corner. There was apparently a neat hole in the top of his skull. You couldn't really see it because the hair was wet, dark, and matted around the wound. But you could see the blood glistening.

Dick Fleming sat cross-legged in the center of the van floor, surrounded by filled pillowcases and mops, buckets, sponges, squeegees, etc. His face was white as paper and his lips were trembling uncontrollably. Clement was stretched out in front of him, his head in Fleming's lap. Dick was jamming one of the spare pillowcases into Clement's ribs, low down, near the stomach. Clement's eyes were closed, and he was sucking in short, harsh breaths, coughing up blood-flecked foam. There was another bullet hole in his right leg, ozzing blood.

I turned away, gagging.

"Son of a bitch!" Jack Donohue said bitterly.

He climbed into the van. He bent down close to Clement's face. He said something but I didn't hear what it was. He took the sodden pillowcase from Fleming's hand, pulled it away gently. He looked at the wound, grimaced, then pressed the cloth back in place.

He climbed out, leaned against the truck. He lighted a cigarette with shaking fingers.

"We've got to get him to a hospital," I said.

They all looked at me with blank faces. Black Jack took a deep breath.

"We would if it would do any good, Jannie," he said quietly. "But it wouldn't. There's something bad cut in there. An artery maybe. He's on his way out."

"You don't know!" I cried furiously.

"I know," Jack Donohue said, nodding, "I know the signs. Ten, fifteen minutes at the most. Listen, if I thought he had a chance, don't you think I'd let you and Fleming get him to a doctor? Go take a look for yourself. Go on, take a look."

I climbed into the van, resolving not to be sick. I steadied myself by putting a hand on Dick's shoulder. He looked up at me, trying very hard not to weep.

"Jannie, he's dying," he said, shocked and anguished.

I looked down at that crimson pillowcase jammed into Clement's chest. Blood was everywhere. The wounded man was soaked with it. Dick's coveralls were stained. The floor of the van was a puddle. I couldn't believe one body could contain so much blood.

I knelt in the mess. I smoothed Clement's wet hair back from his forehead. His face was ashen. Now his breath was coming in great heaving sobs, as if a great weight were pressing him down. I saw his eyelids flutter, his lips move.

I leaned close.

"You're going to be all right," I whispered to him, my lips close to his ear. "We're going to get you to a hospital and get you patched up. You'll see, you'll be fine in a week or so. Strutting around. We'll get you the best doctors and they'll fix you up. Just hang in there, and everything will be all right. You'll be bopping around in your executive suit and . . ."

I went on and on like that. I saw his lips move again. I put my ear close to hear what he was trying to say.

"Bullshit," he said.

Then he was gone. Like that. One instant he was alive, fighting to breathe. The next instant a great gush of blood flooded from his mouth, his head flopped over limply.

I climbed shakily out of the truck. The others had stripped off their coveralls. Jack Donohue was leaning against the truck again, smoking a fresh cigarette. His eyes were narrowed against the smoke.

"He's dead," I said to Donohue. "Satisfied?"

He looked at me without expression.

"It was your idea," he said.

I turned away.

Dick Fleming came climbing out of the van. I helped him get out of his soaked coveralls. Blood had seeped through to make dark stains on his pants and blotches on his white shirt. There were blood smears on his face; his hands were sticky with the stuff. He tried to wipe it all away with his handkerchief. I stood close to him. I put an arm across his shoulders. I could feel him shake.

"I've never seen a man die before," he said in a low, unsteady voice. "I've never even seen a dead person before. That's strange, isn't it?"

No one seemed to know what to do next. They were all looking at Jack Donohue, waiting.

"The problem is—" he started.

"The problem is," I said, "that it's not just armed robbery now. The helper is dead. An innocent man. Now it's felony homicide."

"Shut your fucking mouth," he said without rancor, "and let me think this out."

We waited. The others moved around quietly, putting on jackets, raincoats, topcoats.

"All right," Donohue said. "I've got it sorted out. Clement getting snuffed is too bad, but we all took our chances. Rather him than us—right? The problem is, we were going to Clement's pad up in the Bronx. I never figured on going back to the Hotel Harding. So Clement said we could use his place to hide out and make the split. But with him burnt, that's out. So now we need a new hidey-hole. We got to get out of here, that's for sure. So where we're going is . . ." His head turned slowly until he was looking directly at Fleming. "We're going to your place."

"Dick's place?" I gasped. "Why the hell there? Why not my apartment?"

"No way," Donohue said, shaking his head. "Plenty of witnesses saw the Bonomo cleaning van. How long do you think it'll take the cops to get the rip sheet from Bonomo, go back over the truck's route, and nose around at every stop? Then they find your abandoned Jag in front of that antique shop on Madison Avenue. They check out the license plate and go directly to your apartment. They could be there right now, waiting for you."

"Thanks a lot," I said.

"They'll run a chase on you," Donohue went on. "All your friends and acquaintances. Sooner or later they'll come up with Fleming's name and address. But that won't be for a day or two. Meanwhile his apartment will be as safe as any place in the city. We checked it out. Ten apartments in an old, converted brownstone. Everyone in the place works; right now we'll have the whole building to ourselves. Am I right, Fleming?"

Dick didn't answer.

"Okay," Donohue said, "let's get moving. All the pillowcases out of the van and the Chevy, into the Volkswagen and Ford. We'll go like this: me, Jannie, and Angela in the VW, me driving. Smiley, Gore, the Ghost, and Fleming in the rented Ford, Smiley driving."

It took less than five minutes to transfer the loot to the final getaway cars. While everyone was working, Donohue wiped down the van with a pair of discarded coveralls, smearing door handles, doors, side panels, steering wheel, gear shift lever, the interior of the cab, and the back of the van. Then, for good measure, he did the same smear job on the Chevy.

Finally, just before we left, he climbed into the van one last time and came out with the sodden pillow-case that had been used to jam Clement's fatal wound. Donohue dropped the mess onto the cement floor of the garage and set fire to it. We waited until the soaked pillowcase was entirely consumed by flicker-ing blue flames.

We stood around, watching that sad little fire. It was like a Viking's funeral for poor Clement. (I never did learn if that was his first or last name.) When the fire had burned down, flared up, went out, I thought that was the end of a man who hoped to be something he could never be. Now there was only a small heap of grayish ash on the greasy floor of an abandoned ga-rage.

"Let's go," Jack Donohue said, but not before he transferred my manuscript, Project X, from the back seat of the Ford to the VW. That guy didn't miss a trick.

Fleming's brownstone was empty, just as Donohue knew it would be. Dick handed over his keys without demur, seemingly still stunned by the death of Clement in his arms. We went up to his apartment, a few at a time, lugging the bulging pillowcases. Angela never strayed far from my side, and there was always an armed man close to Dick.

Inside, door locked and chained, everyone collapsed on chairs and sofa, physically and emotionally drained. Donohue asked politely for whiskey, and Dick brought out a bottle of vodka and a half-filled jug of burgundy. Everyone had a healthy belt. It was like drinking hope.

"All right," Donohue said, "now comes the birthday party. Let's see what we've got . . ."

He cleared Dick's desk, piling books, manuscripts, magazines on the floor. He hoisted up the first of the fourteen pillowcases and ripped off the tape. He began to lay out the contents neatly on the desktop. We all clustered about.

I don't care how expertly you describe gems, nothing can match the awe-inspiring sight of the real things in profusion. I admit we all (me included) ooh'ed and ah'ed as the items came out of the pillowcase and were arranged in close rows on the dark walnut top of Dick's desk.

Donohue raised the shade and winter sunlight streamed through to strike sparks from those precious stones. Chokers and rings, pendants and earrings: All flashed, glittered, caught fire and burned. They took the light, ignited, glowed from within. What a display that was! I forgot for the moment that all this was stolen property, taken at the cost of two lives. All I could see were hard white, green, and red flames, twinkling and gleaming.

Donohue picked out a gorgeous bracelet of small cabochon rubies and diamonds set in flowerlike clusters on a white gold band. He handed it to Angela with a courtly bow.

"With our thanks and compliments, señorita," he said solemnly.

"*Gracias,*" she murmured, taking the bracelet and looking down at it unbelievingly. As well she should; it was probably worth more than she had earned in her entire life.

I was about to cry "What about me?" in an aggrieved tone, and caught myself just in time.

"Smiley," Donohue said, gesturing toward the desktop, "how much would you guess?"

"Quarter of a mil," Smiley said promptly. "At least."

"At least," Donohue agreed. "Maybe more. But that's retail value. Still, twenty percent from a fence ain't bad. All right, let's keep score. That's a quarter of a mil."

He swept the jewelry back into the opened pillow-case and set it aside. He pulled up another case and stripped off the tape. This one contained boxes and packets that had been taken from the safe in the vault room of Brandenberg & Sons.

Donohue pulled out a flat, black leather box and set it on the desktop.

"Here we go," he said, and raised the lid.

We all craned forward. Children opening their Christmas gifts.

Inside the case, nestled on puffed velvet, was a gorgeous three-strand necklace of alternating diamonds and emeralds on ornate gold chains. The three strands were joined in front to support an enormous marquise diamond that seemed to have a million facets. They caught the light and gave it back, so that all the faces thrust forward were illuminated. That gem burned.

There were gasps, cries, a few spoken words. Then all sounds died away. We stood in silence. Everyone was staring at a small, chaste metal label fixed to the inside of the case lid.

It read: "Devolte Bros. San Francisco."

"What the fuck?" the Holy Ghost said in a deep, wondering voice.

"Now wait a minute," Donohue said. "Wait just one cotton-picking minute. It could have been a loan. It could have been sent to Brandenberg on consignment. Let's take a look."

The next fifteen minutes were madness. All of us, Dick and I included, tore those pillowcases open, ripped them apart. The sparkling contents were dumped onto the desktop. Cases were jerked open, locked boxes smashed, stock tags stripped away. The pile of gems on the desk heaped higher, slipped, slid, fell to the floor. No one paid any attention; diamonds and sapphires were trod underfoot, wealth scattered, all that fortune treated like so many bargain items in a supermarket: "Damaged merchandise—prices as marked."

Finally, all the pillowcases emptied, the loot piled in a ragged heap, we stopped, breathing hard, and looked at one another.

All the plunder from the Devolte Bros. heist in San Francisco was there, and jewelry bearing the tags of stores in St. Louis, Denver, Chicago, Dallas, and even some from London, Rome, and Rio. Jewelry from all over the world.

I looked at Jack Donohue. He was biting his lower lip and blinking so rapidly I could catch no expression in his eyes. It was Smiley who spoke first.

"A Corporation front," he said dazedly, staring at that mountain of glitter. "A fencing and cutting operation. Working out of a legit East side jewelry shop."

Dick Fleming turned to me in amazement.

"Those weren't salesmen, Jannie," he said. "The guys with attaché cases handcuffed to their wrists. They were couriers, bringing in stolen stuff from all over."

"Sure," I said, nodding. "They'd pry out the stones and melt down the settings in that back room. Reset the rocks on simple, elegant chains or whatever. And the runners would take it away for redistribution. A big operation. All those jewel robberies in the last three years . . ."

"The Corporation," Smiley repeated. Finally, finally, he had stopped smiling. "It has to be the Corporation. Who else could bankroll something that big?"

Donohue said: "No wonder he said we were making a mistake."

"Who?" I demanded sharply. "Who said that?"

"The manager. Noel Jarvis."

"Antonio Rossi?"

"*Who?*" Smiley asked.

"The manager," I told him. "His real name is Antonio Rossi."

Smiley whirled on Donohue.

"*You knew that?*" he yelled.

"Well . . . yeah . . . sure," Jack said, shrugging. "It was in her book."

"Why didn't you tell us?"

"I didn't think it meant anything."

"You stupid fuck!" Smiley screamed at him. "Rossi is a heavy. A *heavy!* Oh my God, we've ripped off the Corporation. We're in the stew. Everyone of us is dead!"

"Now wait a second," Donohue said. "Don't panic. We can still unload this stuff. I got a fence all lined up. Asa Coe. Top man in the business."

He used Dick's phone, dialed the number rapidly.

"Hello there!" he said heartily. "This is Sam Morrison. I met with Mr. Coe a few weeks ago, and he said— What? What? Now just wait a—"

He hung up the phone softly. He turned to us with a sick smile.

"He doesn't know me and doesn't want to know me. The word's out. Already."

"That does it," Smiley said. He tugged his black leather cap farther down over one eye. He gestured toward the glittering heap of stolen gems. "It's all yours. I want no part of it. I'm walking."

"The hell you say," Jack Donohue said.

"The hell I say," Smiley agreed, smiling once again. "I'm including myself out. I want to walk around with something between my legs for a few more years."

We were listening to him, watching the soft, pleasant smile on his face. So when he pulled a gun from his jacket pocket, no one reacted. We were all frozen.

"Nice and easy," Smiley said. "No rough stuff. I'm just taking a walk, that's all."

"No way," Jack Donohue said. "So you can tip the Corporation? Save your own skin and fuck us? No way."

He slid slowly, cautiously toward Smiley. All of the squat man's attention was on him. Maybe that's the way Donohue planned it. Because while Smiley tensed, drew his lips back in an expression more grimace than grin, it was Hymie Gore who moved. Jack hadn't exaggerated when he had told me the big man was fast.

Fast? He was a blur. One big mitt came down on Smiley's wrist and hand, turning the gun inward. Then the two heavy men were pressed close in a straining embrace. It all happened so quickly that none of us had a chance to intervene. Jack Donohue was just starting forward when the gun was fired three times, rapidly.

Simon Lefferts, my editor, had been right: A gun doesn't go *Ka-chow!* But it doesn't go bang, blam, or pop either. In this case, muffled between two thick men, it made a dull, thudding sound, like a side of beef dropping to the floor.

And that's exactly what happened. Hymie Gore released his grip and stepped away. Smiley stood an instant, tottering, his eyes glazing. Then he went down with a thump that shook the room. He straightened. His heels beat a tattoo on the floor. Then his legs stiffened. Then he was still. The black leather cap had fallen off. He was completely bald, freckles on his naked scalp.

Jack Donohue kicked the corpse viciously in the ribs.

"The miserable fuck!" he said furiously. "He'd have sold our asses."

Perhaps I should have fainted or become ill at witnessing this ugly violence. But it was the third dead man I had seen in the past hour, and something had happened to me: I had lost the capacity to feel. I think it was an unconscious reaction. I think it was a self-protective mechanism. The psyche, to protect the organism, shuts off feelings of horror, disgust, despair. You no longer *understand* what has happened, is happening. You see, you observe, but gunshots become merely loud sounds, blood becomes merely a red liquid, a corpse becomes merely a motionless heap. How else could you survive?

"Nice going, Hyme," Donohue said to Gore. "You did real good."

"Gee, thanks, Jack," Hymie Gore said happily. "I never did like that creep. He called me a stupe onct."

Decisions, Decisions

~~~~~~~~~~~~~~~~~~~~~~~~~~~~

Donohue and the Holy Ghost dragged Smiley's body across the floor by the ankles, stuffed it into a closet, closed the door. The passage left a wide, bloody smear that rapidly soaked into Dick's carpet. I saw him staring at the stained path with widened eyes and wondered how long it would be before he came apart.

Donohue poured us all shots of warm vodka. We slumped back onto chairs and sofa. What bemused me was that not one of us, not once, glanced at that mountain of jewelry piled higgledy piggledy on Dick's desk. It didn't seem so much to us now. Just stones.

"Listen," Jack Donohue said, head tilted back, staring at the ceiling, "I don't have to tell you we're in a bind. The cops are looking for us. By this time the Feds are in on it, figuring we're going across the state line. But the worst is the Corporation. They'll be combing the city. And when they're on your ass, believe me they make the cops look like Boy Scouts. I mean they're *everywhere*. I figure it'll take them about a day or two to come up with the Hotel Harding, Fangio's, the whole shmear."

"How will they do that?" I asked curiously.

Donohue shrugged. "That watchman will find Clement in the 47th Street garage. The cops will check out his contacts, which will lead them to me. And what the cops know, the Corporation will know. They'll put out the word. They'll pay off or promise favors. The desk clerk at the Harding will talk. And Blanche. The bartender and waitress at Fangio's. Everyone will talk. That's the way it goes. So I think maybe we better split up. There's no way the six of us can travel together. Ghost, what do you want to do?"

The Holy Ghost, feet and fingers tapping uncontrollably, turned to Angela. They had a brief conversation in Spanish, rapid, harsh, the words spit out at machine-gun speed. Much gesturing. Many expressions: fear, anger, dismay. Finally . . .

"We'll split," the Holy Ghost said to Donohue. "Fade into Spanish Harlem. We'll make it there."

"Sure you will," Jack said, flashing one of his brilliant grins. I hadn't seen that grin for a long time. I don't know why, but it made me feel better. "You and Angela just go to ground. You got a good chance, a real good chance." He gestured toward the desk. "Take whatever you want from that stack of shit. Forget about percentages. Just take. But if you're smart, you'll stick to the small stuff. Rings, unset stones, maybe a bracelet or two. Things you can sell or hock without anyone asking questions. Help yourself."

We watched Angela and the Holy Ghost paw over the heap of sparkling jewelry. They followed Donohue's advice and selected only single stones, rings, earrings, gold chains, cufflinks. Angela filled her purse; the Ghost jammed his pockets.

"Well," the Holy Ghost said awkwardly, "it was a good one, Jack. Just like you said."

"You bet," Donohue said, winking at him. "A nice Christmas for you—right?"

"You better believe it," the Holy Ghost said. "Presents for everyone. We'll be careful with this stuff, Jack. I mean, we won't put on any flash."

"I know you won't," Donohue said. "I know you'll play it smart. You want to take one of the cars?"

"No," the Ghost said. "We'll manage without."

"Sure," Jack said. "I understand. Be lucky."

"Yeah," the Holy Ghost said. "You, too." He went over to Hymie Gore, patted the big man's cheek. "Take care of yourself, Hyme."

"What?" Gore said. "Oh . . . yeah. See you around, pal."

The Holy Ghost turned to Dick Fleming and me.

"Very pleased to have made your acquaintance," he said.

"Likewise," Angela said.

Then they were gone. Donohue locked the door behind them, put on the chain.

"They may make it," he mused. "They may just. The Ghost is smart enough to move the stuff slowly, all over the place. He'll unload it here, there, everywhere. He's no dummy. Hyme, how about you? Want to split?"

Hymie Gore looked up from his tumbler of vodka.

"I'll stick with you, Jack," he said. "If that's okay with you?"

"Sure," Donohue said. "If that's what you want."

He sat down in an armchair. But he didn't sit; he collapsed. I realized what this day had taken out of him. He was drained, shrunken. He seemed to be running on pure nerve; he had no physical strength left. I wondered how long he could go on without rest, without sleep. Until he was safe, I supposed, and wondered if that time would ever come.

He sipped his vodka and regarded Dick and me thoughtfully over the rim of his glass.

"That leaves you two," he said. "You got a couple of choices. I'm going to run, probably south to Miami. I got to get out of the city. They'll burn me here. Me and Hyme. If you want to come along, that's okay. As long as you know that I call the plays. Your other choice is to stay and take your chances with the law. Sorry about that clunk in your closet, Fleming, but it had to be. Then there's the robbery, and those two stiffs in the garage on 47th. You'll have to weasel out of all that. Plus the bomb scares, the stolen Chevy, and so forth. But it's your decision. If you want to stay, we'll tie you up—just tight enough to give us a chance to split. Then you can call the cops and sing your hearts out."

"But you'll take my book?" I asked him.

He grinned at me.

"You bet your sweet juicy little ass. An insurance policy, like. You two want to talk it over, go right ahead. Go over in the corner where Hyme and I can't hear you. Just keep in sight, that's all."

I motioned with my head, and Dick and I moved over to the window. Donohue and Hymie Gore stayed where they were. Both were stretched out, drinks propped on their chests. Their heads were back, eyes half-closed. But I had seen how quickly they could move. I wasn't about to try a mad dash for the phone or the locked and chained door.

"Dick," I said, holding his arms, "what do you think? What should we do?"

"I don't know, Jannie," he said bewilderedly. "Where do we stand on this whole thing? Legally, I mean?"

"It's a mess," I said, shaking my head. "I'm no lawyer, but here's how I see it: We can claim that we acted under duress, that we were forced to take part in the robbery and witness the killing of Smiley against our will."

"It's the truth," Dick said hotly.

"Sure it is. I was threatened by a knife, you by a gun. But the cops are going to ask, 'You claim you were under duress for *twelve* hours? And never once during that time, not for one instant, could you have yelled, screamed, fallen down in fake faint, or do anything else to bring this whole thing to a screeching halt?'"

Dick was silent.

"We'll have the devil's own time proving duress," I went on. "But that's not the worst of it. The worst is that goddamned manuscript of mine, that lousy Project X. Donohue is never going to let that out of his hands, because it proves we were the kingpins in the robbery, the leaders. We planned the whole caper. We picked the target, cased the place. I made nice-nice with the manager, and you checked out police surveillance of the store. With that manuscript in his hands, if he's ever picked up by the cops, Donohue can claim we set the whole thing up and he was just a hired hand. That's what he meant by calling it an insurance policy."

"But you were just doing research for a book."

"Dick, that's the oldest gag going. It's got whiskers. The cops hear that excuse every day in the week. Every john caught with a hooker claims he was just doing research for a book. Burglars, muggers, second-story men, swindlers, kidnappers—when they're caught, all of them claim to be writers, doing research. If I tell the cops the truth—I *was* doing research—they'll fall down laughing. They'll read that manuscript and all they'll see is a day-by-day account of the planning of a spectacularly successful jewelry store heist that left three men dead—so far."

"But we're not criminals," Dick protested. "We have no records. We both earn a good living. We're solid citizens. What possible motive would we have for pulling an actual robbery?"

"Greed," I said. "Sick excitement. A clever DA could suggest a dozen motives. Maybe we did it just to prove how smart we are, to outwit the cops, to defy society and the law. Whatever. But the motive really isn't important if the cops get their hands on Project X. They've got a conviction on that alone."

"Then you figure we don't have a chance if we give ourselves up?"

"I didn't say that. Maybe if we surrender and prove we didn't profit from the crimes, a smart, expensive lawyer could get us off with a fine, suspended sentence, probation. It's possible. You want to take the chance?"

He was silent again, rubbing his blond eyebrows furiously from side to side.

"Jannie," he said finally, "you do what you want to do, and I'll do what I want to do. I mean, we don't necessarily have to do the same thing, do we? If we disagree, we can go our separate ways, can't we?"

I looked at him curiously.

"Sure, Dick," I said. "I'm not going to try to talk you into anything. It's your neck. It's your decision how to save it."

He sighed. "Got a cigarette?" he said.

I went back to the cobbler's-bench cocktail table, picked up a pack of cigarettes and a book of matches, brought them back to Dick at the window. Jack Donohue opened his eyes to watch what I was doing, but he didn't say word one.

"Let me tell you something," Dick said, lighting our cigarettes. "When the bullets started banging through that truck, I flopped down on my face, as flat as I could get. My head was close to the Bonomo helper. He was a young, husky, good-looking guy. I was staring right at him when he was hit. He shuddered and then he was dead. I knew it. And then, later, Clement died while I was holding him. In my arms. And then we opened the pillowcases and saw all that gorgeous jewelry we had stolen. And then Smiley was killed."

"So?" I said, perplexed. "What's the point?"

"The point is," he said, turning away from me to stare out the window, "the point is that there's never been any drama in my life. Never. I'm thirty-one years old and the most exciting thing that's happened to me up to now was a week's vacation in Acapulco, where I got diarrhea. I do all the smart, senseless things a single man in Manhattan is supposed to do. But I never kidded myself that I was living. I mean, nothing was *happening*. I looked forward to a long, safe, uneventful life. Jannie, it wasn't enough."

I stared at the back of his head, wondering why he wouldn't look at me. What he was saying had meaning. I could understand how a guy like him could be shocked, excited, almost exhilarated by the events of the past twelve hours. It was a new world for him. A mild, gentle editor of children's books finds himself in a hypercharged scene of armed robbery, violence and sudden death.

I had been wrong about him; he wasn't about to crack up. But an earthquake had shaken him, changed his perceptions. There was a life he hadn't even envisioned—except once removed in books, movies, television. But this was the real thing. And now he was in the middle of it, part of it. It was raw, sweaty, dangerous. Hadn't he opted for risk and adventure, sensing the lack in his own life?

The thrilling robbery, the careening escape, the

deaths of men close to him—all had given life a savor it never had before. He was feeling now, feeling deeply. Fear, courage, love, hate. Things he had never really felt before. They had been words with dictionary definitions. But now, only now, he knew what they meant.

And there was something else. I wasn't sure about it, but I had to find out.

I put up a hand, stroked his fine hair fondly.

"Dick," I said in a low voice, "do you want to make love with Jack Donohue?"

He didn't answer for a long time, and I thought perhaps he hadn't heard me. But finally he turned. He looked into my eyes .

"I don't know," he said, puzzled, troubled. "Maybe."

"Then you're going with him?"

He nodded.

"Then I'm going, too," I said.

"Jannie," he groaned, "please. Not for my sake."

"Of course not," I said. "I have my own motives."

"Like what?"

"First of all, I want to stay close to my manuscript. I spent a lot of time and work on that thing and I'm not going to give up without a struggle. Second, I want to see how it comes out."

"What? You're crazy!"

"No, no—Sol Faber claims readers want neat, tidy endings. I can't see how this caper can possibly end tidily, but God knows I've been wrong up to now. So I'm coming along. In for a penny, in for a pound. Besides, there's the matter of ego. I don't like being manipulated, and that's what Black Jack has been doing: manipulating us. I want to see if I have the wit and energy to beat him at his own game."

"You voluntarily go now," he reminded me, "and

your duress defense goes out the window. You become a full-fledged accomplice."

"I can always plead insanity."

"You should have done that three months ago," he said. But he was smiling, and leaned forward to kiss the tip of my nose. Then we marched back to stand side by side in front of Donohue.

"We're going with you," I announced.

Jack let his breath out in a long sigh.

"Biggest long-shot gamble I've ever made," he said, grinning. "It's nice to have a winner."

"Would you really have turned us loose to go to the cops?" I asked him.

"Sure," he said cheerfully.

I didn't believe him for a minute. I hadn't told Dick Fleming one of the reasons I had decided we should go with Donohue: I was afraid that if we didn't he'd kill us both. He was capable of it.

"I've been figuring our best bet," Donohue said, standing and pacing around the room. "We've got a day or two before that thing in the closet begins to stink up the joint. But I think we better get out of here tonight, after dark. They won't have very good descriptions of us. Me, Hymie, and Fleming were in coveralls. They had masks, and I had the fake cookie-duster and the Band-Aid. You're the problem, Jannie."

"Me?" I protested. "Why me?"

"Get with it," he said disgustedly. "They find the Jag, trace your apartment, get an accurate description and a photograph from your sister or friends. You'll be all over the front pages of the tabloids and on the TV news shows by tomorrow. So you've got to become Bea Flanders again."

"Not again!" I wailed. "I thought I was finished with

those goddamned falsies. Besides, all Bea's stuff is at my apartment."

"Not to worry," Donohue said. "I'll go out, pick up enough junk for you to change your looks. A red wig, a—"

"Not red," I said. "I hate red hair."

"Will you use your fucking brain?" he snarled at me. "The cops get to your apartment, they'll know what Jannie Shean looks like. The Corporation traces me to the Hotel Harding, they'll make the connection with the blonde who lived next door to me. So now you've got to be a redhead. So I'll pick up a red wig, tight skirt and sweater, a trenchcoat—whatever. Make me out a list. While I'm out, I'll buy some food and booze, enough to keep us going until we get out of town."

"How are you going to pay for all this?" I asked suspiciously.

He flashed one of his 100-watt grins and jerked a thumb toward the pile of stolen jewelry.

"Hock a couple of things," he said. "Rings, watches, earrings—like that. There's no way, *no* way, the cops can have a description of the stuff out to pawn shops already. By the time they do, we'll be long gone."

"Listen," I said, "what about the insurance—" I stopped suddenly. "Forget it. It was a dumb idea. It's not likely Brandenberg and Sons would have taken out insurance on hot jewelry."

"No," Donohue said dryly, "not likely. While I'm gone, Fleming, you get into some clean clothes. That stuff you're wearing is a mess."

Dick looked at him gratefully.

"Another thing," Jack said. "You got any suitcases?"

"A couple," Dick said. "Two leather, and some canvas carryalls."

"Good," Donohue said, smiling at him. "Pack up all the ice. Put some shirts and towels around it so it doesn't rattle. I'll be gone for a couple of hours, maybe more. I'll take your phone number, and if there's any problem, I'll try to call. I'll let the phone ring twice, then hang up. Then I'll call again. That one you answer. But don't answer any other calls. Got it? And don't open the door for anyone. Don't play the radio or TV. And try to move around quiet. And don't worry about me: I'll be back."

Strangely enough, I was sure he would.

"I'll take the Ford," he said. "I'll gas up. We'll leave about midnight. Get some sleep—if you can."

"Where we going, Jack?" Hymie Gore asked him.

"South," Donohue said. "Miami."

"We'll never make it," I said.

"Sure we will," he said. "Dead or alive."

On the Run

We came through the Lincoln Tunnel, worked our way in and out of horrendous holiday traffic, got onto the New Jersey Turnpike and headed south. Dick Fleming and Hymie Gore were snoozing in the back seat. I was driving. Jack Donohue sat beside me, bending over a Gulf Oil map, trying to read it in the light of the dash.

"Don't you ever sleep?" I asked him.

"When it's time," he said absently. "I love this traffic. Safety in crowds, babe."

I was wearing my new wig—a cross between fire-engine red and life-preserver orange. It was a mass of tight curls. I looked like Little Orphan Annie after she had been picked up by the heels and dipped in a bucket of tangerine Jell-O. Jack had done well with the trenchcoat, though. It had a zip-in fleece lining, which was welcome considering that the outside temperature was a few degrees below zero. He had also bought me a tweed skirt and pink angora sweater. The pink went with my orange wig like milk goes with pickles.

"We'll pick up some better stuff along the way," he had assured me. "Also, I'll need clothes, and Hyme and Dick, too. Some more suitcases. Maybe a thermos for coffee, and one of those plastic picnic chests so we can carry food on the road."

"You think we'll make it, Jack?" Hymie Gore asked.

"Can't miss," Donohue had said as he crossed middle and index fingers of both hands and spun around three times.

So there we were, rolling south through New Jersey at about 2:00 A.M. Dick's suitcases and carryalls, stuffed with the Brandenberg loot, were in the trunk. Jack estimated the total take at close to three million, and I didn't doubt it. It gave me a wry satisfaction.

In the passenger compartment, stuffed under the seats, was the arsenal we had accumulated: my gun, Jack's gun, Hymie Gore's gun, Smiley's gun, Clement's gun, and the three guns taken from the Brandenberg clerks.

"We could invade Bulgaria," Jack Donohue said.

The armament was stowed away, hidden, because Black Jack didn't want any of us personally armed during our flight.

"Suppose we get pulled over by some hotshot trooper," he explained. "Chances are he's not going to pat us down. But he might spot a bulge. He might just *feel* something is wrong and give us a quick frisk. But he's not going to climb into the car for a search by himself. So he writes us a ticket and takes off. You've got to figure the percentages. When we hole up in a motel to sleep, we'll go in heeled. But on the road, we're solid citizens."

Following his instructions, I kept to the speed limit and had the frustration of watching cars and trucks go whizzing by. But it didn't seem to bother Donohue. He just bent over his map, tracing routes with his fore-finger.

"Here's the problem," he said musingly, almost to himself. "By tomorrow or the next day the cops and the Corporation will have a handle on me, through Clement. They'll ask around and discover I work out of Miami. The New York cops will drop out and the Feds will take over. They'll cover all the turnpikes, national highways, and so forth, figuring I'll be trying to make time."

"How about airlines?" I asked. "Railroads? Bus lines?"

"Forget it," he said. "They were covered an hour after we hit. No, they'll figure we're heading south by car. So our best bet is to get off the turnpikes whenever we can and use secondary roads. Also, we've *got* to do that. We can't go around Philadelphia and Baltimore, for example. We've got to go into town."

"Money," I said.

He reached out to pat my knee.

"Brainy lady," he said. "Unless you want us to use those credit cards of yours—which would be like leaving arrows pointing 'They went thataway.' So we'll have to go into the cities along the route. Hock or sell enough of the ice to keep us green. Take what we can get. Not carry so much on us that if we're stopped and turned out, the cops are going to get suspicious. But just enough in our pockets so we can pass as vacationing New Yorkers heading south for the season. We can stash extra cash under the seats."

"What if they search the car?" I said.

"Oh shit," he said. "If they turn out the car, they'll find all those irons and the rocks, so what's the diff? I'm just saying what we should carry *on* us. Let's stick to the Turnpike for another hour or so. Then we'll cut over to Camden and Philadelphia. Hole up and get some sleep. Unload some of the stones and buy the stuff we'll need. We'll travel again tomorrow night."

"Drive only at night?" I asked him.

"Morning, day, night," he said, shrugging. "We'll take it as it comes. The important thing is to avoid a pattern so they can't get ahead of us. One day we'll pour on the miles during daylight, the next day a short trip at night. We don't want to give them any tips."

"You're sure they'll be coming after us?" I asked.

"Oh, they're coming," he said grimly. "The Feds and the Corporation. They're coming after us. You can take that to the bank."

We drove awhile in silence, and then I asked a question that was bothering me:

"Jack, if they get onto you, and learn your home base is Miami, then why are we heading there?"

"Where should we go?"

"The Midwest," I suggested. "Chicago. Or LA. Anyplace they won't suspect."

"No good," he said, shaking his head. "Jannie, the feds are an *army*. They'll alert all their field offices. And the Corporation is even worse. They'll put out the word, with maybe a nice prize offered for tips, and they're *everywhere*. I mean, I won't even be able to get a shoeshine without wondering if the kid's made me. So if every direction is equally dangerous, it makes sense to head for a place I know. Where I can find people I trust. Besides, did you ever wonder just what the hell we're going to do with all these big hunks in the trunk? The Brandenberg stuff, and the Devolte loot, and all that?"

"I wondered," I admitted. "The insurance company is out, and from what you said, no fence will touch us."

"Not in this country they won't," he agreed. "That's the other reason we're heading for Miami. With enough of the loot, we can charter a plane to get us out of the U.S. and A. To one of the islands or some-place in Central America. Or South America. Like that. We'll probably have to take ten percent, but down there we can live high off the hog on that ten. And no questions asked if you grease the right palms."

"Why not New England?" I persisted. "Boston? Your home? Surely there are people up there you can trust?"

"Boston?" he said. "My home?" He snorted with laughter. "Holy Jesus, you didn't fall for that fine old family in Boston bullshit, did you, babe? It was all smoke. I'm a cracker. I was born on a farm outside of Albany, Georgia."

I sighed. "Now I don't know what to believe," I told him.

"Not what anyone tells you," he said. "Never believe that. Just believe in what they do. Actions speak louder than words."

"Oh God," I said. "The platitudes! You'd make a lousy writer."

"Sure I would," he said equably. "But I'm a great crook. I'm going to catch a few winks. Wake me up when we get to the Philly turnoff."

In a few minutes I was the only one awake in the car. I had my hands in the 10-2 position on the wheel. I was leaning forward slightly, peering out the windshield. Not the most comfortable driving position in the world (it gets you in the small of the back), but we were running into patchy fog. It was almost an icy mist, enough to make outside lights glimmer but not heavy enough to switch on the wipers.

Like most New Yorkers I can handle midtown Manhattan traffic without a shiver. But get me out on a clear raceway like a turnpike, and I get the fantods. I mean, who *drives* to Miami? I even plane to the Cape and Montauk.

But there I was, Bea Flanders, gunmoll, at the wheel of a getaway car carrying three villains, eight assorted cannons, and about three mil in stolen gems. I'd love to use it in a book, but who'd believe it?

And guess what I was brooding about. My nefarious career? The trail of corpses we had left behind us? The dangers ahead? Nope. I was wondering about what would happen when we did find a motel that raw night. Specifically, what would the sleeping arrangements be? We obviously couldn't ask casually for a room for four adults.

That meant two doubles—and who would bunk in with whom? Did Jack Donohue trust us enough to allow Dick and me to share sleeping quarters? Or would he claim *droit du seigneur?* An interesting problem. It occupied me until I saw the warning signs for the Camden-Philadelphia turnoff and nudged Jack awake with my elbow.

We made the turn and started looking. Just Donohue and I. The two hulks in the back seat were still out, Hymie Gore snoring gently, an occasional soft moan coming from Dick.

We passed up at least a half-dozen hotels and motels, including a Holiday Inn and a Howard Johnson's Motor Lodge. Then Jack found what he was looking for. It was called Flo-Mar's, from which I deduced the owners were Florence and Martin. Or maybe it just meant the toilets worked but the bowls were stained.

An old-fashioned place: a one-story, U-shaped chain of contiguous units. The big advantage for us was that you checked in at the office, then drove around the U and parked right outside your room. Three steps and you were inside. No parking lot, no lobby, no bellhops.

Donohue said, "Leave the motor running," and

went into the lighted office that had a big VAC-NCY sign flashing on the roof. He was out in five minutes and climbed in beside me.

"Perfect," he said. "Two adjoining doubles with empty rooms on both sides. Numbers 8 and 9. I signed us all in."

"Our real names?" I asked.

"You kidding?" he said. "I paid in advance. No questions asked."

"How do we divide up?" I said, trying to keep it casual.

"I figured you and Hymie Gore could share Number 8," he said, just as casually. "Don't worry about a thing, babe. He'll be a perfect gentleman. I guarantee it."

"But he snores!" I cried.

"Naw," Donohue said. "Just breathes heavily, that's all. You're so worn out, you won't hear a thing."

It didn't make me feel any better to know the son of a bitch was right.

"And you and Dick share Number 9?" I said.

"Just for tonight. We'll switch around. Listen, this isn't fun-and-games time. All we want is a good night's sleep."

"Sure," I said.

"Here," he said, fishing in his pocket. "Something I picked out of the take. In case the neighbors get curious tomorrow. I think you better wear it from now on."

It was a gold wedding band, braided, very delicate and very lovely. He took my left hand, slipped it on the third finger. It fit loosely but well enough.

"Does this mean we're married?" I asked him.

I saw his brilliant grin.

"I like you, babe. You're all right. Now let's wake up the clunks, get out of sight and into bed."

"Two beds in each room, I hope."

"What else?"

We took the suitcases and guns in with us. There wasn't a single lighted room in the motel except ours. And we were all in bed, our lights out, doors locked and chained, within ten minutes. I was asleep in eleven.

Jack was right: Hymie Gore was a perfect gentleman, even if his undershorts had small rosebuds printed on them. And if he had any plans to rape a sleeping woman, that was his problem.

I wish I could tell you that I had nightmares of a knife in my ribs, people shooting guns at me, dying men murmuring, "Bullshit." But the truth is, I had a deep, dreamless, wonderful sleep, and awoke a few minutes after 11:00 A.M. on Saturday morning, knowing eactly where I was and what had happened.

Hymie Gore was gone, and when I peeked outside I saw the car was gone, too. It never occurred to me that I had been deserted. I assumed they had left for some good reason, and didn't worry about it. I don't why I had such faith in Jack Donohue, but I did. Maybe that's why he was such a successful bunko artist.

I took a hot shower and realized I didn't have a toothbrush or toothpaste. *That* I worried about. I was just finishing dressing when there was a knock on the outside door.

"Who?" I called.

"Dick."

I let him in. We looked at each other.

"How did you sleep?" he asked.

"Rocksville," I said. "You?"

"Babe in arms," he said. "I thought I'd have nightmares, but I didn't."

"Same here. Where'd they go—you know?"

"Jack said he wanted to scout around with Hymie. I offered to go along, but he said to stay close. Guard the jewels and guns. We could make a run for it now, Jannie—if you want to."

"Do you?"

"No. Do you?"

"No. We've crossed the Rubicon. What are they scouting around for—did Jack say?"

"Not exactly. To buy some stuff, he said. He made out a list."

"I hope a toothbrush was on it."

It was. Donohue and Gore returned around noon with two new suitcases filled with purchases: toothbrushes, toothpaste, aspirin, razors, shaving cream, cologne, powder, two bottles (scotch and vodka), cigarettes, candy bars, boxes of crackers, instant coffee, a quart thermos jug, etc., etc.

"Like a picnic," I said. "You pick up any newspapers?"

"Yeah," Hymie Gore said. "Show them, Jack."

They had bought the *Enquirer*. We were on the front page: "$1M N.Y. Gem Heist." The brief story said that New York police were investigating "several leads."

"One million?" I said. "Who they kidding?"

"The cops," Donohue said. "You didn't expect Brandenberg and Sons to admit they were holding two mil in stolen ice, did you? Y'know, I got to laugh every time I think of it. Crooks ripping off crooks. What a switch! Well, let's get some breakfast. We found a McDonald's right down the road."

It was our first hot meal in I couldn't remember how many hours, and we all had two helpings of everything. Except Hymie Gore: he had three. We sat in a corner booth. I noticed that Jack Donohue positioned us so he could watch the door. Maybe he thought crooks robbing crooks was funny, but he wasn't playing it for laughs.

We were finishing our coffee when he asked us how much cash we were carrying. I had a little over a hundred. Dick had about forty, Hymie had sixty-five. Jack said he was holding almost two grand, proceeds from the jewelry he had sold and pawned in New York before we left.

"Not enough," he said. "We got to spend the day collecting. Here's how we'll handle it . . ."

He spelled it out for us, going over it slowly, in detail. We would head into downtown Philadelphia, all of us in the Ford. Then, at some rendezvous point— say a parking lot in a shopping center—we'd separate and go different ways on foot or in cabs.

Dick Fleming would take men's watches, the beautiful, engraved antique pocket watches and hunters in the Brandenberg loot. He'd select as many as he could comfortably carry—maybe a half-dozen or more— and peddle them in jewelry stores that bought secondhand gold. He would sell one watch in each store he hit. His scam was that the watch belonged to his father, was a family heirloom, and he was selling it regretfully, only because he needed some ready cash.

"Think you can handle it?" Donohue asked, looking at him closely.

"Sure," Dick said.

"Sure you can," Donohue said. "I know you can. Don't volunteer any information unless they ask. Then tell them what I just told you—nothing more."

"Use my right name?" Fleming asked.

"Only if they ask for it, which they probably won't."

"How much should I ask?"

"Five hundred," Donohue said promptly. "They'll laugh and say there's no demand for watches like that. Bullshit. Those watches are works of art; nuts collect them. Come down to two hundred if you have to. If they offer anything less, start to walk out. They won't let you go; take my word for it. The gold in those watches is worth more than that. Jannie, you hit the same type of store. You'll be hawking wedding rings. Solitaires and bands. If they ask, you just got a divorce and don't want anything your sonofabitch husband gave you. If possible, ask them to make the first offer, then you demand fifty percent more. Haggle. Get as much as you can. Clear?"

"Sure," I said. "I can fiddle it, Jack. Can I sell two rings in one store—say a plain band and a diamond?"

"Why not?" he said. "Lots of women have more than one wedding ring. You're a smart twist; I'll leave it up to you."

"Don't call me a twist," I said. "What will you and Hymie be doing?"

"I saw some men's rings in that heap: pinkie rings and heavy gold cufflinks set with diamonds and rubies. Hymie will try his luck in taverns. Bartenders are suckers for a hot buy. Me, I'm going to take some of the bracelets, pins, brooches, cocktail rings—flashy stuff like that."

"Who's going to buy?" I asked him curiously.

"Whores," he said, grinning. "And their pimps. They can't resist the dazzle. And there used to be some good cathouses in Philly. If they're still there, I'll clean up. Now we'll go back to the motel and load up with merchandise. Then we'll get moving; I want to be on the road as soon as possible."

He was a been-around man, no doubt of that. He knew Philadelphia as, I presumed, he knew every big city in the country. We parked the Ford in the lot of a shopping center and agreed to meet there again at 5:00 P.M. If anyone was more than thirty minutes late

—goodbye, Charlie; it would be assumed he had been nabbed and the Ford would take off.

Donohue told Dick and me the best downtown streets to canvass. He saw us into a cab, my purse jammed with rings and Dick's pockets sagging with watches. He waved as we drove away.

"Fun," Dick said.

I looked at him.

He was laughing and excited; that was obvious. He was eager, anxious to test his bravery and wit. He had always been—well, I guess effete is the best word to describe him. But the events of the past twenty-four hours had remade him. He seemed more positive, more thrusting. He leaned forward, a half-smile on his lips, eyes bright and blinking.

I almost asked him about last night, about him and Jack Donohue in Room 9, if anything . . . But how can you ask a question like that?

In all honesty, Dick wasn't the only one enjoying this test of his criminal talents. I admit to a kind of don't-give-a-damn mood. Perhaps because of what had happened, what I had done or participated in. But it was more than that. It was a wild freedom, an absolute kicking over of the traces. Maybe every criminal feels that way; I don't know. All I can do is describe it as an exhilarating madness. With all shackles of habit, logic, and morality thrown off and discarded, you want to see how far you can go. You want to fly, just go with it, push it to its limits: lie and cheat and steal and, if need be, kill.

It's civilization turned inside out. No becomes yes, and black is white. Anything goes.

It went, for me, like a hilarious dream. The first jewelry store I hit was a mom-and-pop shop that had a sign in the window: "We Buy and Sell Gold, Diamonds, Silver." I took off the wedding band Jack Donohue had told me to wear, slipped it into my purse, put on the Mt. Everest of solitaires set in what I guessed to be platinum, but could have been white gold.

"Yes, lady?" the proprietor said, coming forward, smiling. "Can I help you?"

"I want to sell this," I said, sticking out my left hand.

He held my fingers, peered down at the ring.

"Let me have a look," he said, neatly slipping the ring away. It came off easily. "Too big," he said.

"I've lost weight."

"It happens."

"It should happen to you," his wife mumbled, hovering nearby.

"Sha," he said, going behind the counter. He adjusted a lamp, screwed a loupe into his eye, bent over the ring.

"Why should you want to sell this?" he asked casually, inspecting the diamond.

"I just got a divorce. I don't want to own anything that reminds me of that monster."

"He beat you?" the wife asked, horrified.

"You wouldn't believe," I told her.

"Jake, you hear?" the wife said.

"I hear," he said, turning the ring this way and that. "That also happens. Count your blessings."

"Some blessings," the wife said scornfully.

"Well," Jake asked, looking up at me. "How much were you thinking of asking for this little stone?"

"Five thousand," I answered bravely.

"Five *thousand?* Lady!"

"That's what my husband—my ex-husband told me he paid for it."

"He *said.* Believe me, lady, if he paid more than

one, they saw him coming. I could give you maybe five hundred."

"Five *hundred?* No way. Give me my ring back."

"Sha. Sha sha—Don't get angry. Let's talk like civilized people. The ring is worth maybe a thousand in today's market. Retail. All right, fifteen hundred tops. But can I buy it for that? Of course I can't. My rent: seven-fifty a month. Insurance. Utilities. My clerk, he should drop dead already, a cousin yet, who refuses to come in on weekends, another thousand a month. So I give you retail price, and what do I get? *Bubkes,* I get. All right, you're a nice lady. For you, seven-fifty."

I caught on; it was a game. He was enjoying it. To tell you the truth, I was too. I knew he wanted the ring. I had made the sale; the only question that remained was, how much?

We went at it hot and heavy, Mom chiming in now and then when the argument flagged. He pointed out a small scratch in the setting. I pointed out the exquisite cut of the stone. He came up slowly; I came down just as slowly.

Finally we struck a bargain: one thousand, six hundred and fifty.

We smiled at each other, both satisfied.

"In cash," I said.

His smile faded.

"Cash? Look around you, lady. Does this look like a store I get that much money maybe in a drawer? Under the rug? My check is good. Believe me; good as gold."

"I'm sure it is. But the banks are closed today. I'm leaving for Miami tonight. I need the cash."

"Jake, did you hear?" the wife chimed in. "Miami. The children. That's where we should be—Miami."

"Cash," he said dolefully. "I'm sorry, lady. That kind of cash I don't have."

"How much do you have?" I asked. A mistake.

"I could maybe scrape together one thousand five," he said. "Possibly."

So I walked out of there with one-five. Both of them escorted me to the door and wished me the best of luck in my new life in Miami. I knew when I was beaten.

Still, my first sale had netted fifteen hundred dollars. And my first thought was of how proud of me Jack Donohue would be. My second thought was that I wasn't the only thief involved in that transaction. Admittedly I was selling stolen goods. But, in a way, they had stolen, too. Maybe they guessed it was a hot rock. But in any event they had taken advantage of my ignorance and had paid a pittance for a ring I was certain was worth much more.

My other sales weren't that easy, and none yielded as much. In two stores I was turned away rudely when I couldn't produce proof of purchase. A few others offered "take it or leave it" terms, and I accepted. Two others offered checks and refused to pay cash.

The last place I entered was interesting. The proprietor, a youngish, baldish man with bad breath and a black patch over one eye, immediately paid in cash the price I asked for a Victorian gold wedding band engraved with vines and leaves.

"Happy to do business with you, miss," he said with a ghastly smile. "If you have any, ah, comparable merchandise to offer, I'll be happy to take a look at it. Top prices."

"Thanks," I said. "I may take you up on that."

"Then I can expect you to come back?" he asked hopefully.

"We'll see," I told him smiling sweetly.

Are we all thieves?

By that time my feet were aching. I had unloaded seven rings and was carrying almost five thousand dollars in my shoulder bag. It was then getting on to 4:30 P.M., and I figured it was time to start back. I walked two more blocks, caught a cab, and arrived at the shopping center parking lot well before the deadline.

Dick Fleming was leaning against the Ford with a watermelon grin.

"How'd you make out?" he asked me.

"Almost five grand."

The grin faded a little.

"My God," he said. "I did two and thought that was great."

"My stuff was worth more," I comforted him. "Easier to peddle."

We were exchanging stories of our experiences when Jack Donohue and Hymie Gore pulled up in the same cab. They paid off the driver and walked over to us. I could tell things had gone well by the way Black Jack walked: a jaunty, bouncing stride, his arms swinging.

"Have a nice day?" he asked, flashing his dazzling smile.

"About seven grand between us," I told him.

"Lovely," he said. "Beautiful. Much better than I had hoped. A couple of ripe ones, you two are. What nobblers! Hyme and I did all right, too. Unloaded almost everything and were invited to hurry back with more. But we won't be greedy. Not in this town."

"How much?" I asked him.

"I figure we're carrying close to twenty. What a sweet payday this has been! Well, tomorrow's Sunday, and on the seventh day we rest. Let's go back, stash the green, and get cleaned up. We'll find us a nice, classy, expensive restaurant, have a steak and drinks, and relax for a few hours before we hit the road. How does that sound?"

We all agreed that sounded just right.

But the stores and boutiques of the shopping center were still open, and I asked Donohue to give me thirty minutes, no more, for a quick and necessary shopping trip. He agreed to thirty minutes, no more.

So about an hour later I hurried back to the Ford, burdened down with boxes, bags, packages. I had made a whirlwind tour and picked up things I needed: cosmetics, tampons, sweaters, skirts, two simple shirt-waist dresses, a fleece-lined jacket, a velour bikini (for Miami), and even a nylon wig in a strawberry shade a little less frightful than the one Donohue had bought for me.

I thought he'd be furious at my tardiness, but Hymie Gore had had the foresight to bring along the bottle of scotch, and it was obvious the three men hadn't been bored during my absence. They were in a festive, almost roistering mood, and we headed back to the motel with the firm conviction that God was where He should be, and all was right with the world—or at least our small part of it.

Showered, the men shaved, and me dressed in new duds and new wig, we prepared to sally forth to the banquet Jack Donohue had promised. It was then close to 8:00 P.M.

"Hey," Dick Fleming said, "if we're going to hit the road tonight, why don't we pack now? If we get tanked at dinner, we won't feel like it when we come back. The rocks and the guns will be just as safe in the car as they are here."

Donohue thought that over for a few seconds.

"Good idea," he said finally. "As a matter of fact, let's check out now. We'll have our dinner and then take off."

So all the new suitcases were filled with our purchases and stacked in the Ford's trunk, along with the
old suitcases and the loot. The carryalls went into the
back seat, the guns under the seat, and we piled in.

Jack got behind the wheel and pulled up to the motel
office. He beeped the horn twice and the clerk came
out. He was a tall, shambling gink with no chin. But
to make up for it he had an Adam's apple that looked
like an elbow. A fine figure of young louthood.

"We're checking out," Donohue said, smiling and
holding the keys out his opened window. "Many thanks
for your hospitality. Nice place you got here."

"Yeah?" the clerk said in great surprise. "Well, you
come back again, y'hear?"

"We certainly will," Black Jack said, and he said it
as though he meant it. I mean, you could *believe* this
man. "Any idea where we could get a good dinner
around here? Steak, roast beef—like that?"

The clerk never hesitated.

"That would be Uncle Tom's Tavern," he said.
"On the road to Camden. Not real fancy, but real
good. Take a left on the highway. It's about two miles.
You'll see the neon sign on your right."

"Much obliged," Donohue said politely. "Keep up
the good work." Then, after we had pulled out and
turned onto the highway, he said, "Uncle Tom's Tavern? Jesus, can you believe it?"

But it wasn't as bad as it sounded. Larger than we
expected. A big parking lot, well filled, and a ram-
bling, one-story building that someone must have
thought looked like a colonial tavern. The interior
decor carried out the theme: exposed beams in a
whitewashed ceiling, two brick fireplaces with lighted
gas logs, and oak tables set around with captain's
chairs. There was a long mahogany bar down one side,
antiqued mirrors behind it and stools in front uphol-

stered in red vinyl. The bartenders and all the wait-
resses wore colonial costumes, and the maitre d'
was dressed in knee breeches and a powdered wig. He
looked abashed, as well he should.

"Jeez," Hymie Gore said, beaming, "this is cute!"

The food was not bad. Not great, but not bad. We
all ordered the same thing, figuring it would take less
time. The Little Neck clams were fresh and cold (Hymie had a dozen), the salad was crisp, the French
bread hot and crusty. When the entrees were served,
there was plenty of sour cream and chives for the
baked potatoes, the ribs of roast beef (bone in) were
reasonably tender, and the string beans had been
cooked with bacon. Ersatz bacon, of course, but who
cared? Warm apple pie for dessert, with a slice of
American cheese on each wedge. A big pitcher of hot
coffee set in the middle of the table.

It wasn't the Four Seasons, but for Camden, N.J., it
was a pleasant surprise. Or maybe we were all in a
mellow mood from the drinks: two rounds before we
ordered, another with the clams, two bottles of California burgundy with the beef, cognac with the coffee.

By this time, Hymie Gore was burping like a maniac, tapping a knuckle constantly against his lips, and
muttering, " 'Scuse. 'Scuse. 'Scuse."

"And now," I said, "if you gentlemen will pardon
me. Nature calls." They looked at me blearily. "No,
no," I said, "don't get up. I'll manage."

I found the women's lounge, peed, repaired my
makeup, resettled my wig, and headed back to our
table. The restrooms were up two stairs at the rear
of the dining room. As I came down the steps, I
glanced toward the noisy bar. Almost every stool was
taken; the bartenders were hustling.

In the mirror behind the bar I spotted a familiar
face. A man sitting at the far end. I almost stopped.

But if I could see him in the bar mirror, he could see me. I continued my slow walk back to our table, looking at my companions and smiling. I was so goddamned nonchalant, it hurt.

I slid into my chair, pulled closer to the littered table, picked up my napkin. Jack Donohue was seated on my right. I leaned close to him, smiling, put a hand on one of his.

"Jack, darling," I cooed, "we may have trouble. Come toward me, smile and laugh like everything's okay."

I didn't have to cue him twice; he responded immediately. He slid his free arm across my shoulders, pulled his chair closer.

"You two guys go on drinking," he said to Fleming and Gore out of the corner of his mouth. "Don't look up. Don't stare at us. What is it, Jannie?"

And all the time he was laughing, nodding. To an observer thirty feet away, everything would look copacetic: a nice, friendly, somewhat drunken dinner for four.

"Don't look now," I said. "A guy at the far end of the bar. Standing. Youngish. Baldish, wearing a black patch over his right eye."

Donohue took his arm from my shoulders, still smiling. He shook a cigarette from a pack on the table, lighted it, put his head back to blow a plume of smoke upward. I saw his eyes dart.

"Got him," he said.

"Know him?"

"No. Looks like a fink. Who is he?"

"Owner of the last jewelry store I hit. Didn't haggle. Paid what I asked immediately. In cash. Asked if I had any more merchandise like that. Very anxious that I should return."

"I see," Donohue said slowly. "I see."

Dick Fleming and Hymie Gore had been busy with their coffee and brandies. But they had been listening.

"It could be a coincidence," Dick said. "Maybe he's waiting for a date. Maybe he's just here to have Saturday night dinner by himself and is waiting for a table."

"Oh sure," Jack said. "A Philadelphia jeweler drives across the bridge, through Camden, just to have Saturday night dinner by himself in Uncle Tom's Tavern. Some coincidence! What did you do after you left his place, Jannie?"

I thought back, trying to remember.

"It was the last place I hit. After I left, I walked two blocks, caught a cab, went back to the parking lot."

"Was he the only one in the store?"

"Yes. No. I don't know. There was a back room, curtained off. There might have been someone in there. He was the only one I saw."

Jack Donohue sighed. "I don't like it. He could have smelled something. Decided to tail you. Followed you back to the shopping center. Waited. Then tailed us to the motel and here. It's possible."

"I'm sorry, Jack," I said humbly.

"Not your fault," he said shortly. "Mine. I should have warned you. I should have had my head on a swivel, watching for a tail."

"Jack, you don't *know*," Fleming said in an urgent whisper. "It might be entirely innocent. It might be just a coincidence, like I said."

"Might, might," Donohue repeated. "Anything *might* be." He was silent a moment, then: "All right, here's what we're going to do. I'm going to signal for the check, pay it, leave a tip. Then we're all going to get up and move slowly toward the door. *Slowly*—get it? We're all talking and laughing. Not a care in the

world. Now, the moment we're outside, Jannie, you
and Fleming and me, we hightail it for the car, get in,
go screaming out of the lot. Hyme, you fade into the
shadows. Dig? Somewhere on the lot or over to one
side. Somewhere where you can watch the door. Now
if that guy doesn't follow us right away, then it's just a
crazy coincidence, like Dick says, and no harm done.
But if he comes barrel-assing out after us, then you've
got to take him, Hyme. You understand?"

"Sure, Jack," Gore said. "I understand. You want I
should step on him?"

I saw Dick Fleming's face go white, and I clasped
my hands to hide the tremble. The day had been fun,
a lark. The dinner had been a celebration. Now here
was the bleached skull behind the laughing mask.

"Nooo," Donohue said slowly, "don't squash him,
Hyme. That would cause too many problems, too
much heat. We got enough already. Just cold-cock him.
Make it look like your everyday, run-of the-mill
mugging. Turn his pockets inside out. Take his wallet,
credit cards, wristwatch. Try to leave him in his own
car if you can. People coming by will think it's a
drunk sleeping. If not his car, roll him under any heap.
I'll come back for you in about five minutes. Got all
that, Hyme?"

"Got it, Jack. No sweat."

"Good," Donohue said. "Just remember, I'll come
back for you no matter how it turns out. Everyone
knows what to do? Don't look toward the guy as we
leave. We don't know he exists. Let's go . . ."

He called for the bill, paid cash, left a generous tip.
We all rose to our feet, laughing and joking. Moved
slowly toward the door. Reclaimed our coats from
the cloakroom, still chattering and smiling. Went out
the door.

The moment it closed behind us, Donohue, Fleming, and I walked rapidly to the Ford. Jack unlocked the doors, got behind the wheel. Dick and I piled in. We pulled out of the parking lot with a chirp of tires. Hymie Gore was nowhere to be seen. He had disappeared somewhere between the parked cars. We didn't look back.

"What time is it?" Donohue asked harshly.

I was in the back. Fleming was in the passenger seat next to Jack. Dick held his wrist close to the dash.

"About seventeen to eleven." he said, a tremor in his voice.

"All right," Donohue said, "keep an eye on your watch. When it's a quarter to eleven, let me know."

We drove slowly toward Camden. Dick leaned forward, watching the minute hand move around. No one spoke.

"A quarter to eleven, Jack," Fleming said finally.

Donohue let traffic go by, then made a screeching U-turn and headed back to Uncle Tom's Tavern, still driving slowly.

Hymie Gore was waiting for us on the verge of the highway; we didn't even have to turn into the parking lot. I opened the back door, he climbed in. Jack accelerated, speeding toward the Turnpike.

"Got his wallet, watch, credit cards," Hymie said. "Just like you told me, Jack."

"Then he came after us?"

"Oh sure," Gore said. "Like a bat out of hell. I took him just as he was getting into his car. He's in there now. Sleeping."

"Nice work, Hyme."

"A piece of cake," Gore said. "Everything's all right now."

"Un-huh," Jack Donohue said. Then: "We should have killed the cocksucker."

Skin of Our Teeth

It all turned hard. Up to that moment it had seemed like a game, a gamble. And we had won: The hair-breadth escape from New York, the jaunty selling of the jewelry—all had gone well, with grins and laughter.

Now we sensed the presence of an implacable enemy, everywhere, a nemesis.

"I get so goddamned sore!" Jack Donohue burst out. "We made the score; why don't they leave us alone?"

Foolish? Irrational? Of course. But I think that's the way we all felt. Maybe all criminals feel that way. Our planning and daring and bravery were for naught; we were being condemned and hounded. The cops were unfair, the law was unfair, life was unfair.

We drove south on the Turnpike, keeping to the speed limit. I couldn't stand the silence.

"It wouldn't have done any good to kill him, Jack," I said. "He might have already called someone, told them about us."

"No," Donohue said definitely. "If he had done that, there would have been four hammers in that res-

taurant instead of just him. But he'll sure as hell gab
when he comes to."

"The Corporation?" Dick Fleming asked.

"Who else? An FBI man he'ain't."

Silence again while we all thought of what had happened and what it might portend. I had a sudden,
depressing vision of a wild flight south, an endless succession of scrubby motels, pickup meals in out-of-the-
way diners and second-rate fast-food joints. And all of
us, heads on swivels, looking over our shoulders for
the pursuers.

"Hyme," Jack said, "if you were tailing and got the
word we had been spotted in Philly, what would you
figure for our next stop?"

"Baltimore," Hymie Gore said promptly. "Right,
Jack?"

"Right," Donohue said, nodding. "I think that's
what they'll figure. So this'll be just a short trip; we'll
hole up for the night near Wilmington, get some sleep,
drive through to Baltimore around noon. Give us a
better chance to look around. And maybe, if they don't
get a sniff of us in Baltimore tonight or tomorrow
morning, they'll follow their noses on to Washington."

"Jack," Dick Fleming said hesitantly, "I know it's a
crazy idea, but if they're on our tail, the Feds and the
Corporation, and are figuring our route and stops,
wouldn't it make more sense to double back to New
York? They wouldn't be expecting that."

"Never work," Donohue replied immediately. "Too
many eyes in New York, too many big mouths, big
ears. Where would we hole up? How would we peddle the rocks for walking-around money? And then
what would we do—I mean eventually? How would
we get out of the country? No, Miami is our best bet.
We'll get there; don't chew on it."

We crossed the Delaware River, came into Farn-

hurst, just south of Wilmington, and saw signs pointing to Interstate Highway 95. Jack Donohue laughed
delightedly, the first time in the past hour.

"Dear old Route 95," he said happily. "We can take
that mother right into Miami. We're heading home!"

We came down 95, turned off, and found a suitable
motel just east of Elkton, Md. It was called something
or other. I didn't care, and it wasn't important; it was
just a place to sleep. Donohue signed us in for two
adjoining doubles. This time, he said, he and I would
share one, Fleming and Gore the other. No one objected.

We checked entrances, exits, possible escape routes.
We brought in the luggage and guns.

"Uh," Jack said, almost embarrassed, "the situation's changed; I think maybe we should start carrying
when we go out, and on the road. Jannie, you and
Fleming know how to use these things?"

"We can learn," Dick said.

"Sure you can," Jack said. "Hymie will show you
how. It's easy. Hymie, give them the automatic pistols.
Just put off the safety and pull the trigger; that's all
there is to it."

So that night, before we all went to bed, Dick and I
were issued loaded pistols and shown how to use them.
You switched that little dingus up, pointed the gun at
what you wanted to hit, and kept pulling the trigger
until the pistol was empty. You held on tightly because the gun would jerk in your hand, and also you
had to be prepared for the loud noise and not be
startled by it.

"That seems simple enough," I said.

"Yeah," Hymie Gore said. "Nothing to it. You'll
get the hang of it right off."

Later, Donohue and I in our separate beds, lights
out, I called softly, "Jack? You asleep?"

"Can't," he said. "My brain's churning. So much to figure. We'll have to ditch the Ford."

"Why is that?"

"It's got that goddamned sticker of a rental car on it. And maybe the license plate. Can the cops make a rental car from the license plate like they can a cab?"

"I don't know."

"Anyway, the Feds will have your photograph sooner or later. It'll probably be in the papers and on TV. The rental agency guy might spot it. You rented under your own name, didn't you?"

"Yes."

"So then they'll get out a bulletin on the car. That's why we've got to ditch. We'll pick up another heap in Baltimore and just walk away from the Ford. Then we'll make tracks."

Silence in the darkness. I saw him light a cigarette, so I lighted one.

"Jack," I said.

"What?"

"Something I've been wondering about: Why did you bring Smiley into the deal? I thought you owed him money?"

"That's why I had to bring him in," he explained. "I told him I was going to score big and he'd get his five G's. But he wanted to protect his investment, so he declared himself in. It was the only way I could stall him. The bastard didn't trust me."

"Oh."

"Well, he got his," Donohue said vindictively. "I hate people who don't trust me."

The aggrieved plaint of the confirmed liar, con man, cheat: People don't trust him. What was so unbelievable, even to me, was that knowing this, I still trusted him. And so did Hymie Gore, and so did Dick Fleming.

I wondered if we loved him. It was possible. You never love people for their virtues. It's their short-comings that make you lose control.

After a while we put out our cigarettes. We lay awake in the darkness. I could hear him stir restlessly. I thought I heard a groan.

"What is it, Jack?"

"I been on the con all my life," he said, as if speaking to himself. "I admit it. A grifter since I was ten years old. I had to be to survive. Listen, I worked hard at it. Lost my cracker accent. Learned how to wear clothes, order from a menu, who to tip and who to grease—like that. You know?"

"I'm listening."

"So, being on the hustle as long as I can remember," he went on, "it's become my whole life. I mean, I could have been someone else. I keep thinking that with the breaks I could have been someone else. I mean, I'm not a monster, I know how to behave and I got a brain. I know I got a brain."

"I know you do, Jack."

"So, with a break or two I could have been something. Instead of busting my ass on the con every minute. Hitting and moving on. Always moving on. Jesus, what kind of a life is that? But that's not the worst of it. The worst of it is that the con, the hustle, the scam has become such a big part of me that it's a habit. I mean, when does it stop? Am I conning myself? That's what's worrying me. Is this the biggest hustle of my life—swindling myself?"

I thought about that a moment. Then I said:

"You mean about getting to Miami? Getting out of the country with the ice and living happily ever after?"

"Yeah," he said, sighing, "that's what I mean. What do you think?"

I didn't answer. He kept stirring restlessly. I stared

out the window, and in the light from the motel sign I saw that it had started to snow. Big fat flakes were coming down slowly, like petals.

"Jack," I said finally.

"What?"

"Want me to come into your bed?"

"Yeah," he said. "That might help."

The Donohue Gang didn't do much on Sunday, just mooched around, went out for breakfast and lunch. Armed. Then we repacked the suitcases and carryalls, dividing up the Brandenberg loot so if one or two cases were lost or stolen, we'd still have plenty. Hymie Gore cleaned the guns that had been fired during the wild getaway. He used handkerchiefs and a package of pipe cleaners he had bought.

"Jack," he said, "we're going to need more pills."

"I know it, Hyme," Donohue said. "I figured we'd wait till we get a little farther south. Easier to buy ammo down there, and no questions asked. We got enough to see us through, don't we, Hyme?"

"Oh sure, Jack. But, you know . . ."

Late in the afternoon we were all sitting around in the room occupied by Fleming and Gore, watching a football game on television and drinking vodka. The snow had stopped—only an inch or so had fallen—but it was cold enough so that it wasn't melting. We knew we'd have to hit the road again soon, but it was warm and cozy in there: no one wanted to make the first move.

A short news broadcast came on: the usual about the Mideast situation, a famine in Pakistan, a plane crash in Poland, a fire in Bombay that killed 196. All swell stuff. Then the expressionless announcer said:

"New York police admit they have no leads in a particularly gruesome double homicide discovered early this morning in an abandoned butcher shop in the South Bronx. The bodies of a man and a woman were found hanging from meat hooks. Both victims, said police, had obviously been tortured before they died. Identification has not yet been definitely established, but it is believed the woman was of Hispanic extraction. And now, back to today's football scores . . ."

Black Jack Donohue got up slowly. He switched off the TV. We watched him walk to the window. He stood staring out at the snow-covered scene.

"Jack," Hymie Gore said falteringly. "You hear that?"

"I heard it, Hyme."

"You think . . . ?"

"Yeah, Hyme, that's what I think. Angela and the Ghost. They didn't make it."

"Uh . . ." Dick Fleming tried. "Uh . . ."

Donohue whirled on him.

"You mean did they talk?" he demanded. "Is that what you're wondering? Did they talk?"

Fleming hung his head.

"Goddamned right they talked! So would you, so would I, so would anyone. Now they got our names, descriptions, everything. Jesus Christ, we got to dump that car!"

"How did they get to the Holy Ghost?" I asked, hoping to calm him down. "You said he'd play it smart."

"Who the hell knows?" he said, shrugging. "Maybe Angela gave a ring to a relative, a Christmas present, and they flashed it around. It could happen a dozen ways. Oh, those bastards! They didn't have to cut them up. The Ghost would have sung right away. He'd know I'd understand. But no, they had to hurt them. You know why? A warning to us. Oh, yes. An example. You rip off the Corporation, that's what you get. They knew we'd hear about it or read about it. They want us to know what's in store for us."

"Oh God," I said faintly, remembering the finger-tapping, foot-tapping Holy Ghost, the skinny little Angela wrapped around with yards and yards of knitted wool.

"Want to take off now?" Donohue said harshly. "You and Fleming? Turn yourselves in? Go ahead. I wouldn't blame you. Hyme and I will keep the car, the rocks, and split. You call the cops and take your chances."

Dick and I stared at each other.

"No, Jack," he said, looking at Donohue. "We're in this as deep as you are. We'll stick."

"It's your ass," Black Jack said with a mirthless grin. "Let's pack up and get moving. This place gives me the creeps."

Dick drove down to Baltimore, staying on Route 95. Hymie Gore sat beside him, Jack and I in back.

"These short trips are no good," Donohue grumbled. "But we've got to pick up another car and maybe some more cash in Baltimore. Once we're south of Washington, we'll make time. Hell, we could even drive straight through if we want to, taking turns at the wheel. No more motels until we hit Miami."

"I'd like that," I said. "I can do without any more motels."

"Yeah?" Donohue said, in a low voice for my ears only. "Last night I thought you were having the time of your life."

But as he spoke, he was watching the cars that whizzed by, turning to look through the back window, leaning forward to keep an eye on cars we overtook and passed.

I started talking to him about Project X, the manuscript he had been lugging along since we left my apartment in Manhattan. I told him I knew why he wanted it, and that was all right with me. What *I* wanted was to keep it up-to-date, record what was going on.

"Look, Jack," I said, "it can't do you any harm. At least if I write what really happened, they can't get you on a kidnapping charge. You can carry the manuscript under your arm, for all I care. All I want to do is add to it as we go along. I'll need a portable typewriter and some paper. Give me something to do in the motels. Or, if we decide to drive straight through, I can even use the typewriter on my lap in the car, while we're on the road."

"The typewriter is definitely out," he said. "Just more junk to lug along. Also, that's all we'd need: someone next door hearing you typing and remembering, or complaining to the desk."

So I settled for a bunch of ballpoint pens and a stack of long yellow legal pads. I'd bring Project X up-to-date in longhand. I could always rent a typewriter in Miami, or buy one, and transcribe the written record into an acceptable manuscript. Jack promised to pick up pens and paper on our next shopping trip.

I won't describe the motel we stayed in just east of Baltimore. What I can tell you—it was a motel. Drinking glasses in little paper bags, a strip of paper across the toilet seat, an oil painting of geraniums bolted to the wall, a plastic bucket for ice cubes, the smell of pine-scented disinfectant, and mattresses that had been pounded by a thousand strangers.

This time, in our little game of ring-around-the-rosy, I shared a room with Dick Fleming, while Donohue and Gore bunked together. I figured Jack wanted to get some sleep. He sure as hell didn't get much the night before. He had been a wild man.

"You think he's doing it deliberately?" I asked Dick as we undressed.

"Doing what?"

"Schlepping me around. One night with Hymie, one with him, one with you. What am I—the Sweetheart of the Regiment?"

Dick laughed. "I don't think he's doing it deliberately. What would be the point?"

"I don't know," I said, perplexed. "But that lad never does anything carelessly. He's thought these sleeping arrangements through, and it's all part of some deep, dark, devious plot."

"Oh God," Dick said, sighing. "Can't you ever forget you're a novelist?"

"No" I said, "I can't. You like him, don't you, Dick?"

"Yes, I like him. I admire him. He's very strong. A man of action. Takes what he wants. Does what he wants."

"Uh-huh," I said. "Your bed or mine?"

"It makes a difference?"

But he wasn't ready for the traditional scrabble in the hay. I tried, but he backed off. He wanted to talk. All my men wanted to talk. Except Hymie Gore, and he wanted to snore.

"I don't know what's happening to me," Fleming said. "I didn't know I could *do* these things. Taking part in a robbery, running from the cops, learning to use a gun. It's like it's all happening to someone else. Someone I don't know. I can't believe it's me. Jannie, how can you live with yourself all your life and not know yourself?"

"We all do it, kiddo," I said. "Enjoying it?"

"Am I ever! It's like being born again. A second

chance. I'm scared witless most of the time, but that can be exciting too. Like I'm on the edge, the very edge. Jack and Hyme talk so casually about killing and death. 'Should I step on him?' 'We should have killed the cocksucker.' Like that. But they're used to it. To me it's new and scary. But it's a high, a real high."

I asked the question I had wanted to ask and thought I never could. But lying naked in bed with him, with the intimacy that darkness lends, I asked it:

"Dick, did you have, uh, sex with him?"

"Yes," he said, almost casually. "And that's another thing: Where the hell did *that* come from? I mean, I've never swung that way before. Never had any desire to. Consciously or unconsciously, I swear it. But with Jack, it seemed the most natural thing in the world. How do you feel about my making it with him, Jannie?"

"Jealous."

He laughed again. "No reason to. It doesn't affect at all the way I feel about you. But it's part of my whole life turning inside out, of becoming a new person. We could get killed, couldn't we?"

"Easily," I said. "Any day. And hung up on meathooks to dry."

He shivered and moved closer to me.

"I know it," he said. "Maybe that's why I did it. The plague moves closer and everyone copulates like mad. You think that's it?"

I thought a moment.

"Part of it," I said, stroking his soft, velvety skin. "And maybe you just love him."

"Admire him."

"Love him," I insisted.

"If you say so," he said, sighing.

We moved closer, held each other tighter.

"Do *you* love him?" he asked.

"I don't know," I said. "I really don't. I'm as mixed up as you are. Why am I doing all this? The book is just an excuse now; I know that. But here I am wearing a crazy wig and running for my life. Why? Maybe, like you, I was just bored and wanted theater."

"Maybe."

"And maybe, like you, I wanted to discover just what I'm capable of. I suppose those nutty novels I wrote were a kind of sublimation. But this is the real thing. I wanted to see if I can handle it."

"You're doing great so far."

"Thanks," I said. "Can I kiss you here?"

"Yes. That's nice. I like that. My turn now . . ."

And in a few minutes we were at it again: our ritual of lickings, nippings, strokings, pinchings. Ended before it went too far. He snuggled down in my arms, huddled in my arms. He smelled so sweet, so sweet.

"You know," he said drowsily, "I would like it to go on forever."

I knew what he meant. I had the same irrational hope. I thought of what a strange person I was to myself. I searched for clues to my character and couldn't find them. I seemed to be acting from hidden motives, buried passions, I couldn't glimpse an outline of me.

Is everyone in the world like that? I mean, do we plan careers, make out budgets, plot craftily how we will live our lives, and all the time we are being turned and twisted by forces we don't recognize? I don't mean outside forces: chance and accident. There's always that, of course. But I mean powers, surges, whims deep within ourselves, drives we aren't conscious of until we find ourselves wearing a fright wig and running from retribution?

The next day, a Monday, we had a council of war

over a late lunch. The main project was obtaining new wheels. Donohue said that he and Hymie Gore would take care of that.

"How are you going to do it?" I asked, interested. "Steal a car? Jump the wires?"

"Nah," Black Jack said, offended. "We can pay cash on the line. We find a used car lot owned by Honest John, Honest Sam, Honest Abe. Now you've got to know that the biggest crooks in the world are the guys who start a conversation, 'To be perfectly honest—' or 'To be absolutely frank—' Count your rings after you shake hands with those guys. So a used car dealer who calls himself 'Honest Whatever' has got to be a gonif. He'll go for a quick cash deal, no questions asked, and if we plan to use the car to crash the White House, he couldn't care less. Hyme and me, we'll take the Ford until we get the new wheels. Jannie, you and Dick go shopping."

We borrowed a pencil from the waitress and wrote out our list on a paper napkin. My ballpoint pens and yellow legal pads came first. Then the men wanted shorts, underwear, socks. I marked down the sizes carefully. I wanted a new bra, at least one, and some pantyhose. We all needed cigarettes and more whiskey.

"And a plastic picnic chest," Donohue reminded me. "Big enough for a couple of six-packs. Also some nibbles for the road: crackers, pretzels, potato chips, candy bars, gum—like that."

"A bottle of white wine would be nice," I said.

"Why not?" Jack said. "And some plastic tumblers. Don't forget a bottle of gin and a small dry vermouth. Buy the best. I like a martini now and then."

"Olive or lemon?" I asked.

"Lemon," he replied, absolutely serious. "And a small paring knife to take off the peel."

We returned to the motel, packed up, checked out. Donohue drove Dick and me to a shopping center on Moravia Road. As I got out of the car, he leaned close and whispered, "Have a good time last night?"

"Better than I had the night before."

"You bitch!" he said, laughing.

Then they drove away in the Ford, and Dick and I started our shopping spree. It took us almost three hours, and when we had finished, we could have used a strong packhorse. We lugged all our purchases out to the parking lot and settled down to wait.

After about fifteen minutes I said, "You and I decided not to take off. But maybe they have."

"No way," Fleming said definitely. "Jack said he'll be back, he'll be back."

"You're a trusting soul."

"He needs to be trusted."

"Oh?" I said, looking at him. "You found that out, too, did you?"

"Sure," Dick said, nodding. "And if you need proof, here they are now."

They pulled up in a three-year-old black Buick Riviera, Hymie Gore sitting proudly behind the wheel. There were a few nicks and scratches on the side panels, and the right front fender looked like it had been crumpled, straightened, and repainted. But generally the car appeared to be in good condition.

"The hell with the appearance," Donohue said, helping load up. "We don't want a brand-new car that might attract attention. No one will look at this heap twice, but it's got it where it counts: under the hood. I mean, it's a big, *big* engine, with all the power we'll need. We took it for a test drive and it takes off like a goosed jackrabbit."

"Any trouble buying it?" I asked.

"Nah," Hymie Gore said, laughing. "It was like

Jack said. The guy's name was 'Honest Percy.' Jack offered him five hundred less than the marked price, in cash. He couldn't make out the papers fast enough."

"Use your real name?" Fleming asked.

"Yeah," Donohue said sourly. He wasn't happy about it. "I had to show my license. But I asked Percy a lot of questions about the best route to Pittsburgh. If anyone tails us this far, maybe that'll send them on a phony chase. For a while anyway."

We pulled away from the shopping center, headed back to Interstate Highway 95, and turned south. Hymie Gore was driving, Fleming beside him.

"Where did you dump the Ford?" I asked Donohue.

"You're the expert in crime," he said. "Wrote all those great novels. If you had to get rid of a car and didn't want it found and identified, how would you do it?"

"I don't know," I said slowly, thinking about it. "Drive it out to some deserted place in the country, I guess. Heavy woods would be best. Drive it off the road into the underbrush. Try to cover it over with branches. Take the license plates and throw them in the river. Either that or push the whole damned car in the river if you could do it without being seen."

"Too fancy," Black Jack said. "Too chancy, and too much work. What we did was this: I drove the Ford, and Hyme followed me in the Buick. I found the worst neighborhood I could. A real tenement slum down near the river. Talk about Bed-Sty; that place was just as bad, or worse. So I parked the Ford and got out. Left the doors unlocked and just walked away. I got in with Hyme and we took off. I guarantee you that by tomorrow morning that Ford'll be stripped down to the bare bones. They'll take the wheels first, then the battery, carburetor, distributor, fuel pump—anything that can be unscrewed, unbolted, or whacked off. The gang kids will take the seats for their clubhouse and the parts pirates will take everything that's left. In twenty-four hours nothing will be left but a burned-out frame. And that's how to get rid of a car, Jannie. The modern way."

We stayed on 95, and went around Washington, D.C., without stopping. All I saw of the nation's capital was a rosy glow in the sky. We had dinner at Fredericksburg, at a restaurant designed to look like the white, pillared mansion of a southern plantation. They even had plastic Spanish moss hanging from the trees outside. They featured "Southern Fried Chicken," which also might have been plastic.

Back in the car, we switched places. I drove, with Dick beside me, and Donohue and Gore in the back seat. At our last gas stop we had bought a bag of ice cubes and loaded our picnic chest. Now, as we headed south for Richmond, the weather definitely improving, Jack broke out the booze and the tumblers and served as bartender. I had white wine as I drove, Fleming and Gore had scotch on the rocks, and Donohue built himself a martini, complete with a paring of lemon peel.

I drove to Richmond, where we paused long enough to stretch our legs and switch positions again. Donohue and Gore moved to the front seat, Jack driving, and Fleming and I tried to get comfortable among all the gear in the back seat. I wanted to write on the yellow legal pads, bringing Project X up to date, but the light was so bad I gave up.

We continued our flight south, Donohue trying to put on the miles. He said we'd hole up for some sleep at Rocky Mount, N.C., or maybe drive straight through if traffic was light. Dick and I dozed off. I remember hearing Jack and Hymie talking in low voices, and the next thing I knew, the car was slowing. Jack was cutting to the right lane to make a turnoff.

"Where are we?" I asked.

"Rocky Mount," Jack said. "Hyme and me have got to pee."

"Me, too," I said.

"Me, too," Dick Fleming said, rousing, yawning, stretching.

"There's a place, Jack," Hymie Gore said after we were off the highway. He pointed to a sign on our right.

It was in the shape of a rooster, outlined in red neon, with the name spelled out below in blue tubing: "The Game Cock." It looked like a roadhouse, with beer signs in the windows. We pulled into a graveled parking lot. There were a half-dozen cars, a pickup truck, a van, two motorcycles, and an enormous tractor-trailer. We heard a juke blaring country-western.

"A real fun place," I said. "I can tell."

"As long as they got a can," Donohue said, "Who cares? Everyone heeled? Okay, let's lock up and see what the Game Cock's got to offer."

What it had to offer was a squarish room with bare wood floors, scarred and pitted. There was a stained bar along one wall. No stools; strictly for stand-up drinkers. There were tables and booths, and an empty space that apparently served as a dance floor, maybe on weekends.

When I tell you that the most attractive objects in the Game Cock were the juke box and cigarette machine, you'll get some idea of its glories. Ugly seediness? You wouldn't believe. The dim lighting did nothing to hide ramshackle furnishings and a general appearance of spit-on-the floor slovenliness. There was a fly-spotted sign on the wall listing the prices of hamburgers, ribs, chili, ham and cheese sandwiches, apple pie, coffee. The small kitchen was located in the rear. I had smelled it the moment I walked in: a rancid grease odor competing with the stench of stale beer and an eye-smarting disinfectant.

There were five men drinking at the bar, and about twenty men and women at the tables and booths. All the men had a rough, red-faced, outdoorsy look: farmers, construction workers, telephone linesmen—like that. The women looked like—well, to tell you the truth, all the women looked like me, Bea Flanders: blond or red wigs, tight sweaters, hooker's heels, and enough makeup to drive a covey of clowns mad with envy.

Conversation died down when the four of us entered, and heads turned. We got blank, faintly hostile stares, reserved for interlopers who lived more than ten miles away from the Game Cock. But, after we slid into a booth, the regulars went back to their dirty jokes, arm wrestling, and loud arguments competing with the thunder of the juke.

The lone waitress came over to take our order. She looked to be about fifteen years old, but obviously had to be older to be working in a joint like that. She was wearing low-slung, hip-hugger jeans. Her midriff was bare (I should have such a slender waist!), and a puckered bandeau kept her pointy breasts from stabbing a customer in the eye when she bent over a table. She had a great mass of brassy hair swinging halfway to her waist.

She took our order and went sashaying back to the bar. We all watched the swing on that hard, tight ass. A good three-inch displacement there, side to side.

"I bet she does all right on tips," Donohue said. "You like that, Hyme?"

"Well . . . yeah, sure, Jack. You want I should ask her if she'd like a lift to Miami?"

"Oh no," Donohue said hastily, "don't do that. We just don't have the room."

"Whatever you say, Jack," Gore agreed amiably. "But I'm getting—you know. Like lonesome."

"Sure, Hyme, I understand. Hang in there, old buddy. Another day or two and we'll be in the land of the string bikini, and you won't be lonesome anymore. Okay?"

When the hip-twitcher returned with the drinks, Jack asked her where the restrooms were. She said they were in back of the kitchen. Actually she said, "Threw duh kitch'."

"Me first," Donohue said. "I want to check the place out." He slid out of the booth. I watched him walk to the back of the room, and noticed a few of the other women were doing the same thing.

He was back in a few minutes.

"No men's room or women's room," he reported. "Just one closet marked Toilet. Beautiful. Hold your nose. And that goes for the kitchen, too."

He wasn't kidding. How the local health inspectors had missed that dive I'll never know. That toilet was the pits, the absolute pits. There was a sign tacked over the sink that virtuously stated: "All employees must wash their hands before leaving this lavoratory." Very nice. But no hot water, of course, and no soap. The roller towel looked like it had been used to wipe down a coal truck.

There was a back door leading outside, and a little hallway between toilet and kitchen. Two telephone booths in that hall, and a swell vending machine that sold breath-freshening mints, squirts of perfume, combs, pre-moistened tissues, and condoms. The only thing not offered patrons of the Game Cock was a quick cure for leprosy.

And that kitchen! A cesspool. The smell was enough to put you on a starvation diet. The grill was crusted with grease, and grease had coated the walls, hung in the air, and shone on the pimply face and bare arms of the gangly cook. When I walked through, he was poking at a pot of chili, tasting it from a long-handled wooden spoon. Then he used the same spoon to stir the pot.

We took turns using the john and then had one more round of drinks. After a while the waitress swayed over to ask if we wanted anything to eat.

"Yeah," Donohue said, "but not here. Just the check, please."

He paid, left a generous tip, and we moved to the door. Hymie Gore went first, exited, then held the door open for the rest of us. We came out into the night. I looked up: a clear sky, a million sharp stars. After the Game Cock, the air tasted polished and pure.

But Hymie Gore wasn't looking at the stars.

"Jack," he said in a low, hard voice. "On the right."

We all looked. A black car parked head-on. Two men standing close to it, one on each side, hands deep in topcoat pockets. As we stared, powerful headlights came on. We blinked in the glare.

Almost at the same time we were hit by bright lights from the left. Another car, facing the door of the Game Cock. I shielded my eyes. I could make out, dimly, three men standing in gloom. One in particular . . .

"Inside," Jack Donohue said, his voice unsteady. "Everyone inside. Don't panic. Don't run."

We turned, went back into the Game Cock. Black Jack led the way to the end of the bar. We huddled.

"Back again?" the bartender asked, wiping the bar in front of us with a grimy rag.

"One for the road," Donohue said with a ghastly grin. "Four double-Seagram's, water on the side."

"You got it," the bartender said.

"Jack," I said in a low voice, "who are—"

"Shut your yap," he shot back viciously.

"The back door?" Dick suggested.

Donohue showed his teeth.

"You think they won't have it covered?" he sneered. "Those guys are professionals. Don't believe it? Just step outside back there. Bye-bye."

The bartender brought our drinks. Jack paid with a ten, pushed the change back for a tip. No one spoke until the bartender moved away. Then Donohue turned, faced the crowded room. He rested his elbows on the bar. He surveyed the customers.

"They haven't got anyone inside," he said, his lips hardly moving. "I'll bet on it. And they won't come in blasting. They'll wait for us to come out."

"Our car!" I burst out desperately. "They must know our car. Why don't they just break in and take the rocks?"

"You think that's all they want?" Jack said scornfully. "Get smart, kiddo; they want *us*."

"Uh, listen, Jack," Hymie Gore said slowly. "It could be the Feds."

"No way, Hyme," Donohue said. "They'd have searchlights, bullhorns, tear gas, guys in iron vests. No, this is a Corporation gig. How in *Christ's* name did they get onto the Buick?"

"Honest Percy?" Dick asked, with no irony.

"Could be," Jack said. "Or maybe someone made the plates of the Ford when we dumped it. Hell, maybe we've had a tail since that last motel in Baltimore. No use worrying it. Right now we've got to figure out how to blow this joint."

"Jack," Hymie Gore said, blinking slowly, "I could go out the back door. Blasting—you know? Lots of noise. Lots of fireworks. Bring them all around to the back. Then you and the kids—"

Donohue put a soft hand on the big man's arm. "Thanks, Hyme, but it wouldn't work. They'd cut you down in a minute—and for what? They'll keep the front door covered. Drink your drinks, everyone. Smile and talk. Act like everything's just fine."

We tried, we really tried. Stretched our mouths, gabbled to each other, sipped our whiskey. I risked a quick look out the front windows. Darkness out there; those powerful headlights had been doused.

"Hey, Hyme," Donohue said slowly. "Before, when you were talking about going out the back door blasting, you said lots of noise, lots of fireworks. Isn't that what you said?"

"Well . . . yeah, sure, Jack. You want I should try?"

"No, no," Black Jack said. "I was just thinking about what you said. Okay, now here's what we're going to do . . . Jannie, you got change with you? Dimes and quarters?"

I nodded.

"Good," he said. "You and me are going to walk to the back, slowly, easily, not a care in the world. Through the kitchen. To the phone booths in that smelly hallway. You're going to call the fire department. Make it hysterical. The Game Cock is burning down. People trapped. The grease in the kitchen caught fire, and everyone's frying. Get the picture? Tears, howls, screams, sobs—the whole bit."

"I can do it, Jack."

"I know you can. It's a chance. The only one we've got. I'll use the other phone at the same time. A call to the cops. Robbery in the progress. Three bad guys are holding up the joint. Send in the Marines. If it works, in about five or ten minutes this place will look like Times Square on New Year's Eve. Hyme, you and Dick stay right here, drinking and talking. Don't make a move. We've just gone to pee, that's all. Come on, babe; let's get the show on the road."

I did just what he said. I sauntered ahead of him toward the back of the room, smiling and talking to him over my shoulder. Through that grotty kitchen. Into the hallway. I stepped into the old-fashioned wooden telephone booth.

That's when I saw the sign: "Out of Order."

I must have gone white and begun to sway, because Jack stepped close and grabbed my shoulders.

"You cave on me now," he spat out, "and I'll slit your fucking throat, I swear to God."

Still holding me, he peered into the other booth. No sign there. He thrust me into the booth.

"Make the goddamned call," he said furiously. "If they ask your name, just keep sobbing and yelling."

He squeezed into the booth with me and pulled the door shut. It wasn't I guessed, the first time a man and a woman (that nubile waitress?) had been together in that phone booth in the back of the Game Cock.

I got the coin into the slot with slippery fingers. I dialed Operator. It rang three times, then:

"How may I be of service?" a languid voice inquired.

"Fire Department!" I yelled. "Emergency! Oh my God! The fire department. Quick!"

"Just a moment, please," she sang pleasantly, "and I will connect you with your party."

A clicking, and then a man's voice came on, heavy and rasping.

"This is—" he started.

"Fire!" I screamed, my mouth close to the handset. "It's terrible! *Fire! Fire!* People are burning up! We're trapped! The whole place is—"

"Where?" he barked. "Where are you calling from?"

"The Game Cock!" I yelled. "The tavern. Near Route 95. Hurry! Oh God, please hurry! The whole place is on fire! People are burning, and—"

"What's your name?" he shouted.

"Please hurry," I begged piteously, getting into the role. "The flames are snapping, and—"

Donohue's hand clamped down on the hanger, disconnecting.

"Beautiful," he said with a thin grin. "I never realized what a ham you are. Now get out and give me a chance."

He wrestled the folding door open, stepped out into the hallway. I got out of the booth. Then Jack reentered. He fished in the coin box, picked out the coin I had used, returned by the operator. You've got to admire a man who thinks of that at a time like that.

I leaned into the booth, listened to his call. He had the operator put him through to the local police department. He put his mouth close to the phone.

"Listen," he said in an urgent whisper. "I can't talk any louder; they might hear me. Three guys holding up the Game Cock roadhouse. You know where it is? Good. They're doing it right now, got everyone lined up against the bar. Yeah, that's right: three guys. Listen, be careful; they've got these guns. Yeah, right now it's going down. The Game Cock. For God's sake, get here as soon as you can. Yeah. My name is—"

He hung up suddenly. He didn't forget to reclaim the dime. He didn't give it back to me.

"How'd I do?" he asked, grinning.

"I think I gave the better performance," I said loftily.

"Keep your fingers crossed, kiddo," he said, and took me by the elbow.

We walked steadily through the kitchen, across the main room.

"Sorry I got shaky," I said.

"You did fine," he assured me. "Just fine."

We rejoined Dick and Hymie. We picked up our drinks, took deep gulps.

"How'd it go?" Fleming asked in a low voice.

"Okay," Donohue said tersely. "It went okay. With luck we may get out of this. Now here's what we do: The moment we hear the sirens, finish your drinks. We stand around talking for a minute or so. Very relaxed. Very casual. Near the windows. We don't make our move until the fire engines and squads pull into the parking lot. Whichever comes first. The moment they stop, and cops or firemen start toward the place, *then* we go out. We stroll while we're inside. Once we're out, and it looks good, we make tracks for the car. Hyme, you drive. Go for Route 95. Turn south, and pour it on."

"They'll follow," Fleming fretted. "North or south on the highway—what's the difference? Why don't we try the back-roads?"

"Because we don't *know* the backroads, dummy," Donohue said stonily. "We're liable to drive into a dead-end, and then we're up Shit Creek. Pour on the juice, Hyme. If we get enough of a start, we can shake 'em."

"I'll shake 'em, Jack," Hymie Gore said, nodding vigorously. "Put your money on it."

I've got to hand it to the local public service departments. Less than five minutes after Jack and I made our calls, we heard the distant wail of sirens. We finished our drinks. Chatting and laughing, we moved toward the front windows. The sirens were louder now, and we could distinguish the distinctive hoot of buffalo whistles.

"Fire engines," Donohue said quietly. "They're beating the cops."

The sirens were screaming now, close by. Several customers rose to their feet, looked toward the windows. A few started moving to the door.

Then the ear-piercing wail seemed right in the room with us, and that weird, warbling whistle. A red light flashed through the windows as the engines came swinging into the parking lot, spraying gravel.

We went out the door, other customers crowding after us. There were three trucks—pumper, hose cart, a short hook-and-ladder. The firemen started dropping off even before the trucks came to a complete halt. A chief's car, red rooftop light revolving, turned into the parking lot.

Firemen trotted toward us, carrying axes, extinguishers, hook-poles. The sirens were suddenly loud again as two police cars came careening in from the road.

Now all the customers from the Game Cock were spilling out into the parking lot. Firemen and cops tried to push their way through, shouting and cursing.

Donohue looked quickly to right and left.

"Now!" he said urgently.

Hymie Gore led the way, bulling his way through the jostling mob. The big man used his hands, pushing and shoving, and his heavy shoulders. We ducked behind him, rushed along in his wake. Jack Donohue's hand was on my back, hurtling me forward.

We made the car, unlocked, scrambled inside. Hyme got the engine started, pulled away before the doors were closed. He rammed the Buick toward the road, narrowly missed the rear of a fire truck, cut across the path of a third police car just entering the lot, swerved down into a shallow culvert, came up the other side, bounced across a bumpy verge, got onto the pavement, put the car into a tight spin with a squeal of tires, headed toward the entrance to Route 95, accelerating, whipping the Buick around turns, his broad back hunched over the wheel, trees flickering by, a blare of horns from startled motorists as we cut them off, sliced around them, their brakes squealing, our car roaring as we went sailing up the ramp, knifed into southbound traffic, angled across to the lefthand lane, went flying down to Miami, Gore staring ahead, the rest of us craning back and seeing no signs of pursuit.

"We made it!" Jack Donohue yelled, with something between a sob and a cry of exaltation. "Made it, made it, made it!"

A Heavy Loss

~~~~~~~~~~~~~~~~~~~~~~~~~~~~~~~~~~~~~~~

Our euphoria lasted all of five minutes, with loud talk, jokes, hysterical laughter. Then we fell silent. I saw my hands trembling uncontrollably.

"Jack," I said in a small voice, "I'm cold and scared. Can I have a drink, please?"

He was in the back seat with me. He rooted around in the mess, found the bottle of brandy. He poured heavy shots in plastic tumblers, handed them across the front seat to Gore and Fleming. Then he served me. Finally he took his own. We all gulped greedily. No one proposed a toast.

"Slow down, Hyme," Jack said. "Not more than sixty. We can't afford to be stopped."

We had been doing seventy, seventy-five, in that range. Gore slowed, edged the Buick over into the middle lane. It was after 1:00 A.M., but traffic was heavy.

"My God," I said, laughing nervously, "Is *everyone* going to Miami?"

No one answered. We drove on through the night in silence. I was afraid of sleeping.

"It's just a guess," Donohue said musingly, "but I'll

bet it was that scummy bartender at the Game Cock who made us. Anyone see him go to the back, to the phone, while we were in the booth?"

No one had.

"Maybe he did and we just didn't notice."

"Jack," Dick Fleming said, "how could he make us? He didn't see the car!"

Donohue came alive, began to snap his fingers.

"Right!" he said. "He didn't see the car, but he saw *us*. This is how I figure the Corporation worked it: They put out the word up and down the highway —in restaurants, bars, taverns, motels, roadhouses, and so forth. Their local men took care of this. So a mob guy comes into the Game Cock, braces the bartender, and hands him a tenner. 'This is for your trouble' he says. 'Now what we're looking for is four people traveling together, three men and a woman.' Then he gives the bartender our descriptions, which the Corporation cut out of Angela and the Holy Ghost. 'You spot these people,' the local guy says, 'you call this number. If you're right, there's a C-note in it for you.' I'll bet my bottom buck that's how it happened."

I sighed. "In other words, you're gambling the bartender didn't see the car, and that's why there were no Corporation guys guarding the Buick when we made our break. Because they don't know what we're driving."

"Surely they saw us driving away," Fleming said.

"Maybe, maybe not," Donohue said. "That was one fucked-up scene, with the fire engines, cop cars, people running around, cars starting up and taking off in all directions. I'm betting they didn't make us in the darkness. This car is safe."

I sighed again. "Why do you gamble, Jack?"

He whirled on me.

"Why do you write?" he demanded. "I read your book. You called it an obsession, a kind of masturbation."

"You never forget anything, do you? All right, you win."

"Damned right. And we have been winning, haven't we? I tell you I'm on a high streak. When you're hot, you give it all you've got. I've been twisting my brain, trying to figure how to get new wheels. But we don't need them; Honest Percy didn't rat on us, no one saw us dump the Ford and no one's been tailing us. I tell you, this car is safe."

We didn't disagree with him. Perhaps because no one had any better ideas. It was a relief to put our destinies in his hands, let him make the decisions: where to go, when to go, when to stop, how to act.

"Hyme," Jack Donohue said, "we'll make a detour. Take the next turnoff. We'll go over to Raleigh, hole up and get some sleep. Tomorrow we can come east again and get back on the highway at Smithfield."

"Yes, Jack," Hymie Gore said obediently.

We took the turnoff at Wilson and drove west on Federal Highway 264. Got to the outskirts of Raleigh about 2:30. Found a place to sleep. My premonition had been accurate: This flight was going to be an endless succession of sleazy motels. This one thoughtfully provided a can of bug spray in every room. I bunked with Donohue. If he made any carnal noises, I was prepared to use the spray on him. But he was asleep before I was.

We all slept till noon, then went out for a steak-and-eggs breakfast. One of the things I enjoy when you get south of the Mason-Dixon Line is that, in the better restaurants, waiters come over to your table, say, "Good morning," and pour you a cup of hot black coffee. I mean, they don't even *ask;* they *know.* And they're right.

So, with stomachs full, the sun shining in a bland sky, things didn't look so bad. Jack said we should do a little peddling in Raleigh so the day wouldn't be a total loss. We went back to the motel and pawed through the contents of the gem cases. There wasn't much small stuff left. Most of what we had were big pieces: chokers, necklaces, bracelets, tiaras—all heavily encrusted items that could never be pawned or sold in a local mom-and-pop jewelry shop.

Jack picked through the stuff and selected the remaining small pieces: a few simple rings, some watches, brooches, cufflinks.

"I'll see what I can do with these," he said. "I'll take the car. The three of you sit tight. Don't go out. Watch TV. Have a few drinks. I should be back by five at the latest. If I'm not, you'll know I've been nicked. Then just take off and do the best you can."

"Jack . . ." I said hesitantly.

"Yeah?"

"Something I haven't told you. I'm not sure about it, so I decided not to say anything. But maybe I should."

"*What,* for God's sake?"

"Remember when we came out of the Game Cock the first time? The lights of the car on the right went on. Two guys standing there. A few seconds later the car on the left flashed its headlights. I shielded my eyes. I saw three guys standing near it. I might have been imagining it, but I thought I recognized one of the men. Short, heavyset, wearing a bowler. He had on an overcoat, which means he came from up north. I couldn't see his features, but I thought maybe it was him."

He caught on immediately.

"Noel Jarvis?" he asked. "The manager?"

"Rossi," I said. "Antonio Rossi."

"Yeah, Rossi. You sure?"

"No, I'm not sure. It was just a quick glimpse. It was dark out there. I was staring into the lights. But that's the feeling I got."

He thought about that a moment, biting his upper lip.

"Yeah," he said finally, "it's possible. But it surprises me. I mean, they're giving him a chance—probably a last chance—to run us down and waste us. He's lucky."

"Lucky?"

"Because they didn't burn him right away. He goofed. They know it. They know he dated you. They figure he was careless, he talked."

"How could they know he dated me?"

"Oh, Jannie"—he sighed—"use your noodle. By this time your photograph has been circulated. So you went to that West Side restaurant with him, didn't you? It's in your book. So hard guys over there saw you with him. That's why I say he's lucky. They could have figured he was in on it and squashed him without asking questions. But the Corporation's giving him a chance to find us."

"And the stones," I said.

"Fuck the stones!" Donohue said savagely. "You really think the Corporation wants that hot ice? Sure they do, but not as much as they want to fry our asses. We can't be allowed to get away with that heist. Bad public relations. That's why Rossi is on our tail. He'll never give up, because it's his cock if he fails. Lock the door after I'm gone."

We did as he said. Had a few drinks, watched a stupid game show on TV. Then Dick and Hymie dozed off and I got busy on Project X, writing on those yellow legal pads with a ballpoint pen, writing as fast as I could. I took up where I had left off a hundred years ago and tried to catch up. But I had only finished the account of the actual robbery when it was 4:00 and time to put the manuscript aside. I took a shower and dressed, then roused the men. They got up, grumbling, stuffed their gear in suitcases. We settled down to wait for Jack.

He had said that if he didn't return by 5:00, we should take off and do the best we could. I considered what the "best" would be. I had no idea. I literally had no idea. It was the first time in my life that my fate depended on someone else. I said that was comfortable, and it was. But when I tried to imagine what would happen if the sovereign died or disappeared, panic set in.

But he came back, before the deadline of 5:00 P.M. He came into the room quickly, carrying a package. He was trying to smile. His pale forehead was sheened with sweat.

"All set?" he said. "Good. Let's get going. Right now. Let's hit the road."

We all looked at him.

"Jack," Dick Fleming said, "what is it? Something's happened. I can tell. What happened?"

He slumped suddenly into an armchair. He thrust out his long legs.

"I saw him," he groaned. "I *saw* the bastard. Jannie, you were right."

"Rossi?"

"Yeah. Coming out of a hotel. Thank God I saw him before they spotted me."

"They?" I asked.

"Him and two other guys. Heavies."

"You think they was like, you know, bodyguards, Jack?" Hymie Gore asked.

"Sort of, Hyme," Donohue said, smiling wanly. He was beginning to lose his pallor. "I figure the Corporation is keeping him on a tight leash. They're giving him a chance to make good, but they'd hate to see him run. So they assigned two guided missiles to keep him company."

"What's he doing in Raleigh?" I said sharply. "How did he follow us here if no one tailed us?"

"Just an accident," Jack said. "They're covering every city of any size up and down the coast. Him being here when we are is just a coincidence. I'll bet on it."

No one said a thing.

We got back on Route 95 at Smithfield and turned south. Donohue was driving, Dick beside him. Hymie and I stretched out in the back seat. No joking, no talking. It wasn't the happiest of times. I kept turning to look back, expecting any minute to see a long black car coming up behind us, and at the wheel, a chunky figure wearing a bowler, velvet-collared Chesterfield, pinstriped suit, polka-dot bowtie. Eyes cold, thin lips tight. One desire: to murder the woman who had made a fool of him.

That evening we drove through Fayetteville to Lumberton. Southbound holiday traffic was heavy; it took us more than three hours. We got off the highway at Fairmont, had a quick dinner, and started off again, Dick Fleming driving. Donohue was next to him, bending over a map, trying to read it in the dashlight.

We had hardly exchanged a dozen words since leaving Raleigh. I couldn't stand it.

"How did you make out in Raleigh, Jack?" I asked casually. "The rocks?"

He folded the map, put it away in the glove compartment. He half-turned to face me. He seemed pleased that we had decided to talk to him again.

"Not bad," he said. "Another couple of grand."

"What did you buy? In the package?"

"When we get to Miami, we might need some heavy green. For grease—you know? Buy some new IDs for us. Charter a plane. All that. So we're running low on the small ice, the stuff that's easy to peddle and hock. I figure that after buying the Buick and then picking up a couple of G's in Raleigh, we've all got about fourteen-fifteen thou between us. Not enough. So I bought some tools. To cut up the heavy ice if we have to. Now what I got in there is wire clippers, awls, long-nosed pliers, a loupe, a dissolvent they use to loosen the cement when the stone is glued to the setting, a small ball-peen hammer, a few other things. All this stuff is used to break up jewelry. If things get tight, we'll pry out the stones and I'll pick up a little electric kiln so we can melt down the settings. The price of gold's way up these days. Then we'll peddle the individual rocks. No way, *no* way, anyone can identify those. And a hunk of gold is just a hunk of gold."

I looked at him with admiration.

"Jack," I said, "is there anything illegal you haven't done?"

"Not much," he said.

Perhaps it was about then that, for me, our flight began to take on a dreamlike quality. I was aware that we were then in South Carolina. It meant nothing. The highway kept spinning away beneath our wheels. It seemed stretched forever. If someone had said that this ribbon of concrete wound the world, I would accept that. Next stop: Hong Kong. That made as much sense as what we were doing, devouring miles, watching idly as the night fled by: neon signs glimmering in the distance, the faint glow of far-off towns, brilliant headlights of cars passing on the other side, and the occasional roar as a tractor-trailer went grinding by. Some nut in a sports car darting in and out of traffic. Vans. Pickups. Wheezing heaps striving to make the promised land.

I saw it all, and I didn't see anything. I mean, I was *aware* of what was happening, but I was divorced from it. I said, prior to the actual robbery of Brandenberg & Sons, that I was both observer and participant. Now it seemed to me that my role had dwindled to observer only. I had that removed coldness.

Dick driving, we flew south. I remember noting a sign that read "The Great Pee Dee River," and I thought that was mildly amusing. We went around Florence, Manning, Summerton, across Lake Marion.

"How much in the tank?" Donohue asked.

"About a quarter," Dick Fleming said.

"Let's get off," Jack said, sighing. "I thought we'd try to make Savannah, but the hell with it. Any turnoff that looks good to you, Dick. You pick it. We'll get some sleep. I'm beat. Are you beat, Jannie?"

"Beat," I said, nodding. "Jack, can we find a nice place? Something decent—without bug spray in the room? And if we do, can we stay for a day or two? Just rest up? I can't see where it would do any harm. And it might do some good. If they're figuring our travel time, it could throw them off if we take a couple of extra days."

"Right," he said promptly. "We'll do it. We'll relax. Put our act together. Okay with you, Hyme?"

But Hymie Gore was asleep, breathing heavily. His big head was on my shoulder. I endured it. As a matter of fact I welcomed it, and tried to make the Incredible Hulk comfortable. He was really a very sweet man. Another lesson for me: You can be stupid *and* sweet.

We turned off toward a town called Coosawhatchie. "Why here?" Donohue asked.

"I like the name," Fleming said. Jack laughed and let him go.

It didn't turn out all that funny. We drove around for a half-hour, found no motels displaying a Vacancy sign. We got back on the highway, went south to Ridgeland. The same story: No room at the inn. Back on the highway again, and south to Hardeeville, just before the Georgia border.

I have a vague recollection of stopping before a motor lodge that could only be called "imposing" compared to the fleabags we had been frequenting. At least this place had a generous lobby, an elevator, and "All Modern Advantages," just as advertised on the sign outside. These included small refrigerators in every room, central air conditioning and, if desired, water beds. We didn't desire.

We checked in and lugged all our luggage up to our fourth-floor rooms. I was sharing with Jack Donohue that night. After we were settled in, he disappeared for about twenty minutes. By the time he returned, I had finished a hot shower, was dried, dusted, sprayed with foo-foo. I was lying in my bed, spreadeagled beneath a single sheet. I felt like a lump. That's the only way I can describe it: I was a lump.

I heard him, dimly, lock and chain the door. Heard him undress, curse softly as he stubbed his toe. Heard him shower. Saw through half-closed eyes the light from the bathroom as he shaved. I wasn't sleeping, exactly, and I wasn't awake, exactly. Suspended animation—that was me. I wasn't even sure I was breathing. And my brain was mush. I couldn't think, let alone concentrate. A thought would pop up and then just go drifting away before I could grab it.

That's the way I was that night—drifting.

Jack Donohue came into bed with me and I didn't object. He did things to me. I responded, but it was all on a physical level, reactions I couldn't resist. Didn't have the will to resist, or the strength. And all the time my body was leaping, heaving, twisting and thumping, my lumpish mind was going "Uhhhhh." Nothing.

By the time I awoke, Jack was back in his own bed and I was back in my own head. He was still sleeping when I showered, wigged, dressed, and went next door to knock on the door of the room shared by Dick and Hyme. No answer. But I found them in the coffee shop downstairs and slid into their booth.

I ordered what they were eating: scrambled eggs, pork sausages, and grits. Don't knock it if you haven't tried it.

Jack joined us as we were working on our third coffees, and by the time we all wandered outside, things were looking good again. I realized that was a pattern we were running: We were on a goddamned roller coaster, up and down. Right then we were on the rise.

That was quite a layout. It was a *big* shopping center, just off the junction of three roads. An enormous parking lot and a semicircle of department stores, shops, boutiques, a movie theater, a restaurant. Almost a little city. We were in a modern motel at one end of the curve.

It looked to me like the center had started off small, with maybe one or two buildings, and then had just grown, with more structures added over a period of years. Because it wasn't one continuous design; there was space between buildings. And no two buildings seemed designed by the same architect or even by friendly architects; the place was a hodge-podge of crazy façades, Disneylike silhouettes, and clashing signs.

The whole thing was called Wonderland Shopping Center. Good name. It made you wonder.

"Great," Dick Fleming said. "We can live the rest of our lives right here. Supermarket, liquor store, restaurant and bar, post office, laundry, bakery, men's and women's clothing, gas station. Who could ask for anything more?"

That was just about right. The four of us spent a fine, relaxing time there. The weather couldn't have been better: up in the high 70s and sunny during the day, down in the low 60s at night. We went to the movies, ate well at the restaurant and motel coffee shop, wandered the stores and bought a few things, sat around drinking and talking about the robbery and how well it had been planned and executed. No one spoke of the future.

Jack Donohue selected a diamond necklace from the loot and showed us how it could be broken up, using his new kit of tools. The stones were gently pried loose from their settings, using a solvent when necessary, and then the chain in which they had been mounted was cut up into inch-long pieces.

It sounds simple, but it took a long time, Jack working slowly and carefully. Most of the stones were held by claws, each of which had to be gently bent away, and the stone pried out. Small decorative diamond chips he left in their settings, but cut into sections. When he finished, we had a dozen gemstones of various sizes, pieces of chips and pavé, and hunks of gold chain.

"Not worth as much as the original piece," Jack acknowledged, "but a hell of a lot safer to sell.

Nothing can be identified. When you peddle loose rocks, the scam is that you've been buying cut diamonds for investment and want to sell a few for ready cash. No questions asked—believe me."

The only downer during those two restful days was when Donohue picked up a Savannah paper and brought it to the room to show us. There was a small item datelined New York about the discovery of a corpse in the closet of an East Side Manhattan apartment. Dick Fleming's apartment. But the newspaper story didn't mention Dick's name. It said only that police were attempting to locate the tenant.

"Now they have your name, description and probably your photograph," Jack said, looking at Fleming.

"So?" Dick said.

By late afternoon of the second day, fed, rested, rejuvenated, we all knew it was time to move on. I had discovered what Black Jack had been up to when he disappeared after we checked in. He had scouted all the entrances and exits from the motor lodge, and the best getaway routes. He had also decided that as a precautionary measure it would be smart not to park the Buick right outside the motel, but to leave it in the big, general parking lot of the adjacent shopping center.

"The car's safe," he told us. "I'll bet on that. But why go looking for trouble? So we park it in that big lot. Plenty of cars there. And if they do tag us, they don't know where we are—in the motel, shopping, watching a movie, whatever. Am I right?"

We told him he was right. I think that at that time he needed reassurance. Or, as Dick and I had decided, he needed to be trusted.

Anyway, we all had a good dinner at the nearby restaurant, then returned to our rooms, started packing. No hurry. We tried to consolidate the gems, and were able to get them into two suitcases and a canvas carryall. Our clothing and toilet articles went into three more suitcases and two shoulder bags.

It was then about 9:00 P.M.

"Okay," Donohue said cheerily. "Time to hit the road. I'll go down first and check out. Then I'll bring the car around to the front. Give me about ten minutes. Then you start bringing the stuff down. We'll load up and be on our way."

It sounded good.

But he was back in two minutes.

"Trouble," he said tersely. "Son of a bitch!"

"Jack, what is it?" I asked him.

"I saw your lover," he said, showing his teeth. "Him and his heavies. Talking to the guy at the desk."

"How did he find us here?" I wailed.

"Who knows?" he said. And for the first time his face showed despair. "That bastard won't give up until we're all dead."

We all caught his mood and looked at one another with angry frustration.

"They coming up, Jack?" Hymie Gore asked.

"I don't think they'll do that, Hyme. They don't want a shootout inside the motel any more than we do. They'll probably stake out the place, cover all the doors, and pot us as we come out. But there's an easy way to check . . ."

He picked up the phone and called the desk.

"This is Sam Morrison in Room 410," he said briskly. "Have any friends been asking for me? Uh-huh. That's fine. And are they waiting in the lobby? Oh . . . good. Well, I'll be down soon. Thank you very much."

"Like I figured," he reported. "The cocksuckers said they'd wait outside."

"Just the three of them, Jack?" Gore asked.

"That's all I saw, Hyme, but Rossi's probably got more. And if he hasn't, you can bet he's calling up an army right now. They'll sew this place up tight."

"Can we call the cops and fire department again?" I said.

"Won't work twice," Donohue said, shaking his head. "They'll be ready for it and just lay back and pick us off as we come out. Besides, this place is just too big for a juggle like that to work."

He paced up and down, biting at the hard skin around a thumbnail. We all watched him. I wasn't conscious of being frightened as much as feeling an utter lack of hope. I think the others felt the same way: that we had come to the end of our rope, and all our daring and resolve had gone for nothing. I understood then the irrational fury that Donohue had expressed earlier: Having accomplished so much, why couldn't we be left alone to profit from our boldness?

"Uh, Jack," Hymie Gore said, "maybe we should go out blasting? I mean, we got the irons. Maybe one or two of us could make it."

"Suicide," Donohue said bluntly. "I cased all the exits when we checked in. At night, all those doors are brightly lighted. They'll be back in the darkness, take their time, and pop us off, bang, bang, bang, bang— like that. Can't miss."

Silence again.

Finally Black Jack stopped his pacing. He stood in front of Dick Fleming's armchair, looked down at him.

"Well, college boy?" he said. "You got a good nut on you, I know that. Any ideas how we can get out of this mess?"

"Back doors?" Dick said slowly.

"They'll all be covered."

"Basement?"

"The steps come up to the back doors."

"Disguises? We put on some of Jannie's clothes and —ah, that would never work."

"It sure wouldn't," Donohue said, sighing. "Maybe I should make a run for it. I might be able to decoy them away while you three slide out the other way."

"They're too smart for that," Fleming said. "Aren't they?"

"Yeah," Jack said sourly, "they are."

"We could call the cops," I said. "Or the FBI. For real, I mean. No gimmicks. Give ourselves up. Tell them to come get us."

"And face a felony murder rap?" Donohue said. "You really want to do that?"

"No," I said.

"Wait a minute," Dick said.

We all looked at him. He was rubbing his blond eyebrows side to side.

"Look," he said, "it's just a matter of logic. We obviously can't go *down,* so why don't we try going up? The roof."

Jack Donohue took one swift step to Fleming's side, bent over, kissed his cheek.

"Sweetheart," he said. "I knew you had a brain from the start. Sure, the roof. It's a chance. Dick, you come with me and we'll take a look. Hyme, you stay here with Jannie. Lock the door and don't open for anyone, and I mean *anyone.* Not even for me unless I give you the right knock: three short raps, pause, two more. Got it? Let's go, Dick."

They were gone almost fifteen minutes. Hymie Gore and I waited in silence, chain-smoking. We were still wearing our coats, the suitcases packed, locked, and stacked near the door. Gore opened one of the shoulder bags to extract another revolver and slip it into his side pocket. I wondered if I should also take another, but I didn't. I kept thinking of "Two-Gun Jannie Shean," and the idea was just too ridiculous.

Finally we heard Donohue's code-knock: three raps, pause, two more. Gore opened the door cautiously, peered out, let the two men into the room.

I looked at their faces but could read nothing in their expressions.

"It's a chance," Donohue said.

"A *good* chance," Fleming said.

"A chance," Jack repeated. "Just a chance. Here's the situation: We get to the roof up an iron staircase through a fire door. That part's easy. The building next door is a department store about the same height. Maybe a few inches higher. But it's about five feet away. Dick, would you say five feet?"

"About."

"There's just space between the two buildings. Nothing there. Like an open alley. But we jumped it. No problem. All right, now we're on the roof of the department store, hoping no one heard us jump. The building on the other side of the department store is the movie theater. A problem there. It's about five feet away from the department store, but it's also lower. I mean, maybe five, six feet lower. So we not only have to jump across that open space, but we have to jump *down*. Get it? Once we do that, there's no getting back. Naturally we didn't try *that* jump."

"But we saw a door up there," Dick Fleming said excitedly. "If we can make it to the roof of the movie house, and if we can get through that door, maybe we can make it down through the theater."

"Carrying our luggage," Donohue said, and flashed us one of his sparkling grins.

I looked at him in astonishment. I gestured toward the stack of suitcases.

"You're not telling me we're taking all this stuff, are you?" I demanded.

"You're not telling me we're leaving it all behind, are you?" he replied.

So up we went to the roof of the motor lodge, carrying all our luggage. We took the stairs at the end of the corridor because Donohue didn't want to chance meeting anyone in the elevator. Jack led the way, then me, then Dick. Hymie Gore came last. The big man was carrying two suitcases, but I noticed that one was under an arm, and he was gripping a revolver in his free hand.

When we got to the roof door, Jack turned to me.

"It opens outward," he whispered. "It's locked from the outside so crooks can't get in from the roof. Very smart. When Dick and I went out to look around, we left it jammed open with two packs of cigarettes. We'll do the same thing now, just in case this scam doesn't work and we have to get back in."

Then we were on the roof. It was cool up there, a stiff breeze blowing from the north. The sky was clear, the stars diamond-bright. But there was no moon; we moved carefully in the gloom, avoiding protruding pipes and ventilation ducts.

Donohue led the way to the far side. The tarred roof of the department store was across a black open space.

"That looks like more than five feet to me," I said nervously.

"Nah," Jack said, "it's an easy jump. Dick, show her how easy it is."

Fleming put down the suitcases he was carrying. He backed up a few steps, opened his raincoat. Then he rushed forward and leaped. He went sailing, the tail of his coat billowing out behind him. He cleared the chasm easily, by a foot or two. He didn't even fall; just went running forward a few steps, then stopped, turned, came back to the edge. He smiled across at me.

"See?" Donohue said. "Nothing to it. You next, Jannie."

I stood a few steps back from that deep, deep valley between the two buildings.

"Don't look down," Jack said. "Just get a running start and jump."

"I can't do it."

"Sure, you can do it! It's an easy jump. I read in your book how strong you are. Jogging and exercise and all that bullshit. You can do it."

"I can't."

"Come on," he said, beginning to get angry. "If it was a puddle, you'd step across it."

"A puddle isn't six stories up."

"Goddamn it," he snarled furiously, "are you going to jump or am I going to have Hymie throw you across?"

I began to cry.

"I can't," I wept, "I really can't, Jack. Something that wasn't in my book: I'm afraid of heights. Scared out of my wits. I don't have to look down there. I know what's there. Nothing. I just can't do it. Leave me here. The rest of you go ahead. That's all right; I'll take my chances."

"Son of a bitch," Donohue said bitterly. He put his hands on his hips, tilted his head back to stare at the sky, took a deep breath.

We stood there a monent, not talking. So help me, I had the shakes.

"Hey," Dick called softly from the other side. "What's going on? Let's get moving!"

"Hyme," Jack said, "throw all the luggage across to Fleming."

I stood well back from the edge, trembling still, watching Gore tossing the suitcases and carryalls over to Dick. Then everything was stacked on the roof of the department store. And Dick was there. But the three of us were still on the motel roof.

"Go ahead," I told them. "It's all right."

I really thought they were going to leave me.

"Oh, shut your stupid yap," Donohue snapped. "Hyme, let's take a look at that fire door."

They made their way back to the rooftop door. I followed forlornly.

The two men examined the door. It was steel-covered, about two inches thick. Donohue rapped it with his knuckles.

"Think you can pull it off the hinges, Hyme?"

Gore swung the door open wide, examined the hinges.

"Bolted," he said. "But I'll try, Jack."

He reached up, put locked hands over the outer edge of the open door. He let his weight sag, pulling down and outward, trying to snap the top hinge. There was a screak of metal but nothing yielded.

"Let me get inside your arms," Black Jack said. "We'll both put our weight on it."

The two of them put their combined weight and strength on the open door. Even in the dimness I could see their strained faces, cords popping in their necks and clenched jaws.

There was a raw screech of metal that I was certain would be heard for miles. The top hinge pulled loose from the door frame. The two men almost fell. They stepped back. The door hung loosely, held only by the bottom hinge. Hymie Gore gripped it, began to pull it away with ferocious yanks.

"Heavy mother," he panted.

With another wail of twisted metal, the whole door came away in Gore's hands. He carried it back to the chasm between the two buildings, Donohue and I following.

"Work fast, Hyme," Jack said nervously. "That was loud enough for the desk clerk to hear."

Gore set the door on edge on the cornice of the motel roof. He slid it slowly across the five-foot space, leaning his weight on his end to keep it from toppling into the alley. Dick Fleming, kneeling on the department store roof, reached out fearlessly. He grabbed the wavering leading edge, helped drag it across. The two men lowered the door into a flat position. It was about seven feet long and spanned the open gap neatly, with about a foot protruding on each end. It was a steel bridge.

"Shut your eyes and hold my hand," Donohue said. "If you don't do this, I'll shove you off the edge myself."

I did what he said. I shut my eyes. I stepped up when he told me. I took short shuffles. His hand was tight and hard on mine.

"Okay," he said, about a hundred years later. "You made it."

I opened my eyes. I was on the roof of the department store. Dick Fleming slid an arm across my shoulders, smiling at me.

Gore came strolling casually across the door bridge. We worked swiftly. Carried all the luggage to the other side. Then Hymie went back for the door. Dick Fleming helped him. They got a good grip on it, inched it free of the motor lodge cornice, let it swing downward, bang against the wall. Then they hauled it up. Gore carried it across to the other side balanced on his head.

We repeated the process. Fleming made the first

leap to the roof of the movie theater. This time, jumping out and down, he fell, rolled, and got up limping
and rubbing his ankle. Hyme tossed the luggage
across the space between the two buildings. Then the
three men wrestled the door into position again. This
time it barely spanned the gap, by no more than an
inch or so on each side. And because the movie theater
roof was lower, the ramp led downward.

Once again I closed my eyes and Jack Donohue led
me across. This time his arm was about my waist, and
we moved slowly in little, dragging steps. We made it,
and Hymie Gore came dancing across, pausing to spit
over the edge.

"Leave the door here, Jack?" he asked. "Dump it—
or what?"

Donohue looked at the steel door.

"Leave it right there," he said. "Dump it and the
noise will tip everyone. It's no use to us anymore. The
next building is so much lower, there's no chance to
make it."

We went over to the fire door on the roof of the
movie theater. It was also steel covered and worked
just like the rooftop door of the motor lodge: It was
locked on the outside. Donohue struck a match, held
it close to the lock. He sighed.

"I could get in," he said. "Maybe half an hour, an
hour. We haven't got the time, after that racket we
made. Also, I don't like the idea of the four of us cart-
ing all this shit down through a movie theater. This is
a public place; there's got to be a fire escape. Everyone spread out and look around."

I stayed right where I was, close to the middle of
the roof. I wasn't about to go peering over the edge of
a high building.

It was Hymie Gore who found it in the darkness:
iron railings that came curving over the roof cornice.

Donohue leaned far out, peered down. I didn't know how he could do it.

"Looks okay," he said. "A zigzag stairway. The last floor is probably on a slide or gravity pull; that's the way these things are usually set up. Let's try it. Hyme, you go first. Then Jannie, then me, then Dick. Everyone carries."

And that's the way we did it, me lugging only one suitcase and a shoulder bag, my free hand hanging on to that rusted iron banister with a grip that never relaxed, my knees trembling as we went down slowly step after step.

The last floor had a counterweighted swing staircase. As Gore stepped onto it, it swiveled creakily. He went down cautiously until the free end touched the ground. He stepped off and leaned on the handrail, holding the steps steady as we came scampering down that final flight. Then he relaxed his grip; the fire escape swung upward out of reach.

We were in a narrow alley between the movie house and the department store. Maybe five feet wide. Easy for two people to walk abreast, too narrow for a car. It was lighted at both ends with bright bulbs under pyramid-shaped green shades, on the ends of pipes protruding from the walls.

Jack Donohue looked around a moment, getting his bearings.

"That way," he said softly, jerking his chin. "That's the parking lot. We're not too far from the car."

We started off, Hymie Gore leading the way again, carrying two suitcases. The rest of us followed in single file. I couldn't believe we were doing it. Escaping from Antonio Rossi and his heavies. It seemed too good to be true.

It was.

Gore was about twenty feet from the opening to the alley when a man stepped out into the glare of the naked light. He was facing us. He just stood there in the center of the open space. Not moving. We stopped. I saw he was tall, slender. He was wearing a snap-brim fedora but no raincoat or topcoat. I couldn't see his face, it was shadowed by the brim of his hat. But I saw the gun in his hand. It was gleaming.

I heard Hymie Gore say "Aw." I think that's what he said: "Aw."

He started forward. This takes longer to write than it took to happen. Hymie hurtled toward the man. He dropped one of the suitcases he was carrying. He raised the other, vertically, so it was covering him from chin to groin. He was gripping it at the sides with both hands, elbows bent.

I thought I heard him say "Aw" again.

It all happened so fast, so fast.

He was about ten feet away from the gunman when his arms snapped straight. The suitcase went flying forward. At the same time I heard the shot. This time they were sharp cracks, three of them in rapid succession. I didn't know then if the bullets went through the suitcase. It didn't make any difference.

Hymie was hit. I saw him shudder. He paused a brief second, then went falling forward, pawing futilely at his side pocket. The tall, slender gunman was still standing, the suitcase at his feet. I heard two more shots.

Then Gore crashed into him. The two of them went down in a tangled heap. I thought the gunman was trying to squirm free, get out from under the weight pressing him down.

"Run!" Donohue screamed. His shoulder hit me,

spun me around. "Go that way! To the parking lot! The car!"

Dick and I ran, luggage bumping against our knees. We fled down that gloomy, walled alley, sobbing, gasping. I glanced back. Jack dropped his suitcase and shoulder bag. He darted forward. He had his gun out now. I saw him lean over, jam the muzzle into the ear of the gunman, who was still struggling to rise. The sound this time was more like a liquid *splat*. I saw something fly, glistening in the light at the end of the alley.

Jack bent over Hymie Gore briefly. Then he picked up the suitcase Gore had thrown. He came running back toward us. He paused long enough to grab up Gore's other suitcase and the case and the shoulder bag he had dropped. He came stumbling toward us awkwardly, trying to hang on to everything he was carrying.

"Move it!" I heard him screaming. "Move it!"

Dick Fleming dashed around the corner and disappeared. But I stood there. I couldn't move, wouldn't move, not till Jack Donohue came panting up to me. Mouth open, eyes wild and straining, chest heaving. I took one of the suitcases from him. I stumbled with him to the exit from that horrible place. Black Jack disappeared around the corner. I took a final glance back.

I saw a squat, heavy man, guns in both hands, step into the light at the far end of the alley. There was no mistaking that figure: the broad shoulders, deep chest. The pinstriped, vested suit. The bowtie. A British bowler set squarely atop the heavy head.

He looked up briefly. Looked directly at me, as if calculating his chances for a lucky shot. Then he looked down at the two men on the ground. He leaned over, held one of his guns close. I heard a single shot.

A *boom* that echoed back and forth from the walls of the narrow alley.

Then Jack Donohue was back, cursing. He clamped a hand on my arm, jerked me away.

"Jack," I said, sobbing. "He's dead. Hymie!"

"So?" he said. *"Run,* goddamn you!"

Three's Company

Where were we? I didn't know—and I was driving. Dick sat beside me. Jack Donohue was in the back seat, alone, calling out rapid instructions without the benefit of a map:

"After we get through Savannah, take a right onto Route 17. Just below Midway you'll hit Route 82. Make a right on that and go west to Hinesville. Then southwest to Jesup. We'll connect up with Route 301 south of Jesup and go down to Folkston. Then over to Jacksonville where we'll meet up with 95 again. It's a detour. Takes more time, but they'll be patrolling the Interstate. They'll never find us in the backwoods."

I wasn't so certain. I thought Antonio Rossi would follow us through the thickets of hell.

After the death of Hymie Gore, we had made our getaway in a wild, roaring dash across the shopping center parking lot. Jack had been at the wheel, and that escape from the crowded lot had been like running an obstacle course, a heart-stopping careen around startled pedestrians, grocery carts, and moving cars. I remember only lights flashing by, outraged

faces, screams of protest, squealing brakes, the angry
blast of horns, the screech of tires in tight turns.

We made the highway with no signs of pursuit and
headed south again. We paused on the verge just
north of Savannah and changed places. That's when I
got behind the wheel and Black Jack crawled into the
back seat and immediately poured us all drinks.

Dick, I knew, was trying hard to control his trem-
ors. He clutched his plastic tumbler of brandy in both
hands, elbows pressed against his ribs. I was not so
much shaken as numb. Too many things had happened too quickly. When I had asked Donohue the
sequence of events back there in the alley, he had
been cold and laconic.

"I wasted the guy. I think he was one of the clerks
from Brandenberg's. I blew his fucking brains all over
the fucking alley. Then I took a look at Hyme. He
was still alive, but he had at least three pills in him.
He was going; I could tell. So I split."

"I saw Rossi kill him," I said faintly.

"Yeah," Jack said. "Well, that figures."

"He was such a sweet man," I mourned.

"Yeah," Donohue said, "he was okay. Not much
between the ears, but he was a good muscle."

"Did he have a family?" Fleming asked.

"Who the hell knows?" Black Jack said irritably.

I was about to reproach him for his heartless un-
concern—but what was the use? No one would pity a
dead Jack Donohue either, or grieve for his wasted
life. He knew it and accepted it.

But still, the death of Gore was on his mind—or
perhaps it was the implacableness of the enemy who
followed. Whatever he felt, alone there in the back
seat, he drank heavily. He finished the brandy, lowered the window, and tossed out the empty bottle.
He cackled when it smashed to splinters on the high-

way behind us. Then he started on a quart of vodka, drinking from the bottle.

We drove in silence then. We were south of Savannah before Donohue spoke again. His voice was heavy and dull, the words slurred.

"The funny thing is . . ." he mumbled. "You know what the funny thing is? That suitcase Hyme held up in front of him was filled with clothes. The slugs went through it like a hot poker through butter. I got the case right here. I'm feeling the holes, front and back. We got to ditch this case. But if he had been holding a suitcase full of jewelry, it probably would have stopped the slugs or deflected them—you know? It was just bad luck that Hyme had a suitcase full of underwear and shirts. That's what it's all about, isn't it? Luck, I mean."

Then he was silent again. When I glanced in the rearview mirror, I saw that he had stretched out. His chin was down on his chest. I hoped he was sleeping.

I tried to remember all his instructions, but I got lost. I stayed on Route 82, going southwest. Finally, at Waycross, Dick and I saw signs pointing to the Okefenokee Swamp Park, and knew we were on the wrong road.

We discussed in low voice whether we should wake up Donohue and see if he could get us back on course. But it was then almost 12:30 A.M., I was bone-weary, and I knew Dick's ankle was bothering him. It seemed foolish to push ourselves over the edge of complete collapse.

We had to drive another thirty miles before we found a motel that was displaying a Vacancy sign. It was another of the fleabag variety, but I couldn't have cared less. Dick woke up the night clerk and registered for two rooms, paying in advance. Between us we wrestled all the important luggage inside, then supported a stumbling, grumbling Jack Donohue and got him onto a lumpy bed.

Dick said he'd take care of undressing him, and I thankfully went off to my very own room. It was, I thought with a shock, the first time I had slept alone in I couldn't remember how many days. I took my personal luggage in with me, including Project X, and just did manage to take off coat, shoes, wig, sweater, and skirt before I fell on top of the ratty bedspread in bra and pantyhose. I didn't know which smelled worse, me or that bed. But sleep conquered all.

I awoke about 8:00 the next morning because some idiot was emptying trash cans into a dump truck right outside my window, and whistling mightily as he worked. After he left, with a great grinding of gears, I tried to get back to sleep again, but it was no go. So I got up, showered in a stained stall no larger than a vertical coffin, and put on fresh clothes, makeup, and a brushed wig.

Then, feeling reasonably presentable, I ventured outside. A hot, smoky day, the rising sun hidden behind a scrim of white fog. I looked around. Mostly flatland. Some clumps of scrub pine. The earth looked old, baked, worn. And our motel was designed to fit right into that landscape.

The Buick was where we had parked it, and I figured the men were still sleeping. I wandered over to the renting office and found a fat woman sitting behind the desk, filing her nails with a piece of steel as big as a saber. She was about half my height and double my weight, with an enormous purple birthmark that covered one cheek and dripped down onto her neck. But it hadn't soured her: she was perky enough.

"Morning, dearie," she said cheerily. "How you this bright, sunshiny morning?"

I won't attempt to reproduce the Georgian accent.

But that "morning" was more like "mawnin' " and the
"how" was "haow." Still there was a softness to her
speech, a warm lilt. I liked it.

"I'd feel a lot better if I could get some coffee," I
said grumpily.

"Got it right here," she said happily. "Thirty-five
cents a cup. Doughnuts go for two bits each."

"One coffee," I said. "Two doughnuts."

She served me from a ten-quart electric coffeemaker
on the end of the check-in desk.

"We got canned milk," she said.

"Black will be fine."

"Yeah," she said, grinning slyly. "Black is beautiful. Plain, sugared or chock doughnuts?"

"Plain, please."

"Where you folks headin'?" she asked pleasantly
as she filled a plastic container with coffee and wrapped
two doughnuts in a paper napkin.

"South," I told her.

"Most folks is, this time of year. Miami, I bet."

"Uh . . . maybe."

"Me and the old man plan to get down there one of
these days," she nattered on. "Last year we went to
Disney World. Ever been there?"

"No, I never have."

"Don't miss it," she advised me seriously. "Just the
nicest place. I shook hands with Mickey Mouse. Can
you imagine? *Me*, shaking hands with Mickey
Mouse?"

Feeling a lot better, I carried my breakfast back to
my room. I put coffee and doughnuts on top of the
stained maple dresser and pulled up a straight-back
chair. I got out the yellow legal pads and ballpoint
pen. Sipping the hot, flavorless coffee, chewing the
spongy, flavorless doughnuts, I wrote as fast as I could,
trying to bring my manuscript up to date.

I must have worked for at least two hours. I was just describing our arrival at the shopping center motor lodge near Hardeeville, South Carolina, when there was a knock at the door. I peeked through the front windows before I unlocked. I was learning.

Jack and Dick came in, carrying their own coffee and doughnuts. Dick was still limping slightly, but they both looked rested and cleaned up. They sat hunched over on the edge of my bed.

"We missed the turnoff at Jesup," Fleming told me.

"But no problem," Donohue said. "You kids did just right to hole up for the night. There are two or three ways we can get back on the Interstate from here. If we want to."

I looked at him.

"If we want to?" I said. "I thought you were in such a hurry to get down to Miami?"

"Well . . . yeah," Jack said, "I was. Still am. But me and Dick have been talking it over. Maybe it would be smarter to find some backwoods hidey-hole for a week or so. Someplace way off in nowhere. We could lay low till the heat's off. We got plenty of money for that."

"It's Georgia," Dick explained. "Jack says he knows the roads and the land like the palm of his hand. He says he can find us a safe spot."

"What do you think?" Donohue said.

I thought that now the Donohue Gang was reduced to three living members, it was becoming more democratic. Our Leader was consulting rather than commanding.

The idea of holing up for a while seemed more attractive to me than fleeing from our nemesis down Route 95.

"Sounds okay," I said, shrugging. "Where do we find this safe place?"

"I figure we'll go back to Waycross," Jack said. "Then head west toward Albany. I know that country pretty good. I'll find a spot."

"We'll stop for food at the first decent place we come to," Fleming said. Then he added: "Won't we, Jack?"

"Why not? We'll take our time. No one's going to find us in the Georgia boondocks. I'll bet on that."

So we went back to Waycross, then headed north and west to Alma, Hazlehurst, McRae, and Eastman. Jack Donohue was driving. I sat beside him, trying to follow our route on a Mobil map. I thought he was heading toward Macon, but I couldn't be sure.

I wasn't sure because four-lane concrete highways became three- and then two-lane. Then we were on two-lane tarred roads. Then graveled roads. Then one-lane dirt roads. Everything dwindled down until we were running between bare fields so baked and dry that we spun a long plume of dust behind us.

We passed crossroad villages—no more than a filling station and a grocery store that sold beer and snuff. I saw men in faded overalls, women in calico dresses, mule-drawn wagons, and once, like something out of the past, a man in a field following an ox-drawn plow. The land here seemed bleached out, blooded and drawn, and so did the people. In our big Buick, dented and dusty as it was, we were visitors from another planet. To me, this was *terra incognita,* the earth sere and hard, a gigantic sun burning through the morning fog and filling the sky with shimmering heat. That sun looked like it might set right into the cropped fields and char the world away.

I glanced sideways at Black Jack as he drove, and saw the light in his eyes, the twisted smile on his lips. I thought at first that he was seeking the most deserted, malign, and remote spot he could find, thinking of our safety and the enmity of our pursuers.

Then I realized it wasn't wholly that. It was a return for him. He was coming home. After all his travels and adventures, happiness and pain, he was coming home. Yes, I decided, it was that. As paved roads shrunk to paths and we went jouncing over pits and rumbling across dried creek beds, I saw his lips draw back from his teeth and heard his low laugh. He was remembering.

"Ran alky through here," he said, "in a beatup truck. White lightning, panther piss—whatever you want to call it. Clear as water and maybe a hundred proof. Scorch your tonsils, that stuff would. But pure. No artificial additives or flavorings, as the ads say. Vintage of last Tuesday. At least we let it cool off. I had a route. Delivered to some regular customers and some local distributors. All kinds of bottles: milk, medicine, whatever. It had to hold a pint, at least. That was the minimum. With a cork. You got a dime back if you returned the bottle. Two cents back on the cork."

"How old were you then, Jack?" Dick Fleming asked from the back seat.

"Shit," Jack Donohue said, "I was small fry. Thirteen, fourteen, fifteen—like that. They used kids for drivers, figuring if you all got caught, what would they do to you? Whump you up some, that's all."

Something else I noticed: As we got deeper into hardshell Baptist country, Jack's speech subtly changed. Not changed so much as reverted. The rapid New York cadence slowed, a drawl became evident, and I noted the same lilt I had heard in the speech of that birthmarked lady back at the motel. It wasn't "you-all" or even "yawl." But there was only a tiny hesitation between "you" and "all." And humor—dry, wry, and unsettling.

"You heerd about how to handle a mule? First thing you do is to smack him across the skull with a two-by-four. That's just to get his attention. This feller I knew tried the same thing on his wife. She just *wouldn't* stop gabbing. He's still breaking rocks somewheres."

This followed by a mirthless laugh.

So there we were in a foreign country, being chauffeured by a native guide. Only Jack Donohue spoke the language and knew the customs. It was like a time warp, going back to the 1920's, a time of dirt roads, hand-cranked gas pumps, tin signs advertising Moxie and chewing tobacco. All the men seemed to spit endlessly, and the women looked old before their time.

Another thing I noticed as we went slowly through those small, sad, crossroad towns . . .

So many of the males were injured. One-armed men, boys with missing fingers, cripples jerking along on false legs or crutches.

"Farm machinery," Jack said when I commented on this phenomenon. "You get in any rural area, anywhere in the country, you find guys who lost a finger or hand or arm to a tractor or binder or thresher. Happens all the time. One reason why I got out."

We came, finally, to a village no smaller, no larger, no different from a dozen others we had passed through on the packed dirt road, trailing our cloud of dust.

"Yeah," Donohue said, "this is it. Whittier, Georgia. We'll settle in around here."

"Why this place?" I asked. "It doesn't look special."

"It ain't," he said, grinning. "That's the point. Just another spot that the mapmakers forgot. There's a hundred places like this around here. I know them all. One gas station, one general store, one feed and hardware store. Maybe a small branch bank. A restaurant and liquor place side-by-side. A church somewheres. Maybe a school."

"No motels?" Fleming asked.

"Motels?" Jack said. "Who comes through here? Exceptin' folks who go *through*. I mean, this is a nonstop place."

"So where do we stay?" I said.

"What I'm looking for," he told us, "is a private home owned by a spinster or widow lady. It'll have a sign on the front lawn that says, like, 'Tourists Welcome.' Or maybe just 'Boarders.' There's bound to be at least one around here."

He found it, too. A big white house set back on an improbably green lawn. The sign read: "Tourist Accommodations—Day, Week, Month." The house was all fretwork and gingerbread trim: a wedding cake of a house.

On the wide proch, a woman swung slowly back and forth in a rocker, cooling herself with a palm leaf fan. There was a crushed stone driveway that led up to the house, then curved away to a clapboard building that looked like a barn converted into a garage.

We pulled up on the edge of the dirt road. Donohue switched off the ignition, turned to Fleming in the back seat.

"Hyme had a hat," he said. "He wasn't wearing it when he got blown away. Is it back there? Or any hat?"

Dick rooted through the scrambled mess, came up with a stained gray fedora. He handed it over. Donohue clapped it on his head. It slid down to his eyebrows. He shoved it back so it was hanging.

"We leave the car here," he said. "All of us, we walk slowly up to the porch. Just looking around, casual-like. You're a step or two behind me. Let me do the talking. Dick, you limp on that ankle of yours more'n you have to."

"What's the hat for?" I asked.

"So's I can take it off," he said, almost indignantly, like I was the stupe of stupes. "Anyone want to make a bet?"

Dick and I looked at each other.

"What kind of a bet?" I said cautiously.

"I'll bet you a sawbuck her first name is Rose, Opal, Pearl, Minnie, Faith, Hope, or Charity."

"Okay," Fleming said. "I'll take you. It's got to be Rose, Opal, Pearl, Minnie, Faith, Hope, or Charity, or you owe me ten—right?"

"Right," Donohue said. "Let's go."

We got out of the car. Closed the doors to keep in the air conditioning. We walked slowly up the driveway to the porch. The woman in the rocking chair watched us approach. Very calm. That chair didn't pause or vary its rhythm for a second. As we came closer, I saw that she was a big woman in her midsixties. Tall rather than full. Almost gaunt. A face like an ax blade. Strong hands. Eyes as clear as water. Wearing an old-fashioned poke bonnet, calico housedress, thick elastic stockings. The shoes were unusual: unbuckled combat boots from World War II. She was chewing something placidly. Gum or tobacco or whatever. (I learned later it was a wad of tar, which she was convinced would make her remaining teeth whiter.)

As we came up to the porch, Donohue motioned Dick and me to stop. He put a foot lightly on the bottom step of the three stairs leading up to the porch.

"Afternoon, ma'am," Jack said, taking off his hat with what I can only describe as a courtly gesture.

She nodded, quite regally.

"Hot," she said, fanning herself. "For this time of year."

"Yes'm," Donohue agreed, "it surely is. Ma'am, my name is Sam Morrison. This lovely lady is my good wife, Beatrice. And this other feller is my brother, Dick. Richard, that is. We're all from Macon, y'know? Well, we're heading south for a couple of weeks. Figure to do some fishing down in the Florida Keys. But Dick, he up and sprained his ankle just this morning. You saw him limping? Nothing serious, the doc says, but keep the weight offen it a day or more. So we're in no hurry and figured we'd just rest up awhile and give Dick's ankle a chance to heal. Him being in pain, and all. So what we were wondering is this: if you could fit us out with two rooms, me and my wife in one, my brother in the other, like for a few days, a week at most? No trouble, no wild parties, oh no, ma'am, nothing like that. We all been working hard. This is our vacation. Rest is all we want, ma'am. Peaceful rest."

The rocker never stopped. The waving palm leaf fan never stopped. She and Jack Donohue looked at each other. It seemed to me the silence lasted for an eternity. But out there in that deserted countryside, I figured absolute silence was normal: no cicadas, no birdcalls, no passing traffic, no airliners overhead. Nothing.

The stare between Donohue and the woman in the rocking chair never wavered. It was like they were talking to each other with their eyes. I didn't understand it.

"Sam Morrison, you said?" she asked.

"That's right, ma'am," Donohue said gently. "I'm born and bred from up Macon way. My wife and brother, they're from up north."

She nodded as if it were the most natural thing in

the world that a man from "up Macon way" would have a wife and brother from the north.

"Ten dollars a day," she said, still fanning her sharp face. "Per person. That includes breakfast. You all'll have to go into town for your other meals. The food ain't great at Hoxey's there, but it's filling. For a week or so. No cooking in your rooms. I don't hold with hard liquor, but if you want to drink in your rooms, quiet-like, I'm not one to complain. Ice cubes in the kitchen refrigerator. I got myself a TV in the parlor if you're wanting. You're welcome to watch."

"Thank you, ma'am," Jack said softly, taking out his wallet. "That sounds just grand—a nice quiet place where we can rest up, and my brother, he can let his ankle get good again. And what's your name, ma'am, if I may ask?"

"Mrs. Pearl Sniffins," she said firmly.

From slightly behind me I heard Dick Fleming's low groan.

"You can pull in behind the garage," she went on. "The drive curves around to the back. Plenty of room in there. Just my old Plymouth. A few chickens. One goat. Two hounds. They won't cause no trouble."

"We'll take care, ma'am," Donohue assured her. "I'd like to pay in advance. Is Mr. Sniffins . . . ?"

"Mr. Sniffins has passed on."

"I'm sorry to hear that, ma'am," Jack Donohue said, hanging his head. "But it's a glory to know he has gone to his reward."

"I hope so," she said grimly.

Those rooms we stayed in for eight days in the tourist home outside of Whittier, Georgia, really belonged in the American Wing of the Metropolitan Museum. I don't mean they were furnished with valuable antiques or in exquisite taste. But they were a touching

reminder of how middle-class rural Americans lived
fifty years ago.

Wide, waxed floorboards. Gossamer, hand-hemmed
curtains at the generous windows. Maple furniture
with a high gloss. Beds with spindle posts. Armchairs
covered in flowered cretonne. Pressed ferns framed on
the white walls. Oval rag rugs on the floors.

And all so neat, clean, and glowing that I felt like
weeping. Because there was nothing chic, smart, or
trendy about those rooms. They were just reminders
of what home had once meant. The light filtering
through those gauzy curtains seemed to infuse the old
rooms with young beauty. They smelled faintly of
lavender sachet, and sounded of peace, security, and
a sense of the continuum of life.

It was all so different from the speed, violence, loud
noise, and sudden death of the preceding days. We
were doused in peace, lulled by it. We had almost for-
gotten a world without fear.

I don't mean that the past was wiped away. But we
did begin to forget.

We carried all our luggage upstairs to the larger of
the two rooms assigned us. There were three other
bedrooms on the second floor, all empty, and one
enormous bathroom with a tub on legs and a toilet seat
with a needlepoint cover.

"Mrs. Pearl says she finds it hard to make the
stairs," Donohue told us. "Arthritis. So she sleeps
downstairs on a sofa in the parlor. Got a john down
there. A colored lady comes in once a week to clean
up for her." He looked at Dick Fleming meaningfully.
"That's Mrs. *Pearl* Sniffins I'm talking about," he said.

"You son of a bitch," Dick said ruefully, handing
over the ten dollars. "How did you know?"

Black Jack grinned and pocketed the bill.

"Sucker!" he said. "One born every minute. This is

my *home*. Mrs. Pearl Sniffins? She's every aunt I ever had."

"And your mother?" I asked curiously.

"No," he said shortly. "Not my mother."

We were all in the larger bedroom then, not yet having faced the problem of who was going to sleep with whom, and where. The fact that we had the entire second floor to ourselves simplified things, or complicated them. But I wasn't worried; just curious.

I sat in one of those neat armchairs. It was equipped with a crocheted antimacassar, naturally. And how long has it been since you've seen one of those things? The two men sat on the edge of the bed. It was covered with a patchwork quilt that looked like Betsy Ross had had a hand in it, after she knocked off Old Glory.

When the men sat down, the bed sang and rustled beneath them. Donohue was amused and patted the coverlet with his palm.

"Straw-filled mattress," he explained. "Great sleeping—if the noise doesn't keep you awake. I'll bet she bought the material and sewed up the tick herself, then stuffed it. A great old lady."

"And what a con job you did on her," Dick said. "She went for it hook, line, and sinker."

Jack turned slowly to look at him.

"Think so? Think again, sonny. She knows we're on the run."

I gaped at him.

"Jack," I said, "how in hell would she know that? Your spiel sounded believable to me. I thought she went for it."

"Use your head," he said. "We pull up here in a big, dust-covered Buick. We say we're on our way to Florida. If we were going from Macon to Florida, we'd be nowheres near this place. We'd be on Route 16, going over to 95. Or going straight south on 75, and then cutting over to 95 at Orlando. Listen, that lady's no idiot. She knows we're running and need a place to hole up for a while."

"Then why—" I began.

"Needs the money!" he said, shrugging. "Wants the company. Whatever. When she was looking at me, it was nip-and-tuck; she knew but couldn't decide. Finally she figured we were good for the green and wouldn't cop her knitting needles. But that's why she's clipping us ten each per day. I'll bet her regular rate is five."

"She won't talk?" Fleming asked nervously.

"Nah," Donohue said. "It's no skin off her nose who we are or what we done. If we behave ourselves she'll keep her mouth shut. Most of the folks around here are like that; they mind their own business. It's some of the white trash in town who'll sell us out. But not Mrs. Pearl Sniffins. She's a lady, she's seen a lot, and there's no way you can surprise, shock, or scare her. Hey, listen, let's take a look around this place. The land's hers, but she's got tenant farmers. She says it's mostly peanuts and corn. Some okra. And she's got a mud crick back aways. That I gotta see. Let's go."

As we walked slowly across the stubbled fields, it seemed to me that day was so splendid that we would live forever. A fulgent sun filled a blue, blue sky, and even that hardscrabble land took on a warmth and glow that made me want to lie down naked in the dust and roll about. I began to understand why people might choose to live in such a bleak landscape—for days like that one, when the sun seemed created for that plot alone, coming low to bless, the firmament serene, the air as piercing as ether, the whole universe closed in and secret.

We paused in the middle of an empty field, swallowed in silence. We followed Jack's pointing finger and there, high up, saw a black thing no more than a scimitar, wheeling and soaring.

"Chicken hawk," Donohue said somberly. "Big bastard."

We watched that dark blade cut through the azure. Then it came between us and the sun and was lost.

"See that line of trees?" Jack said. "That's gotta be the crick. We'll just go that far. How's the ankle, Dick?"

"I'll live," Fleming said. "If there's a drugstore in town I'll pick up an elastic bandage."

"If not," Jack said, "Mrs. Pearl will wrap it in rags for you. These country women can doctor anything from an ass boil to a mule down with colic."

I've seen bigger creeks than that after a water main break in Manhattan. But Donohue was enchanted with it and we humored him. It was a muddy stream, no more than twenty feet across, and looked to be about waist-deep.

"Smell that?" Jack demanded. "Catfish in there—I'll bet on it."

"Where does it go?" I asked him. "I mean, does it run into a deeper river?"

"Who the hell knows? The Oconee maybe, but I doubt it. Probably just pisses out in a field somewheres and disappears. Most of them do." He looked around. Not a soul in sight. Not a sound. He began to unbutton his shirt. "I'm going in," he said.

"In that?" I said, astonished. "It's a mudpuddle."

"So?" he said, continuing to undress. "It's wet and it's cool. Used to be a crick just like this where we lived when I was a tad. A big old hickory hung over from the bank. My pappy rigged up a rope and an old tire so we could swing out and drop off. Jesus, those days!"

Dick Fleming looked at me doubtfully, then sat down on the dirt bank and began to pull off shoes and socks. I sat down too, lighted a cigarette, watched the two men undress and wade, white-bodied into the shallow stream.

They plunged and began to shout, laugh, splash, dunk each other. They floated awhile, then leaped up into the air, glistening, and then slipped below the surface again. I watched them awhile, smiling. Then I ground out my cigarette, kicked off my shoes. I rose, stripped down. Took off my wig. Waded cautiously into the muddy water. It was colder than I expected. I took a deep breath, closed my eyes, belly-flopped in.

I think we spent about a half-hour in that shallow stream. I never knew muddy water could wash you clean, but that creek did. Washed away fears and tensions, terrors and regrets. We played with each other, then lay side by side, drying, on the dirt bank. I wanted the moment never to end. Thought was lost, thankfully, and all I could do was feel the hot sun on my bleached skin, feel a finger-touch breeze, feel the closeness and the intimacy. No one spoke.

After a while we rose, brushed ourselves off as best we could, dressed, and went straggling back across those shaved fields, still in silence. We heard Mrs. Pearl moving about in the kitchen, and Donohue called to tell her we were back. She didn't reply.

We trudged upstairs, all of us weary with a divine, sunbaked tiredness. We took turns in the big bathroom, showering away the dust and the sun-sting.

Then we went back into the big bedroom, locked the door. Got out a quart of vodka and drank it warm, passing around the big bottle like a loving cup. Then we all, the three of us, threw back the patchwork quilt and the top sheet (unbleached muslin, many times laundered) and got into bed together.

It wasn't the sex, but it was. What I mean is that it just wasn't randiness that drove us together. It was sweet, loving intimacy. We had been through so much, shared so much. And perhaps we were all frightened; there was that, too. Whatever it was, we huddled, and were kind, solicitous, and tender with each other.

I think that's what I remember most—the tenderness. We comforted each other. I make no apology for having sex with two men at the same time; it was a delight. There was nothing vile, sweaty, or grunted about it.

I think, after a while, we all slept for an hour or two. When we awoke, in a tangle of limbs, the room had cooled, and darkness was outside. We hadn't banished that.

That night we drove into town for dinner. We knew where we were going; as Mrs. Pearl had said, "In Whittier, it's Hoxey's or nuthin'."

Hoxey's looked like it had been designed by the same benighted genius responsible for the Game Cock. It had identical scarred wood floor, bar, tables, booths, kitchen in the rear, raucous jukebox, and glittering cigarette machine. Even the odor was similar, although now the grease had a fried chicken flavor. In addition, Hoxey's had a pool table off to one side and a table shuffleboard up near the bar.

Just as at the Game Cock, conversation temporarily ceased and heads turned as we walked in. But things got back to normal when we slid into a booth, and the waitress came over to take our order. She was an older and plumper version of the Game Cock's houri, and looked a lot jollier.

"Evenin', folks," she beamed. "My name's Rose. You drinkin', eatin', or both?"

"Both," Donohue said. "We'll have vodka on ice to cut the dust. Then we'll take a look at the menu, if you got one."

"Sure, we got one," she said. "Whaddya think, this is some kind of a dump? Don't answer that question!"

She left us three sheets of dog-eared paper, spotted with grease, that looked like they had been ripped from a memo pad. Each sheet was headed, in longhand: "Hoxey's: Where the Elite Meet to Eat." The menu read: "Soup. Bread and but." Then it listed the entrees, followed by: "Pots. and vegs. Ice cream or Jello. Coffee." Across the bottom was a stern admonition: "Don't take this menu for a suvenire."

"Too bad," I said. "I wanted it for my Memory Album."

"Sounds like a real banquet," Dick Fleming said. "Should we start at the top and work our way down; a different entree every day? If we stay around here more than six days, we're in trouble."

Rose came back with our drinks and a bowl of peanuts in the shell.

"Just throw the shells on the floor, folks," she advised us breezily. "Keeps out the termites. You decided yet?"

"What're catfish balls?" I asked, consulting my scrap of a menu.

"Delicious," Donohue told me. "And very hard to find. They can only get them from the male catfish, y'see."

"Oh, *you!*" the waitress said, slapping his ear with her order pad. "You'd make me blush effen I hadn't heerd that joke a hundert times before. Honey, they're ground-up catfish meat, deep-fried."

"What's the soup?" Dick asked.

"Tomato," she said. "Campbell's best."

"How's the breaded veal cutlet?" Jack said.

"I ate it tonight, and I'm livin'."

"Any veal in it?" he wanted to know.

"Some," she said.

We all took the soup and cutlet. The pot. and vegs. turned out to be home fries and string beans. If we hadn't been so hungry, we would have starved. The ice cream was warm; to make up for it, the coffee was cold.

But the drinks were big, and for every two rounds we bought, the house bought one. A pleasant custom. When Rose brought our coffee, Donohue asked her, "That guy behind the bar, is he Hoxey?"

"Nah," the waitress said. "Hoxey was smart, sold out to us and moved to California. We never got around to changing the name."

"The bartender—he's your one and only?"

"That's what *he* thinks," Rose laughed. "Yeah, that's my hubby. Ben Lufkin."

Donohue slid out of the booth, went over to the bar. In a minute the two men were shaking hands. Then they leaned toward each other, their heads together. I saw Jack slip him money, so neat and quick and smooth, I think I was the only one in the restaurant who noticed it. Donohue came back to the booth.

"Think we could get a couple of cold six-packs, Rose?" he asked.

"I think maybe I could fix you up. Anything else?"

"Not right now, thank you, ma'am. The food was fine."

"I always did like a cheerful liar," she said, adding up our bill. "Please pay at the bar. Ben won't let me handle the money. He figures if I see more'n five bucks, I'll take off after Hoxey."

We drove slowly back to Mrs. Pearl's, watching a

lemon moon come bobbing into a cloudless night sky.

"Nice people," Dick Fleming said.

"Uh-huh," Donohue said. "Most of them. Some ain't so nice. Like everywheres."

"I saw you give Ben some money," I said.

"Yeah. He's going to keep his eyes and ears open. Give us a call out at Mrs. Pearl's if anyone comes around asking for us."

"You trust him?" Fleming asked.

"Got no choice, do we?" Donohue said. "But I think he's straight. Hell, let's forget it and just relax. That bastard Rossi is probably knocking on doors in Jacksonsville right now."

Mrs. Sniffins was rocking on the porch, a white wraith, when we arrived. Jack parked on the crushed stone driveway alongside the house. We walked around to the front, Dick carrying two cold six-packs of beer in a brown paper bag.

"Evenin', ma'am," Donohue said. "Right pretty night, with the moon and all."

"Right pleasant," she said, nodding. "If you're of a mind to set a spell, there's plenty of chairs."

We thanked her and pulled up wicker porch chairs with thin sailcloth cushions.

"Would smoking bother you, Mrs. Sniffins?" I asked her.

"Land, no," she said. "I smoke a ciggie myself ever' now and again."

So we lighted up, Black Jack holding a match for Mrs. Pearl's cigarette. She gripped it between thumb and forefinger of her left hand and smoked it importantly. I don't think she inhaled. But it was obvious she was enjoying the smoke, and enjoying our being there. Donohue had been right: She wanted company.

"Ma'am," he said, "we picked up some cold beer at

Hoxey's. It'd be a downright pleasure if you'd share it with us."

It wasn't hard to persuade her. So there we were a few moments later, all four of us sipping Budweiser from cans, smoking our cigarettes, and talking lazily of this and that. I couldn't remember when I had been happier.

After a while, Jack got Mrs. Pearl talking about her family's history. It wasn't difficult; it almost seemed as if she had been waiting for the opportunity to tell the story. She didn't want it to die with her.

She herself was from Alabama, but this piece of land had been in her husband's family since before the War Between the States. She had met her husband, Aaron, at a church convention in Athens, Georgia. They had corresponded and then he had traveled to Evergreen, Alabama, to meet her family. She and Aaron had been married a year later, in Evergreen, and she had returned to live with him in the big white house in Whittier. Aaron's mother was alive then, living with them, and it was evident the new bride and the mother-in-law didn't hit it off.

"I won't say a word against that woman," Mrs. Pearl Sniffins said firmly, in a tone of voice that implied if she ever started, she might never stop.

She accepted a second can of beer graciously from Dick Fleming, and said, "I thank you kindly," when he removed the tab for her. She took a deep swallow and belched gently before continuing her story.

She and Aaron had six children. One boy died at childbirth, one girl died at the age of three months from a respiratory ailment. "Just coughed up her pore little lungs." Another son died aboard a battleship in World War II. The others, three girls, married and moved away. They were all over: Arizona, Chicago, Toronto. Mrs. Pearl had eleven grandchildren.

For a few years after they were married, the girls came back to Whittier to visit with their husbands and new babies. But they didn't come so often anymore. But they wrote regular, Mrs. Pearl assured us, and sent pictures of the children and gifts on her birthday.

"I already got their Christmas gifts," she said proudly. "All stacked up. I'll open them Christmas morning."

We didn't say anything. Just sat there in silence on a balmy night in Georgia, staring at moon shadows.

"What about your own family, ma'am?" Jack Donohue asked softly.

"All gone," she told him. "I was an only child and my folks passed. Uncles and aunts passed. Cousins passed or scattered. We just lost track."

"Yes," Dick Fleming said slowly, "that's what happens: We just lose track."

"I don't know," Mrs. Pearl Sniffins said. "It just seems a shame that a family should break up like that. It wasn't always so. My land, my husband's family just went on for years and years. I've got all the pictures. Tintypes, they called them then. And some little paintings framed in velvet. And bundles and bundles of letters, so faded now you can hardly make them out. But that was a family that lasted. Now it seems like they bust up so fast. People die or move away. No one stays in the same place anymore. So we lose track. A name used to mean something. People knew who you were. They knew your people. But no more. Well . . . I ain't one to pity myself; don't you go thinking that."

"No'm, Mrs. Pearl," I said, "we'd never think that of you. But times change, and customs, and the way people are. And we've got to go along with the changes, like it or not."

"You maybe," she said sharply. "You're young

enough. Not me. I don't hold with the new ways, and don't have to. I just wish I had my children around me, that's all. My own sons working this land that's been in the family so long. Great-grandchildren I could see and hug. This house is big enough for all. But it's not to be, and that's God's will, and we must accept it and believe it's for the best. And now I do believe that delicious sip of nice cold beer had made me drowsy enough to sleep, so I will excuse myself and go off to bed. You all set out here just as long as you like."

We all stood up and Dick Fleming helped Mrs. Pearl out of her rocker. She smiled at us in the dimness.

"Good night, all," she said in a tremulous voice. "Sleep tight. Don't let the bedbugs bite. Now that's just a little saying we have. You won't find any bedbugs in this house, I do assure you."

Then she was gone. The screen door closed behind her. We sat down again. I took Mrs. Pearl's rocker, the cushion still warm. I closed my eyes, rocked back and forth and saw it all. I hoped no one would say anything, and no one did.

After a while, the beer finished, we went inside, locked the door carefully, and went up to bed. We heard Mrs. Pearl snoring in the parlor, and we moved on tiptoe, not talking, so as not to wake her.

That night we all slept naked together in the double bed in the big bedroom. I was glad I was between two men, being held by both. I never wanted to be alone again. I fell asleep, the old straw rustling gently beneath me: a derisive whisper.

Our stay in Whittier was twenty-four-hour champagne, the days sun-crisped, the nights moon-cooled. It was a shared dream that changed us all, in ways we could not understand. Something deep was happening to us, but what it was we did not know.

Our daily routine was simple enough. We slept together, although I kept my personal suitcase in the small bedroom. I rumpled the bed, scattered toilet articles about, left cigarette butts in ashtrays, gave the room what I fancied was a lived-in appearance. All this to mislead Mrs. Pearl in case she made an unexpected climb to the second floor, and to fool the cleaning lady when she appeared.

But we slept together. Every night but one.

We rose before 8:00, dressed, went downstairs to have breakfast with Mrs. Pearl in the big kitchen. And the size of the breakfasts matched that room: orange juice; oatmtal; eggs; bacon, ham, or pork sausages; pancakes; grits; corn muffins, blueberry muffins, toast; waffles; sweet butter; jams, jellies, and homemade preserves; milk or coffee.

Mrs. Pearl bustled about, talking a blue streak, and seemingly delighted with our appetites and praise for her cooking. She told us (three times) that her quince jelly had won a blue ribbon at the county fair. I could believe it; it was nectar.

After breakfast we usually drove into Whittier to shop. We knew what those gargantuan breakfasts were costing Mrs. Pearl, so we took her shopping list into town and paid for the milk, coffee, pancake flour, ham, and all the other goodies. We also loaded her refrigerator with beer, cola, and tonic water, and put two quarts of vodka in the freezer.

By the second day of our stay, practically everyone in Whittier knew us, and we exchanged "Howdy" and "Have a nice day" a dozen times as we went from general store to liquor store to gas station to Hoxey's.

At Hoxey's, Rose would have a bag of sandwiches made for us. Really dreadful sandwiches: processed cheese on dry white bread, pressed ham on stale rye. But we didn't care. Everyone was just so *nice,* it would have been cruel to suggest to them that a luncheon of Twinkies and Yoo-Hoo wasn't really the best food American agriculture could offer.

Then back to Mrs. Pearl's with our purchases, usually including a special treat for her. (She doted on licorice-filled mints.) Then, around noon, we took our sandwiches and six-pack of beer across the fields. We dunked naked in the muddy stream (even Dick and I were calling it the "crick" by then), and ate our sandwiches and drank our beer, kept cold by immersing the cans in the running water.

On one of those trips Donohue carried our lunch in the emptied, bullet-riddled suitcase that had provided no shield for Hymie Gore. Jack and Dick scooped out a hole under one of the oak trees near the stream and buried the case.

In the afternoon, back at Mrs. Pearl's, I worked on my manuscript, and wrote enough so that I was up-to-date and describing current events. The men washed down the Buick, then cleaned up Mrs. Pearl's seven-year-old Plymouth. They also consolidated all our gear into four suitcases and three canvas carryalls.

One afternoon they left me at Mrs. Pearl's and drove away, ostensibly to have the Buick gassed, oiled, and tuned. But when they returned, Jack had extra ammunition for all our guns and a complete cleaning kit. He and Dick spent hours stripping down the guns, cleaning them, and reloading. Donohue said Dick was very good at it and could become an expert if he applied himself.

Something else they brought back from their trip were two unlabeled pint bottles of colorless liquid which, Jack assured me, was the finest white lightning in the State of Georgia. I tried a sip and it felt like my vocal cords had been given a shot of Novocain, while sweat ran down from my armpits. I said, when I recovered my voice, that I'd stick to eighty-proof vodka.

But that night, after we returned from Hoxey's and had a beer with Mrs. Pearl on the porch, we retired to our bedroom, and the two men demolished the pints of alky. Fortunately, they were sitting on the edge of the bed as they drank, and all they had to do was fall back.

I lifted up their legs and left the louts, fully clothed, to their groaning unconsciousness. Then I went into the smaller bedroom. It was the only night I slept alone. In the morning they were full of that crazy macho boasting about which one had the worst hangover. I wasn't sore at them—just amused, and amazed at the way Dick Fleming was acting.

Because, of the three of us, he had changed, was changing, the most. Some of it was physical. He was leaner and harder. The sun was burning his pale, freckled skin a bronzed tan. His hair was bleached to the color of wheat, and his blue eyes seemed deeper, steadier, more knowing. I saw the looks he got from the women in Hoxey's and on the streets of Whittier.

But less obvious were the changes within. He took a more active role in our sexual shenanigans, frequently as initiator. He insisted on driving the car more often, ordered for us at Hoxey's, offered his opinions on a multitude of matters in a firm, decisive manner.

I looked at him with astonishment: a new man. When, alone with Donohue, I mentioned something of this, Black Jack flashed me one of his wise grins and said, "He's found his balls." Whatever had happened, was happening, I knew Dick and I would never again indulge in those tickle-and-squirm games. The pistilless and stamenless man had become more than a neuter. I was glad for him, I suppose. I wasn't certain about my own reaction.

So the days passed in a dream, peaceful, golden, and each hour separated us further from what had gone before. We sniffed security like cocaine, certain that the chase had cooled, pursuit had ended, and we could leisurely accomplish all that we had set out to do.

Christmas was on a Sunday that year, and on the preceding Friday we bought a sad, lopsided tree in the gas station lot in Whittier. We brought it home to Mrs. Pearl, lashed on the roof of the Buick. We were certain she would have all the ornaments and tinsel necessary. Women like Mrs. Pearl Sniffins don't throw away Christmas tree ornaments. She didn't disappoint us.

So on Friday evening, after our return from Hoxey's, we gathered in what Mrs. Pearl called the "sitting room" and decorated our tree. It was, I suppose, a kind of party. We all drank a bottle of port wine. There were jokes, laughter, remembrances of past holidays. It seemed strange to me to be celebrating Christmas in such a warm climate. How can you lie naked on a muddy crick bed on Christmas day? But that wine made everything seem quite normal. I think we sang some carols, more for Mrs. Pearl's sake then ours. She surely was partial to "Silent Night."

Later, in bed together, Mrs. Sniffins snoring peacefully downstairs, we talked quietly of our plans. We decided to spend Christmas day with Mrs. Pearl (she had invited us, promising to roast a turkey "with all the trimmings"), and maybe even go to church with her. Then we would take off on the following Monday. We still had plenty of cash, and Black Jack said we could take back and secondary roads all the way down to Miami, just to play it cool. We'd probably arrive Wednesday or Thursday.

It all sounded good to us. After those glittering days and perfumed nights, it was impossible that anything could turn sour.

On Saturday morning, after breakfast, we drove into Whittier to buy Christmas gifts for Mrs. Pearl. There wasn't much choice. In the general store I found a quilted bed jacket I thought she might like, and the men bought her perfume, a five-pound box of chocolates, and two palm-leaf fans.

We decided to forego our afternoon swim, so we didn't stop at Hoxey's for sandwiches and beer. We drove directly to Mrs. Pearl's, planning to spend the afternoon wrapping our gifts and getting a gentle buzz on in honor of Christ's birth.

And that's exactly what we did, until about 2:00 that afternoon, Christmas Eve. Then we heard Mrs. Pearl calling from downstairs. Donohue opened the door and went to the top of the stairs.

"Mr. Morrison," we heard her say, "you got a phone call. It's Ben Lufkin at Hoxey's."

Jack went down the stairs.

Dick Fleming turned to look at me with bleak eyes.

"Start packing," he said harshly.

We heard Donohue come up the stairs. He stalked into the room. He took two guns from a canvas carryall, a revolver and a pistol. He pulled back the slide of the pistol, let it snap forward. He put the revolver in his belt, the pistol in the side pocket of his jacket. Then he started helping us with the packing.

"Two guys came into Hoxey's looking for us," he reported. "Ben Lufkin says one was wearing a gray suit, vest, hat. Young, clean, fresh-shaved. Doesn't sound like one of Rossi's boys. Sounds like a Fed. The other guy was wearing a star, a deputy from the county sheriff's office."

Even while I was listening, the worm of fear beginning to gnaw, I noted his accent: "deppity" and "shurf."

"Ben says he told them nothing," Jack went on. "Maybe he didn't, maybe he did. But someone in town sure as hell will; you can bet on that. They had photos of you two, descriptions on all of us."

"How could they trace us here, Jack?" I asked him.

"Got a line on me, I suppose," he said wearily. "Found out I came from the Macon area. So they're covering this part of the state, figuring I might head for home, like some animal going down its hole."

"That's what you did," Fleming said. "What *we* did. You figure they know we're here—at Mrs. Pearl's?"

"I'd make book on it," Donohue said. "By now, someone's talked."

"Why should they talk?" I asked. "Why betray one of their own?"

"A reward maybe," Black Jack said, shrugging. "Maybe from envy—us driving a big car and throwing money around like we did. Maybe just to see the excitement. A shoot-out. Nothing much happens in Whittier. Who knows *why* they did it? But someone did, bet on it."

"A Federal agent and a county deputy?" Fleming repeated. "The two of them won't try to take us. Not right away. They'll call in more men, more cars."

Donohue looked at him with affection.

"You're learning," he said. "You're beginning to think like a pro. You're right; we've got some time. Not a lot, but a little. All finished? Got everything? Okay, you bring the bags down. I'll bring the Buick around in front."

When we carried the luggage downstairs, Mrs. Pearl

Sniffins was leaning against the frame of the kitchen door. Beyond her, I could see the big turkey on the kitchen table, ready for stuffing. There were bowls and pots and pans. Potatoes and yams, stringbeans and corn. A pile of chestnuts. A pumpkin pie.

Mrs. Pearl wore an apron over her housedress. Her hands were floured. She just stood there in those unbuckled combat boots. She watched us. She didn't say anything.

Donohue came in and helped us carry out the suitcases. We stowed everything in the trunk and back seat of the Buick. Then we all came back inside.

"Ma'am," Jack said, trying to smile, "we've got to be moving on. We're just as sorry as we can be, looking forward to that fine Christmas dinner like we were. But we got no choice."

"No," she said, still staring at us. "I don't suppose you do."

"Uh, Mrs. Sniffins," Dick said, "we got you a few little things. Christmas presents. Not much. But we do appreciate all you've done for us."

"Your kindness," I said. "Your friendship. We'll never forget it."

We held the gifts out to her.

"Leave them in the hall," she said, her face stony.

So we piled our packages on the hall table. We went outside. We got into the Buick, Donohue behind the wheel. We started up, pulled out of the driveway. I looked back. Mrs. Pearl Sniffins was standing on the porch. Her hands were clasped under her apron. She looked like a statue. Something carved.

Jack turned to the left.

"Through Whittier?" Dick said.

"The shortest and fastest way out," Donohue said. "Maybe they haven't got a roadblock set up yet."

But they had. We sped toward the town, trailing a

cloud of dust. Then Jack slammed on the brakes. The car slewed sideways on the dirt, half-turned, skidded, came to a stop, rocking.

About five hundred yards ahead we saw a car and a Jeep blocking the road. They were in a V-formation, nose to nose, pointing toward us. No space between them. Men behind them with rifles and shotguns. On both sides were deep ditches, and then barbed wire fences along the bald fields.

Donohue backed, swung, backed, swung. We accelerated in the other direction, speeding by Mrs. Pearl's again. I craned sideways. She was still standing on the porch, hands under her apron. We flashed by, went about two miles. Then slowed, slowed, and stopped.

Ahead of us, parked sideways across the road was a heavy tractor. No way around that. Two men behind it, peering cautiously over the treads.

"Boxed in," I said.

"They're waiting for more men," Dick said. "More cars. More guns. Then they'll move in."

Donohue didn't say anything. He was leaning forward over the wheel, staring through the dusty windshield.

"Take off across country?" Fleming suggested. "Bust through the fence and cut across the fields? It's a chance."

"Where to?" Black Jack said dully. "It's miles to the nearest backroad, over fields, culverts, crick beds. Meanwhile we'll be leaving a dust cloud so big a blind Boy Scout could tail us."

He put the car in reverse. We began to back up slowly. No reason. Just for something to do. Just to be moving.

"Let's run the roadblock," I said. "The one near

Whittier. Just plow right on through. What the hell."

Jack Donohue took a deep breath.

"Suits me," he said. Then he turned, flashed his electric grin. "I love you, Jan," he said. "You too, Dick. If you're all game, let's go for broke."

"Wait a minute," Fleming said. "Stop here a minute, Jack."

The car halted. Donohue and I looked at Fleming. His eyes were half-closed. He was breathing deeply, blowing air through pursed lips. His face had gone white. Freckles stood out on nose and forehead.

"All right," Dick said, opening his eyes wide, "here's what we do. Not much of a chance, but some. We go back to Mrs. Pearl's. Get her Plymouth. Pay her for it or just take it. Whatever's needed. Unload the Buick, put everything in the Plymouth. Jannie drives the Plymouth, and, Jack, you're hunched down in the back seat, out of sight. Wait—another idea: Jan, you borrow one of Mrs. Pearl's bonnets. Get it? You're driving an old Plymouth in a bonnet. You look like Mrs. Pearl alone. They're going to let you get close to the roadblock. They're not going to shoot. They're waiting for two men and a woman in a big black Buick. Okay, so now Jan, in a bonnet, is driving toward Whittier in the loaded Plymouth. Raising a big cloud of dust. And I'm right in the middle of that cloud of dust, driving the Buick. They'll be watching the lead car—right? So at the last minute, just before the roadblock, Jannie, you pull as far over to the side as you can get. Not down in the ditch, but give me room to pass. I go roaring by in the Buick and crash the roadblock. Bam, biff, and pow! I'm going to bulldoze a way through; you can bet on it. Then, Jannie, the moment you see the opening, step on the gas and whiz through. What do you think?"

We were silent. I looked at Black Jack Donohue.

He was staring out the side window at the cropped fields of Georgia.

"Only one thing wrong with that idea," he said.

"What?" Fleming demanded.

"*I* drive the Buick," Jack said. "*You* hunker down in the back seat of the Plymouth."

"No way," Dick said. "It was my idea; I get to have the fun."

"We'll flip a coin," Donohue said. "Heads you do the hero bit, tails I do."

He fished in his pants pocket, brought out a fistful of change. He selected a quarter.

"Bullshit!" Fleming said. "I'd never let you flip a coin, you lousy crook. Jannie, you flip it. Heads, I drive. Tails, Jack does."

I flipped the coin, caught it, closed my fist over it. Opened my fingers slowly. Heads.

"Beautiful," Dick said. "My lucky day. Let's go."

We drove back to Mrs. Pearl's. No one on the porch. But when we pulled up in front with a scattering of crushed stone, she came out. She must have been watching from behind the screen door.

"Let me do the talking," Jack said in a low voice.

She watched the three of us come up the steps. Those water-clear eyes regarded us gravely.

"Another man called you," she said to Jack. "Said he was from the Federal Bureau of Investigation. Wanted to talk to you. I said you was gone."

"Uh-huh," Donohue said. "Ma'am, we need your car, we surely do. We don't mean to harm you, no ma'am, we don't but we do need that car in the worst way. And there's no trouble for you in it, see'n as how we're desperate characters and forced you to give us your keys. Leastwise, that's what you can say. And we'll pay you good money, ma'am, we surely will."

She looked at him sorrowfully.

"I'll get the keys," she said, "and I don't want no money."

It took about five minutes to bring the Plymouth around and transfer the luggage. Mrs. Pearl handed over one of her poke bonnets without asking why I wanted it. I supposed she guessed. Then we were ready to leave her for the second time. We stood close on the porch, me wearing the bonnet pulled down over the red wig.

"Ma'am," Jack Donohue said, "there's just no way we can thank you for all you done for us. You'll get your car back sooner or later, I promise you that. I know you won't take any cash for yourself, but I'd be much obliged if you'd let us make a contribution to your church."

"Yes," she said, "I'll take it for the church. For good works. And I'll say a prayer for you all."

"Thank you, Mrs. Pearl," I said, and stepped close to kiss her leathery cheek.

The men did the same. She just stood there, expressionless, not moving.

Jack took out his wallet, counted out a thousand dollars. He folded it, put it into her palm, closed her fingers over it.

Then we went down to the cars. Black Jack and I turned to Fleming.

"Well . . ." Dick said. "Everything straight? Jannie, get as close to the roadblock as you can before pulling aside. Then I come roaring past and you pile it on the moment you see the opening."

I nodded dumbly. I looked toward the sky. I didn't want to look at him. If I looked at him, I'd burst, collapse, and die.

"After you bust through," Donohue said to him, "get out of that car in a hurry. I'll cover you and I'll have the back door open. We'll pick you up on the other side. Real bang-bang stuff. The Late Show."

"Sure," Dick Fleming said with a radiant smile. Then he said lightly, "Take care."

We climbed into the cars. I drove the Plymouth. Donohue got down on the floor in the rear. When I glanced in the mirror, I saw he already had both his guns out. Dick Fleming followed us in the Buick."

Mrs. Pearl Sniffins watched us go. I thought she waved a hand in farewell, but I may have been imagining that.

Jack gave me a series of commands from the back seat. So many, so rapidly, I knew I'd never remember them all . . .

"Keep it under forty. Before we get in sight, swerve back and forth all over the road. Kick up the dust, slow down, then speed up suddenly. Try to churn up the road. That dust has got to be thick. Figure about thirty feet from the roadblock. Then stand on the brakes. You'll skid in the dirt. Be ready for it. Try to stop fast. Turn to the left. Get it. The *left!* So when Dick goes by, he can see how much room he has. The moment he's past, tell me. Yell or something. I'm out of sight; I won't be able to see. After you yell, I'll start popping away to keep them down. Don't get spooked by the noise. You pour on the gas. He'll hit and then you go through. Go fast! Brake on the other side. Wait for Dick. Then—"

"All right," I said, "all *right!* You're telling me too much too fast. Just let me do it my way."

He was silent a moment. Then, when he spoke, his voice was surprisingly gentle.

"Sure, babe," he said. "Do it your way."

I glanced in the rearview mirror, then ahead, then in the mirror, then ahead. I gave Jack a running commentary . . .

"Dick's right behind us. About fifty feet back. Lots

of dust. I can hardly see him. We're coming to the
final turn. Now we're around. Now we're on the
straightaway. I'm slowing a little. I'm sitting up. I'm
leaning forward so they can see the bonnet. Soon now.
Get set; I'm going to turn off to the left. They see us.
They're standing behind the cars. A two-door and the
Jeep. They're waving their arms. I'm slowing. I'll count
down. *Five, four, three, two, one* . . . NOW!"

I jerked the wheel to the left. I felt the rear end
break away. I fought the skid. The Plymouth started
down into the ditch. I wrestled it back. Then we
slowed, slowed. Stopped, tilted slightly, on the verge.
The black Buick went roaring by. So close, so close.
I caught a quick glimpse of Dick Fleming bent over
the wheel, his face impassive.

It all should have gone in a flash. But it didn't. It
went in slow motion. I saw everything.

Dick aimed the accelerating Buick at the Jeep. Men
scattered. One dived into the ditch. I pulled back onto
the road. Donohue was up. He leaned out the open
back window. He fired the pistol as fast as he could
pull the trigger. Dick hit the Jeep just back of the right
front fender. The crash deafened me. The Jeep lifted
into the air. It rolled. The Buick spun and spun. A
tire blew. The Jeep rolled over. The Buick plunged
down into the ditch. There was room ahead. I aimed
for the opening, sobbing, cursing, whatever. Jack held
the back door ajar. He fired the revolver. I heard
screams. Crack of rifles. Boom of shotguns. Dust
everywhere. A reddish haze. Screech of torn metal.
Sudden *whumpf!* as the Jeep exploded in a blossom of
orange flame. I swerved to avoid the other car. Then I
was through, past the mess. I stood on the brake,
skidded to a halt. Jack Donohue was out and running
back. I twisted to see. The Buick was crumpled in the
ditch on its right side. The hood and trunk lid were

sprung. The driver's door was thrown back. Dick
Fleming crawled out. He jumped to the ground. His
left arm was dangling. I found the gun in my shoulder
bag. I opened my door, stepped out onto the road. I
held my gun with both hands. I aimed at the sedan
and the men behind it. I pulled the trigger. Again.
Again. Donohue was close to Dick. So close! His arms
reached out. Shotgun boom. Dick lifted into the air.
Literally lifted. Flew. Smacked down. Rolled. Jack
halted, turned. He came running back. White face,
white eyes, white teeth. All of him leached and straining. I stood there clicking the trigger on an empty
gun. Donohue came gasping up. He pushed me
sprawling onto the front seat of the Plymouth. He
jammed in beside me, behind the wheel. He shoved
the car in gear. We took off. Spinning wheels. Shouts.
Rifle fire. Something spanged off the roof of the
Plymouth.

We went careening down the road. Through Whittier. Pedestrians and dogs scattered before us. Blank
faces turned to us. Cars pulled onto sidewalks. I
dragged myself from the floor. I sat upright on the
seat.

Jack Donohue was singing a hymn, banging on the
steering wheel . . .

"Brighten the corner, where you are," he bellowed.
"Brighten the corner, where you are . . ."

Journey's End

Now I knew I was changing. I knew *how* I was changing. Up to this point I had been a war correspondent, accredited to report but not to play an active role. Oh, I could, willy-nilly participate, but I could not influence.

But now I had planted myself on a dirt road in Georgia and fired a lethal weapon at duly appointed representatives of the law. It was really, in my mind, my first act of conscious illegality. I might have killed someone, although I doubted it. I couldn't have cared less.

"How old was he?" Jack Donohue asked.

"Thirty-two," Jannie said. "I think. Maybe he had a birthday. Maybe thirty-three or -four. Around there."

"You don't *know?*" he said incredulously.

"No," I said.

"Sheesh," he said.

At the same time my role as war correspondent came to an end, I became dissatisfied with what I had written in Project X. It seemed to me I had not told the whole truth about Dick Fleming, Hymie Gore, Angela, the Holy Ghost, Clement, Smiley, Antonio Rossi. Or even Jack Donohue. Or even myself.

As a journalist, I had limned us all as two-dimensional characters, cardboard cutouts. But reading back over what I had written, remembering the contradictions and complexities of everyone involved, I yearned for a larger talent so I could do justice to their humanness. Not only their frailties and inconsistencies, but their constancy and brave humor.

"Where was he from?" Jack Donohue asked.

"Somewhere in Ohio," Jannie Shean said. "He never spoke of it. Never went back, as long as I knew him."

"Have a family?" he said.

"A mother living, I think. Never mentioned his father. I had the feeling the father had deserted or maybe he was dead. Dick never said and I never asked."

"You didn't know much about him," Black Jack said. Accusingly.

"No," I said wonderingly. "I didn't."

Hadn't wanted to, I almost blurted out. Hadn't wanted to pry, probe, ask questions. If he had wanted to tell me about himself, he would have, wouldn't he? Or was that a cop-out? Did he interpret my lack of curiosity as lack of interest? I thought him a very private man. Perhaps he was, not from choice but because that was the kind of friend he thought *I* wanted.

Donohue was right: I hadn't really known Dick Fleming. Who he was, what moved him. I saw his body flung into the air, then crumpling, rolling. I wanted him back. I wanted to hold him naked in bed, stare into those guileless blue eyes, and whisper, "Who are you?" I think he would have told me.

"He had class," Jack Donohue said.

"You have class," Jannie Shean said.

"No," he said sadly, "all I got is front. I know it."

At the same time I realized I had been hardened. I could feel it in my bones. I am speaking now not of Jannie Shean, a novelist, mother of Chuck Thorndike, Mike Cantrell, Buck Williams, Pat Slaughter, and Brick Wall. I am speaking of Bea Flanders, née Jannie Shean, refugee, criminal, and most-wanted. I had learned the argot, habits, fears, precautions, cruelties, and cunning of the lawbreaker on the run.

When I had been casing the Brandenberg job, I had felt something of that: me against society, everyone's hand raised against me. I had found a kind of wild exhilaration in it: rebel versus the establishment. Now I felt no excitement. Only a savage resolve. Simply to exist. Acknowledging that I had turned a corner in my life and could never go back.

"He was a marvelous lover," Jack Donohue said. "You know?"

"Yes," Jannie Shean said. "I know."

"He was so fucking *elegant*," Black Jack said.

He wanted to talk about Dick Fleming, to remember him. Bea Flanders didn't. I wanted to forget the dead and get on with the perilous business of living.

After that bullet-studded getaway at Whittier, we fled along backroads to Homerville, Donohue threading a maze of dirt lanes he remembered from his rumrunning days. The Plymouth had no radio, but at Fargo we ditched the car and stole a Chevy pickup, the keys kindly left in the ignition. There was a scratchy radio in the cab, and we heard hourly broadcasts of the hunt that had been organized, the net drawing tight around us. "An arrest is expected momentarily."

We took turns at the wheel, and north of Lake City in Florida ditched the Chevy pickup and caught a bus into Jacksonville. There, after spending half a day in a fleabag hotel, we bought a rackety heap in a used car lot. It was a ten-year-old Dodge. We paid cash, gassed up, and headed south on Route 95 again.

In all these switches and changes, we had carefully transferred all our luggage. There was never a question of leaving anything behind; we didn't discuss it. We even brought along the suitcase containing Dick Fleming's clothing, and toilet articles.

During the time we spent in Jacksonville, I found a drugstore that was open and bought hair bleach, dye, and some other things. We changed Donohue to a straw-colored blond, a process that took more than six hours. His eyebrows were lightened with white mustache wax and he donned a pair of mirrored sunglasses.

The next day, at St. Augustine, Jack bought maroon slacks, white socks, leather strap sandals, and a short-sleeved sport shirt in a wild tropical print. He wore the tails loose, over his belt, not only to look like every other tourist on his way to Disney World, but also to conceal the revolver carried at the small of his back.

We knew there had been no photos taken of Bea Flanders; the best they'd have would be a police artist's sketch or a retouched photo of Jannie Shean. So I stuck with the curly red wig, heavy makeup, falsies under a tight sweater, and floppy slacks with wide cuffs above high-heeled shoes.

Also, for additional camouflage, we bought a cheap camera which Jack wore suspended from his neck on a leather strap. And I put away my Gucci shoulder bag, and carried a straw tote bag that had "Florida" and a palm tree woven on the side. The only thing we lacked were three messy-faced kids, screeching and blowing bubblegum.

We spent the next night at Daytona Beach, and realized Christmas had come and gone. We went out separately the next morning and bought each other gifts. I gave Jack an electric shaver and he bought me a string bikini (too small) and a blue velour beach coverup (too large). But we kissed, and it wasn't the worst day-after-Christmas I've ever spent.

We cut over to Orlando, traded in the ancient Dodge, and bought a two-year-old Oldsmobile Cutlass. In all these trades and buys, Jack had to use his identification. We had no doubt that our trail would be picked up eventually. All we hoped to accomplish was to confuse our pursuers long enough for us to get to Miami. There we could hole up in a safe place and figure our next move. We were still carrying more than five thousand in cash, plus the big, valuable pieces from the Brandenberg heist. It was, we figured, enough to get us through with maybe another switch of cars before we arrived in southern Florida.

Got back onto Route 95 again and headed south past Cocoa, Palm Bay, Vero Beach. We stayed the night in West Palm Beach, dined well on broiled dolphin, and went to a disco late in the evening. We didn't dance; just watched. Then we went back to our motel and made love.

It wasn't the first time we had had sex since Dick Fleming's death, but the intensity hadn't diminished. We coupled like survivors, like the plague was abroad in the land and we had to prove we were alive. Between paroxysms I questioned Jack about his family, his youth, what he had done, how he had lived. Never again did I want to mourn a stranger.

But reticence had become such an ingrained part of him that I couldn't break through. And even when he did reveal something—an event, an incident, a triumph, a failure—I never knew whether or not to be-

lieve him. He had told me to doubt everything he
said, and he had taught me too well.

He did say this . . .

"I used to go to the track all the time. In the grand-
stand, you know, or standing at the rail. And I'd turn
and look up at the clubhouse, and I'd see these men
and women. No different from me and you. I mean, in
my head I knew they were no different. They ate
and shit. They were going to die. But to me, they
were different. The way they dressed. Moved. Watching the race through binoculars worth more than I
owned. Laughing and drinking their champagne from
those swell glasses. Class. I mean, they had *class.*"

"Bullshit," I said. "They had money."

"Yeah, well, maybe," he said. "But with some of
them it was more than that. I mean, you can look at a
good colt and see the breeding. The build, the way
it carries its head, the way it steps out. You just
know. Good blood there. Good breeding. Well fed and
cared for, of course. That's where the money comes in.
But also, a thoroughbred could be hauling an ice
wagon, thin as a pencil, bones sticking out, sores, and
you'd still spot it. If you knew what to look for. It's
class, Jannie: the greatest thing in the world. And the
people in that clubhouse had it."

"An accident of birth."

"Sure," he said. "I agree. Not something they did.
Something they were born to, just like that frisky colt
bouncing along and tossing his beautiful head. But
that's what I wanted. To be. To have. All my life.
When I was in the bucks, I bought the right clothes
and went to the right places. I learned how to act.
The small fork for the salad—right? But the headwaiter always knew, and I knew he knew. Slip him
enough and you'd get a good table and good service.
You'd think you were in, until you saw how he treated

the class people. Maybe they didn't even tip him dime one, but he kissed their ass. They were something special, you see. And no matter how much I paid him, he knew I was just a redneck in drag, with punk between my toes and calluses if you looked close enough."

"Just shut up and lie back," I said fiercely. "Let me pleasure you."

"All right," he said faintly.

After a while, just before he fell asleep, he murmured, "I'll never make it."

"Sure you will. We'll be in Miami tomorrow."

"No," he said drowsily, "not that."

Jack drove the Cutlass on the final leg south toward Miami. For some reason, I couldn't fathom, the closer we came to journey's end, the slower he seemed to move. He cut over to Federal Highway #1, and we got caught in heavy seasonal traffic. We were stopped at traffic lights every mile or so, instead of buzzing along on Route 95 where signs warned of going too *slow*.

Also, when we halted for breakfast and lunch, he dawdled over his food. I asked him why he was stalling. He just shook his head and wouldn't answer. I wondered if he feared what awaited us in Miami. I wondered if he was plotting to ditch me and take off with the Brandenberg gems. I even wondered if he was planning to kill me.

You see, in my new role as veteran criminal, I had learned mistrust. I carried a loaded pistol in my totebag and slept with it under the pillow. The same gun I had bought from Uncle Sam ages and ages ago.

We were driving through Boca Raton when Donohue said:

"Listen, babe, maybe it would be smart not to go right *into* Miami. They're sure to be looking for us there. So why don't we stay outside the city and only drive in to do our business—arrange for the plane and new ID and all. But we won't actually stop in Miami. Just drive in and out. Cut the risk."

I thought about that a moment. It made sense.

"Where do you want to stay, Jack?" I asked him.

"Maybe Pompano Beach," he said. "I know the area. It's like forty-five minutes, maybe an hour from Miami, depending on the traffic. We'll take a place right on the beach."

"Sounds good," I said. "We can get some sun, do some swimming."

"Uh, I can't rightly swim," he said. "Not more'n a few strokes in a mud crick. But I like the beach. Especially at night. I really go for the beach at night. Wait'll you see the moon come right up out of the water. It's so pretty. Just like a picture postcard."

We turned left onto Atlantic Boulevard and drove toward the ocean. The bridge was up over the Intracoastal Waterway, and we waited about ten minutes in a long line of cars while a beautiful white yacht went by.

"Four people on that boat," I said, "and they're holding up about a hundred cars."

"So? They own a yacht; they're entitled. This place we're going to is called Rip's. I stayed there a couple times when I was playing the local tracks. I mean, it's right *on* the beach. Step out the door and you're in the water. Rip's gets a lot of horseplayers and a swinging crowd. Guys boffing their secretaries—like that."

"Swell," I said. "We'll fit right in."

"That's what I figured," he said seriously. "We'll try to get an efficiency. That's got a refrigerator and a little stove. So we can cook in if we like. Mostly we'll eat out, but we can have breakfast in and keep sandwich stuff handy."

He wasn't exaggerating about Rip's being close to

the water. It wasn't more than fifty feet to the high-tide mark, a two-story structure of cinder blocks with a Spanish-type tile roof, all painted a dazzling white. It was built in a U-shape, with a small swimming pool and grassed lounging area between the arms of the U. I thought that was crazy: a swimming pool so close to the Atlantic. But I learned later that most beachfront motels had pools, and they got a bigger play than the ocean.

I went into the office with Jack to register. He signed the card "Mr. and Mrs. Sam Morrison." Residence: New York City. The clerk looked down at it, then looked up.

"Hey," he said. "Mr. Morrison? There was a guy here just the other day asking for you."

Donohue played it perfectly.

"Oh?" he said coolly. "When was that?"

"Let's see . . . not yesterday, but the day before."

"A short, heavyset man? A real sharp dresser? Wears a vest, hat, bowtie?"

"Yeah," the clerk said. "That's the man. Said he's a friend of yours. Wondered if you'd checked in yet."

"I'll give him a call," Jack said. "I told him we'd be here, but we got tied up a couple of days with car trouble."

We rented an efficiency, a ground-floor corner apartment. We could look out a big picture window, and there was sand, sea and, if we could have seen it, Spain.

"Is this smart?" I asked Donohue. "Staying here? If Rossi has been around?"

"Sure it's smart," he said. "He's already checked the place out, so he probably won't be coming back. It's safer than a place he hasn't been yet."

That made sense, logically. But I had been doing some heavy, heavy thinking. Part of the changes I was going through. I was evolving a new philosophy, and logic didn't have much to do with it. Well . . . maybe not a philosophy, but an awareness of how things were, and how things worked.

It seemed to me I had come into a world totally different from the one I had known before. That had been a world that, despite occasional misadventure, was based on reason. Bills arrived and were paid. Traffic lights worked and most streets and avenues were one-way. I paid my rent, bought gas, had sex, wrote novels, traveled, read books, went to the theater—all with the expectation of waking the next morning and finding the world, *my* world, relatively unchanged. It was a stable existence. There was order, a meaningful arrangement of events.

I thought, in my ignorance and innocence, that all life was like that. It was the way society was organized.

But now I found myself in a netherworld where irrationality reigned. It wasn't only that I had become a creature of chance and accident, although they were certainly present. It was that my world had become fragmented, without system or sequence. There was no clarity or coherence. I couldn't find meaning.

Perhaps we would succeed in leaving the country with the Brandenberg jewels. Perhaps not. Perhaps I would marry, or at least form a lasting relationship with Jack Donohue. Perhaps not. Perhaps he would desert me or kill me. It was possible.

Anything was possible. And, I discovered, an existence without order, in which anything might happen, is difficult to live. Nerves tingle with rootlessness. The brain is in a constant churn, attempting to compute permutations and combinations. One unconsciously shortens one's frame of reference. The pleasure of the moment becomes more important than the happiness

of the future. The future itself becomes a never-never
land. The past is pushed into fog. Only the present
has meaning.

That's how we lived for almost two weeks—in the
blessed present. We woke each morning about 8:00,
had either a small breakfast in our room or walked
down to Atlantic Boulevard for pancakes or eggs in
a restaurant. Then we bought local and New York
newspapers at the Oceanside Shopping Center and
walked back to Rip's.

There was nothing in any of the papers concerning
us or the Brandenberg robbery. Nothing on TV.
More recent crimes had been committed. There were
wars, floods, plane crashes, famines. The north was
gripped in a cold wave that sent thousands of tourists
and vacationers flocking south.

At about 10:00, we went out to the beach or sat at
the motel pool. Jack usually stayed in the shade of a
beach umbrella, wearing Bermuda shorts and a short-
sleeved polo shirt. I broiled myself in direct sunlight,
wearing my too-small string bikini, a scarf tied
around my hair so I didn't have to sweat in that
damned wig.

I doused myself in oil (Jack obligingly layered my
back), and I grew a marvelous tan, the best I've ever
had. We rarely ate lunch, but usually had a few gin-
and-tonics in the afternoon. We met a few people,
tourists staying for a few days, and talked lazily of
this and that.

Then, when the sun had lost its strength, we went
into our little efficiency apartment and napped, or
made love, or both. In the evening we showered,
dressed, and went out for dinner, a different place
every day. Later we might stop at a bar or disco for a
few nightcaps. Then home to bed, usually before
midnight.

It was a totally mindless existence. I felt that, under that hot sun, my brain was turning to mush—and I loved it. Occasionally, during our first few days at Rip's, I'd ask Jack when he was going into Miami to make arrangements. "Soon," he'd say. "Soon." After a while I stopped asking. It didn't seem important. The money hadn't run out yet.

I think that, in a way, we were both catching our breath at Rip's. I was toasting my body brown and swimming in the high surf. Jack was lying slumped in blued shadow, as torpid as a lizard on a rock. He wanted to go to the local horse and dog tracks, but didn't. I wanted to go shopping, but didn't. We simply existed, and woke each morning secretly pleased at our good fortune in being alive for another day.

But one morning we awoke and, while Donohue was checking his wallet, realized our cash reserve was shrinking. Hardly at the panic level, but low enough to require replenishing. When money is going out freely, and nothing is coming in, the bankroll dwindles at a ferocious rate.

So Donohue decided to drive into Miami the next day. We discussed timing, procedures, and contingency plans. It was agreed that he would go alone, leaving the bulk of the Brandenberg loot in our apartment at Rip's. But he would take one big necklace of startling beauty and value, just as a sample to show an interested fence, if he was able to locate one. Also, we would cut up one of the heavy chokers, prizing out the individual stones. These he would attempt to peddle wherever he could, for ready cash.

"I'll be back by 7:00 in the evening at the latest," he said. "Remember, that's the cut-off time. If I'm not back by then, or haven't called, it means I've been nobbled. Then you grab what's left of the ice and take off."

"Take off?" I said. "How? Where to?"

"Cab. Bus. Plane. Train. Walking. Do what you have to do. Just get out of here. Fast. Because if Rossi grabs me, I'm going to talk. Eventually. You know that, don't you?"

I leaned forward to kiss him.

"I know," I said, nodding. "But you said your luck's running hot. You'll come back."

"Sure I will, babe," he said, pouring on one of those high-powered grins. "I'm too mean to die; you know that."

I looked at him critically. His bleached hair was now combed straight back from his forehead. His eyebrows were lightened, and he had grown a wispy mustache that we had attempted to dye with indifferent results. But I doubted if anyone would recognize him from a reported description.

I had an odd thought: that with his lightened hair and eyebrows, he resembled Dick Fleming. They could have been brothers.

We spent that evening cutting up the choker and prying out the diamonds. Then we went to bed early. Our sex that night was like our first time together when he had been fierce, hard, filled with desperate energy. He was a one-way lover again, taking what *he* wanted. He wore me out. Almost.

The next morning he left most of the remaining cash with me, wrapped the big necklace and loose stones in handkerchiefs and slid them into his inside jacket pockets. He carried a revolver in his belt and concealed an automatic pistol under the front seat of the car.

It was time for him to go. He paused a moment, frowning.

"What is it?" I said.

"Listen," he said, "I may call you and tell you to

bring the rest of the jewels to a certain place. You know?"

"Sure."

"But I might be under a gun when I make that call. If I call you 'Jan' or 'Jannie,' you'll know it's okay and you can bring the stuff. But if I call you 'Bea,' you'll know someone's forcing me to make the call. Got that?"

I nodded dumbly.

Then he kissed me.

"See you around," he said.

"Stop in any time," I said.

He smiled and was gone.

I went out to the beach and spread my towel, as far away from other sunbathers as I could get. I had brought along a quart thermos of chilled white wine, and I sipped that all afternoon and thought of nothing. Two men spoke to me, but I didn't answer. After a while they moved away to easier pickings.

It was a smoky day, the sun in and out of clouds shaped like dragons. I lay there and felt myself, felt my skin burning and tight. I wanted to be naked. I wanted that sun inside me, searing and consuming.

I went back to the motel about 3:00 and took a hot shower to take the sting away. Then I put on a loose shift and did more typing. I had persuaded Donohue to let me buy a portable, promising to type only during the day. Now I continued converting the handwritten legal pads to typed manuscript pages.

It was a mechanical job: no thinking required. If I wondered why I was doing it, what importance Project X could possibly have other than representing a horrible danger if the cops ever got hold of it, I suppose I thought of it as the last slender link with my past, with a world lost and gone, evidence of a corner turned.

The truth, I now believe, was that I didn't want to die in an alley, as Hymie Gore had, or to be blown away on a dusty backwoods road, like Dick Fleming, without leaving this account of what had happened to me and how it happened. Project X was really my last will and testament.

I finished my typing for the day. Straightened up the pages, locked the ms. away in one of the suitcases. Then I poured myself a vodka over ice and settled down to wait for Jack Donohue.

By 6:00 P.M., I had started to think coldly of what I would do if he didn't return. I would consolidate my personal belongings, trying to jam clothes, the Brandenberg stones, Project X, and the guns into two suitcases and maybe into one shoulder bag. Then I'd call a cab. I'd go to the Ft. Lauderdale airport and get a seat on a plane going anywhere. It really didn't matter. I'd just go as far as I could. When the money ran out, I'd cut up more of the jewelry and peddle the stones. I'd change my name and try to change my appearance again. I'd start a new—

There was a key in the lock. Jack Donohue walked in, looking drained. I burst into tears and flew to him. I almost knocked him over.

"Jesus Christ, baby," he said, "take it easy. I'm still in one piece."

He wouldn't tell me what had happened in Miami until we had eaten, saying he hadn't had a bite all day and was famished. So we went to a seafood joint on the Intracoastal and ordered red snapper amandine. I picked at my food, but Donohue gobbled and went to the salad bar three times. The place was too crowded and too noisy for a private conversation.

Then we returned to Rip's and mixed tall brandies with soda. We took our drinks out onto the beach. We went barefoot, Jack rolling up his cuffs. There were a few other beach strollers, but it seemed to me the sand and sea belonged to us alone.

There wasn't a full moon—that would have been too much—but we watched a silver scythe come out of the ocean, and that was as pretty as Donohue had promised. The surf was pounding. Black waves rolled in and then crashed into white foam. We could feel the spray on our skin, driven by a moaning wind. There were scudding clouds, hard stars, a sky that went on forever.

There was a chill in the air, even in Florida, but the brandy helped, and the sand was still warm beneath our toes. It was such a *natural* scene: beach, ocean, sky, clouds, stars, moon, wind. It could have been perfect. But there were people.

"There's good news and bad news," Jack Donohue said. "I'll give you the bad first."

"Thanks."

"The guys I thought I could depend on, I can't. The few I called hung up on me. The few I saw turned around and walked the other way. A few who would talk told me I'm poison. The word's got around. The Corporation was very heavy on this: You help Jack Donohue and you spend the rest of your life with busted kneecaps, pushing yourself along on a little platform on wheels. If you're lucky. Listen, I don't blame the guys; they've mostly got wives and kids. Or girlfriends anyway."

"Sure," I said.

"Also the charter planes," he went on. "The outfits that will fly anyone anywhere for a price. The Corporation had tipped them, too. Jack Donohue goes *nowhere*. Ditto the fences. They won't touch me. That Rossi had been one busy little boy. As far as Miami goes, I got leprosy."

"If we give back the Brandenberg jewels?" I asked.

"No go. The Corporation wants the Donohue jewels. My family jewels."

"How about the good news now? I think I could stand some."

He halted and I stopped beside him. We took a few sips of our drinks, looking up at that sparkling night.

"The good news is this: I unloaded about half those loose stones in jewelry shops. More than twenty grand."

"That's fine," I said faintly.

"So we're not hurting for cash. But you know where I peddled most of the rocks? In the Cuban section. Miami is full of Spics. And not only Cubans, but from all over South America. A lot of loose money there. I figure the smart guys are getting out of those banana republics before they get stood up against a wall and shot. Also, there's a lot of cash around from the dope trade. They're running gage and coke in every hour on the hour. All cash deals, of course. But money like that is hard to spend or get to Switzerland, say. That's why I was able to get top dollar for the loose rocks. You can go anywhere in the world with a diamond up your ass."

I remembered what Antonio Rossi had told me when he was Noel Jarvis: how easy it was to take precious gemstones across a border.

"But the best thing is this," Jack said. "The Spics have their own organization. They're not under the thumb of the Corporation. Oh sure, I guess they make deals now and then, but the South Americans are running the drugs on their own. And they got their own lotteries, cathouses, loansharks, betting parlors, and so forth. They don't need the Corporation."

"You think maybe we can make a deal with the Cubans?" I asked.

"I think maybe we can," he said slowly. "I got onto a guy named Manuel Garcia. That's like John Smith, in American. I flashed that big necklace I was carrying and I saw his eyes light up. I told him what we needed: a plane out of the country, passports, and visas, complete new IDs, no hassle in the country we're going to. He said maybe it could be arranged. He said he'd talk to his people."

"How much would they want? The big necklace?"

"Oh hell no. More than that. He mentioned a hundred G's, casual-like, before I told him it would be for the two of us. Then he said a quarter of a mil, knowing my woman was involved. I figure I can get it for less than that. Maybe two-hundred thou."

"You trust him? This Manual Garcia?"

"That's the trouble with this business," he said fretfully. "You've got to trust *someone* to get what you want. No, I don't trust that greaser. Jesus Christ, he wears *perfume!* But right now he's the only game in town."

"How did you leave it? What happens next?"

"This Garcia is going to talk to his people, to see if they can deliver. I've got a Miami number to call. Every day at noon. I ask for Paco. If they've got no word for me yet, Paco will be out. When they're ready to talk money and how the whole thing will be set up, Paco will tell me when to come back to Miami and where to meet."

"Two hundred thousand is a lot of money," I said slowly.

"Sure it is," Donohue agreed. "Until you remember we've got a couple of mil in those suitcases. At least. Also, it's not all profit for them. They've got to pay the paper guys, the clerks in the consulate, the pilot of the plane, the guys on the other end. Everyone's got to be oiled. So the two hundred G's isn't all that much. Not if it gets us out from under the Feds, Rossi, and the Corporation."

"I'll drink to that," I said, draining my brandy.

Donohue finished his drink. Then he took the empty glass from my hand. With a wild, whirling motion, he threw both glasses as far out to sea as he could. I saw the glint in the moonlight. Then the faint splashes as the empty glasses hit the water and disappeared. Then there was only the dark, rolling ocean.

"You think it'll work?" I said.

"It's got to work," he said fiercely. *"Got* to!"

We went back to our daily routine—breakfast, beach, drinks, dinner, sex, sleep—except that each day at noon Donohue called the Miami phone number he had been given and asked for Paco. For five days Paco was out and hadn't left any message. On the sixth day there was a different reply, and Jack motioned to me for a pad and pen, saying into the phone: "Yes. I've got it. Repeat that address. Okay. Yeah. Sure. Uh-huh, I understand. Fine."

He hung up and looked down at the scrawled notes he had made.

"I go to Miami tomorrow. They claim they can deliver what we need."

"You want me to come with you?"

"No," he said, "this is just to negotiate the deal. What they want, what we'll pay, the timing, and so on."

"Are you going to take the loot with you?"

"My God, no! I'll leave it here with you."

"Just make sure you're not followed back here."

He looked at me disgustedly.

"My pappy didn't raise me to be an idiot."

It started raining that night, and in the morning the TV weather forecaster spouted technical jargon about a stationary low-pressure area off the Florida coast. He remarked cheerfully that the rain would continue for at least another forty-eight hours, driving conditions were hazardous, small-craft warnings were in effect from the Palm Beaches south to the Keys. And of course he added: "Have a nice day!"

Jack Donohue took off for Miami in a heavy rainstorm whipped by a twenty-mile-an-hour wind that tore at palm fronds and rattled the motel windows. There was enough to eat and drink in our refrigerator; no way was I going to venture out until that crazy weather calmed.

After breakfast I started typing again, and just before noon finished transcribing my handwritten manuscript. Now I was up to date on Project X—462 pages ready for posterity. I then tore up the pages written in longhand and dumped the pieces in the garbage. One copy of that damning manuscript was all I needed—or wanted.

I took time out for a sandwich and a can of beer, then got started on the luggage. I put aside all of Dick Fleming's clothes and personal belongings, plus a few things we still had that belonged to Hymie Gore. There was a Salvation Army bin outside one of the local supermarkets, and I figured that would be a good place to dump what we didn't want.

That left one suitcase for Jack, one for me, and a third for the Brandenberg loot. The guns went into two shoulder bags, wrapped in towels stolen from various motels along our escape route.

Then I tidied up, showered, washed my hair, did my nails. I was tempted to call Sol Faber, call Aldo Binder, call my sister. But their phones could be tapped—it was possible—and besides, what could I say—"It's raining here; how is it there?"

All these activities, I told myself, were just a way

of killing time until Jack Donohue returned. But there was more to it than that. I was preparing for departure; I felt it. The storm had hidden the sun and ended the days of mindless basking. We had caught our breath, rested, and let time dull the memories of what had happened. Now we had to move on.

Antonio Rossi wasn't lolling in the sun or walking the beach at night, and I knew the Feds sure as hell weren't. They were all busy, every day and every night. Sooner or later, if we stayed where we were, they would zero in on us.

It was as simple as that: We couldn't hide; we had to run.

Donohue returned about 4:30 P.M. He was soaked through, his face drawn, his teeth chattering. He peeled off his wet clothes and got under a hot shower. By the time he came out, I had a cup of hot black coffee and a big glass of brandy waiting for him. He gulped both greedily, cursing when the coffee scalded his tongue. He solved that problem by pouring brandy into his cup.

We sat awhile without speaking, listening to the rain smashing against the windows. The wind was a low moan, like a child crying. Occasionally lighting flared over the ocean; thunder rumbled like distant guns.

I looked at Jack. He had stopped shivering, but kept both hands wrapped around his coffee cup. His wet hair was plastered to his scalp. He had lost his color; his face was pale and shiny. His eyes showed tiredness and strain. He slumped at the table, shoulders bowed, head hanging. My hero.

"Are you hungry?" I asked finally.

He groaned. "I had lunch with those *banditos*. Chicken and rice, with a pepper sauce hot enough to bring the sweat popping. It didn't seem to bother them, but it sure as hell did me in. I can still taste that crap."

"Where was this?"

"A little grocery store on a rat-trap street in the Cuban section. It had a small restaurant in back. Four booths. I think the grocery part was just a front. Lots of traffic, but no one bought any groceries that I could see. Might have been a betting drop, or maybe they were peddling happy dust. Anything is possible on that street."

"How did you make out?"

"I wish I knew," he said, sighing. "What they want is this: that necklace I showed Manuel Garcia the first time we met, plus another one of equal value."

"My God, Jack, that's almost half a million!"

"Retail value maybe," he reminded me. "About thirty percent of that from a fence. And worth absolutely nothing wrapped up in a towel in our suitcase."

I couldn't deny that, but it was hateful that others should profit from our suffering and fear.

"What do we get out of it?"

"Passports, visas, Social Security cards, drivers licenses—the works. For Arthur and Grace Reynolds, residents of Chicago. That's us. Plus a plane ride, all expenses paid."

"Where to?"

"How does Costa Rica grab you?"

I thought a moment.

"I've heard of it, of course, but I don't know where it is, exactly."

"Central America. Between Nicaragua and Panama."

"And we can live there?"

"With the right papers, which they'll furnish. The permits will have to be renewed every so often, but they claim they've got some local *officials* in their pocket and we'll have no problem."

"We're taking a lot on faith," I said.

"We got a choice?" he demanded.

"You agreed to everything they asked for?"

"Not all of it. We kicked it around for a while." He showed his teeth in a cold grin that had no humor in it. "Those were hard boys, babe. There was this Manuel Garcia plus two other desperadoes who I would not care to meet in a dark alley. When the argument was going hot and heavy, one of them took out a shiv big enough to gut a hog and started cleaning his nails. He just kept staring at me with those black button eyes and using this sticker on his filthy nails. Nice, civilized people. Made me feel right at home."

"I hope you had your gun handy."

"Handy? In my lap, babe, in my lap! Under the tablecloth. One wrong move and there would have been three greasy clunks, believe me. I think this Garcia knew it, because he told the other guy to put his blade away."

"What were you arguing about?"

"First of all they wanted both necklaces before they delivered the papers and we got on the plane. I said no way. One necklace before we left and the other handed over to their man in Costa Rica when we got there safely. Garcia finally agreed. Also, I insisted that at the final meet here, Garcia come alone with the passports and stuff. I figured that would cut down the possibilities of a cross. But he said we'd have to have passport photos made, and his paperman would have to be there to trim them, paste them in, and put the stamp on them. So I okayed the one guy but no one else. Garcia agreed to that. Finally we argued about where the final meet would be made.

Garcia wanted it right there at midnight, after the grocery store closed. I wasn't about to go into the back room of that place after dark. So they jabbered awhile in Spanish. I know a few words, but not enough to follow what they were saying. Finally Garcia suggested an old wreck of a hotel on Dumfoundling Bay. I think that they use it for a dope drop. It's somewhere between Golden Shores and Sunny Isles."

"Golden Shores and Sunny Isles?" I said incredulously. "You've got to be kidding!"

"What's so funny? That's what they're called. So I said I'd look the place over this afternoon, and if it was okay I'd call him and the deal would be on."

Manuel Garcia had given Jack very exact directions on how to find the deserted hotel on Dumfoundling Bay. It was just east of North Miami Beach, less than ten miles from where they had met in the Cuban grocery store. But still, Jack got lost twice and it took him almost an hour to find the place.

He had spent another hour driving around the area in the rain, reconnoitering approach routes and roads that could be used for an emergency escape. Then he had parked the car and inspected the wrecked hotel on foot, which was when he got soaked through.

He said he figured the hotel had been built in the 1920s, during one of the first Florida booms. Originally it had been an ornate white clapboard structure with a lot of gingerbread trim. There was a main building with a pillared portico, and two wings. But one of the wings had been destroyed by fire and was not just a mess of blackened timbers fallen into the basement. The rest of the hotel had been beaten gray by wind, sun, and rain.

All the windows were broken, part of the roof of the main building had collapsed, and the outside doors

hung crazily from rusted hinges. Donohue said the
hotel grounds were separated from other buildings
and lots in the area by a high chainlink fence with a
padlocked gate. There were No Tresspassing signs
posted all over.

But the fence had been cut through in several
places, and Jack thought the grounds and falling-down
building were used by local kids for picnics, pot parties and—from the number of discarded condoms he
saw—for what he called "screwing bees."

He said the hotel was on about a four-acre plot,
and back in the 1920s there must have been lawns,
gardens, brick walks, palm trees, and tropical shrub-
bery. But at some time, maybe during a hurricane,
the waters of the bay had risen, inundated the
grounds, and lapped at the base of the hotel.

"You can still see the high-water mark," Jack said.
"About halfway up to the second-floor windows."

Now the ruined building was in the center of a mud
flat—nothing left but patches of scrub grass and a
few ground creepers. The palm trees were all gone,
and any other plants of value had died or been
stolen. Even the bricks from the walks had been dug
up and carted off. The grounds were dotted with piles
of dog feces, so local residents were probably using
the place to run their hounds.

The front door had a faded legal notice tucked
onto it, warning that trespassers would be prosecuted.
It was closed with a chain and padlock, but that was
silly since all the first-floor windows were broken and
the French doors leading to the wide porch were
swinging open.

Jack went in and found more evidence of picnics,
barbecues, and bottle parties. The place was littered
with moldy garbage, burned and sodden mattresses,
empty beer cans, and bird droppings. He saw birds

flying in and out of the upper windows and heard them up there. He figured they were nesting. In the rain, the whole place smelled of corruption and death.

He went outside again and picked his way down to the bay, where more offal floated in the water. There was a rotting dock, the piles covered with slime and a thick crust of barnacles. There was no beach worth the name; just garbage-choked water lapping at garbage-clotted land.

"I'll bet Garcia and his laughing boys are using it for a drug drop," Donohue said. "A mother ship comes up the coast from Central or South America. It's in International Waters, so the Coast Guard can't touch it. Small boats go out at night and the cargo is off-loaded. Or maybe they just dump it overboard in waterproof bales. The small boats pick it up and run it in. That cruddy dock would be a perfect place to unload the small boats and transfer the grass and coke to vans and trucks."

"Well . . . what do you think?" I asked him. "How safe is it?"

He shrugged. "Not perfect—but what is? The thing I like about it is that there's only one narrow road coming up to that front gate. There's no way to get to the place except by that road. What I figure we'll do is get there an hour or two before the meet. We'll go through every room to make sure no one's been planted to wait for us and then jump out and shout 'Surprise!' Then, if it really is empty, we'll pull out and watch the place from a distance through my binocs. If one car pulls up, and only two guys get out, then we'll go in. But while we're in there, one of us will be watching that road all the time. Another car comes anywhere near and we take off."

"Then what?"

"We play it by ear," he said. "We're going in there with enough guns to take Fort Knox."

"All right," I said, "suppose this Garcia is there with the passport forger, just like he promised. We hand over the necklace and he gives us the papers. When do we get on the plane?"

"He said he'd tell us when we hand over the rocks."

I groaned. "Jack," I said, "there's a dozen ways he could cross us."

"A dozen? I can think of a hundred! The papers can be so lousy they wouldn't fool a desk clerk. Garcia and his paperman can pull iron on us. They can let us go and mousetrap us on the road out. Maybe the plane will be rigged to blow up over the water. Maybe the pilot will bail out after takeoff and just wave goodbye. Maybe we're being set up on the other end. We step off the plane in Costa Rica and the whole goddamned army is waiting for us. Jesus Christ, Jan, if they want to cross us, they can do it. You want to call it off? I haven't phoned Garcia yet."

I thought a long time, trying to figure the best thing to do. But there was no "best thing," no right choice. All our options were dangerous, all possibilities tainted.

"I told you," Donohue said, "if you want to take half the ice and split, that's up to you. I won't try to stop you."

"No," I said, "I'll stick with you. But if we don't go for this Costa Rica deal, then what?"

"You know what," he said grimly. "We go on the run again, maybe across country to L.A. Never staying more than a few days in one place. Trying to keep a step ahead of Rossi and the Feds. Prying out stones and peddling them when our cash runs out. Is that what you want?"

I had a sudden dread vision of what that life would be like.

"No," I said, "I couldn't stand that. There's no chance at all that way. The Feds or the Corporation would catch up with us eventually; I know they would. All right, Jack. Call Garcia and tell him it's on."

"It'll be okay," he said, patting my cheek. "You'll see."

"Sure."

Donohue called the Paco number in Miami. He spoke a short time in guarded phrases. That day was Tuesday. The meet was set for 3:00 P.M. on Thursday. That would give us time to have passport photos made. After we handed over the necklace and received our new identification papers, Garcia would give us the details of where and when to board the plane for the flight to Costa Rica.

After Jack hung up, we started on a bottle of vodka. Neither of us felt like eating. I suppose we were too keyed up. Read "frightened" for "keyed up." Anyway, we drank steadily, talking all the time in bright, hysterical voices, laughing sometimes, choking on our own bright ideas.

What we were trying to do was to imagine every possible way Manuel Garcia could betray us and what we could do to prevent it. We devised what we thought were wise precautions and counterploys. We had no intention of crossing Garcia. We would play it straight. All we wanted to do was stay alive.

When we finally fell into bed around midnight, we were too mentally and emotionally exhausted to have any interest in sex. All we could do was hold each other, shivering occasionally.

We listened to the storm outside, heard the lash of rain and the smash of thunder, saw the room light up with a bluish glare when lightning crackled overhead.

That's the way we fell asleep, hearing the world crack apart.

The next day the thunder and lightning had ceased, but the sky was low and leaden. Vicious rain squalls swept in from the southeast. Even when it wasn't raining, the air seemed supersaturated. My face felt clammy, fabrics were limp and damp. Water globules clung to the hood of the Cutlass, and all the cars on the road had their headlights on and wipers going.

We got rid of all the last possessions of Hymie Gore and Dick Fleming. We found a place that took passport photos and waited there until they were processed and printed. We bought a few things we thought might be hard to find in Costa Rica: aspirin, vitamin pills, suntan lotion, water purification tablets —things like that. We really had no idea of what the country was like, where we would be living, what modern conveniences might be available. We were emigrants setting out for an unknown land.

In the evening we continued our packing, trying to discard everything not absolutely essential. Winter garments from up north were eliminated: gloves, scarves, knitted hats, wool skirts and shirts. We set aside the necklace we would deliver to Manuel Garcia and selected another we thought of equal value. It was about then we got into a brutal argument. It was about time; our nerves were twanging.

On the following day, Thursday, when we left for our meeting with Garcia at the deserted hotel, Jack Donohue wanted to take all our luggage (including the Brandenberg loot) in the Oldsmobile, checking out of Rip's.

I said that was foolish. If we were bushwhacked at the hotel, we stood to lose everything. The smart thing to do, I said, was to go armed, taking only the single necklace we had promised. If everything went according to plan, we could then return to Rip's and load up before we departed to board the plane.

"Listen," Donohue said, "we've got to allow at least an hour for the trip from here to the hotel. What if we deliver the rocks and Garcia says we've got to get on the plane right away? Then where are we? No time to come back here and pick up our stuff."

"Then we'll stall," I said. "Tell him no deal. Tell him we need at least two hours to get our luggage."

"Jesus Christ!" he said angrily, "you think they run these Micky Mouse flights on a regular schedule? We get on the plane they've got lined up at the time they say or we don't go at all."

"Then we don't go at all!" I said, just as furiously. "We're not walking into that lion's den carrying everything we own. That's just plain stupid. We'll go down there with—"

"*Well!*" he shouted. "*We'll* do this. *We* won't do that. Who the hell voted you the great brain? *I* call the shots!"

"In a pig's ass you do!" I yelled, spluttering in an effort to get it all out. "You really did a swell job of calling the shots, you did! Heading for Miami when every cop in the country knew it was your home base. Getting Hymie and Dick killed because of some nutty dream that you'd be treated like King Tut once you got to Miami. And then you discover they don't want to know you."

"You think I couldn't have made it if it hadn't been for you?" he screamed, white with fury. "Fucking woman! I had to nurse you along, hold your hand while you jumped a roof a ten-year-old kid could have stepped across. You've been a goddamned jinx. You and Fleming. All the way. Without you two schmucks, I'd have been out of the country right now, living high off the hog. What an idiot I was! I should have known better. I should have ditched the two of you in New York. Left you for Rossi to take care of. You've been nothing but trouble. You junked me up. And now you're telling *me* how to run things? Take off. Go on, beat it. I'm sick of the sight of you."

"You shithead!" I said. "You're going to get yourself killed. Go ahead. I couldn't care less. You've got no goddamned brains. Go on. Take all the stuff to Garcia and just hand it over. 'Here it is, Mr. Garcia, and I hope it's enough.' And don't forget to kiss his ass. But include me out, you fucking . . . *peasant!*"

We stood there trembling, glaring at each other. I think if one of us had said another word, we would have been at each other's throats. Perhaps we both knew it, because we said nothing. Just bristled. Then Jack turned away. He walked to the window. He thrust his hands into his pockets. He stood there, staring out at the rain-whipped night.

I slumped into a chair, leaned back. I stretched out my legs. I lighted a cigarette with shaking fingers. I wasn't thinking straight. I wasn't thinking at all. Just trying to regain control. Telling myself it was nerves. That's all: just nerves. But I hadn't cried, I reminded myself grimly. I was proud of that: I hadn't wept.

Jack Donohue spoke first. He was still staring out the window, his back to me. And he spoke in such a low voice I could hardly hear him.

"That week at Mrs. Pearl's," he said. "You and Dick and me. Together. That was the happiest time I ever had in my whole miserable life."

I stubbed out my cigarette. I rose and went to him.

I took him by the shoulders and turned him so that we were facing. Close. Staring into each other's eyes.

"It was the happiest time for me, too," I told him. "Absolutely the happiest. No matter what happens we had that, didn't we?"

"Yes," he said wonderingly. "That's right. We had that. No matter what happens."

He sighed deeply. "We'll do it your way, Jan. We'll go down there tomorrow with just the one necklace. Fuck 'em. We'll get on that goddamned plane when *we* want to. We're paying for it."

"Whatever you say, Jack," I said gently. "You're the boss."

The rain had stopped by Thursday morning, but a clumpy fog had moved in. It was like living in a murky fishbowl. We could hear the ocean but couldn't see it. When we walked down to Atlantic Boulevard for a pancake breakfast, we saw a dead pelican on the road, all bloodied and muddied. A great way to start the most important day in our lives.

Back at the motel, Jack cleaned and reloaded the guns we'd take: a pistol in his raincoat pocket, a revolver in his belt. Another pistol concealed in the car. I would carry a pistol in my raincoat pocket and a small revolver in my shoulder bag.

"Babe," Jack said, "if you have to blast—you won't, but if you *have* to—don't, for Christ's sake, take the time to pull the iron out of your pocket first. Just aim as best you can and blow right through the raincoat. It may catch on fire, but that'll be the least of our worries. Keep your hand on the shooter in your pocket every minute we're in there. Got it?"

"Got it."

We started out at noon, paused to gas up, then went south on Federal Highway #1. Jack was driving, leaning forward to peer through the murk. Traffic was moving very slowly; most of the cars had their lights on.

After we got below Golden Shores, I couldn't follow the twists and turns Donohue was taking, except that I knew we were off Federal and generally heading eastward. There were no road markers. We seemed to be passing through an area of tidal flats, vacant fields, and fenced lots choked with palmettos, scrub pines, and yellow grass.

"You're sure you know—" I began.

"Don't worry," Donohue said tensely. "I *know*."

He did, too. We finally turned into a single-lane road. It might have been tarred originally, but now it showed bald patches of sodden earth and weeds sprouting from cracks. We followed the lazy curves going slowly. Then, on the right-hand side, I saw a chainlink fence, bent, dented, and rusted.

"That's it," Jack said. "This is the only road in, the only road out."

We came up to the sagging gate and stopped.

"Take a look," he said.

I looked. In that swirling fog, the hotel was a ghosts' mansion. It was silvered with age, glistening with damp, and it *loomed*. That's the only way I can describe it: It loomed through the mist, enlarged and menacing. I saw black birds circling and darting into upper windows. I saw the nude grounds, puddled, still shining from the past two days' rain.

I tried to imagine how it had been, white and glittering, a place for ladies in long gowns with parasols and men with straw boaters and high, starched collars. People laughing and moving slowly along brick walks under lush palm trees. I tried to imagine all this but I couldn't. It was all gone.

"Think they've got a suite for us?" I said, laughing nervously. "Two rooms with a view?"

"Let's go take a look."

We got out of the car and crawled carefully through a cut in the fence. We tried to avoid the puddles, but the ground squished beneath our steps. My shoes were soaked through before we got to the porch.

We stepped up the rotting stairs, keeping close to the sides where the sag wasn't so apparent. Then I smelled it.

"Jesus!" I breathed.

"Yeah," Donohue said. "And it's worse inside. Breathe through your mouth."

We went in through one of those broken French doors. It was just as Jack had described it: soaked garbage, offal, all the detritus of a dwelling place abandoned and left open. We went up to the fourth floor, the top except for an attic that appeared open to the lowering sky.

We sent colonies of birds into a flurry of activity. I was certain I heard the scamper of rats. And once I did see a small snake slither behind a baseboard.

We looked hastily into every room, not a difficult job since most of the doors had been removed. There was evidence, as Jack had said, of pot and bottle parties, of fires and wanton destruction, of the terrible inroads age makes. On buildings. On people. Everything goes.

Back on the ground floor, we wandered about until Jack selected a large, high-ceilinged chamber that had probably been the dining room. Broken French doors opened out onto the sagging porch and a side terrace. Most important, from two sides we had a good view of the access road. We could see our own car dimly, parked at the gate.

"This is where we'll meet," Donohue decided. "I'll do the talking. I mean," he added hastily, "if you want to say anything, you say it. But mostly you keep an eye on that road beyond the gate. You see another car pulling up, or anything fishy, you let me know."

"Don't worry," I said. "I'll scream."

"Good." He looked at his watch. "We got a little more than an hour. We'll go back to the junction and park where we can watch who comes in."

And that's what we did, retracing that cracked road until we came to the paved junction that, Donohue told me, led eventually back to the Federal Highway. We were in a neighborhood of one-story cinderblock homes, some with front yards of green gravel, a few with boats on trailers in their garage driveways.

We parked there, settled down, lighted cigarettes, and waited. Jack had brought his binoculars, but they were of no use. That misty fog was still so thick we could see no more than twenty or thirty yards. But we could make out the turnoff to that road leading to the deserted hotel.

Sitting there, closed around by the fog, swaddled in silence, we talked slowly in murmurs. Jack wanted to know all about my life. Mostly my childhood. Where I had been born, where I lived, the places I had visited.

But mainly he wanted to know *how* I had lived when I was growing up. How many rooms did our various homes have? Did we have servants? How many cars did we own? Did we belong to a country club? Did I attend private schools? How much money did my parents spend on my clothes? What kind of presents did I get for Christmas?

It wasn't just curiosity, I knew; it was a hunger. He wanted a firsthand view into a world he coveted, a vision of moneyed ease. He saw it as a life in sunlight. Beautiful women and handsome men sat around on a seafront terrace, sipped champagne and nibbled caviar served by smiling servants. It was *class*.

I didn't have the heart to disabuse him. So I embellished my descriptions of what childhood was like when there was money for everything, people were polite and kind, and life was a golden dream in which every wish was granted. He kept smiling and nodding away, as if what I told him was no more than he had envisioned. I wasn't telling him anything he hadn't imagined a thousand times. There was a world like that; he *knew* it, and he couldn't get enough of it.

But then, a few minutes after three, he straightened up behind the wheel.

"Car coming," he said in a tight voice.

We both leaned forward, squinting through the fogged windshield. It was a big black car, a Cadillac, and it came to the access road, slowed, then made the turn.

"How many men did you see?" Donohue demanded.

"Two. In the front seat."

"That's what I saw. We'll follow them in."

He started up. We turned into the tarred road leading to the hotel. The black car ahead of us was lost in the mist. We found it parked outside the gate in the chainlink fence. We saw two men picking their way across the littered grounds to the hotel.

Jack grunted with satisfaction.

"The short guy is Garcia," he said. "I'm sure of that. The tall gink must be the paperman. We'll wait till they get inside."

When the two men disappeared into the hotel, Jack pulled up ahead of the Cadillac. Then, with much backing and hard cramping of the wheel, he turned the Cutlass around until we were heading back the way we had come, away from the hotel. Then we got out of the car. Donohue left the key in the ignition and the doors unlocked.

"Just in case we wish to depart swiftly," he said with a thin smile.

We walked back to the Cadillac, inspected the back seat. Empty. Jack tried the trunk lid. It was locked.

"Looks okay," he said. "We'll go in now. You all set?"

"Sure."

He gave me one of his flashy grins, pulled me close, kissed my lips.

"Win, lose, or draw, babe," he said, "it's been fun."

"Hasn't it?"

"Let's go."

We stooped through the cut in the fence. We started toward the hotel. We both had right hands in our raincoat pockets. We must have looked like a pair of assassins.

Donohue paused a moment on the porch. He took a final look around. No one in sight. Nothing stirring.

"Remember what I told you," he said in a low voice. "Keep an eye on that road. If I make a play, be ready to cover my back. And be ready to run."

I nodded dumbly. Suddenly I needed to pee.

They were waiting for us in the hallway. The little one, Manuel Garcia, was wearing a clear plastic raincoat over a suit of horrendous green plaid. His pointy shoes were two-toned, yellow and brown. He wore a ruffled purple shirt with a wide tie in a wild carnation print. The knot was as big as my fist. His black hair was slicked back with pomade. He wore diamond rings on *both* pinkies, and when he grinned, gold sparkled in his front teeth.

Donohue had been right; I could smell his fruity perfume from six feet away.

The taller man, presumably the passport forger, was dressed like an undertaker: black shoes, black socks, a shiny black suit, a not-too-clean white shirt, a black tie hardly wider than a shoelace. He had a long, coffin-shaped face, badly pitted with acne or smallpox. He never looked directly at us. His pale eyes kept darting—left, right, up, down. I thought he was just shifty-eyed, but then I realized he was scared witless. He was carrying a brown paper bag and his hands were trembling so badly that the paper kept crackling.

No introductions were offered, none asked.

"Let's go in there," Donohue said, gesturing toward the open door of the room he had selected.

"Why not ri' here?" Garcia said. His voice was surprisingly deep, almost booming.

"Too open," Jack said and cut short any further argument by leading the way into the dining room.

We trooped after him. I took up a position in the corner, away from the others. I stood at an angle where I could see the gate and the access road and also keep an eye on what was going on in the room.

I gripped the pistol in my raincoat pocket tightly, but kept my finger out of the trigger guard. Jack still had his hand in his raincoat pocket. Garcia, in that clear plastic coat, obviously had nothing in his pockets. And he carried his arms slightly out to the sides, palms turned outward, as if to prove his peaceful intentions.

"You got the necklace?" he asked, grinning.

"Sure," Jack said. "Right here. You got the papers?"

"Joe, you show him," Garcia said.

The three men were standing in a close group. There was no place to sit down, no chairs, no table, no sofa—nothing.

The undertaker fumbled open his paper bag. He pulled out a sheaf of documents. In his nervousness he dropped a card to the littered floor. He swooped quickly to retrieve it and tried to smile apologetically at Garcia. He held out the papers to Donohue.

I looked out at the gate and road. Only the two cars standing there. Nothing moving.

Donohue examined the papers carefully, taking his free hand from his gun pocket. If they were going to make a move, this would be the time to do it. I watched carefully. But they made no move. Just waited patiently while Jack shuffled slowly through the documents, examining every page of the passports, the Social Security cards, the drivers licenses, the birth certificates.

He stopped suddenly. Raised his head. Glanced quickly toward me.

"Road clear?" he said.

I looked again.

"Okay," I said. "Nothing."

He frowned. "Thought I heard something."

"Maybe the wind," Garcia said, grinning. "Maybe the rain."

"Maybe," Jack said shortly. He went back to examining the papers.

"You bring the pictures?" Garcia said. "For the passports?"

"Sure," Donohue said, nodding. We got them."

"Good," Garcia said. "José, he's got glue and the stamp. Firstclass work."

Then I heard it. A dull, sodden thump.

"Jack," I said.

He looked up.

"I heard something," I said. "A low thud."

"A shutter banging," Garcia said, grinning. "That's all."

Donohue stared at him.

"This place ain't got shutters," he said.

Manuel Garcia shrugged. "A rat maybe. A big bird. A place like this, it's got all kinds of noises. I think maybe you're a little anxious—no?"

Donohue didn't answer. He just stood there, his head cocked, listening. I looked again toward the road. Nothing moved there.

We all stood frozen, silent. Jack was still holding the papers.

Then we all heard it. Unmistakable now. A footfall on soft ground. I imagined I could hear the squish of the sodden earth.

"You prick!" Donohue screamed.

He threw the papers at Garcia's face. But the other man was just as fast. He ducked. When he straightened up, miraculously there was a long knife in his hand. He held it flat, knuckles turned down. The blade glittered wickedly.

Jack started to reach into his pocket for his gun.

Garcia moved forward with little mincing steps. The knife point swung back and forth.

The passport forger gasped and dropped onto the filthy floor.

Garcia lunged.

Jack leaped backward.

"Run!" he yelled at me.

I fired through my raincoat pocket.

Garcia was suddenly slammed backward. He didn't fall. He looked down at himself, not believing.

Jack had his gun out now.

He leaned toward Garcia, his arm out straight. He fired twice.

The man's face swelled enormously. His mouth opened. His eyes popped. His tongue came lolling out. Then blood gushed from nose and ears. He melted down.

The paperman cowered on the floor. His arms were over his head.

Jack grabbed my arm. We ran.

I saw crouched figures coming across that dreary landscape. From the bay. From a boat on the bay. From the rotting dock.

Donohue yanked me back inside. We turned. Dashed to the other side. Climbed out a broken window. Jumped off the porch. Bolted toward our car.

Then I was alone. I stopped, turned. Jack was standing between me and the hotel. He had both his guns out. He was firing at men darting between pillars on the porch. Men racing to one side to cut us off. Men lying on the wet ground, aiming carefully, firing their weapons methodically.

I saw a familiar figure, short, heavyset, big shoulders, barrel chest. Wearing a black raincoat buttoned to the chin. A black fedora, the brim snapped low.

He came around the corner of the hotel and walked slowly, purposefully toward us. His hands were in his pockets. He fired no guns. But that deliberate, implacable advance frightened me more than all the shouts, screams, the hard snaps and deep booms of the guns.

I had my pistol out now and emptied it toward that advancing figure. Still he came on. I heard the pistol click and flung it from me. I fumbled in my shoulder bag.

Then Jack turned and came dashing back. I saw the widened eyes, open mouth, the chest heaving.

"Jan—" he gasped.

Then something hit him. Punched him forward.

He went down on one knee. He reached slowly around behind him.

I was at his side. Grabbed his arm. Hauled him up. Staggering, stumbling, we made it to the fence. I pushed him through the cut. He fell flat on his face. I saw the bloodstain spreading over the back of his raincoat.

Sobbing, I wrenched him to his feet again. He couldn't stand erect. He was doubled over. I heard gnats singing about us. A buzz. There were whispers in the air. Things spanged off the bodies of both cars.

I pushed Jack into the back of the Cutlass. Just threw him onto the floor. I doubled his legs, jammed them in, slammed the door.

I got behind the wheel, started the engine. I accelerated in a jackrabbit start, spun the wheels, slowed until I had traction. Then I pushed the pedal to the floor, swerving around the parked Cadillac.

I had a hazy impression of more shouts, curses, explosions of guns. Men running toward us.

And, from the corner of my eye, saw that black trundling figure coming on. Not running. Not firing a gun. But just coming on, coming on . . .

A Walk on the Beach

His first words were: "Are you all right?"

I tried to smile, bit my lower lip, blinked rapidly. I put a hand on his forehead. Fevered. I soaked a towel under the tap, wrung it out, draped it softly across his brow.

"They came by boat," he breathed painfully. "We should have watched for that." It was an old man's voice: faint, harsh, bubbling with phlegm —R WORSE

I nodded. He was right; we had been out-guessed.

"Was Garcia in on it?" I asked.

"Sure." Speaking was an effort for him; I could hear it. "His price was probably the necklace. Or more. Did you see him?"

I knew whom he meant.

"I tried to kill him," I said. "I emptied my pistol at the bastard. But he just kept coming toward us."

"You did fine. Just fine. Real class. What happened after I caught it? Tell me everything."

He closed his eyes. I hoped he was sleeping. But I kept talking.

"I found Federal Highway," I said. "But I made a mistake; I turned south instead of north."

Then I knew he was awake and listening. And understanding. But his eyes were still closed.

"Road blocked?"

"No. I thought it would be, but it wasn't."

"They were so sure," he said. "So sure. Followed?"

"No, Jack, we weren't. I kept looking back to make certain. Garcia probably had the Cadillac keys. Anyway, I took a turnoff and went east to A1A. Then I came directly home."

"Home," he repeated faintly. "Was I out?"

"Half-and-half. I thought that I'd get here and look in the back seat and you'd be—you know."

Something like a cruel smile moved his mouth.

"Not me. I'm too mean to die. How'd you get me in?"

"You leaned on me," I told him. "Arm around my neck. We passed a couple coming in and I yelled at you about drinking too much. They smiled at me sympathetically. No one else saw us."

"Blood?"

"Not as much as I thought. Very little in the car."

That was a lie. There had been a flood.

"How does it look."

"Okay. It looks fine. Just a small hole, kind of puffed up. I got a towel around you and tied it tight. Then I went out and found a drugstore that was still open. I bought pads and bandages and tape. Antiseptics. Things like that. I've got you all bandaged up now. I gave you some brandy and aspirin."

"A small hole? Where?"

"Under your ribs. A few inches left of the spine. Above your waist."

"Did it come out?" he asked in a low voice.

I was silent.

"Did it come out?" he repeated.

"No. The bullet's still in there. We've got to get you to a doctor, Jack. To a hospital."

"No. No doctor. No hospital. No need for that. I feel grand."

He didn't look grand. He was lying in bed, naked, covered with a sheet and light blanket. Because frequently he would get the shakes. In spite of the fever, his whole body would tremble, stricken with a sudden chill.

"Jack," I said. "Let's give it up. I'll call the cops. We'll get you to a hospital."

He opened his eyes. He stared at me.

"After what we've gone through? Give it up now? Don't say that, Jan. I can take this. This isn't so bad. I feel better already."

"You're lying."

"I'm not lying," he said patiently. "I really feel better. Hardly any pain at all. Listen, one pill is nothing. It could heal by itself. It doesn't have to come out."

I didn't say anything. He closed his eyes again.

"Promise me," he said faintly.

"What, Jack?"

"You won't call the cops or a doctor unless I say okay. Promise?"

"I promise."

He fell asleep smiling. I washed out the bloody towel and tried to rinse the stains from his shirt, jacket, and raincoat. There was blood on his pants, undershorts, socks. There was blood in his shoes. I didn't want to think of that puddle caking on the back floor of the Oldsmobile.

I poured myself a brandy and sat in a chair alongside the bed. I watched him breathe: slow, almost lazy breathing. I told myself it was normal: no coughing, no gasping. Maybe the wound would heal by itself.

I know now that during that night and the day that followed, I wasn't thinking. I *couldn't* think. The outside fog was inside me now. A thought would drift into my mind—doctor, hospital, police, escape—and then it would just fade into smoke and cobwebs. I couldn't concentrate. I could not pin down a single rational idea. All I could do was float in the swirl, numbed, moving like a zombie.

I did what had to be done. I made food for myself and ate it. I made food for Jack and fed him. I bathed him and myself. I mixed drinks. I made certain the door was locked and the blinds drawn. I mean, I *functioned*. But all the time I wasn't aware, either of myself or what I was doing. Those twenty-four hours were a mindless blank.

I think now it was nature's way of protecting me. I think that somnambulism was a mechanism to preserve my sanity. I didn't weep. No hysterics. I just felt divorced from what was happening. I was a stranger in a foreign world. I breathed, ate, slept, and never once did I ask, *why?* I was Jannie Shean, the mechanical woman. Wind her up and away she goes.

That night, Thursday, I slept sitting up in an armchair. Jack woke me once, and I brought him more brandy and water and put another wet cloth across his forehead. He muttered something I couldn't understand, then slept again. I thought his sleeping was a good sign. I thought everything was a good sign.

There was sunshine in the morning—another good sign. Not much brightness, but the clouds were breaking up and there were patches of blue. I locked Jack in and ran out to buy some food, orange juice, the Miami papers. There was nothing in the papers about the shoot-out at the deserted hotel on Dumfoundling

Bay. And nothing on the TV news broadcasts. I figured Antonio Rossi had cleaned up neatly behind him.

Jack woke about 10:00, and I fed him some hot beef broth with bits of bread soaked in it. He got a few spoonsful down, then turned his head away.

He didn't look at all good. His face was waxen, sheened, white as the pillow. His features seemed to be shrinking, tightening. He was getting a hawk profile. I had to roll him over to change the dressing on the wound. The bleeding had stopped; the bullet hole was closing. It was a blue pucker. But his body was a shock: pale, flaccid, bones jutting. And there was a smell. Not just sweat and blood and soiled sheets. But something else. Something sweetish, curdled, and piercing.

He drowsed, fitfully, all that Friday. He had an enormous thirst, drank water, milk, coffee, brandy, orange juice. Four times I had to help him into the bedroom. He wouln't let me stay with him in there. I wanted to; it didn't bother me. But he insisted on closing the door. Then I would assist him back to bed, half-carrying him, his arm around my shoulders.

Once he forgot to flush the toilet, and I saw he had been passing blood. Around 5:00 P.M., he awoke again and said, "Give me a cigarette."

"Jack," I said, "are you sure you should—"

He looked at me. I lighted a cigarette and put it between his lips. He caught my hand and kissed my fingers.

"My mom," he said. "She run off. I never did know her."

"Don't try to talk, Jack. Just finish your cigarette and get some more sleep."

"It wasn't all bad," he said. "Most of it was, but not all of it."

His hand fell limply. The lighted cigarette dropped

to the floor. I picked it up, snuffed it out. When I looked at him again, his eyes were closed. But the blanket across his chest was rising and falling steadily.

"The mud crick," he said. "I told you?"

"Yes, Jack. You told me."

"Dick," he said. "Dick Fleming. What a brain on that kid. Style. Real class."

"Yes, Jack."

"Where did Ernie go?"

"Who?"

"Ernie. He was here just a minute ago."

"He'll be back."

"The track in the morning. When they were working the horses. The sun coming up. Dew on the grass. That was something."

I was silent.

"I cried," he said, "when I was a kid. But that don't do no good. That fucking Rossi."

"Yes."

"Dick and I talked about you. He liked you dressed like a hooker. I liked you best when you were you, Jannie."

"Thank you," I said faintly.

"Have you seen Al lately?"

"No, I haven't seen Al."

"Peters is in town for the season," he said. "And the Carter boys. They're all coming in. Shumsky was out on the Coast. Hit it big in Vegas—he says. But you know Shumsky."

"Shh," I said. "Try to sleep."

"I wonder where she went? I thought I'd bump into her someday, but I never did. You want another drink, Alice?"

"No," I said, "thanks. I've had enough."

"We'll have to put that hound down. Too bad, but

he's hurting. I'm running a load to Athens tonight, Pop. We'll do it when I get back."

"Okay, Jack."

"A sweet caper. The best—am I right?"

"You're right, Jack."

"Jesus, I'm tired. I've got to get to the track, but I think I'll take a little nap first."

"You do that. Take a little nap."

Then he slept, and I think I did, too. When I awoke, he was sitting on the edge of the bed, his feet on the floor.

"Jack," I said, "for God's sake, lie down. Get under the blanket."

"I'm thirsty," he said in an aggrieved tone. "I want some orange juice."

"You finished the juice," I told him. "But there's milk, beer, cola, coffee, brandy, water—whatever you want."

"Orange juice," he repeated.

I looked at the wall clock. Almost 8:00.

"Jack, where am I going to get orange juice this time of night?"

He looked at me steadily. When he spoke, he was perfectly rational, perfectly lucid.

"There's an all-night 7-11 Store right across the bridge. You can be there and back in fifteen minutes. I really would like some fresh, cold orange juice."

"If I go, will you get back in bed?"

"Have I got a choice?"

He fell back into bed. I lifted up his legs. I covered him up to his chin. I leaned down to kiss his dry lips.

"Be right back," I said. "I love you, Jack."

"Yeah," he breathed. "Say it again."

"I love you."

"Yeah."

I looked back from the door just before I went out.

His eyes were closed. He seemed to be breathing slowly, steadily. I locked the door behind me.

I bought three quarts of orange juice. I came speeding back. I wasn't gone more than twenty minutes. The door to our motel room was wide open.

I knew then. *Knew*. But I went through the motions. I went inside, put the juice in the refrigerator.

The note was on the drainboard of the sink. Written in a scrawled, wavery hand:

"Babe, It's no good. I'm filling up with blood. I can feel it. I think I'll take a walk on the beach. Take everything. Do what you have to do. Get out. Keep moving. You got a chance. I'll bet on it. I love you, Jan. Did I tell you? I love—"

The pencil line drooped, fell away.

I went outside. I walked down to the black sea. I thought I saw the dragging track he had made, but perhaps I was imagining it.

I waded into the pounding surf until the water was up to my knees. I stared into the darkness. But all I could make out were the rolling waves, the white crests, the milky foam. There was no moon. But I could see stars twinkling between patches of cloud. An airliner droned overhead, lights flashing.

After a while I went back inside and started packing.

Letter to Sol Faber

~~~~~~

Dear Sol,

I know you only read the first 50 and last 50 pages of the books you peddle, but even you must have guessed that this is Project X, the manuscript I began a hundred years ago in another world.

You'll also notice that this package is postmarked from New Orleans. If the Feds have a mail cover on you, as they probably do, they'll have noted the same thing. It's not important; by the time you receive this I'll be a thousand miles from New Orleans.

Sol, please try to sell this. I'm not hurting for money; I've got plenty of cash plus the Brandenberg jewels. But I'd like to see this published, just so people will know my side of the story in case something happens to me. If you do sell it, hold the money. I'll work out some way of getting it without the Feds knowing. If Jack Donohue taught me anything, it's that the system can be fiddled, one way or another.

Please call my sister and tell her I'm alive and well. Call Aldo Binder and tell the old fart that he was right: I didn't know what reality was all about.

Sol, I'm going to drop this off at the post office on my way to the airport. The reason I'm leaving New Orleans is that about an hour ago the room clerk tipped me that someone had come by asking for me. A squat, heavyset man wearing a vested suit, topcoat, and British bowler. A man with wide shoulders and a barrel chest.

The clerk kept his mouth shut (he says!), but it doesn't make any difference; that guy will be back.

And he'll find me wherever I go; I know that. But the next time things will be different. Remember when you told me readers like a nice, tidy ending to a novel?

I'm going to tidy this one up.

The next place I go to, I'm going to let Antonio Rossi find me.

And then I'm going to kill that son of a bitch.

Love. Jan